THE HURRICANE . . .

There was no escape for them now. *Shearwater* was driving straight on to a coral reef and would leave her bones upon the coral as many a tall ship had done before. He had not the remotest idea where they were.

He leaned across and kissed his wife. "I'm sorry."

She kissed him in return. "It's not your fault."

There were now only a few minutes to go. She could only think of Janice, Janice whose future happiness lay buried in the concrete beneath her feet. The concrete would survive upon the coral reef, but nobody would ever know of it but Keith. Keith, who had never made much of his life; Keith, who had never been anywhere or done anything. Keith, to whose keeping she had trusted Janice.

In those last moments the power of prayer came to her and she muttered in the accents of her childhood, "Lord, gie Keith a bit o' guid sense."

Then they struck.

Also by Nevil Shute
published by Ballantine Books:

Trustee From The Toolroom

NEVIL SHUTE

BALLANTINE BOOKS • NEW YORK

Library of Congress Catalog Card Number: 60-9545

ISBN 0-345-27191-2

This edition published by arrangement with William Morrow & Co., Inc.

Manufactured in Canada

First U.S. Printing: August 1967
Second U.S. Printing: May 1969

First Canadian Printing: August 1967
Third Canadian Printing: September 1978

An engineer is a man who can do for five bob what any bloody fool can do for a quid.

Definition—origin unknown

1

WEST EALING IS A SUBURB to the west of London, and
Keith Stewart lives there in the lower part of No. 56 Somerset Road. No. 56 is an unusual house and a peculiarly ugly
one, a detached house standing in a row but in a fairly
spacious garden, four storeys high if you include the basement, a tall, thin slip of a house. It was built in the spacious
days of 1880 when West Ealing stood on the edge of the
country farmlands and was a place to which Indian Civilians
retired after their years of service, but it was built of a
particularly ugly yellow brick, now toned to a drab grey, at a
period when English suburban architecture was going through
a bad patch. The years have not dealt kindly with West
Ealing; the farms are now far away. Most of the big old
houses have been split up into two or three flats, as Keith
Stewart had converted No. 56.

He had bought it when he married Katie in the middle of
the Second War. That was soon after he moved down from
Glasgow to the London area to work as a toolroom fitter
with Stone and Collinson Ltd., who made subcontract parts
for aeroplanes at Perivale. It was, of course, the first house
that Katie or Keith had ever owned, and they were very
proud of it. They contemplated quite a family so that they
would need quite a house, the upper rooms for nurseries and
children's rooms and playrooms while the garden would be a
nice place for the pram. When, after a few years, it became
evident that that was not to be, they had separated the two
top floors from the remainder of the house and let them off
as what the agents called a maisonette, retaining the ground
floor and the basement for themselves. On the ground floor
they had a bedroom in the front, the living room and kitchen
at the rear overlooking the garden, and a bathroom at the
side. In the basement they had adapted what had once been
the scullery as a small spare bedroom; the whole of the rest
had been taken by Keith as his own domain.

Here he made models, and here he wrote about them
weekly for the *Miniature Mechanic,* a magazine with a
considerable circulation in the lower ranks of industry and

with a growing popularity amongst eccentric doctors, stock-brokers, and bank managers who just liked engineering but didn't know much about it. All his life he had made models, little steam engines, little petrol engines, little speedboats, little locomotives, little Diesels. He was a considerable horologist; in his time he had made many clocks with motions of antiquarian interest and had written full directions for constructing them, always in the *Miniature Mechanic*. He had made little beam engines which would have delighted James Watt and still delighted those who are fascinated by such things; he had made little jet engines which would have delighted Frank Whittle. He had made pumps and boilers and carillons that played a tune, all in the miniature scale. He was a quick worker and a ready writer upon technical matters and he delighted in making little things that worked. He had now so ordered his life that he need do nothing else.

All through the war he had written about his hobby after the long hours of overtime in the toolroom. The coming of peace had given him more leisure for his models and his articles about them, and two years later he had taken the great plunge of giving up his job in favour of his avocation. It had not benefitted him financially. He would have made more money in the toolroom progressing up from charge-hand to foreman; he would have made more money as an instructor in a technical college. He would not have made more happiness than he had now attained.

He was a very serious and well-informed student of engineering matters, though he would have been amazed to hear himself described in such terms. He read about techniques for pleasure. One morning in each week he would spend in the Ealing Public Library browsing through the technical magazines, slightly oppressed by a sense of guilt that he was not working. On Fridays he always went to London to deliver his weekly copy to the editor of the *Miniature Mechanic* and arrange about the blocks and, being in London, he would take time off and sneak away for three or four hours to the library of the Patent Office for a period of interest and pleasure before going home to catch up with his work. He worked normally till eleven or twelve each night.

He called the front basement room his clean workshop, and this was his machine shop. Here he had a six-inch Herbert lathe for heavy work, a three-and-a-half-inch

Myford, and a Boley watchmaker's lathe. He had a Senior milling machine and a Boxford shaper, a large and a small drill press, and a vast array of tools ready to hand. A long bench ran across the window, a tubular light system ran across the ceiling, and a small camera and flashgun stood ready for use in a cupboard, for it was his habit to take photographs of interesting processes to illustrate his articles.

The other room, which once had been the kitchen of the house, was considerably larger. He called this his dirty workshop, but it was in this room that he had his desk and drawing board for it was usually free of oil. Here he did what small amount of carpentry and woodworking might be necessary for his models. Here he welded and brazed, here he tempered and hardened steel, here he did steam trials of his steam engines so that it had been necessary for him to fit an extractor fan into the window. It was in this room that he stood talking to his brother-in-law, Commander Dermott, the red leather jewel case in his hands.

The copper box that he had made stood on the bench before them, the rectangular sheet of copper that was to be the lid loose beside it. "I've left room for packing this asbestos card all round it," Keith said. "I'll braze it up with a small oxyacetylene flame, but I'm afaid it's going to get a bit hot inside. I'm afraid it may scorch the leather, even with the asbestos."

"I don't think that matters," said the naval officer. "It won't set it on fire?"

Keith shook his head. "The top is a good fit, and I'll clamp it down all round while I'm brazing. There won't be enough oxygen inside to support combustion. I'm just worried about the look of it when you take it out. It could be a bit brown."

"That doesn't matter."

Keith shook the case; it was fairly heavy, but nothing rattled. He glanced at his brother-in-law. "What's it got in it?"

"All Jo's jewels," John Dermott told him. "You're only allowed to take so much out of the country."

"This is going somewhere in the yacht?"

The other nodded. "Somewhere where nobody's going to find it."

Keith said no more but took off his jacket and hung it on a

hook at the back of the door. He put on a leather apron that covered his body from the neck down, and turned on the gas at the cylinders, picked up the torch, and went to work. He never questioned anything that his brother-in-law said or did; they came from different worlds. John had been a regular naval officer, and Keith was a modest little man.

His sister had done a good job for herself, he reflected as he brazed the seam, when she married John Dermott; it had turned out well in spite of the social disparity. Jo had been a pretty child with good Scots sense; she had been fond of dancing and at the age of twelve she had become one of the Tiller Girls. Her first part was one of nine Elves in the Magic Wood, in pantomime. She had stayed with the organization and had played in theatres and music halls all over the British Isles, with occasional runs in London. It had been partly upon her account that Keith had left Glasgow and come down to work in the south, to see more of his only sister. It had gone on till at the age of nineteen she had been in the Christmas pantomime at Portsmouth. She was playing a small speaking part by that time as the Widow Twankey's maid, more noticeable than in the chorus. She had gone with a party of show girls and young naval officers to the Queen's Hotel after the performance; she told Lieutenant Dermott that she was going to see the *Victory* next day. He took her there in pouring rain, which neither of them noticed. He followed her to London. Six weeks later, in the Palm House at Kew Gardens, he asked her to marry him, and she accepted. It wasn't till nearly a month afterwards that she learned that she was marrying the nephew of Lord Dungannon.

Inevitably she had drifted somewhat apart from her brother Keith, the toolroom fitter in the factory at Perivale. She had the makings of a good actress in her; she was observant and could project herself into a part. It was no effort to her to take up the part of a young naval officer's wife, abandoning her Renfrew antecedents; with the Tiller Girls she had learned to abandon or assume her Scots accent at will. She married Lieutenant Dermott in 1939 and almost immediately the war came, taking him away from her for the best part of five years. In those years she saw him only for brief spells of leave. They did not start a family during the war. She lived in a small flat over a shop at Cosham and

worked as a woodworker with many other girls in a small
dispersal aircraft factory at Havant. In the evenings she
attempted to catch up on education to be on equal terms with
other naval wives. She attended classes at the Polytechnic in
French and history and geography and English Literature;
the latter she found infinitely tedious, but struggled on with
it.

John Dermott came back to her in 1946, a lieutenant-
commander with greying hair and a face lined on the Mur-
mansk convoy route; in 1947 their only child, Janice, was
born. They bought a little house in Southsea and lived mod-
estly, as naval officers do. They could have lived better for
John Dermott had a private income of about a thousand a
year, but already the shadow of an early retirement from the
Navy lay upon him. He was a general duties officer, a salt
horse, impatient with the rush of new techniques that were
invading his service. Early retirement lay ahead of him as he
passed out of the promotion zone. They saved their money
but for the extravagance of two years in Hong Kong for
Joanna and the baby Janice when he was drafted to the
China Station, and for the mild extravagance of duty-free
gin in increasing quantities as John Dermott passed out of
the zone. Early in 1957 the axe fell and John Dermott was
retired from the service to which he had given his life; he
was then forty-five, the same age as his brother-in-law,
Keith.

Joanna sat talking to Katie while the two men worked in
the basement room below. "It's terribly kind of you to offer
to look after Janice," she said. "I do want you to know how
we feel about that." She paused. "I wouldn't feel very comfortable about leaving her for all that time with the Dungannons."

Katie said anxiously, "I do hope she'll be happy, though.
Ealing isn't very exciting, not after what she's been used to.
Do you think she will? I mean, never having had any myself,
one doesn't know . . ."

She was a plump little woman in her early forties; she
worked in the Household Linen department of Buckley's
drapery shop, in Ealing Broadway. She had been in Household Linen as a girl, but in the war she had been directed to
running an automatic lathe at Stone and Collinson, at
Perivale. Here she had met Keith Stewart in 1941; they had

married in 1942, and she had gone back to her automatic lathe after a week's honeymoon. They had no children. The purchase and conversion of the house had taken all their savings and left them with a heavy mortgage. She had tried it for a year after the war as a lady of leisure and had tired of it; when Keith gave up his job and took up free-lance writing and construction for the *Miniature Mechanic* Katie went back gladly to the Household Linen, a red-faced, dumpy little woman, well liked by the customers.

Joanna said, "I think she'll be very happy with you, very happy indeed. I wouldn't leave her if I thought she wouldn't. I think you'll spoil her, though."

"She's such a dear little thing," said Katie. "I was saying to Keith, perhaps we ought to have a kitten."

"You'll be landed with a cat for the rest of your lives," Joanna said practically. "She'll only be with you for about six months. I don't think it will be longer. Then you'll just have to take her to London Airport and put her on the aeroplane to us in Vancouver."

"Would that be somewhere in America?"

"In Canada," Jo said. "It's on the other side, on the Pacific coast. Everybody says it's a lovely place to live in, and John thinks he can get a job there. It's got quite a mild climate, but it rains a lot."

"My ..." The thought of the aeroplane was troubling to Katie. "I don't like the thought of her going all that way, all alone. Would she have to change, like at a station?"

Jo shook her head. "She goes right through in the same aeroplane, over the North Pole."

"Fancy ..." Katie said. "Is that the way you're going, in the yacht? All in among the ice?"

Jo shook her head. "You couldn't go that way in a boat." Katie was a dear and she was going to look after Janice for them while they travelled, but she had lived in Ealing all her life. "We're going to go southwards into the warm seas," she explained. "When we leave Hamble on Thursday week we go to Falmouth to clear Customs and to pick up anything that we've forgotten. Then John wants to make a passage straight for Las Palmas in the Canary Islands. From there to Barbados, and then to the Panama Canal. When we get into the Pacific, first of all we go to the Galapagos Islands, and then to Tahiti. We do want to see that, and it's not much out of

the way. Then we go up to Honolulu and from there to
Vancouver. It ought to take about five months. A bit less, if
we're lucky with the winds."

The string of foreign names perplexed Katie; she did not
know where any of them were, except the Panama Canal.
The whole venture was entirely alien to her experience; she
struggled to make sense of it. "Will there be anyone to help
you with the boat?" she asked. "With the sails, and that?"

Jo shook her head. "We won't need anybody," she said.
"John and I can sail her by ourselves."

Katie was perplexed. "But what happens at night, when
you want to go to bed? I mean, do you anchor or something?" A sudden doubt assailed her. "You have *got* beds,
haven't you?"

"We've got very good beds," said Jo. "I sleep marvellously
on board. No, we couldn't anchor. It's too deep. Sometimes
we can let her sail herself while we both sleep." She tried to
make the matter simple, but it was rather difficult. "She'll do
that with the wind forward of the beam, or running under
the twin spinnakers. Otherwise we keep watch and watch—
one up in the cockpit steering and the other one down below
sleeping." She smiled. "It's quite all right. We're very used to
it."

"You wouldn't be sailing all the way, though, would you?"
Katie asked. "Keith was saying you could go some of the
way with the motor."

Joanna shook her head. "We shall sail all the way," she
replied, "except perhaps just getting in and out of harbour.
We have got a small motor, but we don't use it at sea. It's
only a little one, and it's dirty, and it makes a smell." She
paused, and then she said, "John's such a *seaman*."

Presently Katie reverted to her own problems. "It's just the
holidays," she said thoughtfully. "School time—well, I'm
back in the house by a quarter to six, always. School finishes
at four so she'd be back here by a quarter past, but Keith is
almost always here then, unless it's a Friday. It's really just
the holidays."

"The Christmas holidays," Jo said. "We don't sail till the
first of August. I'm going to take her up to the Dungannons in
Tyrone next week. I think school starts—Miss Pearson's
school, here—I think she said term starts on September the
15th. That means she'd be coming to you about the 13th, I

suppose. I think you'll have to meet her at Euston, but I'll make sure that the Dungannons let you know."

Katie nodded. "Keith would meet the train and bring her down here. He'd like doing that."

"I think we'll be sending for her about February," said Jo. "We should be there by then, and if we haven't got a house she can live on the boat with us. But anyway, I'll be writing to you from each place. It's just the Christmas holidays."

Katie said, "Of course, Keith is in the house most of the time, down in the workshop. They're not very long, the Christmas holidays."

"I don't want her to be a burden on you and Keith."

"She won't be that—honestly she won't." Katie paused. "I think it would be nice to have children's parties, and crackers, and presents, and all that."

Joanna eyed her uncertainly, wondering how far she meant it. "I'm sure Margaret would have her."

"Do whatever you think would be the best for her," said Katie. "But don't do it for us. Keith's always wanted to have kids about the place. I mean, with a great big garden, like we've got . . ."

In the room below Keith turned off the gas at the two cylinders, hung the torch up on its hook, took the copper box to a sink in one corner of the room, and scrubbed the brazing with water and a wire brush. He dried it on a dirty towel, and examined the seam carefully, inch by inch. Then he handed it to his brother-in-law. "She's tight now," he said briefly.

John Dermott took it from him. "No chance of sea water getting into it? Corrosion?"

"Not in a hundred years." He paused. "When you want to open it, just cut the top off with a hacksaw—round here."

The naval officer hesitated. "I'm going to set it in concrete," he said diffidently. Keith stared at him, surprised; he had thought the box was to go into the yacht. "Do you know how to mix it?"

"I know how to mix concrete," the mechanic said. "You mix it different proportions, depending on what it's for— what it's got to hang on to. How much would you want?"

The naval officer hesitated, and then indicated the box upon the bench before them. "About as much as that, or a bit more."

Keith frowned; this was getting difficult. "I should grease it before setting it in concrete," he suggested, trying to be helpful without knowing the job. "Come out easier when you want it out."

"I see." The naval officer hesitated, irresolute; he had never had to do this sort of work before and he wanted a good job made of it. "You wouldn't like to come down to the boat and do it for me?"

"Down to Hamble?" John Dermott nodded. "When?"

"We're going down tomorrow, in the car. Would it take long?"

"If it's a straight job it might take about an hour," Keith said. "Then you ought to leave it for a while to set—two or three days. I could come tomorrow, but I'd have to be back tomorrow night." His eyes strayed to a corner. "I've got half a bag of cement there, but I'd have to slip up to the builder for some sand. Got some aggregate down there?"

"What's that?"

"Little clean stones—just a few pounds. Not salty—washed in fresh water."

"There's plenty on the beach. We could wash them under the hose, couldn't we?"

Keith nodded. "Doesn't matter if they're wet."

They left it so, and turned to go upstairs. The naval officer paused by the littered desk with the drawing board beside it. "This where you do your stuff?"

Keith nodded. "I used to do it up in the parlour, but it's better down here. You'd be surprised at the number of letters that there are—all over the auction. I save the foreign stamps and give them to the boy next door—Jamesie Morris, he collects them. Six or seven in a day, some days. You'd be surprised."

John Dermott opened his eyes. "How many letters do you have to write—say, in a week?"

"Twenty or twenty-five," the mechanic said. "It's letters all the time, and then there's the articles each week. I spend more time writing than I do working." He paused, and added a little resentfully, "It's fifteen bob a week for stamps— more, sometimes. Of course, one has to do it. Some of them send international reply coupons, though."

"Do a lot of them come from foreign countries, then?"

"About a third."

John Dermott went back to the bench and picked up the copper box. "I'll take this along with me," he said. He hesitated. "You'll keep this under your hat?" he enquired diffidently. "I mean, it's quite all right. They're just Jo's rings and bracelets and things—they're all her own property. But the regulations are so stupid about taking things like that out of England, and she'd be miserable without them. I mean, a woman sort of values her little bits and pieces when she's away in a strange country. And we may be away for years."

Keith said, "Oh, that's all right. I shan't talk about it." He paused, and then he asked, "You're going to live out there?"

"I think so—if we like it. Jo says she wants to live in Tahiti, but I don't go much on that, myself. It's French, and it's a very little place, you know. Still, she wants to see it. I think we'll probably end up in British Columbia—it's a grand country, that. I'd like to buy a house in Victoria, on Vancouver Island."

Keith nodded. He had only the vaguest idea where Vancouver Island was, but it was the sort of place that people like his brother-in-law who sailed about the world in little yachts would want to go to. "Suppose I tell Katie that I'm going down to rig up an electric light over the compass, so you can see it at night?" he suggested.

John Dermott smiled. "That's just the thing."

They went up the narrow wooden basement stairs to the main floor and Keith went to wash the grime off his hands. When he rejoined them in the parlour his sister and her husband were standing, ready to leave, having pleaded a somewhat formalized dinner engagement to Katie. He did not press them to stay for tea, because he had learned long ago that they pursued different meal habits. Katie and Keith had their main meal in the middle of the day. Their evening meal was high tea at six o'clock when Katie got back from work, a meal of perhaps a kipper, bread and jam, and a piece of plum cake, washed down with tea. They knew that Jo and John ate differently at eight o'clock, favouring perhaps potted shrimps followed by soup, a grilled steak, and mushrooms on toast, the meal preceded by a couple of gins and followed by coffee. The couples got on well together, but they had long ago accepted differences springing from their ways of life.

Jo and John Dermott called for Keith at about nine o'clock next morning, driving their vintage sports Bentley open four-seater, nearly thirty years old and with many prosecutions for noise and speeding to its credit. They loved it very dearly. Katie had already left for work so she did not see the two small sacks that Keith put into the back compartment beside him, or she might have wondered why a small electric light required cement and sand. It was a warm summer morning in late July, and Keith enjoyed the drive through southern England. They got to Hamble on the creek that runs into the east side of Southampton Water, parked the car near the entrance to Luke's Yard, and carried the sacks out on to the long wooden walkways above the tidal mud, the yachts moored bows on in tiers. Presently they came to the Dermotts' ship, *Shearwater IV*.

Shearwater was a healthy-looking, modern Bermudian cutter about twenty-eight feet on the waterline and nine feet beam. On deck she was practical and well equipped for deep sea cruising, the dinghy stowed upside down over the cabin skylight between the mast and the aft hatch, the twin spinnaker booms in chocks beside it. She had roller reefing to the mainsail and a very short bowsprit no more than four feet long for the jibstay. Aft, she had a self-draining cockpit well protected by the vertical extensions of the cabin top, and a sail locker in her canoe stern. Below, she was conventional in her arrangement. A roomy forecastle served mainly as a sail store. Aft of that there was a washroom and toilet to starboard, a galley and pantry to port. Aft again came the saloon with the settees on each side and a table in the middle; a small chart table was arranged against the forward bulkhead. Aft again there were two quarter berths, the companion ladder leading up on deck, and a small petrol motor underneath this ladder, rather inaccessible. *Shearwater* was such a yacht as is to be found by the hundred cruising the south coast of England, though rather better equipped then most.

John Dermott led Keith down below. The linoleum on the deck of the galley and the washroom had been taken up, and the floor boards lifted. What was exposed to view was a smooth level floor of concrete into which the frames disappeared and in which the mast was stepped. About two feet behind the mast step was a fairly deep, rectangular recess in the concrete, large enough to hold the copper box that Dermott carried, and about two inches deeper.

"That's the place," he said. "That's where I want to put it."

Keith wrinkled his brows. "What's all this concrete doing here?"

"Internal ballast," said the naval officer. "They often do it like this. Pour it in when she's building, and bury pig iron or any old scrap iron in it. She'd be too lively with all the ballast on the keel. She's got about three tons of lead outside, as well."

"I never knew that," said the mechanic. "What's this hole been left here for, then?"

"I don't really know. She's got another like it at the stern, but that's used for a sump; the bilge pump suction goes down into it. Perhaps they thought she'd want another sump up here. I don't know. She never makes any water, anyway."

Keith knelt down and fingered the concrete hole. "It's a bit oily," he remarked. "I think I'll chip it a bit first—clean it up and make a sort of rebate, so it'll hold." He fetched his tool bag, and set to work with hammer and cold chisel.

Half an hour later he was mixing a little concrete of cement, fine stones and sand. He made a bed of it at the bottom of the hole, greased the copper box, and set it carefully in the middle. Then he filled in the spaces round it with the wet mixture, working it carefully into the corners and the newly cut recesses. "Look your last on it," he said, and covered it over with a smooth layer of the mix, patting it, working it with a little builders' trowel, taking up the surplus, till it was smooth and level with the original concrete floor, only the darker wetness of the new material showing the difference. He gathered his tools and the remainder of the mix in new paper, cleaned up the mess, and got up from his knees a little stiffly. "I'd leave the floor boards up for a day or so, till it's set hard," he said. "It'll take a week to harden properly, but you can put the boards back."

His sister asked, "What do we do when we want to get it out, Keith?"

"Just cut around the edge with a cold chisel and a hammer, like this," he said. "You'll probably be able to see where the concrete's a bit different, but even if you can't, it'll sound hollow when you tap it with a hammer. The top layer of concrete'll come off easy enough, because it's only an inch or so thick. Then when you can see the box you'll have to cut around with the chisel till you can get it out. You won't have any trouble."

He stayed for a cold lunch with them on board, and while the meal was in preparation he examined the ship, a short, white-faced, plump little man completely out of his element. He knew nothing of yachts and the sea. She seemed to him to be cosy enough downstairs, though a bit cramped; upstairs he was confused by the complexity of her and by the unfamiliar materials, the sisal, nylon, flax, cotton, hemp, and teak. He was unfamiliar with the sea and did not like it much; it was a place that made you cold and wet and sick. His brother-in-law was a sensible man in most ways though not in matters technical, and he liked the sea so there must be something in it for some people, though not for him. They had asked him once or twice to go down with Katie for a weekend on the yacht in the Solent, but he had always made excuse, and they had not pressed the point. The Stewarts had their way of life, and the Dermotts had theirs.

After lunch John Dermott drove Keith into Southampton and put him down at the West station to catch a train to London. They would meet again before the Dermotts started off across the world in *Shearwater;* they parted cordially, the naval officer grateful to his dissimilar brother-in-law for his help. He drove back from Southampton to Hamble; they would live on the yacht now till they sailed but for one last trip to London. There was still much to be done.

He parked the car and went on board. Jo met him in the cockpit. "Catch his train all right?"

He nodded. "Ten minutes to spare."

"Oh, good. I've just put on the kettle for a cup of tea."

They had their cups of tea sitting in the cockpit in the sun. The naval officer glanced down into the forward end of the ship, to the rolled-back linoleum and the floor boards piled beside it. The dark wetness of the concrete patch was already drying, turning a lighter grey at the edges that would match the original surface. "Well, that's the most important job done," he said with satisfaction. "I was worried about that, but it's all right now."

Joanna nodded. "Keith's awfully good at that sort of thing," she said quietly. "When he's got somebody to tell him exactly what to do."

She seldom talked openly to him about her brother; now in their shared satisfaction and relief that remark had slipped out. He glanced at her. "I know," he said. "Not much initiative."

She sat silent for a minute. "Poor old Keith," she said at last. "I always feel he's missed the boat, somehow. That I've had everything, and he's had nothing."

"Everything?" he asked. He was morbidly conscious of his truncated career, of the failure inherent in his early retirement, of the forty years of idleness that might lie ahead of him unless he could reorganize his life.

She knew what he was thinking, and he mustn't think it. She turned to him. "Oh, yes," she said. "I've had Janice, and money, and the Navy, and this boat. And I've been to China, and to Italy, and Malta. And now we're going off across the world, and we'll see the coral islands, and Hawaii, and Canada, and the States. I've had everything. But poor old Keith, he goes on in that ghastly half-a-house in Ealing and just makes his models and gets practically nothing for them, and Katie has to work in the shop. And he's so good at what he does. It isn't fair."

He tried to comfort her. "I don't think he's unhappy."

"No," she agreed, "he's not. Nor Katie, either. They're neither of them a bit jealous of the things we've got. I think it's going to do Janice a lot of good to be with them for a bit. But he's so much better than I am, he ought to have so very much more."

He smiled. "Wants somebody to put a squib up his behind."

"He always has to be told what to do," she agreed.

"Apart from making models," he remarked. "He seems to be original enough in that."

"Yes," she agreed. "But that doesn't get him anywhere."

Keith Stewart got to Waterloo at about half past four, and travelled out to Ealing Broadway on the Underground. From there he took a tram to West Ealing and walked up to his house. He got in about ten minutes before Katie and put the macaroni cheese into the oven as she had told him to, and took the mail from the letter box in the front door and shuffled it through; there was one letter for her and eleven for him, three from the United States. He sighed a little. You could produce an induced current on the surface of a metal sphere that would act as a gyroscope, and from this you could devise a tiny automatic pilot for ship or aircraft models that would weigh only a few ounces. He was aching to get on with the experimental work on that, but first he had to write the last instalment of his serial upon the Congreve clock. After that this heavy mail must be dealt with, and he would be too tired then, and it would be too late to start off on experimental work. He was already inclined to be sleepy from his unaccustomed day in the open air.

He sat with Katie at the kitchen table over the macaroni cheese and the cups of strong tea. "Get the light fixed up for them all right?" she asked.

"The light?" And then he recollected. "Oh, the compass light. Yes, I fixed that for them."

"What's it like in the boat?" she asked. "How do they cook anything?"

"It's like a caravan," he told her. "They cook on Primus stoves."

"Oh. With everything rocking about?"

"I suppose so."

"It must be ever so uncomfortable."

"I think it is," he agreed. "It looks all right when she's tied up in calm water, like she is now, but even then she goes up and down a bit. I don't know what it's like when she gets out to sea, where it's rough. Wouldn't suit me."

"Would the water come in, say in a storm?"

"I think it would. Of course, she's all decked in. I don't suppose that much would get inside."

"It sounds awful. I mean, Jo was saying that one of them must be on top to steer. Why do they want to go like that, K? I mean, they've got plenty of money. Why don't they take a cabin on a proper ship, or else fly?"

"I dunno," he said. "I think they just like doing it."

They sat in silence; they would never understand the Dermotts and there were times when they abandoned the attempt. At last Katie said, "They won't get shipwrecked, will they?"

Keith shook his head. "That's one thing they won't do. John's a naval officer and he knows all about it. They've got two sextants to take sights with to tell them where they are, and all the rest of it. They'll be safe enough. But if you ask me, they'll be darned uncomfortable."

Katie gathered the plates together and put them on the draining board. "I'm glad it's not me going with them."

"So am I," he said. "I can't imagine anything much worse."

2

Shearwater ROLLED LAZILY UP ON THE ocean swell as she forged ahead under her twin spinnakers, making about three knots and towing the log line behind her. It was early in the morning and John Dermott was taking a sight upon the sun on their port quarter, dressed only in a pair of faded shorts. Jo sat at the tiller in blue jeans and shirt, watch in hand and pad and pencil at her side, taking the time for him.

They were three and a half months out from England, and now it was the middle of November. They had crossed the Atlantic to Barbados without incident though more slowly than they had anticipated; they had been delayed a little in the West Indies for a broken gooseneck to the boom, and they had been delayed for a long time at Panama after passing through the Canal waiting for a permit from the Ecuadorian Government to call for water at the Galapagos Islands. In the end they had sailed without a permit, had watered at Floreana without trouble, and proceeded on their way. They were thirty-four days out from Floreana, and all was well.

They had not hurried on their way. Thirty-six hours previously they had lain hove-to all night rather than approach the island of Reao in the darkness, their first landfall in the Tuamotu group of islands. With the coming of the dawn they had seen cloud forming above it and had sailed close enough to see the tops of the trees; then they had borne up and resumed their course towards the south and west, leaving the island ten miles to the north. They would not set foot on land until they reached the island of Tahiti, more than eight hundred miles ahead. They did not particularly want to do so; they had settled into the rhythm of their life at sea, the rain squalls, the warm easy days, the unending maintenance of sails and gear, the cooking and the housework down below. They had grown accustomed to this routine and liked it. For John Dermott it meant full occupation in the way of life that he preferred; shore life to him was now a matter of frustration and unwanted idleness. For Jo, this way of life meant a happy John.

She jotted down the altitudes as he called them out and the exact time from the watch in her hand, and gave the pad to him. He disappeared below to work the sight and plot it on the chart. He came on deck again after ten minutes. "It *was* Reao?" she asked.

"It was Reao all right," he replied. "I think we're getting set just a bit to the north, though. You're still steering two four zero?"

She nodded.

"Make it two three five," he said. "Pinaki should be showing up upon the starboard bow before long. I want to pass about ten miles south of it."

"There's a bit of cloud there now," she said.

He stood looking at the little white patch on the horizon with her. "Could be." He went below, entered the change of course in the log, and came up again with the hand-bearing compass and squatted on the cabin top with it, sighting upon the cloud. "That's probably Pinaki."

They sailed on all the morning over a long swell before a moderate southeast breeze, under a hot sun shrouded by occasional clouds. In good conditions such as these it was their habit to take their main meal in the middle of the day; Jo cooked a corned beef stew and an apple crumble from dried apples, and they had it in the cockpit. Then she went down to sleep. In the middle of the afternoon the sky clouded over, the wind got up suddenly, and a vicious rain squall swept down on them. They were accustomed to these short-lived tropical squalls and before it started John at the helm could see clear weather behind it. He carried on, the ship scudding before the strong breeze with everything taut and straining, but a seam in the port spinnaker suddenly let go, the sail ripped across, and there was nothing but a flapping shambles of loose sail and wildly flailing boom across the foredeck forward of the mast. John shouted but Jo was already awake and coming out on deck to take the helm; such incidents were part of their daily life and she was well accustomed to them. By the time John had got the sail down and the boom under control the sudden wind had dropped down to a gentle breeze, and they could see the squall driving away to leeward. They set the mainsail and the second jib, took in both spinnakers, and went on. Jo went down to finish her sleep before taking the first watch, and John spread out the damaged sail to dry in the cockpit with him while he measured and cut new sailcloth on his knees for the repair, sailing the ship as he did so.

They sailed on easily all night. Under twin spinnakers they could perhaps have slept at the same time, but running under the mainsail they had to steer the ship. Jo took the first watch until midnight, sailing easily under a bright crescent moon with little to do but to keep awake. She roused John as he had instructed her and he put on the Primus and made cocoa; they had it together in the cockpit before she handed over to him and went down to sleep.

At dawn they were still sailing easily. She relieved him at the helm, and presently when the sun was high enough he took another sight and went down to work out the position line. When she saw him plotting it upon the chart down in the cabin she called out, "How do we go?"

"Not bad." He brought the chart to the companion, and standing on the cabin ladder he showed it to her in the cockpit. "We must be about *here*." He made a little cross upon the chart. "We might be a little south of the course now. I'll take a noon sight today, I think, and see if it makes sense." He did not trust a sight with the sun practically overhead.

"How far before we change course, John?"

He took the chart back to the chart table and measured with dividers, and came back to the companion. "About forty miles. Sometime this evening, if everything goes well."

They had been sailing substantially the same course since leaving the Galapagos Islands thirty-five days before. "What will the new course be?"

"Two hundred and seventy. An easy one."

"That's for Tahiti?"

He nodded.

"I don't suppose the compass will work," she said. "It's

probably got rusty and stuck up, we've been on this one for so long."

He smiled. "Like me to get breakfast?"

"No, you come and take her. I'll get breakfast. After that we'll have to mend that spinnaker."

He nodded. "We'll be bringing the wind more aft when we change course."

All morning they worked on the spinnaker together in the cockpit. It was finished before the noon sight had to be taken but they did not set it, for the wind was still well on the quarter. The noon sight confirmed their position for what that was worth, but when they went to check it with the reading of the log they found the line trailing idly; the rotator had been taken by a fish. They had left England with a dozen spare rotators and were now reduced to three; they fitted one of these last ones and started to get dinner.

They slept in turns all afternoon in overcast, rainy weather without much wind; in the hot humidity they paid little attention to getting wet at the helm save to wear a hat to keep the rain out of their eyes. The overcast prevented an evening sight. John stood for a while at the chart table weighing the doubtful evidence of the noon sight and of the log, the more certain evidence of the morning sight which did not give much indication of the latitude, the landfall that they had made the day before at Pinaki. Eight o'clock, he thought, would be a convenient time for the change of course, when Jo took over for the first watch; if the wind held as it was they would take in the main and the jib then and set the spinnakers. They should be far enough by that time to make the turn, but he was very conscious of the massed coral islands of the Tuamotus over the horizon to the north. He didn't want to get mixed up with that lot.

They followed on this plan, and started to change sails at half past seven, the wind still moderate from the east-south-east. By eight o'clock they had her settled under the twin spinnakers on the new course. "I think this deserves a drink," he said. At sea they drank little alcohol.

She smiled. "Whiskey and lime juice for me. The compass seems to be working, anyway."

They had the sheets of the spinnakers rigged to the tiller and the ship would steer herself before the wind without attention. They watched her for a few minutes, and then went down into the cabin and sat with their drinks in the light of the oil lamp. "What are the hazards, John?" she asked.

He pulled the chart over and showed it to her. "Ahunui," he said. He showed her the island. "Should be about twenty miles to the north, and abeam about three in the morning. We probably shan't see it. After that there's nothing much until Tahiti."

They finished their drinks and put their heads out on deck at the companion; the ship was sailing easily on course in a gentle breeze and a long swell, the tiller moving now and then to the pull of the sheets. In those waters there was little chance of meeting any other ship and they sailed without lights as one chore less to do. They went below together and slept intermittently, one or other being up on deck every hour or so.

All next day they sailed on placidly under the twin spinnakers, and the next night. The massed chain of islands constituting the Tuamotus now lay a hundred miles to the north of them; there was nothing in their path before Tahiti and they were making good about ninety sea miles each day. Rain squalls came occasionally without much strength in them. The barometer, which John watched unobtrusively but closely, pursued its regular diurnal variation according to the book. They began to make plans for cleaning the ship up, including themselves, before entering the harbour of Papeete.

Jo had been reading the sailing directions for entering the port. "We can lie alongside there, at the Quai du Commerce," she said. "It's going to be good for getting the stores in, but we'll have to get everything all tiddley."

John said, "Going to be bad for little boys spitting on the deck. I think we'll lie off if we stay for any length of time."

On the second morning after they changed course the barometer displeased him. It was two millibars lower than it should have been according to the book; he tapped it gently, mindful of the delicacy of the mechanism, but it showed no difference. Jo was on deck at the helm when he made this discovery for the wind had got up a bit and veered towards the south, and *Shearwater* was now careering along with the spinnakers at a cockeyed angle fore and aft, and needed someone at the helm. He bit his lip, and looked again at the barometer, but there was no sense in trying to argue with the evidence. They were late at Tahiti, and the hurricane season was now on.

He sat down on his berth and turned to the sailing directions. He knew the part about tropical revolving storms pretty well by heart, for he was a careful seaman and had briefed himself before entering these waters. He read the page again. It fitted with his observations of the barometric pressure and the wind. Now it was up to him.

The wind had already veered a little, so the centre of the storm, if storm it was, must lie away to the northeast, two or three hundred miles away from them. It would probably move west-southwest towards them at about ten knots, far faster than they could sail to escape it. At some time it would turn towards the south. The wind direction showed them to be south of its path now. The course of safety was to run north and west before the increasing wind ... and north of them lay the coral islands of the Tuamotus. If they escaped the eye of the storm the wind would go on veering to the south and then to the southwest, blowing them dead on to a lee shore.

They must make towards the west, every mile they could, to gain sea room.

He put the book back in the bookcase, and went on deck. He looked around; the spinnakers were straining. It would be unwise to carry them much longer, anyway. He said to Jo, "I think we'll put the trysail on her, and take these in."

The trysail was their storm mainsail. "The trysail?" she asked.

"Barometer's dropping a bit," he said.

"Oh." She knew the situation almost as well as he did. "Want any help?"

"Not yet." He went below and bundled the heavy canvas up on deck through the fore hatch, brought it aft of the mast and began to reeve the lacing, the halliard, and the sheets. It was work that he was well accustomed to and liked; while you were doing something physical like that you couldn't worry about falling glass and veering winds. He hoisted the sail in the calm air before the spinnaker and made the halliard fast, and pulled the sheet out to the cockpit, putting weight into the sail. Then he got down the lee spinnaker, and then the weather, stowing them both below. Finally he set the storm jib. Under the reduced canvas the yacht went more easily, with little reduction in her speed.

He came aft to the cockpit. Jo asked, "Is anything bad coming?"

"I don't know," he said. "She's going all right like this, anyway."

It was an hour since he had looked at the barometer. He went below and found that it had dropped another point; it was now three millibars below normal. He went back to his wife at the helm. "I don't much like the look of it," he said. "We may be in for something."

She smiled at him. "Too bad." She remembered that you steered in certain directions to avoid the path of a tropical storm, but it was different in the northern and the southern hemispheres, and all a bit complicated. "Ought we to change course?"

He shook his head. "I think we'll keep on as we're going for a bit. See what the wind does. Like me to take her?"

She relinquished the helm to him. "I think I'll go below and make some sandwiches and put some coffee in the thermoses, if we're in for something." She knew storms.

All morning the wind rose steadily, veering a little as it rose. The sun grew weaker, covered over with a thin layer of cloud. Before it disappeared for good John took a sight and came to the conclusion that they were in about latitude 19° 30′ south, longitude 142° 35′ west. The wind was now south of southeast blowing about Force 5 or rather more. By noon the barometer was five millibars lower than the normal reading.

There was now no doubt of the position in his mind, and he braced himself for what was coming. The wind would continue veering to the south and would increase in strength, driving them to the north on to the Tuamotus. A hundred and forty miles ahead of them and a little to the south of west lay an isolated atoll called Hereheretue; there was no harbour there, no entrance to the lagoon, and no safe landing in this weather. Yet if he could reach it he might shelter behind it from the fury of the storm, using it as a breakwater; in any event a more southerly course would take him further from the Tuamotus. He altered course to 245°, and his ship went racing along with a beam wind, making about six knots. At that rate they would reach the shelter of the atoll in about twenty-four hours, but from the first he doubted if they would make it.

They put on their waterproof storm clothing with bright orange life jackets and waist life lines that they could clip on to the rigging. They locked the forehatch down, and fitted the weatherboards over the glasses of the cabin skylight under the dinghy.

All day the wind increased and veered towards the south. They could take in one reef in the trysail with a lacing round the boom, and they took that in with difficulty towards evening. With the reduced canvas they made much more leeway, and now John Dermott gave up the attempt to reach Hereheretue. With the last of the light he backed the foresail a little and hove his vessel to on the port tack in the increasing wind; she lay fairly quietly making about two knots to leeward in the direction of the Tuamotus. At any rate, he thought, they had made some useful offing.

They sat together in the cabin, dimly lit by the swaying oil lamp turned down low because it smoked with the motion, listening to the crash of the seas against the bow as the vessel rode the waves. Jo asked, "Where do you think we are, John?"

He showed her on the chart.

"It's a bad one, this, isn't it?" she asked.

He nodded.

"The worst we've ever had?"

"It might be," he admitted. "I'll tell you when it's over."

"I suppose it's because we're late in getting here," she said. She had known in theory that hurricanes were apt to happen in those waters from November onwards. Now that theoretical knowledge was being translated into fact.

"We're not so late as all that," he said a little resentfully. "This is an early one."

She knew that he had first proposed that they should leave England in June. "We had to see Janice settled for the summer holidays."

He nodded. "We couldn't have started any earlier."

Presently they lay down on their berths to get what rest they could. From time to time Dermott got up and put his head out of the hatch; the wind seemed stronger every time he looked, and the sea higher. Each time the ship's head pointed, on the wildly veering average, a little more towards the west and north.

At about three in the morning there was a great crack, the ship's motion changed, and a wild beating of heavy canvas was heard above them. They tumbled out on deck, and saw in the light of a flashlight through the flying scud that the jib had gone; only the bolt ropes remained with tattered streamers of canvas flying from them. Without the jib the ship had come up to the wind, and the heavy blocks of the trysail sheets were flailing the cockpit, threatening death to anybody in their way.

Without the jib he could not lie the vessel to in such a wind. He shouted to Jo to get a warp from the forecastle, and went forward carefully himself on deck, clipping his life line on to something fresh at every two or three steps. At the mast he slacked off the main halliard and let the trysail down and quietened it; with the warp that Jo had brought up to him from below they furled the trysail on the main boom, wrapping it round with the rope.

Without any sail at all the yacht now lay rolling wildly in the trough of the waves, safe enough for the time being, but blowing to the north. John Dermott sent his wife below to get some rest, and stayed in the cockpit himself to watch his vessel and assess the situation. The wind was now only about a point to the east of south and this was good so far as it went, for it indicated that the centre of the storm might pass southwards of them. The sea, however, was rising very high; in the grey of the dawn it seemed to be breaking everywhere around him. He judged that his ship was drifting to the north at the rate of three or four knots.

The line of the Tuamotus to the north of him ran about northwest to southeast. The more he could get towards the west, the more sea room he would have to the north. He took the helm and set himself to sail his vessel under bare poles as much towards the west as he could manage. He found that he could steer about northwest upon his compass paralleling the line of islands, and at that he seemed to make about five knots with the wind on his quarter. But now, running in that way, the seas behind were menacing and occasionally the top of one came on board, lukewarm, flooding the cockpit and drenching the helmsman. From below, Jo put the fashionboards in the companion.

"How are we doing?" she asked.

"All right," he said. "If we can keep going like this I think we'll be all right. It's doing what they tell you in the book, anyway." Deep in his heart he knew that they could not maintain that course much longer.

At seven o'clock in the increasing wind and sea he could no longer run towards the west, taking the seas upon his quarter, without fear of broaching to and being overwhelmed by the rising sea. Each time a big sea came, and they now came very often, he had to run off before it taking it dead stern-on, so that now he was making about five knots towards the Tuamotus in the north.

This could not go on. He had a sea anchor in the forecastle, a conical canvas drogue stiffened by a hoop of iron, and he called Jo up from below to come and take the helm while he rigged this thing. *Shearwater* was a cutter with a shape below the waterline that was cut away at the bow and deep at the rudder, making her easy to tack and manoeuvre in the narrow seas and waterways of the Solent, for which she had been primarily designed. Running before the wind she was very stable by reason of the windage of the mast, but held up to the wind by a sea anchor from the bow she would not be good, unlikely to lie closer than forty-five degrees to wind and sea. She had a canoe stern, however, fairly well tucked up. He decided to put out his sea anchor from the stern, battening the companion down and retiring below, using the fore hatch for getting out on deck.

He bent his heaviest warp on to the sea anchor, made the other end fast around both pairs of stern mooring bitts, and put the drogue overboard, taking a turn of the warp round one of the bitts as he paid out to ease the strain. The warp strained like a bowstring as the drogue sank in and took hold of the water; then the ship slowed, the strain eased, and he paid out the remainder slowly.

He sent Jo down below and stood himself on the companion steps for a while behind the fashionboards, his head out of the hatch, watching the seas. The ship was riding well to her sea anchor, her buoyant stern lifting to the seas so that little came on board. The wind had steadily increased, however, and he judged that now it was blowing at about Force 8. It was so strong that it seemed to be blowing the tops off the seas in the form of flying scud beneath the heavily overcast sky, flattening the very seas; the warp stretched taut behind the vessel to the submerged drogue, hard as a bar. With this increasing wind the speed of the ship through the water did not seem to be very much reduced; she still seemed to be making about three knots towards the north. Visibility was now only a few hundred yards.

He went below and secured the companion hatch behind him. In the cabin it was dark and stuffy, lit only by one small glass port, tight shut, at the galley, and another at the companion. He went forward and lifted the fore hatch a little, letting some air into the ship, and then came back and sat upon his berth, opposite Jo. He pulled the chart over to him from the chart table and sat studying it.

Jo leaned across in the dim light. "Where do you think we are?"

He did not know with any certainty. "I should say we're about here." He laid his finger on the chart. Actually he was further to the north and not so far to the west, but he did not know that.

"What happens next?" she asked.

"We'll just have to lie like this now till it moderates," he said. "I think the centre will pass south of us."

"How long before it moderates?" she asked.

"Two days, I should think," he said. "Two days. Maybe, three."

"Have we got that much room?" she asked.

He shook his head. "No," he said. "No, I don't think we have."

"Too bad." She smiled a little, and then said, "Tell me, do you think we're going to pile her up?"

He glanced up at her. "I hope not," he replied. He ran his finger down the line of the Tuamotus. "The line of islands isn't very thick, and there's deep water all between them. We can steer her a bit down wind, running. If there's any visibility we should be able to run through them." He paused, and then said a little bitterly, "Like a drunk crossing the traffic in the Strand."

"We aren't drunk," she said gently. "A bit out of luck, perhaps, but not drunk."

He glanced at her. "I'm sorry about this, Jo."

"We'll be all right," she said. "Lie down and get some sleep."

They lay down and rested, if not slept. The motion of the ship was too violent for any cooking, but in the course of the afternoon Jo managed to light a Primus and to brew some strong, sweet chocolate, and this revived them a little. She still had a few sandwiches left, but neither of them could eat. The bilge water was slopping over the cabin floor; inevitably a wooden ship will leak a little under such strains, and in the last two days a good deal of water had found its way below.

In the middle of the afternoon John Dermott decided to pump the ship out. He pulled up the floor boards near the engine and left Jo to keep the suction clear of any debris in the bilge, and went out on deck himself by the fore hatch. He was startled and concerned at the strength of the wind now, and the steepness of the seas behind them. As the yacht's stern rose upon the forward slope of each great wave the warp to the sea anchor stretched out taut behind her, the water pattering off it with the strain; then the crest passed, the surf filling the cockpit, and the rope relaxed.

He crept aft on hands and knees on deck against the wind and the loose surf of each wave crest that slapped at him. With each step he refastened his life line, for the danger of being swept overboard was now a real one. He gained the cockpit, but he did not immediately begin to pump the ship. The sea anchor warp was more urgent, and he turned his attention to that.

He had wrapped three teacloths around the rope at the stern fairhead, tying them to the warp with marline, to take the chafe. They were just about worn through; he cut the marline, working mostly under water, and remade the packing. The rope below the cloths did not seem to be damaged. He crouched waist deep in water in the flooded cockpit, watching it for a time. Everything seemed to be holding, but the strain was immense. If the sea anchor went—or when it went—there would then be nothing to be done but to come to the helm and steer the ship, running under bare poles before the storm towards the islands.

He turned and started work upon the pump. There was a little opening glass porthole in the aft side of the cabin top by the companion, and from time to time Jo opened this to tell him how the water level was before shutting it again. It took him about an hour to clear the ship of water, sitting

mostly in lukewarm water up to the waist in the force of
the gale. By the time he had finished and the pump had
sucked he was exhausted, but he did not immediately go
forward to the hatch.

He made another inspection of the sea anchor warp; it
looked all right. He sat for a time looking round the horizon.
An early dusk was creeping down upon the scene. He could
see nothing but blown spray and breaking towering seas; he
did not think he could see further than about two hundred
yards. There was nothing to indicate the presence of land,
but then he knew there wouldn't be until they saw and heard
the breakers.

He glanced around at his ship. She seemed to be in perfect
condition, but for the tatters of the sail upon the jibstay. The
helm swung quietly and loose. The ends of halliards and
sheets were streaming overboard; they did not matter. Seeing
the strength and order of his ship, he felt suddenly tired. As
usual, he thought, the ship was stronger than the people in
her.

He took a final glance at the compass; the wind had gone
round further, and was now west of south, blowing harder
than ever. The eye of the storm would pass to the south of
them now, though pretty close; before the wind eased it
would haul round into the west. Before then, he knew, they
would be in among the Tuamotus. He left the cockpit and
crawled forward to the fore hatch, waited his chance, then
opened it and slipped below, pulling it down behind him.

He was shivering a little, more from fatigue and shock
than from cold. They heated up the remainder of the cocoa
and drank that, and then lay down fully clothed with life-
belts on, in their sodden clothes upon their sodden berths.
There was nothing further to be done on deck; it was more
important now to conserve their strength.

Darkness came swiftly, but they did not attempt to light
the lamp. They had electric torches, and there were still dry
spare batteries in sealed tins. They lay trying to rest, listening
to the struggle of the ship, the wash of waves along the deck
over their heads, and the insensate screaming of the wind.
Presently they may have slept a little.

At about ten o'clock John Dermott went out on deck again
to adjust the wrappings round the warp. Conditions were
similar but it was dark as pitch and raining hard, or so it

seemed to him for it was only possible to distinguish rain from the blown spume by the taste. He worked largely by feel, renewed the wrappings, and returned down below.

"We'll have to stand a watch as soon as it gets light," he said. "We may be getting pretty close to something by tomorrow."

"Would you like me to go up now?"

He shook his head. "We're all right for tonight. You can't see anything up there, anyway. Hardly the ship's length."

"What's the wind doing?"

"Seems to be a bit more over in the west."

They lay down on their berths again, but not for the whole night. Soon after midnight the yacht surged forward on the forward slope of a wave, a motion they were well accustomed to, and did not check her run. Instead she went surging forward wildly and then round in a crazy turn to port, throwing John out on to the cabin floor. Then she was thrown on her beam ends and buried in the seas; everything fell down on to the starboard side within the cabin, John on top of Jo in a mass of tins, books, tools, bedding, sextants, and cooking gear. The ship lay on her side for what seemed an age till gradually she rose again as they struggled free and to their feet in a foot of water over the cabin deck.

They knew what had happened; the vessel had broached to. In fact, the sea anchor warp had chafed and parted at the drogue end, and now the yacht was lying broadside on and at the mercy of the waves. They ripped the companion hatch back and struggled into the cockpit, and as they did so she went over again in a breaking sea.

She came up again more slowly, sluggishly, and they were both still there in the cockpit. The companion hatch had been half open, and she had taken much water in through it; she now lay heavily and sluggishly at least a foot deeper in the water, in the trough of the waves. But Dermott had the helm now and was steering her round down wind, and Jo had slammed the hatch shut and bolted it. When the next wave came they took it stern on and she rose to it with far less than her normal buoyancy, but rise she did; the top of the crest swept green across them but they did not broach again. There was now a little faint light on the scene, probably due to the moon above the clouds.

John said quietly, "Start pumping, Jo. We'll take it in turns."

She bent to the pump and began the endless, back-breaking motion on the handle. Presently he gave her the helm and took the pump himself; so they continued alternately pumping and steering for the rest of the night, while the wind screamed around them and the surf beat on them. From time to time the suction blocked with debris in the bilge; then John had to wait his chance to open the companion hatch for a moment to get down into the flooded cabin, shut the hatch above him, and working with his hands and arms deep in the water in pitch darkness clear the pump. The night passed like this, but when the grey cold light began to make things visible the ship was buoyant again, almost clear of water.

In the cockpit as they rested, Jo asked, "Did you think we'd had it that time, John?"

"I don't know that I had time to think of anything, except getting her straight and running," he replied. "When we got her running I knew that we were going to make it all right."

She said, "I've been thinking so much about Janice."

"Don't," he said gently. "We'll have her with us in a month or two."

"If we get out of this."

"We'll get out of it, all right," he said. "But if anything should happen, if we buy it, she couldn't be with anybody better than Katie and Keith."

"They'll look after her," she said. "But she's only ten. And John, they haven't any money."

"She'll have money," he replied. "It's all left in trust to Keith for her, until she's twenty-five. She'll get as good an education as anyone can get, and after that she'll have a good lump sum. Don't you remember how we made our wills?"

"But John, she won't have anything! We've got it all here!"

He stared at her in the half light. "I never thought of that." This was another disaster that had come upon him, and one that hit him far harder than any that had come so far. The approach of the storm, the parting of the jib, the chafing of the sea anchor warp, the broaching to, the near-

ness of the Tuamotus—these were challenges to his seamanship. When you went to sea and crossed the world in a small
yacht you wagered your courage and your skill against the
elements with your life as the stake, and if you were good
you usually won. It was what you went to sea for in this
game; if you didn't like the game you needn't play it. He had
wanted to play it because the sea was his whole life, and Jo
had wanted to play it with him because she loved him. Now,
suddenly and without warning, his small child's future had
been added to the stake.

Inevitably, perhaps, he held strongly right-wing views; he
was a conservative in politics. He held that if a man worked
hard and well and saved money he had a right to pass some
of it on to his children, especially if they were girls, who
usually got a raw deal anyway. He approved of moderate
death duties because he did not hold that grandchildren
should live in idleness because grandfather had worked; all
people ought to work, as he had worked for the Navy
himself. He held, however, that it was the duty and the right
of every decent man to give his children as good a start in
life as he had had himself. He had been blessed with money
from the start and he had tried to use it wisely and to save it
for his child so that she should grow up in the way of life he
was accustomed to. That she should go to the council school
and be fed and clothed by charity was quite unthinkable.

Joanna did not follow him in all of this. For twenty years
she had lived as a naval officer's wife and she had absorbed a
good deal of it, but she had come from a labourer's home
and had gone to the council school herself in Renfrew. She
had raised herself when she went on to the stage with a
serious, well managed troupe of girls; she had raised herself
again when she had married John Dermott. In many ways
she was now more conservative than he. The slum streets and
the council school were not terrifying novelties to her for she
had come from them, but she had long been determined that
Janice was going to have no part of them. She had borne
Janice into a different world, a world of naval officers and
impoverished noblemen in Northern Ireland, and she was
going to stay there.

As the full daylight came they could see the binnacle, and
see that the wind was now about west-southwest by their
compass. At the same time, it had risen higher than ever, and

was now screaming in their ears, deafening them, so that John judged it to be Force 10 or more. The sky cleared with the morning so that they could see much further than before, and away to the south there seemed to be a line of blue sky just above the sea. John pointed it out to Jo, and put his lips to her cold ear. "That'll be the eye of the storm," he shouted.

"Passing south of us?"

He nodded. There were no great waves now, just a smoking, hissing sea flattened by the insensate torrent of the wind. To talk was an effort and a strain; it was better to conserve their strength. They sat in silence, each busy with their thoughts turning over slowly in their stunned minds.

John Dermott was thinking always of the ship. She was still sound and practically undamaged. The mainsail and the trysail were still lashed firm upon the boom, ready for use. No sails could stand a minute in such wind; it was no good thinking about them. There was one resource still left to them, however. They still had a little engine.

He had scant faith in it, but it was there. In dead calm weather it would give the ship a speed of about four knots for going in and out of harbour or up windless estuaries, but the wind was now blowing sixty knots or more. This puny little engine, if he could make it work, could not affect the major issues of their course, yet if he could get it going it might serve to pull them out of trouble somehow. It was the last resource still left unused.

He gave the helm to Jo and went below, shutting the companion after him. In the light of his torch he saw that the battery had been thrown from its crate when the ship broached to and was lying on its side; everything was streaming with sea water. He stood the battery upright, checked the leads, and tried a light switch. There was the faintest of red glimmers from the filament, which faded as he watched.

There was no help in the starter. He wiped the magneto and the plug leads with a wet handkerchief, having searched in vain for a dry cloth, and tried her on the handle. For a quarter of an hour he laboured over her, and never got a kick. Finally he gave up the effort and went back on deck. There was no help in the engine.

While he was below, Jo sat at the helm in dull despair. The huge efforts needed to pull the tiller continuously one way or the other to keep the ship stern on to the seas were draining the last of her strength; she could still make them mechanically but she was now near collapse. There was no ending to this storm and would not be for days and days and days; the ship might see it through if she had fresh hands at the helm, but they would not. She was near failure now, she knew; half an hour longer or perhaps an hour, and she would be no longer able to swing the tiller. Then the ship would broach to and lie swept by every sea; they would be drowned. *Shearwater* would fill and sink, and Janice's future would sink with her. She was too tired now to care about themselves, but Janice was a sharp pain. Keith would look after her and bring her up, and he would do it well. But he would have to bring her up into his own way of life, not theirs; at sixteen she would have to start work in a shop.

John Dermott came back to the cockpit and took the helm from her. "No good," he shouted in her ear.

She shouted back, "Won't it go?" He shook his head, and she settled down beside him, listless.

About the middle of the morning something in the water ahead drew John's attention. He gave the helm to Jo and stood up against the companion, the wind tearing at his clothing, lashed by the spray. Visibility was between one and two miles. There was something different half a mile or so ahead of him; the backs of the seas looked different in some way. Then, over to the left a little, in a quick, passing glimpse, he saw what looked like the tops of palm trees above the waves.

He turned with a heavy heart, and went back to his wife. "There seems to be an island dead ahead," he shouted. "I think we're driving down on to a reef."

She nodded. She was now past caring.

He took her hand. "I'm sorry about this, Jo."

She smiled at him. "It doesn't matter."

"Can you take her a bit longer?" he asked. "I want to see if we can dodge it."

She nodded, and he stood up again by the companion. It was clearer now for they were closer. What he had seen was the backs of great combers breaking on a coral reef; the line of different surf extended both on port and starboard hands as far as he could see. He searched desperately for a break in the surf, something to indicate a passage through the reef into the sheltered lagoon that might lie beyond. If there were any break he would try and steer her off and run in through it, even though they might be overwhelmed in the process. He could see no break at all; it all looked just the same on either hand as far as he could see. There was no escape for them now. *Shearwater* was driving straight on to a coral reef in the Tuamotus somewhere, and would leave her bones upon the coral as many a tall ship had done before. He had not the remotest idea where they were.

He came back to her and took the helm. In bad moments in the last forty-eight hours he had imagined this situation, and had thought it out. Better to take the coral straight, head on, than to be thrown on to it on their beam ends, to have the hull crushed like an eggshell by the fury of the waves. Better to take it head on, taking the shock on the lead keel and trying to keep stern on to the seas. Reefs were seldom uniform in height; if they had the luck to strike a fissure, a patch where in calm water the coral was a couple of feet or more below the surface, they might possibly be driven over it into the lagoon, and still float, and live. He bent to explain this to his wife.

"I want you to go below," he shouted. "When we strike, stay in the hull. She'll probably get full of water, but stay in the hull. Just keep your head above the water, but stay inside."

She shouted, "What are you going to do?"

"I'm going to stay up here and steer her on. I'll join you down below as soon as she strikes. It's our best chance. I don't think she'll break up."

"If she breaks up, she'll stay on the reef, won't she?"

He knew what was in her mind. "The keel will, and probably the frames." He paused, and then leaned across and kissed her. "Now go below. I'm sorry to have got you into this."

She kissed him in return. "It's not your fault." She stood up, waited her chance, opened the hatch and slipped down below, leaving it open for him to follow her.

She sat down on one of the settees, the first-aid box in her hands. There were now only a few minutes to go. She thought she ought to say a prayer, but it seemed mean to have neglected God and her religion for so long and then to pray when death was imminent; the words would not come.

She could only think of Janice, Janice whose future happiness lay buried in the concrete beneath her feet. The concrete would survive upon the coral reef, but nobody would ever know of it but Keith. Keith, who had never made much of his life; Keith, who had never been anywhere or done anything. Keith, to whose keeping she had trusted Janice.

From the cockpit John Dermott shouted above the screaming of the wind, "Next one, Jo!"

In those last moments the power of prayer came to her and she muttered in the accents of her childhood, "Lord, gie Keith a bit o' guid sense."

Then they struck.

3

AT ABOUT ELEVEN IN THE morning the telephone bell rang upstairs. Keith Stewart stopped his lathe, wiped his hands, and went up the narrow wooden stairs to answer it. The girl said, "Mr. Stewart? This is Gordon and Carpenter. Just one moment—Mr. Carpenter is calling."

In a moment the solicitor came on the line. Keith had met him once before, a heavy, methodical man whose office was in Bedford Square. He said, "Mr. Stewart, have you had any news of your brother-in-law and your sister? Do you know if they have reached Tahiti yet?"

"I haven't heard anything. Not since they left Panama."

"Nor have I. I would have thought that they'd have cabled their arrival by this time."

It seemed an unnecessary extravagance to Keith. "An air letter would do. That's what they've been sending all along."

"Yes, I know. The airmail to Tahiti is very infrequent, though. All mail seems to be infrequent to Tahiti. They're building an aerodrome there now, but it's not working yet. I would have expected a cable to say they had arrived. But you haven't heard anything?"

"No, I haven't. They should be there by this time, though, shouldn't they?"

"The last letter I had was from Panama posted on Sep-

tember twenty-ninth. Commander Dermott says in that they
expect to arrive in Papeete on November the twentieth.
Well, here we are, and it's December the first. We should
have heard something by now."

They discussed the possibilities of delay in arrival and
delay in mails for a minute or two. Finally Mr. Carpenter
said, "There's no British consul in Papeete. I think I'll send
the Governor a short cable asking if there's any news of
their arrival."

Keith went back to his lathe, vaguely disquieted. He had a
great respect for John's solicitor. In his lifetime he had never
had much to do with the Law. He had met solicitors from
time to time; some that he had met in pubs were clearly not
so good. Others had been better; one had come to see him
once because he was making the little Burrell traction engine
and was in trouble with the governor, and because of that he
had handled the purchase of the Ealing house for Keith. Mr.
Carpenter, John's solicitor, was different again, part of the
wider world, John's world, infinitely competent and infinitely
courteous. Keith would have hesitated to suggest that Mr.
Carpenter should take his work.

When Katie came in she gave Janice and Keith their tea,
and then he read an Enid Blyton book to Janice for half an
hour till it was time for her to have her bath and go to bed.
Katie looked after that, and he went down to his desk in the
basement to write an article about fusible plugs. He sat for a
long time fingering the four little screwed pieces that had
been loaded with the different solders, the paper ready to his
hand, but the words would not come. It was incredible that
anything could have happened.

When Janice was safely in bed in the room beside his
workshop, he went upstairs and told Katie all about it in the
parlour. "I don't think anything could have happened," he
said uneasily. "It's just that they haven't got there yet."

Katie said, "They wouldn't have got jammed among all
that ice, would they?"

He knew that she had it in her mind that John and Jo had
taken a course somewhere over the North Pole, but how she
had got hold of that idea he did not know. He pulled out the
school atlas that they had. "They didn't go that way," he
explained. "It's hot the way they went." He turned to the

map of the Pacific. "Down here." He traced the route from Panama to Tahiti with his finger.

"Oh, I remember. It looks an awful long way, Keith. All that blue would mean it's sea, wouldn't it?"

"That's right," he said. "It *is* a long way." He studied the longitudes with an eye well accustomed to calculations. "It's— it's seventy-five degrees. That's more than a fifth of the way round the world." He checked the figures in wonder.

She stared at him. "All in one trip? I mean, not landing anywhere in all that way?"

"I don't think so."

"Well, they might take any time. I mean, the wind might be against them."

"I suppose so," he said doubtfully. "I think it's quite all right. Still, we'd better not say anything in front of Janice."

"There couldn't be anything wrong, though, could there?"

"I dunno. I don't like that Mr. Carpenter sending cables all about the world. Don't look as though *he's* any too happy."

For the next two days he was restless and ill at ease, mainly because he felt himself to be quite incapable of assessing the situation. He knew nothing about yachts or the sea; the oceans to him were something painted blue upon the pages of the atlas and no more. He had never been out of England. He had sailed once on an afternoon's excursion in an old paddle steamer from Weymouth to Lulworth Cove, a distance of six miles; he had liked the look of the cliffs from the water but had been appalled at the machinery and interested in its antiquity till the smells of the engine room coupled with the slight motion of the vessel made him sick. He knew that this experience was no guidance for assessing any hazards that might lie around his sister on her voyage, and his ignorance distressed and worried him.

Mr. Carpenter rang him up again on the morning of the third. "Mr. Stewart," he said, "I wonder if you could come up and see me? I've got an answer to that cable, and there's a good deal that I think we should discuss."

"Have they got to Tahiti?"

"Not yet," said the solicitor. "I'm having further enquiries made out there. But in the meantime, I would like to see you if you could look in."

"I can come up now, if you like," said Keith. "I don't punch a clock."

They fixed a time; Keith took off his apron and washed his hands, put on his dark suit, and started off toward the tram. It was raining with a cold December drizzle; he wore a greasy old raincoat and an equally greasy old soft hat; he had a shabby muffler round his throat. He was pale with lack of sun and exercise, and running a bit to fat. He looked, as he sat in the tram taking him to Ealing Broadway, like any one of thousands of men to be seen in trams in any industrial district, and he was.

He got to the solicitor's office at about half past eleven, and he was shown straight in. Mr. Carpenter got up from his desk to meet him. "I told you that I had an answer to that cable, Mr. Stewart," he said directly. "I'm afraid it isn't very satisfactory."

He passed the flimsy to Keith, who could not read it without the steel-rimmed spectacles he always had to use for close work. He undid his shabby coat, fumbled for his spectacle case, and put them on. The cable was in English, and it read:

Natives from Kautaiva Island report small vessel wrecked in hurricane November 19th on reef off Marokota Island bodies one man one woman buried Marokota stop Shearwater now much overdue making further enquiries.

Administration Papeete

The solicitor, watching closely, saw the fat, pallid lips quiver a little. The shabby little man stood motionless, staring at the cable. "Sit down, Mr. Stewart," he said gently. "I'm afraid this isn't very good news." He went on talking as was his habit upon these occasions. "There's nothing very definite in that," he said. "As you see, it seems to be just a rumour brought to Tahiti by natives from another island. We can't come to any conclusion till we get more news."

Keith sat down heavily, loosening his muffler. "It's terrible," he muttered. "I never thought anything like this could happen."

"We must hope that it isn't true," the solicitor said. "I thought it was sufficiently serious to ask you to come up, though. I didn't want to read this out to you upon the telephone."

Keith said, "Thank you, sir."

He raised his eyes. "I've got their daughter staying with us in the flat," he said. "I'll have to tell her, won't I?"

"How old is she? Twelve, is it?"

"Ten. Only ten."

The solicitor tightened his lips. "If it's true, she'll have to be told sometime, Mr. Stewart," he said. "I should talk it over with your wife. When you've had time to think this over for a little you may decide it's better to wait until the news is definite."

Keith asked, "You think it's definite now, don't you? I mean, you think they've been drowned?"

"I think the Governor thinks it's definite," Mr. Carpenter said carefully. "I don't think that he would have cabled quite in those terms unless he was fairly sure."

Keith laid the cable down upon the desk. "It's got to happen to us all, some day," he said. "It's when it happens suddenly, to your own people—it comes as a bit of a blow."

"I know."

The solicitor picked up a sheaf of papers from his desk. "I don't know if you want to talk about the future just now, Mr. Stewart, or if you would rather come up again when we know more. If, unhappily, your sister and her husband should be dead, a new set of circumstances come into being, as you probably know."

"I know they wanted us to take care of Janice if anything happened," Keith said. "It might be better if we talk about that now."

"You know the contents of their wills?"

"I think so. They wanted me to be trustee or something. I said I would."

"Yes. That was at our previous meeting, in this office. It was after that meeting that I drew up these wills." He handled them upon the desk before him. "They are very simple wills, Mr. Stewart. I don't think I should show them to you till the deaths are established, but as you are already acquainted with the most important features I think we can discuss what may arise from them." He paused. "Both wills are in identical terms, as perhaps you know. That seems to

make it immaterial which spouse died first. Each will leaves
the entire estate to the surviving spouse. If the spouse should
be already dead, then the entire estate passes to the daughter
Janice, to be held in trust for her until she attains the age of
twenty-five. You are appointed the sole trustee, and you and
I are appointed joint executors to the wills. In consideration
of your trusteeship, you are to receive the sum of one
thousand pounds from the estate." He paused. "If the daughter should decease before the expiration of the trust, or if
she should be already dead, you receive the same legacy of
one thousand pounds, but the balance of the estate passes
back to the Dungannon family."

"That means, I'd have to sort of look after the money for
her and give it to her when she gets to be twenty-five, does
it?"

"That is correct, Mr. Stewart. Both wills name you as the
guardian of the child Janice and both wills appoint you as the
sole trustee. You would have to invest the money for her in
certain selected securities that we call Trustee Stocks, and
you would devote the interest to her education and general
benefit during the period of the trust. In case of necessity
you have power to realize some of the capital for her
benefit."

"I've never had to do anything like that before," Keith
said doubtfully.

The solicitor nodded. "You may need a little help. I realize
that. If you have confidence in your own solicitor he would
be the best person to assist you. Otherwise, I should be glad
to."

Mr. Cannon had made a nice little model of the Burrell
traction engine, but privately Keith did not think that he had
handled the purchase of the house at Ealing any too well. It
had taken a long time and there had been trouble with the
Council over the alterations, which might not have been his
fault. "I'd be grateful, if it's not putting you out." He meant,
if the scale of the business was worth the time of a man like
Mr. Carpenter. "Do you know how much money there might
be?"

The solicitor turned over the papers on his desk. "I hold a
power of attorney both for your sister and for her husband," he said. "I know of three bank accounts. Your sister
has an account at Southsea, your brother-in-law has one at

Alverstoke, and he has another at the head office of the bank here in London, in Throgmorton Street. When I began to get troubled about their non-arrival at Tahiti I wrote to all three banks for a statement of account and list of securities that they might be holding on behalf of my clients, using the power of attorney."

He paused. "The Throgmorton Street office report a credit balance of fifty-six pounds eighteen shillings and fourpence," he said. "Your brother-in-law's account at Alverstoke is three pounds four shillings and tenpence in credit. Your sister's account in Southsea shows a debit balance—that is to say, an overdraft—of four pounds sixteen shillings and fivepence. Adding those up, there seems to be a total credit balance of fifty-five pounds six shillings and ninepence. All three banks state that they are holding no securities."

Keith stared at him. "But that's daft! I mean, they've got more than fifty-five pounds!"

"I have always imagined so, myself," said Mr. Carpenter. "I must say, at the moment I am perplexed. Do you know of any other bank accounts that they might have had, or where they might have deposited their securities?"

Keith shook his head. "They never talk of things like that. Not to me, anyway."

"Oh. I had hoped that you might have the answer." The solicitor paused in thought. "I have a number of Commander Dermott's papers in my keeping," he remarked. "When he gave up his flat he left a suitcase full of receipts and correspondence with me, with instructions to send it to him later on in Canada, or wherever he decided to settle. Probably I shall find the answer in that." He thought for a moment. "He certainly told me that the contents were receipts and correspondence. But probably the share certificates themselves are there. I shall have to look and see."

"That's where they'll be," said Keith. "Do you know how much money they might have left? I mean, if they *are* dead?"

"Commander Dermott gave me to understand that the estate would be between twenty and twenty-five thousand pounds."

"That's about what I thought," said Keith.

They left it that they would meet again when Mr. Carpenter had received further news from the Administration in

Papeete, by which time he hoped to have found the missing securities. Keith lunched absent-mindedly in a Lyons cafeteria, and went back all the way to Ealing down Oxford Street, through Notting Hill Gate and Shepherd's Bush, on top of a bus, deeply troubled in his mind. He had loved his sister though in recent years he had seen little of her, and he had felt honoured when John Dermott had suggested that he should be their trustee and guardian of their daughter, rather than one of their naval friends or one of their relations in North Ireland. They had chosen him, he knew, because of his stable life, because he was always there, in the same place, with the same wife, doing the same things; the Dungannons fell in and out of marriage with the greatest alacrity and *savoir faire;* their naval friends were apt to uproot and go to Kenya or Hong Kong. They knew that through wars and rumours of wars, whatever happened in the greater world, Keith Stewart would go on living at No. 56 Somerset Road, Ealing, because his workshop was there, built up and established over the years. To uproot all his machine tools and remove the whole of his equipment to another house would mean a dislocation to his work that was unthinkable. He was anchored firmly in the same place by his workshop, and by his own inclinations.

He got back to his house an hour before Janice was due back from school, his mind full of his little niece. If her parents were indeed dead, they would have to tell her, but he could not imagine how they were going to do it. Katie might have some ideas; Katie was good with children. His mind ranged on beyond the bad half-hour to the part that he could play. Janice would have to have something to play with, to take her mind off death. A doll's house? She already had one, and was getting a bit old for it. A bicycle? Not old enough, and children didn't seem to have them nowadays, perhaps because of the traffic. A scooter? Somerset Road was a quiet bye-street that carried no through traffic; she could use a scooter there and be in no danger, and it would take her out of doors, and keep her warm. His mind ranged over the job. He had a couple of eight-inch rubber-tyred wheels left over from a little traction-engine passenger truck, and he could bore them out to take a ball race each side. Inch-and-a-quarter steel tube for the steering head, parallel five-eighths tubes for the frame; he could braze that up in no time. Make the handlebars first, because they would have to be chrome plated. He had some red paint for the rest of it, which would make it look gay. He went down to the workshop directly he got home and took the little bronze sphere of the automatic pilot from the bench and packed it carefully away in rags in an old cigar box with its tiny transistor rectifier and the delicate relays, clearing the decks for a more mundane job, and started work upon the handlebars. Better to work at something than to sit thinking of Joanna and their childhood together in the Renfrew streets.

When Janice came in he suggested that she should draw a farm with all the animals for him, and he took her down with him to the workshop and settled her down at his desk with a large sheet of paper, clearing away letters from Cornwall and Colchester and California to make a space for her. He went on working at the handlebars, which were too immature as yet to draw her notice, and as he worked he measured her furtively with his eye for the height of the steering head. Thirty-two inches from the ground ... From time to time he stopped work to admire her picture.

That evening, after Janice was in bed, he told Katie all about it. "This chap in this place Papeete—the Governor—he thinks they're dead," he said heavily. "There's no doubt of that."

"It might have been some other boat," she suggested.

"They buried two people," he replied, "a man and a woman. On this other island, Maro . . . something or other."

They looked for it on the atlas unavailingly. "Ought we to tell her?" he asked.

She shook her head. "Not now. Wait till we know for sure. She's not old enough for things not being certain."

"I started to make her a scooter," he said. "I'll keep it under cover, all in bits, until we know."

"That'll be nice for her," she said. "She can use it up and down the pavement, not in the road."

He told her about the missing securities. "He'll find them, all right," he said. "I mean, they must be there somewhere."

"They couldn't have taken them with them, in the boat?"

"That's possible," he remarked. "They might have done that. But then, that wouldn't matter, because they'd still be the owner of the shares in companies in England, or where have you. It just means that the lawyers would have to get copies. Be a bit more expense. The money would be there just the same."

She did not fully understand this, but let it pass. "Until it's all squared up, though, there's just fifty-five pounds."

He nodded. "Not much to bring her up on, not in the way they'd want. But it'll be all right. The money must be some-where."

"It's enough," she said. "She'd live with us till she's grown up, like as if she was our own kid. I don't want any money with her."

"Be a bit tight," he said.

She smiled. "We'll manage."

He was content with that; if Katie said that they could manage, it was so. He himself had never cared much about money, or wanted it, or taken any interest in it except so far as it controlled the equipment of his workshop. That was very largely over now; the tools he had would last his lifetime and only minor additions would be necessary from time to time. He was content to take what income he could derive from the work he loved and live on that without complaint; the management of the *Miniature Mechanic* knew all about him and gave him just enough to keep him in a very modest way of life, the finances of their magazine allowing no more. He kept no car, drank very little, and hardly smoked at all. Each year they took a fortnight's summer holiday in Cornwall and went for motor coach rides, but that was only possible because Katie worked. She managed all of their finances and saved about a hundred pounds a year for the gradual repayment of the mortgage.

It was a week before Mr. Carpenter rang again, again at about ten o'clock in the morning. He said, "I have a further cable from the Governor in Papeete, Mr. Stewart. Could you come up and see me again, do you think?"

Keith said, "I'll come up right away. Can you tell me what's in the cable?"

"Not very good news, I am afraid."

"Oh. They're dead, are they?"

"I am afraid so. The vessel that went on the reef at Marokota Island was undoubtedly *Shearwater*. They have some of the clothing from the bodies."

Keith said dully, "I'll come up right away, sir."

He was sitting with the solicitor in Bedford Square an hour and a half later, reading the cable. "There doesn't seem to be any doubt about it now," he said. "This full report he says he's sending. We haven't had that yet, I suppose?"

Mr. Carpenter shook his head. "This only came in during the night."

"Well, that's the end of it." He sat in silence for a minute. "We'll have to tell Janice now."

"I am afraid so." The solicitor paused, and then said, "If I may speak from my experience, don't be too much influenced by the child's first reaction, Mr. Stewart. It will be very painful, because there will be floods of tears. They will go on for a day, and then they will dry up. A child's wounds heal very quickly—or appear to, anyway. The thing is patience, and enduring kindness."

The engineer glanced at him gratefully. "I know. I've been making her a scooter."

"A scooter?"

"You know—what kids have, to push about on with one foot. I've got it painted red. She hasn't seen it yet."

"A very good idea, Mr. Stewart. You say you made it yourself?"

Keith nodded. "I can do that sort of thing."

"How fortunate you are . . ." The solicitor turned back to the papers on his desk. "I have been going into my client's financial affairs since I saw you last," he said. "I am afraid they are rather unsatisfactory."

"You haven't been able to find the securities?"

"The securities that John Dermott held were all sold, Mr. Stewart, between February and April of this year. The proceeds were paid into the Throgmorton Street branch of his bank. They totalled—" he glanced at a paper "—twenty-six thousand eight hundred and forty-four pounds, eleven shillings and tenpence."

"What's happened to that money, then?"

"Between March and the end of May," said the solicitor, "cheques were drawn in favour of a firm called Rosenblaum and Franck totalling twenty-seven thousand nine hundred and thirty-eight pounds, sixteen and twopence." He raised his eyes and looked at Keith. "Rosenblaum and Franck are dealers in precious stones, Mr. Stewart—principally diamonds, I think. They are quite a reputable firm."

Keith stared at him. "What on earth did they want with those?"

Mr. Carpenter said, "I know no more than you do, Mr. Stewart. But I have talked to a partner in the firm, Mr. Franck."

"What did he say?"

The solicitor leaned back in his chair. "Mr. Franck is still a youngish man, under forty, I would say. He told me that he knew Commander Dermott well. He served under him in the recent war, when he would have been between twenty and twenty-five years old. He has a very high opinion of your brother-in-law. I am telling you this in order that you may understand the background of this business."

He paused. "I would say that Elias Franck is a Jew, and a very good one. He inherited the family business from his father. He told me that Commander Dermott came to him last spring and wanted to buy diamonds that would be readily saleable in any part of the world. Mr. Franck told me that they sometimes get enquiries of that sort, and in such cases they avoid asking questions. It is no business of theirs what the purchaser wishes to do with the gems. Their business is to sell precious stones in London."

Keith nodded. "I see. They don't want to get mixed up in anything."

"Exactly." The solicitor went on, "Commander Dermott bought diamonds to the value I have stated, twenty-seven thousand pounds odd, and took them away with him."

"Just like that?"

Mr. Carpenter inclined his head. "Mr. Franck tells me that he was very careful in his selection of the gems for Commander Dermott on account of the sincere regard that he feels towards him. He thinks that your brother-in-law might well make money on the resale, and if the diamonds should come again upon the market he would like to have the first refusal of the business." He paused. "There is just one other thing. Commander Dermott asked him for the name of a reputable broker on the west coast of America. Mr. Franck gave him an introduction to a firm in which he has confidence, in Los Angeles."

He paused. "I have been wondering if Commander Dermott took these diamonds with him in the yacht."

Keith stared at him. "I suppose he might have done. But why would he want to do a thing like that?"

Mr. Carpenter sat in thought for a minute. "I can only surmise, Mr. Stewart," he said. "But as I understand the matter, it was the intention of your brother-in-law to settle permanently in the dollar area, perhaps in British Columbia. There are restrictions on the transfer of capital from England to the dollar area, as perhaps you know. Under the present regulations your brother-in-law could only have transferred a very small part of his capital into dollars each year. It might have taken ten years, or more, to transfer the whole of it."

"You think he bought diamonds and took them with him in the yacht, to sell them in America and get his capital that way?"

"I think it possible."

"Did he ever tell you he was going to do that?"

The solicitor placed both hands on the desk in front of him. "Mr. Stewart," he said, "if Commander Dermott did that, it was an illegal act. It was very highly illegal, and would have resulted in a considerable prison sentence if he had been detected. A solicitor must not allow a client to tell him that he intends to commit a felony. If the client should do so, the solicitor must refuse to advise him or to handle his case; in certain circumstances his duty would be to inform the proper authorities. Commander Dermott never told me or gave me any indication that he intended to do such a thing."

Keith said, "I'm sorry, sir. I didn't know."

"That's all right, Mr. Stewart." He smiled. "If your brother-in-law had such a thing in mind, he knew enough not to come and tell me about it."

"I don't understand why it should have been so illegal," the engineer said. "It was his own money."

"That is the law of the land," the solicitor replied. "Dollars are short in this country. I am not allowed to buy a Buick car, or even to spend more than a hundred pounds in America if I wish to go there for a holiday. In the same way, your brother-in-law was not allowed to take twenty-six or twenty-seven thousand pounds to spend in the United States or Canada."

"I see." Keith glanced at the solicitor. "He did tell me once that he wanted to buy a house when he got to a place called Victoria, on Vancouver Island."

"He told you that?"

Keith nodded.

"I doubt if he could have done that very easily by any legal transfer of capital. Not unless the payments could have been deferred over an excessive period of time."

"He didn't say anything about that. He just said that he was going to buy a house there."

"I see." They discussed this for a time, but Keith could remember nothing more. Presently the solicitor said, "If in fact these diamonds were with them in the yacht, I am afraid that the prospects of recovering them do not seem very rosy."

"We don't know yet how badly the yacht was wrecked," Keith said. "Things might have been saved off her—luggage, or things like that."

"From a yacht, a wooden yacht, wrecked on a coral reef some distance from the land, in a tropical hurricane? I think she must have broken up, Mr. Stewart, otherwise the bodies of the crew would hardly have been washed ashore. In that case all her contents would have been scattered over the sea floor. But we shall know more of the condition of the vessel when we get that report. I do not personally feel very hopeful."

Keith glanced at him. "It's fifty-five quid, then?"

"I am afraid it looks rather like it. Do you think that you can manage with the daughter, without any appreciable money, Mr. Stewart? In the circumstances I should have no hesitation in approaching the Dungannon family on her behalf."

"Katie says that we can manage," said the engineer. "Katie —that's my wife. After all, it's no more than if we had a kid of our own."

"There would be no difficulty in approaching the Dungannons. I could write to Lord Dungannon personally."

"If they paid for her schooling and that," said Keith shrewdly, "they'd want to have her, wouldn't they? I mean, they wouldn't want for her to go living with Katie and me, and going to Miss Pearson's school down the road, and Ealing High School after that? Holidays, they'd want her to be with them in North Ireland?"

"They might," the solicitor agreed.

The engineer shook his head. "That's not what Jo wanted for her," he said. "Nor did John. When they left her with us, they did it of a purpose. They could have left her in North Ireland with the big house and people with titles and ponies to ride and all of that. But they didn't do that. They didn't even like her going there last summer much, but they kind of had to. What they wanted to do was for her to stay with us."

"Do you know why they took that line?" asked Mr. Carpenter. "I know that that was their intention, but do you know why?"

"They had ideas," Keith said awkwardly. "I mean, people getting divorced two or three times, and mess and muddle over the children. They didn't want Janice to grow up thinking that was the usual way people did. They thought she'd be better off with Katie and me in Ealing, seeing it was just for a short time."

"It's going to be for a long time now," said the solicitor.

"I know. But Katie says we can manage." He paused. "I'd like to find out all we can about things that might have been washed up from the yacht."

"It's just possible that the diamonds might have been recovered," said Mr. Carpenter. "If so, they would be in the hands of the French authorities." He sat in silence for a minute, and then said, "I will find out everything I can, Mr. Stewart. But I shall have to word any enquiry rather carefully. If the diamonds were taken out of the United Kingdom it was a most illegal act."

Keith sat with his brows wrinkled. "How do the French come into this?" he asked.

"Tahiti and the Tuamotu Islands are a part of French Oceania," the solicitor told him. "Just as if they were French colonies."

"I didn't know that," the engineer said humbly. "I thought that they were Japanese or something."

He left the solicitor's office a few minutes later with the thought dominant in his mind that now either he or Katie would have to tell Janice that her father and mother were dead. He had the red scooter finished and painted, hanging up in what had once been the coal cellar of the house and now was used as a box room. He had made it with pleasure for her, but now that the moment had come to use it as an anodyne it did not seem to be quite the right thing after all. He walked down to Holborn and then eastwards looking in the shop windows till he came to Gamages. He went into the big store mingling with the crowd of Christmas shoppers till he found the toy department and browsed around there, a pale-faced, rather fat little man in a greasy raincoat. He was already conscious of the need for economy, and finally he bought a yellow and blue plastic duck that would float in the bath. He knew as he bought it that it was much too young a present for a child of ten, but he bought it feeling that somehow it might be the right thing in the circumstances.

He got back to the flat in Ealing early in the afternoon, carrying the duck in a paper bag. He had thought of stopping at the store in Ealing Broadway and discussing the position across the counter with Katie in the Household Linen, but he had abandoned that idea. Katie would want to come home early in order to be at home when Janice got back from school, and it did not seem quite fair to him to throw all the dirty work on Katie. He felt that he would rather tell Janice himself and get the back of the job broken before Katie got home; enough would fall upon her later, anyway.

He was sitting in his chair before the fire in the parlour when Janice came back from school, a slim, dark-haired child in a thick blue overcoat and a blue hat with the school ribbon on it. He called, "That you, Jan? Take off your coat and come in here. I've got something I want to tell you."

She came in, and he sat up in his chair. "What do you want to tell me?" she asked.

"Come over here," he said. She came close, and he put his arm around the slender little waist in the gym tunic. He could only take this straight. "Look, Jan," he said. "I've got something serious I've got to tell you. You know about boats and yachts, and how they get wrecked sometimes, running on shore, on rocks?"

She nodded.

"Sometimes," he said, "the people in the boats get drowned when that happens."

She stared at him, and he knew that the realization was already with her. She asked, "Drownded dead?"

"That does happen sometimes, in a shipwreck," he said gently.

"Has that happened to my Mummy and Daddy?"

"I'm afraid it has, Jan," he said steadily. "They got into a terrible storm, a long, long way from here. And they were wrecked."

"Are they drownded dead, Uncle Keith?"

"I'm afraid they are, both drowned," he replied. "Come and sit up on my knee."

He had thought that she would burst into tears, but that did not happen. She came up on his knee and he held her close, and so they sat in silence for ten minutes. At last she asked, "Do you think my Mummy and Daddy were very frightened when the ship got wrecked?"

The adult quality of the question amazed him; children were so much older than you thought they were. "No," he said. "No, I don't think that they'd ever have been frightened. They weren't that sort of people. And you won't be frightened of things either, I don't think."

She shook her head. He reached down beside his chair and brought up the paper bag. "I bought you a duck," he said. "I'm not sure if it's a very good present, but I wanted to bring you something and this was all that I could think of."

She pulled it out of the paper bag upon his knee. "It's a lovely duck," she said. "Can I have it in the bath?"

"Of course," he said.

She wriggled round upon his knee and kissed him. "It's a lovely present," she said. "Thank you ever so much for it."

He held her for a moment, and then said, "What about a cup of tea?"

She got down from his knee. There were still no tears. "Can I come and watch you make a bit in the workshop?"

"Why, yes," he said. "I'll make a bit specially for you. What sort of a bit shall we make?"

Her eye fell on the duck, clutched close in her arms. "Can you make an egg for the duck to lay?"

His mind ran quickly over techniques and materials to hand. "I can make you all sorts of eggs," he said, "but none of them would be quite the right colour. A duck's egg ought to be a sort of bluey-green." He thought rapidly. "We could do a silvery egg in steel, or a yellow egg if we heated a steel egg a bit, or a blue egg if we heated a steel egg quite a lot, or a gray egg if we case-hardened it. Or we could make a coppery-coloured egg if we made it out of copper. But I can't just see how we could make a proper coloured duck's egg, unless we painted it."

She smiled at him. "It isn't a proper coloured duck, so it wouldn't have proper coloured eggs, would it? But it's a lovely duck." She stroked its plastic hide. "Can I have one egg of each sort, so that we can make a nest for her to sit on?"

"I can't make them all before your bedtime," he said. "We can make one now, and then I'll make the rest after you're in bed, and then I'll put them on the table by your bed and you can have them in the morning." He paused. "Which one would you like me to make now?"

"The blue one," she said.

He got up from his chair. "All right, we'll go down and make a blue egg."

He took her by the hand and they went together down the steep wooden stairs into the front basement room that was his clean workshop. He pulled out the high stool that he sometimes sat upon before the bench and sat her up upon it so that she could see everything that he was doing at the three-and-a-half-inch lathe, and began a running commentary on his operations. He picked a three-inch end of inch-diameter steel rod out of the scrap box, put it in the three-jaw chuck, started the lathe, and chamfered the end to forty-five degrees. A lifetime of such work had made him very quick; in a minute he was working with a hand scraper on a rest turning the end of the steel to form the large end of the egg, talking to the little girl all the time. Three emery sticks of successive fineness followed the scraper, and the large end was finished. He brought forward the parting tool and parted off the piece one and a half inches long down to a diameter of about a quarter of an inch, and chamfered the small end shape roughly by the careful manipulation of a knife tool in the four-tool post. Then came careful work again with the hand scraper, then the final parting off. He gave the warm, nearly finished egg to the little girl to hold while he found a one-inch-bore copper collar and put it in the chuck. Then he put the egg in it small end outwards and pinched it up using the tailstock centre to set it roughly true, started the lathe again, and went to work very gently with the hand scraper and the emery sticks till he had it finished to his satisfaction. Then he took it from the lathe, gave it a final burnish on a rouge polishing mop at the tool grinder, and gave it to her to hold, a new, silvery, shiny egg. It had taken him less than twenty minutes to make.

"There'll be another one like that in the morning," he said, "and a grey one and a yellow one and a copper one. But now we'll make this one blue."

He helped her down from the stool, still clutching the plastic duck and the new, shiny egg, and led her into his dirty workshop. He lit a Bunsen burner and arranged a tin filled with about an inch of sand above the burner on a little metal stand and began to heat the sand. Presently he took the egg from her and dropped it on the sand and began to stir the sand expertly with a small pair of tongs, always keeping the egg on top of a good layer of the hot sand, turning it over and over. As the heat increased it took a yellow tint which grew darker as they watched, and began to turn to blue. He made the little girl stand back, turned out the Bunsen, put on a thick leather glove ready on the bench beside him, picked the hot egg from the sand quickly and dropped it into a tin of oil upon the bench. It made a sizzling splash and a little spurt of hot oil; he waited a moment, took off the glove, and fished it out of the oil, and wiped it carefully on a clean rag. Then he gave it to Janice, a deep, brilliantly blue egg.

"It's a *lovely* egg," she said. "It's such a pretty colour, just like Diana's frock. Thank you ever so much, Uncle Keith."

There was the sound of the front door upstairs, and Katie's step in the hall. "Lord," he exclaimed. "There's Katie, and we haven't done anything about the tea!"

She scurried to the stairs, the duck held firmly in her arms, the egg clenched tight in one hand. "I'll go and put the kettle on."

He followed her more slowly, and arrived in the hall in time to hear her greet Katie. "Uncle Keith bought me a duck and I can have it in the bath and he made me a blue egg for it to lay and he's going to make me more eggs tonight, a silver one and a yellow one and a grey one and a copper one so she'll have five eggs to sit on in a nest."

He heard Katie say, a little dazed, "What a beautiful duck and what a lovely egg. Keith spoils you."

Janice said, "He made the egg in the lathe and I watched and we forgot all about the tea. But I'll run and put the kettle on now."

She scurried off into the kitchenette, duck and egg held close. In the hall Keith said in a low tone, "It's true enough, old girl. I went up and saw Carpenter again this morning. They were both drowned, and buried on the island." He paused. "I've told her."

"You've told Janice?"

He nodded.

"How did she take it?"

"She didn't cry," he said. "She just sat quiet on my knee for a bit, and then we went down and made the egg."

"She didn't cry at all?"

He shook his head.

"Oh, that's bad," she said in a low tone. "You're sure she understood?"

"She understood all right," he replied.

She stood in silence. "Well, I dunno," she said at last. "We'll talk about it tonight after she's in bed. In the meantime, don't let's say anything unless she brings the subject up. Let her take it her own way." She paused. "I think I'll give her one of those phenobarbitone tablets tonight."

She went into the kitchenette to run up a dish of scrambled eggs, and Keith went down into his clean workshop to sweep away the steel shavings from the lathe and to start work on another egg. He had it nearly finished by the time the meal was on the table, and was halfway through a third one by the time the meal was washed up and he was called upstairs to see the duck swimming with Janice in the bath. He went downstairs and worked till he had finished the fifth, and brought them up to the parlour. He found Katie sitting and darning a hole in one of Janice's stockings.

He put the eggs down on the table by his chair. "Did she say anything?"

Katie shook her head. "Only about the duck and the eggs. It's as if she's kind of closed her mind to the other thing." She sat in silence for a moment, and then said, "I think I'll put my coat on and run round and have a talk with Miss Pearson, so that if anything happens at the school tomorrow you could go round and fetch her home. You wouldn't mind doing that, K, if she rang?

"Of course not. These eggs all ought to have a coat of lacquer before they get scratched. I might do that tomorrow, while she's at school. You think it's all right for her to go to school, Katie?"

"I'm sure it is, the way she's taking it. It's just in case anything comes out in the newspapers, and the other children start asking her—that might set her off crying or something."

"You'd think there'd be a fair chance that the newspapers won't get hold of it," he said. "It's all in a French colony on the other side of the world." He paused, and then he said, "I've got that scooter I made for her. When do you think she ought to have that?"

"Tomorrow's Friday," she said. "Give it to her Saturday morning and she can play with it all morning if it's fine. And then in the afternoon she can have Diana Soskice round to play. I'll see Mrs. Soskice, or else ring her up."

"There isn't any money, Katie," he said. "If there was, they had it in the yacht with them."

She darned on placidly. "Mr. Carpenter couldn't find the securities?"

"They sold them," he told her. "Seems like they turned everything they had into cash, and then bought diamonds, and took them in the yacht. Kind of illegal it was, so he says. Seems like they meant to sell the diamonds in America or somewhere and buy a house."

"That doesn't sound illegal to me," she said, her eyes fixed on the darn.

"Well, it is," he told her. "It's about the worst thing you can do, apart from murdering somebody."

"And now the diamonds are lost, so she'll have nothing?"

"That's about the long and the short of it," he said. "He asked if he should ask the Dungannons to help with educating her and that, but I said, no."

She shook her head. "I wouldn't want that, and we can manage." She dropped her busy hands down to her lap, and they were still. "I know we can't give her all that John and Jo would have wanted her to have," she said quietly. "I'm sort of sorry about that, in a way. But it does make it more as if she was our own child now, and maybe that's for the best, things being like they are."

He stirred uneasily in his chair. "Those diamonds are her diamonds now, and they must be somewhere," he said uneasily. "I mean, I'm the trustee."

She picked up her darning again. "You can't be a trustee for what's at the bottom of the sea," she said.

"The ship's not at the bottom of the sea," he said stubbornly. "She got wrecked on a coral reef near an island."

"Same thing," she said, and went on darning.

She went out presently to see Miss Pearson, and he went down into the basement. He looked into the little bedroom off his dirty workshop and saw Janice sleeping deeply, the plastic duck clutched in her arms. He laid the other four eggs down beside the blue one on the table by her side, and pulled the bedclothes gently up around her shoulders, for the night was cold and the window open. He closed the door, and sat down at his desk. There was the morning mail, seven letters still unopened. Amongst them was one from the United States in an ornate airmail envelope, the back of which announced to him in neat print that it was from Solomon P. Hirzhorn, Box 6507, Tacoma, Washington. He sighed a little. Mr. Hirzhorn was an enthusiast who was building the Congreve clock from Keith's serial in the *Miniature Mechanic*, and Mr. Hirzhorn couldn't read a drawing very well, and Mr. Hirzhorn evidently had a secretary with an electric typewriter to whom he could dictate because each letter was about fifteen hundred words long; this was the third that Keith had answered patiently, though not at such length. He settled down to work, and worked till midnight.

The succeeding days passed anxiously, in a state of inarticulate tension. Janice never cried so far as they could see, and she never once spoke of her father and mother, but she lost appetite and got very pale. Katie went to see Dr. Simmonds about her, and he came round and stethoscoped her chest and put her on cod liver oil and malt, which she liked, and approved the phenobarbitone at night for the next week or so. Nothing happened at school because no parent of a child at Miss Pearson's school happened to read *The Times*, the only paper which picked up and printed a short account of the yacht wreck in the Tuamotus. Janice played with her scooter in Somerset Road on Saturdays, and achieved some distinction amongst the other children in the road because her uncle had made every bit of it himself, instead of buying it in a shop. But she continued pale and peaky in appearance.

Katie said, "She'll pick up as the spring comes on." But she took her down each Saturday morning to Mr. Evans, the chemist, to weigh her on the machine in the shop, and kept a careful record of her weight.

The Christmas holidays came. It seemed better to Katie and to Keith to cancel the arrangements that had been made for Janice to go and stay with her Aunt Margaret at Tunbridge Wells and to keep her with them in Ealing, to the extent of disrupting their own routines a little for the period of the holidays. Mr. Buckley agreed to let Katie go on half time, working mornings only till school started again, and Keith suffered an influx of children into his workshops at all hours, sometimes working on till one o'clock in the morning to keep abreast of his current jobs. They did their work in a welter of children's parties, parties in their own flat, fetching Janice from parties in other people's homes loaded with little presents, with paper caps and unpulled crackers.

In the middle of all this a letter arrived from Mr. Carpenter enclosing the report from the Governor in Papeete, and suggesting that Keith might like to come up for another discussion when he had digested the contents.

It was a fairly long, typewritten report. It said that the vessel in question was undoubtedly the yacht *Shearwater,* and the two bodies were those of Cdr. and Mrs. Dermott. The yacht had struck on a reef about two miles to the southwest of the island of Marokota, which was only intermittently inhabited by natives from Kautaiva Island according to the demands of the copra harvest. The yacht had struck at the height of the hurricane and at that time there were about ten natives on Marokota who had seen the vessel as she struck the reef, but could do nothing to help. She had apparently broken up in a few hours; all that now remained was the keel and some of the frames wedged firmly on the reef, from which most of the planking had been washed off. There was no question of salvaging the yacht. The engine had remained attached to its bearers and had been removed by the natives three days later and placed under cover on the island. Much of the remaining heavy articles which were within the hull had been recovered by the natives by diving, including the two Primus stoves and the binnacle, and had been taken for their own use. The same applied to lighter articles that had been washed ashore, such as bedding, spars, planking, sails, etc. The Governor did not consider it practicable to recover these things from the natives. He would, however, appreciate instructions whether any attempt should be made to salvage the engine or whether it should be disposed of at his own discretion. He also asked for instructions regarding the marking and the upkeep of the grave.

Keith showed this letter to Katie one evening when the turmoil of the current party was over. She read it carefully, and then said, "I should think the best thing would be to let him sell the engine for what he can get for it, and put the money towards the cost of a headstone for the grave. There's nothing much else that we can do."

Keith said, "There's no hurry. It all wants a bit of thinking about." To his mind, it certainly did.

She said no more. To her the matter was perfectly clear and straightforward; put the money for the engine to the cost of the headstone and everything would be cleaned up, neat and tidy and done with. But Keith was handling all this with Mr. Carpenter, and she knew her husband to be slow and vacillating in matters of business. Let the men settle it in their own way. It didn't matter.

On New Year's Eve Keith went up to see Mr. Carpenter. In the solicitor's office they went through the report together. Finally Mr. Carpenter said, as Katie had, "I think we should instruct the Governor to set the cost of the headstone against what he can get for the engine, and accept the balance either way. Would you like me to write to him in those terms?"

Keith sat in silence. Finally he said, "I think I'd rather leave it be, if you don't mind, and think things over a bit longer."

The solicitor glanced at him curiously. "There is no immediate hurry, of course."

The engineer looked up. "That's right," he said. "John and Jo, they're buried and all decent, far as I can see. Suppose they had a headstone, well, there's no one there to read it." He paused. "I'm not against a headstone," he said. "Don't think that. But there's a lot of things in this that want some thinking over."

The solicitor sat in silence. "I'm here to help you, Mr. Stewart," he said at last. "I know that you are keeping something from me, and you may have very good reasons for doing so. I'd just like you to remember that your brother-in-law was not only my client, but a friend. Just bear that in mind."

Keith smiled, and said shrewdly, "Unless it came to telling you I might be going to do something illegal."

"There are degrees ..." said Mr. Carpenter. And then he smiled, and said, "Are you trying to tell me that you see some chance of getting back those diamonds?"

"I don't know where they are," Keith said defensively. "I don't know anything. I'd like to leave the whole thing rest a while until I think it out, what's best to be done." He got to his feet.

The solicitor rose with him. "As you like. Just remember that I'm here to help." He picked up the report from his desk. "Would you care to take this with you?"

Keith took the report and thrust it deep into the pocket of his greasy raincoat. "I don't want you to think I don't appreciate everything you've done, sir," he said. "But there's just one thing sticking out like a sore thumb, and that's that I'm the trustee. I don't want to do things in a hurry. Like selling anything."

He left the office and walked down to Holborn. He stood at the Kingsway corner waiting for his bus, and from habit he bought a copy of the *Evening Standard*, but he did not read it. He stood in a doorway in the milling crowd deep in thought, trying to resolve his problem. Twelve thousand miles away there was a coral reef in French territory, washed by the sea, not far from a coral island. Wedged upon that reef there was a three-ton lump of lead surmounted by another lump of concrete. Deep buried in the concrete probably would still be the copper box that he had brazed up for John Dermott. In the copper box was Jo's jewel case, red leather, and he was now certain in his mind that in her jewel case were twenty-six thousand pounds' worth of diamonds that belonged to Janice, who had made a little basket-work nest at school to hold the coloured eggs for the plastic duck to sit on.

And he was the trustee.

4

PETER JAMES SANDERSON WAS A navigator with the British Overseas Airways Corporation. He lived in South Ealing, convenient to London Airport, and at that time he was working the London-Karachi sector of the Eastern route, flying in Britannias. This gave him about a fortnight of each month at home with his young wife and baby, and plenty of time for his hobby, which was model engineering. He was a devoted reader of the *Miniature Mechanic* every week. He had fitted up a workshop in a garden shed, and in it he had built a Stuart Turner steam engine and two of Keith Stewart's designs, the 5-cc. Hornet single-cylinder compression ignition engine with its built-in reduction gear, and the more ambitious 20-cc. Gannet four-cylinder horizontally opposed four-stroke engine. He had exhibited the latter at the annual exhibition of the Ealing and District Model Engineering Society which had been judged by no less an authority than Keith Stewart, and he had received a bronze medal from the hands of the great man himself. He treasured this medal and valued it more highly than any of his professional certificates.

It was therefore with surprise and pleasure that he received a telephone call from Keith Stewart asking if he could come round and have a word with him. "Of course," he said. "Any time you like, Mr. Stewart. Now? That's fine. As a matter of fact, I was just reading about your Congreve clock, but I'd rather talk to you yourself."

He hung up and went to tell his wife of the honour that was to befall them, and she was duly impressed, and hurried to make some hot scones for tea.

Over the scones and tea Keith Stewart unburdened himself partially. "I'm in a kind of an awkward position, and I don't know what to do for the best," he said, and he proceeded to tell Mr. and Mrs. Sanderson about John and Jo and *Shearwater*. The navigator said softly, "I remember reading about this . . ."

"Marokota was the name of the island they got wrecked on," Keith told him. "It's not marked on our atlas, but seems like it's somewhere near a place called Tahiti or Papeete or something. Sometimes they say one, and sometimes the other."

"Tahiti is an island," said the navigator. "Quite a big French island. In the Pacific. Papeete is the town on it. Wait a minute, I think I've got a chart here that would show it."

Maps and charts were his specialty, the tools of his trade, and he had acquired a considerable private store. He pulled out a blue volume, the *Pacific Islands Pilot,* and consulted it. "Nine nine two," he said. "I haven't got it. But seven eight three—I know I've got that somewhere." He pulled out the bottom drawer of a long chest, rummaged, and pulled out a chart and laid it on the top of the chest. "Well, there's Tahiti," he said. "Now, Marokota." He turned again to the *Pilot* and extracted the latitude and longitude of the island. He laid these off upon the chart with pencil and parallel ruler, and marked the position with a little pencil cross. "There's your Marokota," he said. "About three hundred sea miles more or less due east of Tahiti."

Keith Stewart studied the chart. He had never seen one before, but he had heard about them, and he was a technician. "All these little bits of figures," he said. "They mean depths?"

"Depths in fathoms," said Mr. Sanderson. "A fathom is six feet."

Keith nodded, and stood looking at the chart. He pulled out a packet of Players and offered one to his host. "How would a chap set about getting out there?" he asked. "I mean, there's things to be done—the grave, and that. I don't kind of like to let all that go, if you understand me. If it was just over the way, in France—well, of course one would go there and see everything done right. What would it cost to get to a place like that?"

The navigator stood in thought. "By air, tourist, it might cost about three hundred pounds. You might be able to do it for a little less by sea. Perhaps two hundred."

"That's just for the one way?"

Mr. Sanderson nodded. "The return fare would be double."

Keith Stewart said, "I was afraid that that might be the size of it. The *Miniature Mechanic* doesn't pay that sort of wage packet."

"You feel it's very important that you should go there to tidy things up?"

The engineer nodded. "Yes, I do. But there's things you just can't do, and that's all about it."

They talked for a little while. Finally the navigator said, "Take that chart, if it's any good to you. Let me have it back when you've done with it."

Keith Stewart said good-bye and walked off down the street in the grey dusk, the chart under his arm. Mr. Sanderson watched him go from the front door, and went back into his sitting room where his wife was clearing away the tea. "What did you think of him?" he asked her.

"I liked him," she said. "He's a very genuine little man."

"That's what I thought," he replied.

"He didn't mind a bit telling you straight out that he hadn't got the money to go out to the Pacific."

"I know," he said. He leaned against the mantelpiece in thought. "Of course," he said, "there *are* ways."

"Ways to get to Tahiti without any money?"

"Of course there are," he said smiling. "People get all over the world without any money."

"How, Peter?"

"In aircraft, when the load factor's a bit down," he said. "It's just a question of working the right racket."

Two nights later he rang up Keith Stewart. "I don't know if this is any good to you," he said. "Do you remember a chap called Oliver Thorn, who had a model of the Petrolea locomotive in the Ealing and District exhibition?"

"I remember him," said Keith. "Fair-haired chap, shortish, with glasses. Works at Blackbushe airport or somewhere."

"That's the chap," said Mr. Sanderson. "He's chief store-keeper to Albatross Airways. I used to work for Albatross before I got into the Corporation. He thinks a lot of you."

"Nice of you to say that," muttered Keith.

"Well," said the navigator, "the point is this. Albatross have a job coming up to fly a generator rotor to a ship that's stuck at Honolulu. The *Cathay Princess,* fifteen thousand tons. She's a tanker, I believe. She can't move till she gets this rotor, and she's costing the owners God knows how much a day. They've got to make a new one up in Lancashire, and Albatross are flying it to Honolulu one day next week. They're sending it in one of their DC-6B freighters, but it won't be a full load. It struck me that it might be possible to wangle you a ride."

Keith was startled. "To Honolulu?"

"Yes." Distances meant nothing to the navigator; one day he would be in Singapore and the next in Sydney. The world to him was a succession of indifferent hotels united by long, dreary stretches of cloud.

"How far would that be from Tahiti?"

"About two thousand five hundred sea miles. It's not very close, but it's a good deal closer than you are now."

"Can one get from Honolulu to Tahiti?"

"Ah, now," said the navigator, "that may be the snag. I can tell you this much—there's no air line. You'd think there must be some sort of a shipping line, but honestly, I just don't know. It could be that you'd have to find out that in Honolulu. Mr. Thorn told me that the aircraft would go straight through by way of Frobisher and Vancouver, and that it would load the generator rotor at Speke. Well, Speke to Honolulu must be close on thirty hours, so the crew would want at least forty-eight hours' rest before starting home. There should be plenty of time in Honolulu for you to find out about sea passages to Tahiti. If there aren't any, then you could come home again with Albatross. The machine's got to come back empty, as I understand it."

"You don't think they'd want any money?" asked Keith, still a little dazed.

"You'd have to talk to Oliver Thorn," said Mr. Sanderson. "There may be some accountant in Albatross who'd cut up rough, but I don't see why there should be. After all, if a journalist wanted to go and write up the trip and Albatross Airways, they'd take him fast enough. You're a journalist, aren't you?"

"I suppose so," said Keith uncertainly.

"Well, there you are!" They talked a little more, and Mr. Sanderson gave Keith the address and telephone number of Mr. Thorn, and rang off.

Keith Stewart hung up, and went down to his workshop to sit down at his desk. He had Janice's school atlas there, and he traced the route so far as he was able. Speke—he did not know where that was, nor had he heard of it before; it would be somewhere in the north because the generator rotor was being made in Lancashire. Somewhat to his surprise he

found Frobisher Bay without difficulty, but it was in Baffin
Land, up further north than Hudson Bay. Then to Vancouver; he knew where that was. And then to Honolulu, girls in
grass skirts and not much else. He knew about great-circle
courses, and though he had not got a globe he could visualize
this as the shortest route. Besides, when Jo had been speaking
to Katie about Janice's journey, she had mentioned that the
aeroplane went near to the North Pole.

He had never been out of England. It was incredible that
he should even be contemplating such a journey, with all its
expense, all its uncertainties. He would have to have a passport, and he had no notion how to set about getting such a
thing. Still, he knew that the bank manager would tell him.
He would have to have money, quite a lot of money, for if
he succeeded in getting to Tahiti from Honolulu that would
cost a lot. Then he would have to pay his own fare back to
England. That might perhaps be possible if he were to find
the diamonds. But if he didn't, then he would be stranded out
there, in this outlandish place, Papeete.

He thought perhaps that he could raise about a hundred
pounds without increasing the mortgage on the house. But
Katie would have to know.

If he took a hundred pounds from their bank account it
would drain it to the very bottom, to the utmost limit of
overdraft that the bank manager would allow. There was a
little money owing to him from the *Miniature Mechanic,*
perhaps about fifteen pounds. Katie, in theory at any rate,
could carry on for a month or two upon her salary to meet
the living expenses of Janice and herself; they had just paid
the school fees for the coming term. Without his earnings
they could not pay off the debt on the house, or maintain
anything; they could not paint the windows or replace sheets
or blankets or pillowcases or clothes. If he were to take a
hundred pounds and go off on a trip like this, Katie would be
down to the barest of bare bedrock.

He got up and walked about the workshop, uncertain in his
mind. Presently it occurred to him that by his movements he
might be waking Janice, who slept in the little room off the
workshop that once had been the scullery. He opened the
door gently, and looked in. Janice was sleeping deeply, the
plastic duck on the table by her side perched hazardously on
its basket-work nest stabilized by the weight of the metal

eggs. She had thrown the bedclothes off from her shoulders and one arm was out. The room was cold; he went over to the bed and gently put the arm inside and tucked the bedclothes up around her shoulders. She did not wake, and he went back into the workshop, closing the door softly behind him.

The diamonds *must* be in the jewel case, safe buried in the lump of concrete that had once been *Shearwater*. It was the only place where they could be. It was just a matter of someone going there and getting them, without attracting too much attention.

And he was the trustee.

He sat down at his desk again, irresolute. Suppose he didn't go. With the help of Mr. Sanderson and Mr. Thorn and Albatross Airways he might have enough money to get there—just—but he certainly hadn't got enough money to get back. He would be leaving Katie with little or no money for an indefinite time, with Janice to look after. John Dermott and his sister Jo wouldn't have wanted him to do that . . .

If he didn't recover her little fortune, well, Janice would be all right. Katie had said that they could manage, and Katie knew. She'd have to work like any other girl as soon as she could leave school; probably Mr. Buckley would give her a job in the shop. It would be just as if she was their own daughter. She'd never be a fine lady, but who wanted to be a fine lady these days, anyway?

He sat there in mental torment, knowing that he couldn't take it that way. Unless he made a real effort to get back what belonged to her, he'd never be able to look at her without feeling ashamed of himself. He'd never be able to think of John and Jo without feeling ashamed of himself. They had made him the trustee.

But dear Lord, what was Katie going to say about it all?

He went upstairs presently, conscious of a bad half-hour ahead of him. Katie was still up, sitting by the fire knitting something for Janice and looking at the television. He sat down opposite her, and said, "I've got something I want to talk about."

"I know what that is," she remarked, turning off the set.

"What's that?" he asked, startled.

She said complacently, "You want to go out to this place

Tahiti. I heard you talking about it on the telephone. I think it's silly."

"Better wait to say that till you know all about it," he replied, a little nettled.

"What don't I know?"

"Everything," he said. "You remember that time when I went down to the yacht with them to fix up an electric light over the compass?" She nodded. "Well, it wasn't an electric light at all. It was something quite different."

"I guessed that much," she said. "What was it?"

"Jo's jewel case," he said. "Sort of building it into the boat." He started in and told her the whole thing; it took about a quarter of an hour. "Course, I believed what John told me," he said. "He told me it was just Jo's rings and things like that. But now we know that they took twenty-six thousand pounds of diamonds along with them, I bet that they were in that jewel case, too."

Katie got up from her chair. "Make a pot of tea," she said. She went and busied herself in her little kitchenette while she thought it over. She came back presently with two cups of tea. "Suppose you went out there," she said. "What's it all going to cost?"

"Everything we've got and probably a bit more," he replied. "That's just to get there. Getting back would cost as much again."

She stared at him helplessly. "But that's crazy!"

He rubbed his hand across his eyes. "I know. The other way is to do nothing and just leave it be."

She sat in silence for a minute. "That don't seem right," she said at last. "I can't say I like that much better."

He looked up at her gratefully; Katie was coming round to the unthinkable course he had proposed. "I like it a bloody sight worse," he said. "I'd never be able to think of John and Jo again if we just sat tight on our fannies and did nothing."

"That's enough of that shop language," she said. "Drink your tea while it's hot." He obeyed her. "This governor in this place Papeete," she said. "Suppose you were to write to him and tell him all about it. Couldn't he go there and get the box out of the keel?"

Keith nodded. "I thought of that. Tell you the truth, I don't just know what a governor does. Would he be the top man? An asylum's got a board of governors, but they aren't top of anything."

"I think he's the top man," said Katie. "I read about a governor in a book once."

"That's what I thought," said Keith. "If that's right he'd be paid by the government—the French Government, I suppose, in Paris. Well, when John and Jo took those diamonds out of England they could have gone to prison for it—that's what Mr. Carpenter said. Maybe the diamonds would have been confiscated if they'd been found out." She nodded. "Well now, who's to say that if this governor got his hands on them they wouldn't be confiscated again? I just don't know, and what's more, I don't know who to ask, safely. I mean, twenty-six thousand pounds is worth while anybody going after, if they know it's there. I don't feel like telling anyone about it, least of all this governor."

She nodded slowly. Twenty-six thousand pounds was an incredible sum of money to her, but if it existed at all it belonged to Janice, and no one else was going to lay a finger on it. She knew from her Sunday newspaper that many a bank manager had fallen from grace for much less than that, and who was to say that a French governor would be any better? She was reluctant to admit it and to face the infinite difficulties that would ensue, but Keith had the right idea. Better to say nothing to anybody and go after this himself. She asked him, "What were you going to do in this place Papeete, if the island's three hundred miles away?"

"I don't honestly know," he said. "But look at it like this. Suppose we had lots of money, enough to do whatever we wanted without thinking about it." She nodded. "Well, I'd go out there and get a headstone for the grave made in this place Papeete, and then I'd hire a ship with a crew that knew the way around, and I'd go to this island and get the headstone set up on the grave and everything done proper. And I'd take a lot of photographs for Janice to see when she's older. Well, while I was there I'd go out to the wreck upon this reef in a small boat, and I'd know soon as I laid eyes on it if the box was still there in the concrete. Just behind the mast it was, towards the rudder end. I'd be a poor sort of a fish if I couldn't lay my hands upon it then, and get it away."

"Well, we haven't got lots of money," she said. "Not for

hiring ships and that. I suppose you'd say that if you can get a free ride out to this place Honolulu you can do the rest of it free, too."

"I could try," he said simply. "Maybe I could do some work out there or something, if I get into a jam. How much money do you think I could take with me? I was thinking I could take a hundred pounds."

She laid her teacup down. "I'll get the bank book."

They discussed finances for a time, upon the basis that he would be away for three or four months. "You forgot about the rent of the top flat," she said. She figured with a stub of a pencil on the back of the cheque book. "I think it would be all right if you took a hundred and ten pounds," she said. "But we'd have to have money coming in by the middle of April or we wouldn't be able to pay school fees for the summer term for Janice at Miss Pearson's."

"She'd have to go to the council school."

"I know. But Jo was against that."

He nodded. "That gives me a deadline, anyway."

She sat deep in thought. At last she said, "It'll be hot out in those parts, Keith. You'll have to take your cricket shirts and your blazer."

On that note they went to bed.

He knew shop hours, and he knew that half-past six on a pitch dark January morning was no time to ring a busy man hurrying to catch the transport out to work at Blackbushe, forty miles from London. He waited until eight o'clock and rang Mrs. Thorn, and got from her the telephone number of Albatross Airways, and the extension number. He inquired a little delicately if it was all right to ring Mr. Thorn at his work, and got a somewhat affronted reply. "Of course it's all right," she said. "Mr. Thorn has a secretary." He apologized and hung up, well pleased. Mr. Oliver Thorn apparently was somebody at Albatross Airways Ltd.

Ten minutes later he was speaking to the man himself. He got a courteous reception, somewhat to his own surprise. "Nice to hear your voice, Mr. Stewart. We met last at the Ealing and District exhibition."

"That's right," said Keith. "I liked your Petrolea—liked it very much. If I'd been judging the locos I'd have given it a bronze."

"It wasn't worth it, Mr. Stewart, not really. I should have

fluted the connecting rods, and it's got cheesehead screws all over where they should be hex. I'll do better next time. But it goes all right."

"Well, that's the main thing," said Keith. "Tell me, Mr. Thorn, did you hear anything from Mr. Sanderson about me?"

"Sure. He said you wanted to know if there was any chance of a ride with us to Honolulu."

"That's right."

"Well now, there is and there isn't, Mr. Stewart. What I mean is, we don't carry passengers; we aren't allowed to. We run a freight service. We do sometimes stretch a point, but then it's for someone special like yourself, and we sign them on as crew—second engineer under instruction, or something like that. It's all at the discretion of the chief pilot, Captain Fielding. He'll be taking this Honolulu flight, and he's the one you'd have to get round."

"You have got a machine going to Honolulu?"

"Oh, yes. Thursday or Friday of next week, as soon as the component is finished. We load at Liverpool, at Speke." He paused. "Are you doing anything today, Mr. Stewart?"

"Nothing urgent."

"Think you could come out here to Blackbushe and meet the boys? Captain Fielding, he's taking off for Ankara about three o'clock with four jet engines and spare parts and that, and then on the way back he picks up a load of cut flowers at Nice. He'll be gone three or four days. Then his next trip is the Honolulu one. He'll be here at dinner time, and you could have a talk with him."

"What's the best way for me to get out to you at Black-bushe?"

There was a pause, and Keith heard, "Daisy, what time is that truck leaving Belgrave Road with the manifolds? . . . Why not? . . . Okay." He came back on the line. "We've got a truck leaving Belgrave Road, that's by Victoria, about ten-thirty, Mr. Stewart. One of our red trucks with Albatross all over it. If you wait for him on the Great West Road at the corner of South Ealing Road, say—say about ten-fifty, I'll ring him and tell him to pick you up there then."

"I'll be there waiting for him."

"That's fine, Mr. Stewart. There's four or five of the boys

in the maintenance shop would like to meet you. I'll have a word with Captain Fielding, tell him what it's all about."

There was plenty of time before he had to meet the truck. Janice went off to school, and Katie to the shop, and he went down into his workshop to find something that would entertain the fitters at Blackbushe. A couple of years before he had been doing some research upon miniature electric generators in connection with the Showman's version of his traction engine. He had evolved a little six-volt generator no more than an inch and a half in diameter running at three thousand revs. For research purposes he had adapted the basic castings of his Hornet engine to make a new four-stroke 7-cc. engine running on petrol with a little carburetor, and in place of the reduction gear he had fitted a governor; ignition was by a tiny magneto of his own design and a miniature sparking plug. The whole lot mounted on a little baseplate was about four inches long, two inches wide, and two and a half inches high. It was an easy starter. He could flick it into life by swinging the flywheel at one end with his thumbnail, and as it speeded up to the governed revolutions a pea bulb at the other end glowed with the electricity it generated. It had always been a great success in workshops, and he put it in a little box and slipped it into his pocket.

By half-past eleven he was sitting in the office with Mr. Thorn, drinking a cup of tea. Albatross Airways Ltd. were an independent company operating three ten-year-old Vikings and a couple of DC-6B's, one of which was permanently on a trooping contract. Their offices in an old wartime hutment were not luxurious, but their shops were clean and adequately equipped.

Mr. Thorn said, "Glad to see you again, Mr. Stewart. Look, before we start, would you mind telling me what this is all about? Do you just want to go to Honolulu, or was it your idea to go there and come back with the aircraft?"

"I don't really know." Keith Stewart pulled the newspaper cutting from his wallet and showed it to the chief storekeeper, and told his story. "I've got to try and get to this place Tahiti and fix up about the grave and the salvage and all that," he said. "I haven't got the money to get there in the normal way—it's too expensive. But I did think if I could get a lift to Honolulu it would be a help."

"Sure." Mr. Thorn handed back the cutting to him. "You

want to show that to Captain Fielding," he said. "I won't say we've never done this before, Mr. Stewart, because we have. But I can tell you now, we'd have to have it both ways if Captain Fielding agrees to take you. We'd have to sign you on as second engineer under instruction at a salary you wouldn't get, and at the same time you'd have to sign our legal form of indemnity to say that there'd be no claim against us if you get killed or injured on the flight."

Keith nodded. "Fair enough."

"You haven't got any ground engineer's tickets, I suppose?"

Keith shook his head. "I'm afraid not. You know what I do."

"I do indeed. I don't know if Captain Fielding does, though. We'd better get along down to the hangar and see if we can find him. He's down there somewhere."

Keith pulled the box a little shyly from his pocket. "I brought a bit along with me I thought the boys might like to see."

Mr. Thorn took the tiny generator set and examined it with interest. "My . . ." he breathed. "That really is something. Does it go?"

"Of course it goes." Keith took it from him, primed the tiny carburettor by turning the model upside down, and flipped the little engine into life with his thumbnail. It buzzed like an infuriated wasp as he made delicate adjustments to the jet and settled to an even note as the pea bulb lit up.

Mr. Thorn gazed at it entranced. "Have you ever shown it?"

Keith shook his head. "I only made it up for research, when I was working on the generator." He paused. "The commutator is the tricky part. The rest of it's quite simple."

He stopped the little engine by shorting the plug with his propelling pencil. "Bring that down into the shop," Mr. Thorn said. "The boys will like to see it."

Ten minutes later the little generator set was running on a workbench in an annexe to the hangar, surrounded by a crowd of mechanics attracted by the noise and by the rumour that Keith Stewart of the *Miniature Mechanic* was actually there in person. He faced the barrage of questions that he was accustomed to at exhibitions, dealing with them one by one, a little shyly. In the middle of all this a man in uniform, dark haired with a small dark moustache, pushed his way through the crowd. "What's all this going on?"

Mr. Thorn said, "This is Captain Fielding, Mr. Stewart."

Keith stopped the engine with his pencil, and turned to the newcomer. "Glad to meet you, sir."

The pilot nodded, smiled, and fixed his eyes on the little model on the bench. "Don't you know we aren't supposed to run engines in the hangar? Start it up again—if you can."

"She usually starts all right," Keith said diffidently. He flipped it into life again with his thumbnail; the note steadied, the pea bulb lit up, and it went on running evenly.

The pilot bent to examine it. "I wish our engines started as easily as that."

"She's warm," Keith said apologetically.

"Ours are worse when they're warm." The pilot moved Keith's hand and studied the tendency of the running model to move about the bench. "Not badly balanced. What revs is she doing?"

"About three thousand."

"Where did you get the dynamo from?"

"I made it."

Someone in the crowd said, "And designed it. He wrote an article about it in the *Miniature Mechanic*. Two years ago, was it?"

"About that," Keith said.

The pilot grunted. "What about the magneto?"

Somebody said, "He designed that, too."

The pilot looked at Keith. "What *didn't* you design and make in it?"

Keith said, "The sparking plug." He added diffidently, "Working in ceramics is a bit specialized, and you can buy them so easily." He stopped the little motor again with his pencil, and the pea bulb glowed red and went out.

Captain Fielding took it in his hand and examined it closely. Then he passed it to somebody else, and it went from hand to hand. He said to Keith, "Just a minute, Mr. Stewart." He turned and they walked together out into the main hangar under the wing of the DC-6B. "Mr. Thorn was saying something about you wanted a ride with us to Honolulu."

Keith started in to tell his story again, and showed the pilot the cutting from *The Times*. "I don't know anything about the services from Honolulu to Tahiti," the pilot said at last. "Do you?"

"No. I was thinking I'd find out in Honolulu, and if it wasn't any good or expensive, then perhaps you'd let me come back with you."

Captain Fielding stood in thought. "That's possible."

"How long will you be there?"

"Two days at least. Probably three—or four. It's over thirty hours from Speke to Honolulu, and there's such a thing as crew fatigue. I've told the directors it'll be a week's job altogether." He paused. "The officers of the *Cathay Princess* might know about services to Tahiti—or they could find out." He turned to Keith. "All right, Mr. Stewart—you're in. Mr. Thorn told you the conditions?"

"Yes, sir," said the new second engineer under instruction.

"Okay. You'll need a passport and an American visa and a vaccination certificate. Got any of them?"

"No."

"Well, you'll have to hop around. I can't take you in the aircraft without them. Keep in touch with Mr. Thorn. We'll probably be leaving here for Speke on Thursday morning."

Keith made a good start on his formalities before he left Blackbushe. The provision of passports at that aerodrome was a matter of routine; the Ministry of Civil Aviation had a supply of application forms and a tame justice of the peace to witness signatures. He presented this at the Passport Office in Westminster next day, got himself vaccinated, and was well on the way through the formalities by the weekend.

He saw Mr. McNeil, the managing editor of the *Miniature Mechanic*, and told him that there would be a gap of several weeks in his articles. Mr. McNeil was disgruntled, but less so when Keith had told his story and had shown him the cutting from *The Times*. "Well, if you've got to go, I suppose you've got to," he said reluctantly. "I think I'll put a para in the book to say you're on holiday. Or—wait now. Think you could do a piece upon the flight to Honolulu and mail it when you land? Flying to Honolulu . . . right from the flight deck, over the North Pole . . . The readers might like that as a change."

"I think I could do that," said Keith. "I'd have to get the permission of Albatross, of course. The trip's a bit irregular, you see, because they aren't allowed to carry passengers. I'll ask them."

"When do you think you'll be back?"

"April, I hope," said Keith. "It's got to be early April, somehow or other, because of the school holidays. My wife works, you see."

The editor opened his eyes. "I never knew you had any children."

"I haven't," said the engineer. "This is my sister Jo's little girl, Jo who got drowned." He indicated the cutting from the paper. "She left her with us to look after till they got to Vancouver," he explained. "She's ours for keeps, now."

The editor's eyes softened a little; it was just what a silly unbusinesslike mutt like Keith Stewart would let himself in for. But a fine engineer in his own line . . . "Going to make things difficult?" he asked.

Keith shook his head. "Katie says we can manage."

Mr. McNeil sat for a moment in thought. "You know what it's like with the book," he said. "We just scrape along. We have to use such a hell of a lot of blocks. Still, we *do* scrape along. If while you're away you want a bit of an advance on stories that you'll do when you come back, let me know. If there's any cash in the kitty, I'll do my best."

Keith thanked him, and went back to Ealing. Janice was now one of their main problems because school ended at four and Katie did not get home much before six; moreover there were Saturday mornings to be considered when Katie worked and there was no school. What to do for Janice in those periods perplexed them very much indeed; always before Keith had been at home. It worried Keith far more than the problem of how he was to get from Honolulu to Tahiti.

"I might ask Mr. Buckley if she could come to the shop just for the hour before closing," Katie said doubtfully.

"John and Jo wouldn't have liked that," said Keith uneasily.

"I know. I'll find out about that dancing class from Miss Pearson. Some of the children do go to that, I know. Miss Grayson, or Gleeson, or some name like that."

The dancing class filled one evening and the Saturday morning, and Mrs. Soskice, mother of Diana, filled the rest; Janice could go to Mrs. Soskice and play with Diana till

Katie called for her. With that problem cleared away, it then remained to tell Janice that Keith was going to the island. They decided that they had to tell her where he was going to rather than to fob her off with some indefinite journey. She was too intelligent, and would probably find out where he had gone to, and lose confidence in them.

They told her together. "Going to the place where my Daddy and Mummy was drownded?" she asked. It was the first time, so far as either of them knew, that she had spoken of her parents. She had been putting on a little weight, however, and was no longer quite so peaky.

"That's right," said Keith. "We've got to see about selling the engine and the bits and pieces from the wreck and that."

"Can I go too?"

Katie shook her head. "No, darling. It's too far, and it costs too much."

"Mummy and Daddy took me to China when I was little."

"That's right," said Katie. "But you were very little then, just a baby, and you know a baby doesn't have to pay a fare on the tram or the Underground or anything. But you're a big girl now, and you'd have to pay."

Janice nodded thoughtfully. "I have to have a half ticket. Diana's much bigger than me, but she has a half ticket just the same."

"We couldn't afford even a half ticket," Katie said. "It's going to clean us right out if Uncle Keith goes there. But we think it's necessary."

Janice nodded again. Already she had become accustomed to the straitened finances of the Stewart household; the free spending ways of her father and mother were already fading from her memory. She turned to Keith. "Are you going to see that my Daddy and Mummy are buried right?" she asked.

"That's one of the things I was going to do," he replied.

She wriggled on his knee, and prompted by some obscure chain of thought she asked, "Would you like to take one of my eggs with you?"

"Why, yes," he said. "That would be a lovely thing to take."

"Which one would you like to take?"

"Which one can you spare most?"

"No," she said. "You choose."

The case-hardened one would take the friction of a long journey in his pocket best. "I'd like the grey one," he said.

She clapped her hands, laughing. "I was so afraid you'd choose the blue one because I like the blue one best because it's the prettiest and because I saw you make it right from the start." She slithered down from his knee. "I'll go and fetch the grey one now." So that moment passed.

In the last day or two problems of health in the tropics obsessed Katie's mind. "Pith helmets," she said. "That's what people out there wear in the sun. You must buy one of those as soon as you get there, Keith. You don't want to go getting sunstroke. And mosquito nets to sleep under at night, else you get malaria. Perhaps you ought to take one of those along with you."

"There's some kind of a pill you can take for that," he said. "I'll ask at Evans' in the morning."

They decided that he should travel in his best blue suit and the heavy woollen overcoat that he had bought after the war and kept for best, and wear the imitation Panama hat that he reserved for his annual August holiday in Cornwall. He packed a suitcase with his cricket shirts, blazer, and grey flannel trousers, two suits of heavy woollen underwear, and a clean grey workshop coat. He got from his bank a hundred pounds' worth of dollar travellers' cheques, and took with him a few pounds in notes. He put the small petrol-electric generator set into his pocket in its box. Then he was ready to go.

5

THE JOURNEY TO HONOLULU IN the DC-6B was an unmitigated, sheer delight to Keith Stewart. He had never been out of England and though he had flown once or twice as a passenger he had little practical knowledge of aircraft. He had, however, an almost encyclopædic knowledge of things electrical and mechanical, and to be given the free run of the big Douglas was to open a glittering storehouse of technical interests to him. He caught a transport down to Black-

bushe very early on the Thursday morning, and entered his
Wonderland.

The aircraft had been stripped of all passenger seats and
upholstery. Behind the flight deck was a crew rest room; on
the port side two pairs of seats faced across a table, on the
starboard side there were two bunks. Behind again there was
a toilet to port and a small galley to starboard, and aft of
that the cabin was an empty shell right to the aft bulkhead.

Keith spent an hour in the office with Mr. Thorn and
Captain Fielding, putting his signature on various documents.
In the course of the formalities he learned the names of the
other crew members, and was a little surprised at their
number. There were six apart from the captain and himself;
three co-pilots of varying experience and standing, a navigator, a radio operator, and an engineer, Dick King, who knew
all about Keith Stewart. The formalities over, he carried his
suitcase down to the aircraft with Mr. King, who showed
him where to put it, and changed, putting on his grey workshop coat.

Presently, soon after eleven o'clock, the crew came
aboard, led by the captain, who told Keith to sit in one of
the unoccupied rest seats and strap himself in. The doors
were slammed shut, the steps withdrawn, and two of the
younger pilots came and joined him in the other seats. On the
flight deck the crew commenced the pre-flight checks, the
engines whined and started one by one, the captain spoke to
the Tower and got clearance to taxi. Engines were run up at
the threshold of the runway, and presently the aircraft
moved forward, lined up, and took off.

She got off very quickly with no load on board, and only
half fuel. As the flaps came up the two young pilots undid
their belts, indicating to Keith that he should do the same.
They all moved forward to the flight deck, Keith keeping
behind out of the way.

There was nothing to be seen out of the windows or
through the pilot's windscreen but the grey January cloud.
Everybody on the flight deck seemed to be busy; though they
sat relaxed and motionless he could sense the nervous tension. The grey wisps of cloud whipped past and once they
emerged into clear air between two layers of cloud, and
entered cloud again, so that he knew that they were climb-

ing. From time to time the captain spoke to Dick King, who made adjustments to the throttles and the prop controls; from time to time the navigator or the radio officer left his seat and spoke to the captain, who nodded, sometimes glancing at the clock on the instrument panel.

Keith had never before been on the flight deck of a large aircraft, or been in any aircraft at all while it was flying blind. He was impressed and somewhat amazed by the things he did not know. These men were working as a team, doing things together quickly and accurately, things that he could only guess at. He knew that on their teamwork the safety of the aircraft depended. All his own skill and ingenuity could not assist them by one iota; the most that he could do to help them in their work was to keep right out of their way.

He went aft again into the rest quarters and examined the galley. That was understandable, at any rate; there were tins of coffee and tins of tea, and tinned milk, and tinned meats and vegetables, and bread and butter and cheese and jams. This was within his competence. He could not assist these people in their work, mechanical though it was, and that was humiliating, but he could keep them well supplied with coffee and biscuits. He set himself to discover where everything was stowed.

Presently he sat down again; there was nothing to be seen at all but the gray fog. One of the young co-pilots came and sat beside him. "Half an hour to go," he said. "He'll be starting the let-down in a few minutes."

"How high are we?"

"Fifteen thousand. We're going to do a GCA approach."

Keith asked timidly, "What's that?"

"Ground control. They get us on the radar screen and talk us down on to the runway. It's quite interesting. You can hear it all on the loudspeaker if you come forward. But don't get in anybody's way."

The note of the engines changed as the let-down began, but nothing else seemed to alter. When the young man beside him got up and went forward Keith followed him. A trickle of remarks was coming from the loudspeaker over the windscreen between the pilots, half heard by Keith at the rear, one quarter understood. "Delta November, you are cleared down to six thousand feet, six zero zero zero feet, QFE nine

nine eight, nine nine eight, course three two zero." And then, "Delta November, Roger."

He could not understand any of it. The co-pilot seemed to be flying the machine; Captain Fielding sat relaxed, watching the instruments and fingering a black hand microphone, occasionally raising it for a short remark. Everyone was standing or sitting very quiet. Nobody was peering from the windows, for there was nothing to see. Once Captain Fielding, turning to say something to the navigator, noticed Keith Stewart at the back of the standing officers, and smiled slightly at him. Then he turned and faced the instruments again.

The stream of half-heard, quiet orders from the loud-speaker brought them lower, lower, upon changing courses. "Delta November, you are cleared to descend to two thousand feet. Check your QFE, nine nine eight." Keith saw the captain raise the microphone, and heard, "Delta November, Roger." They sat in motionless tension. Then, "Delta November, turn now, right, on to heading zero four zero." And presently, "Delta November, you are now on final and eleven miles from touchdown. Commence your descent at six hundred feet per minute. Check your wheels and flaps for landing."

There was activity in the cockpit; the wheels went down with a thump, the flaps crept halfway out, the note of the engines rose higher as the pitch decreased. There was still absolutely nothing to be seen but the grey fog outside. There was dead silence on the flight deck. "Delta November, you are four miles from touchdown, closing with the centre line. Turn left now five degrees on to heading zero three five." The captain said laconically, "Roger."

"Two miles from touchdown now, and on the centre line."

Suddenly the fog was ripped apart, and streaks of it flew past the windscreen and the windows. The quiet voice said, "Turn right two degrees on to zero three seven; you are one and a half miles from touchdown. Can you land visually?"

The runway, broad and long and comforting, lay immediately in front of them. The captain lifted the microphone and said, "Delta November is visual. Thank you." He hung the microphone upon a little hook and placed his hands and feet on the controls, nodding to the co-pilot. One of the juniors turned to Keith and said, "Captain likes everyone strapped in for landing." They went back to the seats, and as they settled down in them the wheels touched the runway.

The engines roared suddenly in reverse pitch and died again, the brakes squealed a little, and the aircraft slowed, turned from the runway, and taxied to a remote part of the tarmac where the batsman waited. One of the lads by Keith grumbled, "They're putting us the hell of a way from anywhere. I got an aunt in Allerton. I told Ma that I'd try and get to see her."

The other said, "They're putting us over here so that truck can get to us to load, and be out of the way."

The machine came to rest, and the engines stopped. On the flight deck the crew entered up their various logbooks and forms; one by one they came down the cabin to the door, now open. The captain stopped by Keith. "Saw you watching the talk-down," he said. "Did you understand it?"

Keith smiled. "Some of it. Not very much."

"Everyone to his trade," the officer said. "As soon as we get clear of this foggy muck you can come and sit up front."

He passed on, and Keith left the machine with Dick King. "How did you enjoy the flight?"

Keith smiled. "Like being on the Underground."

"It was a bit. Not much to look at, is there? The Met says we'll be out of this by the time we're over Ireland."

"What time do we take off?"

"Depends what time we finish loading. I don't see any sign of the truck yet. We'd better get some dinner while the going's good."

They made for the restaurant. "That's one thing I wanted to ask you," Keith said. "Who cooks and dishes out the food while you're in flight?"

"I do," said the flight engineer.

"All the way? You've got to sleep sometime."

"Oh well, one of the others does it if I've got my head down, or they go without."

"I could help with that," Keith said. "I can serve coffee and biscuits or heat up a can of stew. I don't know that I can help in any other way."

"Well, that might be a help. I'll show you what we do."

The loudspeaker broadcast a call to the telephone for Mr. King while they were having lunch. He came back to the table. "Bloody truck's arrived," he said, and gulped down his cup of tea. "See you later."

He made off back to the machine. Keith finished his lunch quickly and followed him, anxious to miss no moment of the play. The semi-trailer stood by the aircraft with the sausage-like component on the tray swathed in hessian, twelve feet long and weighing about five tons. Beside the truck Dick lounged with one of the co-pilots, idle. "Needn't have hurried over dinner," he said to Keith. "Waiting for the bloody crane now. Captain, he knew better."

Presently the mobile crane arrived, and a Land Rover loaded with baulks of heavy timber, and the slow, delicate business of loading the rotor into the cabin through the door began, and positioning it in the right part of the cabin when it was in, and straining it down to holding lugs with steel ropes and turnbuckles. Keith could do nothing technical to help these men who knew their job so well, but he worked all afternoon as a labourer for them, moving heavy timbers under their direction and passing wires. It took three hours to get the load in place and secured. Then the tank wagon came to refuel the aircraft. It was half past five before everything was finished.

"We'll have a meal before we go," said Captain Fielding. "Take off at seven o'clock."

A foreman electrician from the works was to accompany them and install the rotor in the *Cathay Princess,* a man called Adams. Dick introduced Keith as they walked towards the restaurant again. "This is Mr. Keith Stewart," he said. "Writes for the *Miniature Mechanic.*"

Mr. Adams stopped dead in his tracks. "Not *the* Keith Stewart?" he enquired.

"That's right."

Mr. Adams put out his hand. "Well, did you ever! Wait till I tell the lads in the shop I met Keith Stewart!"

The words comforted Keith, assuaging something of the inferiority complex that had begun to descend upon him; there was so much here that was technical that he did not know. Here, in Dick King and in Mr. Adams, were two who recognized what he could do in the little technical field that he had made his own. He went on to the restaurant with them with restored confidence in himself. Technical fields, he reflected, of necessity were small; if you were expert in one

subject you could not be expert also in all the others, for no
man's mind was big enough. The man who designed the radar
presentation that the controller had used to talk them down
that morning would not, himself, have been able to bring
them into a safe landing, for he would not have known
sufficient about aeroplanes.

They ate together at a long table in the deserted restaurant, all nine of them. The navigator sat next to Keith. In
reply to a question, he said, "Be about midnight, local time,
when we refuel at Frobisher. Nine hours' flight. Be just the
same if it was daytime, because they don't see the sun there
much this time of year. Say it's an hour to refuel. Another
nine hours to Vancouver gets us there around dawn. After
that it's daylight down to Honolulu."

In the cold, windy January darkness they walked back to
the aircraft at about half past six, and climbed on board, and
made their way forward through the cabin, climbing over the
many securing wires of the rotor. Lights were switched on,
the steps were withdrawn from the door and the door itself
was slammed shut and secured by one of the young pilots.
Mr. Adams and Keith settled in a couple of the seats and
strapped themselves in, and the routine of pre-flight checks
began on the flight deck.

"You done this often before?" asked Mr. Adams.

Keith shook his head. "I've never been out of England."

"You don't want to either," said Mr. Adams decidedly.
"Last year the missus and the daughter kept on at me, would
I take them to the South of France. They'd read about it in
the books, and Grace Kelly and all that. Well, I did. God
love us, what it didn't cost, flying to Nice and flying back
again! And when we got there, not half so much fun as we'd
have had at Blackpool. But they liked it . . . Gave them
something to talk about in Salford."

"That where you live?"

"Aye. Ever been there?"

Keith shook his head.

"The Salford and Eccles Model Engineers would like it
fine if you could come up to judge one of their exhibitions,
Mr. Stewart. They had the last one in the Town Hall—
October, was it, or November? A lot of your designs were
there . . ." They went on talking model engineering while the
starters whined, the motors caught and ran, and the Douglas

turned and taxied slowly to the runway, framed in amber lights.

They took off down the runway, and were airborne. For a moment or two Keith saw the lights of Liverpool away over on the left; then they were blotted out by cloud and only the bright glow of the exhaust manifolds could be seen, and the rhythmic pulsations of the red wing-tip light reflected from the mist. "Looks like we're in cloud again," said Keith. "It was like this all the way up from Blackbushe."

Mr. Adams stirred from a post-prandial doze. "Wonderful the way they find their way about," he said comfortably, and dozed again.

Keith was too technically interested to follow his example. He got up and stood in the dim alley leading to the flight deck, watching what was going on. Nothing much seemed to be happening; the pilots sat relaxed and he judged that the machine was on the automatic pilot, for neither of them seemed to be flying it. The pilot's microphone hung idle on its hook, but now and again the radio operator seemed to speak to someone from his desk. Dick King sat upon a folding seat between and behind the pilots, but he did not seem to be doing anything.

As he watched, the darkness ahead through the windscreen seemed to lighten for a moment, darken again, and lighten. Suddenly a wisp of white cloud ripped by the windscreen and they were momentarily in moonlight. More cloud rose up ahead and enveloped them, and that in turn was ripped away. Then they were flying in full moonlight over a white, moonlit floor of cloud and climbing away from it. It seemed to Keith the most wonderful sight that he had ever seen, for it was new to him.

He could not repress his technical interest. He moved forward and spoke to Dick quietly, "How high are we?"

The engineer said, "Thirteen thousand five hundred. Have a cup of coffee presently, when we level off to cruise."

The captain heard the question, and the answer. "We're going up to twenty-one thousand," he said. "I'll let you know when we've settled down at cruising altitude, and you can come and sit up front here, if you like."

Keith went back to his seat, and sat looking out on the moonlit clouds below, at the serene, untroubled security of the wing. Presently the note of the engines altered, the nose

of the machine dipped slightly, and she seemed to take a
new, stable, and rather quieter flight. He judged that this was
the change to the cruising condition, and this was confirmed
when Dick came aft to the galley. Keith got up to help him
with the coffee and biscuits.

"Captain says we'll have a meal for anybody who's awake
and wants it at twenty-three zulu—at eleven o'clock English
time. Then another sometime after we leave Frobisher.
Breakfast on the ground at Vancouver. Coffee and biscuits
every couple of hours or so."

"When are you going to sleep?"

The engineer smiled. "Pretty soon, mate. Take-off, landing,
and refuelling—those are my busy times. I'll take one of the
inside chairs soon as we've cleared this coffee."

"Show me what you do about the meal. I can look after
that, if you're asleep."

When coffee was over and the cups rinsed, Keith went
forward. The captain got out of his seat and stretched, and
at his invitation Keith got into it and sat relaxed, watching
the wide, dim panorama of deep blue sky and moonlit cloud
far below. He studied the instruments massed on the panels
in front of him, examining them one by one. Most of them
were familiar to him in theory; some of the others were
explained by the legend on the dial. When prolonged cogita-
tion failed to yield the function of a lever or a dial he asked
the first officer beside him, who explained it to him. He
passed over the radio equipment without questions, knowing
that the explanations would be quite beyond his understanding.

His day had been a long one, and at the conclusion of an
hour he found that he was growing sleepy. He got out of the
captain's seat, and one of the young pilots took his place.
The navigator smiled as he brushed past him, and Keith
paused to look at the chart. "We'll be about *here* now," the
officer said, putting his pencil on the thin pencil line that led
across the North Atlantic to Greenland.

Keith studied the line. "Do we go over Greenland?" It
seemed incredible that he, Keith Stewart, should be doing
this.

"That's right. We might be over the ice cap about one in
the morning, Greenwich time."

"Shall we see it?" Eskimos and explorers, and the dogs

with tails curled up over their backs that they called huskies.

"I doubt it. There's usually a lot of cloud cover. We might. Like me to call you if there's anything to see?"

"I would." Keith hesitated. "Are you going to be up for the next hour or two?"

"Captain's having a ziz now," said the navigator. "Supper's at eleven o'clock, Greenwich. He's getting up for that. After that I'll have mine."

"Don't wake Dick King to get the supper if he's asleep," Keith said. "Give me a nudge. He showed me what to do."

"Okay."

He passed aft to the rest quarters. The captain and the radio operator were sleeping in their clothes in the two bunks. Keith settled down in a vacant chair and pushed it back to the reclining angle. So many technical interests that he could not absorb because of the need for sleep. Janice and Katie in the flat at Ealing all seemed very far away; his many years of work for the *Miniature Mechanic* were something that had happened in a previous existence, quite unreal. The even murmur of the engines, the motionless flight, wrapped him round, and presently he slept.

He was roused by Dick climbing over him from the inside seat to start getting the supper. He got up and lent a hand. The whole crew seemed to come to life with the smell of the meal heating on the stove. Captain Fielding and the radio operator got down from the bunks, shook themselves, and put on their shoes. Keith realized for the first time that the aircrew were divided virtually into two watches, that the pilots could do the routine navigation, and the routine radio checks. The meal, served in two sittings, signified a change of watch.

He rinsed the dishes when Mr. King went forward, and put everything away. Mr. Adams slumbered again, uninterested in the flight, and Keith went forward to the flight deck again. He sat at the navigator's desk for some time, but presently he grew sleepy again and went back to his seat.

He was roused by the changed note of the engines as they began the let-down an hour out from Frobisher. He knew what was happening from the slight pressure difference in his ears, and from the time. He went and washed his face to clear his mind, and then went forward again to the flight deck. The navigator was back at his desk. "Clear for landing," he said. "Cloud two-tenths at three thousand. Temperature on the ground minus ten Fahrenheit. Good and cold—forty-two degrees of frost. I should stay in the machine, if I were you."

Keith was startled. "What's the outside temperature here, now?"

"I don't know." The officer leaned back and glanced at the panel. "About minus thirty."

"I'd like to do anything I can to help—if there's anything I can do."

The navigator shook his head. "It's just the refuelling, then we'll be off again. Get your bloody nose frostbitten if you go outside."

They landed presently upon a white, snow-covered runway lit with amber lights, using the brakes very little and the engines in reverse pitch a great deal. They followed a blue-lit taxiway to the few buildings constituting the base and came to a standstill in front of the control tower. Steps were wheeled up and the door opened; the captain and the flight engineer and the two youngest pilots put on heavy coats and leather gloves, and went down on to the snow. Keith followed them to the door and stopped in the entrance, checked by the bitterness of the cold.

The moon was bright upon the snow plain of the airfield and the snow-covered buildings, the lights brilliant. He saw the captain and the navigator hurrying to the control tower. He saw a refuelling truck drive up and stop by the port wing, he saw a ladder erected and Dick get up on to the wing with one of the refuelling crew and commence to sound the tanks. Then he could bear the cold no longer, and retreated forward into the machine across the web of cables lashing down the rotor.

In the rest quarters warmth still lingered, though cold air was seeping forward from the rear. Refuelling took three-quarters of an hour. The crew made a quick external inspection of the aircraft and came hurrying into the fuselage again. The door was slammed shut, the steps removed, the motors started again, and the machine moved out on to the runway and took off with a slow, careful acceleration on the icy surface till she was airborne on the long flight over the northern wastes of Canada to Vancouver.

Presently Keith went forward and spoke to Dick King, seated between the pilots at the console. "What time for the next meal?" he asked in a low tone.

"Nine or nine-thirty, Greenwich," the engineer replied. He pointed to the clock above the navigator's table. "That time, there." It showed about five-thirty when Keith looked. "We'll have coffee and biscuits soon as we level off."

"I'll start getting that ready. What are you having for the main meal?"

"There's some pre-cooked steaks in a carton on the lefthand side, up at the top." They went on to discuss the detail of the meal. "I'll probably be up for it," the engineer said. "Get my head down for a bit presently, but I'll be up."

"You don't have to be," said Keith. "I can do all that."

In spite of his bold assertion, he was growing tired. The flight from Frobisher to Vancouver was a repeat of the flight to Frobisher, a night flight without incident, with nothing to be seen. The four pilots, the radio officer, and the navigator took their turns in the bunks; the flight engineer slept in one of the seats. These men were all younger than Keith Stewart, physically more fit and accustomed to long hours of flight and irregular sleep. They seemed to stand it well, but for the first time Keith realized the meaning of crew fatigue. By the time they reached Honolulu, he knew, he would desire nothing so much as sleep in a bed. He could well understand the necessity for two or three days' rest before the crew flew home again to Blackbushe.

He slept most of the way to Vancouver, only rousing himself to help to serve the meal. Few of the aircrew ate much during that stage of the flight, but the demand for coffee and biscuits was brisk. They landed in from over sea on the long Vancouver runway in the darkness at about six in the morning of local time, refuelled and inspected the machine in misty rain, and walked wearily to the airport restaurant.

"You won't get bacon and eggs, English fashion, here," the engineer told Keith. "Hot cakes and syrup with a side order of bacon. I'll show you."

Where everything was strange this seemed no stranger than the rest; he accepted the North American food and enjoyed the novelty, though Mr. Adams grumbled at the little tea bag hanging in the cup of hot water. They ate together sitting up in a long row at a stainless steel counter, while outside the grey dawn showed in the rain. "Might as well be in England," Mr. Adams said.

The navigator heard him, and smiled faintly. "You'll be gasping for breath tonight in Honolulu."

In the grey morning light they walked through the rain to the machine, and settled in their places. The clock over the navigator's desk showed either 4 or 16; both seemed quite inapplicable to Keith and which it was he had no means of knowing. They took off to the west down the long runway and climbed away over water till they entered cloud. "Eleven more hours," the navigator told him. "Then we'll be through."

Half an hour later they broke out into sunshine over a cloud floor; the pilots reached for their sunglasses and put them on. Presently while the first cups of coffee were being consumed the cloud beneath them thinned into holes through which they could see the sea, corrugated with waves. By the time the empty cups had been collected, rinsed, and placed in their racks to dry the cloud had practically disappeared, and they flew on under a cloudless sky, over a blue sea. Later they met cloud again.

The day passed in boredom and fatigue for Keith. He had long exhausted those technical interests of the aircraft that were within his comprehension, and he was growing very tired indeed. He dozed wearily much of the day with his shoes off, for his feet and legs were swelling with the continued sitting and lack of exercise. He ate little of the midday meal. As the hands of his watch moved gradually past twelve and on to one he began to come to life again, for three was the hour of landing, English time, when this slow purgatory would be over. Since they were nearly half-way round the world and they were to land in the late afternoon, he guessed that his watch still cherished the opinion that it was the middle of the night.

Soon after two activity began on the flight deck, and the let-down began. He went forward, and the captain pointed out a very small cloud dead ahead of them and very far away. "That could be over Oahu," he said. "It's either that or Maui. But I think it's Oahu. We're on the range now."

Keith nodded and went back to the navigator's desk to

look at the chart. Honolulu, it appeared, was the name of a town and not an island, as he had supposed. It was on an island called Oahu, by no means the largest of the group. He went back to his seat and sat down, wondering for the first time if he was not absolutely crazy to be here at all. Ealing was his place, and writing articles for the *Miniature Mechanic* was his job. These wastes of sunlit sea, these islands with strange names like Oahu, were no part of his life. He owed it to Janice to try to get back her inheritance . . . but still . . . Ealing was his place. He could stay with the aircraft, of course, and presently the crew would take him back to Blackbushe, only forty miles from Ealing; a truck or a coach would take him up the Great West Road, a red bus up the South Ealing Road, and he would be home again, home in his workshop, in his own routine.

Abruptly he realized that he was afraid, afraid of the unknown that lay before him. He must do better than that for Janice before he could have licence to go home.

The island grew ahead of them, and there was more activity upon the flight deck. Dick King was in the folding seat between the pilots and the captain was talking into the small microphone. They dropped off height as they approached the island and approached it from a little to the south of east. A considerable town with docks and shipping lay upon the southern shore, and to the west of this there was an enormous airport, apparently about five miles long. They made a wide circuit of this and approached from the southwest, and touched down upon a runway halfway up the length of the field. They taxied to the Customs entry building near the garlanded civil airport building, and stopped the motors.

Keith asked the flight engineer, "What time is it here?"

"Ten minutes to five—in the afternoon."

Steps were wheeled up to the aircraft, the door opened, and they made their way out on to the tarmac, carrying their luggage. The humid heat hit Keith like a blow. He was wearing a blue serge suit with a waistcoat, a woollen shirt, and thick woollen underwear, clothes that had been reasonable enough in England thirty-six hours before but which were intolerable in the tropics, where everybody seemed to be wearing a light shirt and trousers and little else. Moreover, he was carrying his suitcase and his raincoat. He stood with the crew in a small group while a small Oriental man in charge of a brawny Customs officer came up and greeted Captain Fielding.

"Very good afternoon, Captain," he said. He spoke with a slight American accent. "I am Harold Yamasuki, of the Yamasuki Trading Company, Incorporated. We are agents for the tanker ship, the *Cathay Princess*. You have had a good flight? You arrived exactly on time."

Captain Fielding put out his hand. "Nice to meet you, Mr. Yamasuki," he said. "Yes, we had a good flight—no troubles." He turned around. "This is Mr. Adams, who is to superintend the installation of the rotor. You had a cable about him?"

Mr. Yamasuki stopped shaking hands with the captain and shook hands with Mr. Adams. "Very glad to know you," he said. "Yes, we had the radiogram about Mr. Adams. He will be great help. Now, everybody must go to the entry formalities with passports and vaccination certificates ready, please, and after that the Customs. You give bags to the boy here and he will meet you with them in the examination room. There are nine? Yes, nine. I will now call the Beachcomber Hotel and arrange accommodation. You will not mind if two must share a room, a room with two beds? I will meet you as you come from Customs, and we go to the hotel. Then we can talk more. Now you go with officer to passport examination."

The captain said, "They'll want us to shift the aircraft away from here before we go to the hotel. Are you unloading tonight?"

"It is too late now," said Mr. Yamasuki. "Tomorrow, I think, at seven o'clock we will begin to unload. By the time we could begin tonight it will be dark, and there would be the possibility of accident and damage to the rotor. I think it will be better in the day."

Mr. Adams said, "I'm with you there, mate, all the way."

They went from the brilliant sunshine into the cool shade of the air-conditioned examination room. Keith passed through with the crew without difficulty and emerged into the Customs shed with them. Nobody had anything to declare and only a cursory examination was made. The bags were loaded into an elongated motor car, the captain spoke to the

control tower and to Shell upon the telephone, and the crew
went back to the machine to move it to the park. Keith
Stewart went with them, leaving his coat, jacket, and waistcoat in the car. Even so, he sweated profusely as he walked
out to the aircraft in his braces and blue trousers.

There were palm trees by the foreshore, and the sea was
glittering and blue. It was incredible that he, Keith Stewart,
should be in a place like this.

Moving the aircraft nearly a mile away and refuelling it
took an hour. The sun had set and the quick darkness was
covering the airport when the last man got down from the
aircraft, slammed the door, and locked it. In the fading light
the aircraft movements seemed to be continuous; they took
off and landed with their winking navigation lights in the
soft, velvety dusk, in what appeared to be an endless stream.
Keith stood watching them, fascinated. "Busy place, this,"
remarked Mr. King.

The long car appeared with Mr. Yamasuki and took them
to the hotel. The agent consulted with the desk clerk about
the rooms, and then turned to the captain. "I will now leave
you to rest," he said. "Tomorrow, at half-past six in the
morning, I will come back with a car, and the truck will be
beside the airplane at seven."

They talked about the mobile crane. "I will arrange," said
Mr. Yamasuki. "One thing. I have called the ship, the *Cathay
Princess*, to say you have arrived. I think some of the officers
may come here tonight to meet you, and to talk about the
electrical work with Mr. Adams."

As he was going down the steps to the car Keith Stewart
stopped him. "You can tell me, Mr. Yamasuki. Is it possible
to get from here to Tahiti?"

"To Tahiti? There is no regular service. The Matson ships,
they go Tahiti to Honolulu but not from here to Tahiti.
There are rumors that they will change, but I do not know.
There are Norwegian cargo steamers which call sometimes
from Vancouver to Tahiti. They carry a few passengers."

"Will one of those be going soon?"

Mr. Yamasuki shook his head. "I do not think so. One was
here last week. Perhaps in two months' time. I will find out.
Sometimes there is an island trading schooner going to Tahiti. They take passengers, not very comfortable. Sometimes,
to sleep on deck."

"Would one of those be going soon?"

"I do not know. I will ask tonight, and tell you in the morning. You wish to go from Honolulu to Tahiti, yourself?"

"That's right."

"I do not think it will be easy. But I will ask."

Keith Stewart was depressed, and tired, and very, very hot in his unsuitable clothes. He went back to the group at the desk and signed his name in the register, and found that he had been allocated to share a room with Dick King. They went up in the elevator to the fifth floor.

The Beachcomber was a fairly modern hotel on the unfashionable, dockside side of the city, much used by aircrews and ships' officers on account of its nearness to the airfield and to the docks. It had no swimming pool, but it commanded a pleasant view out over the ocean in the front and the mountains at the back. Keith and Dick King found themselves in a back room with a shower, two beds, converted into lounges for the day, and a wide, deep verandah furnished with wicker chairs and table. The door of the room was louvred for the full height, permitting the cool trade wind to blow through the room continuously.

"I'm for a shower," said Dick King, throwing off his clothes and making for it.

Keith Stewart had never had a shower in the whole of his life. He had seen them in shop windows and had read about them, but one had never come his way. As a boy and a young man in Renfrew he had had a bath once a week, and though he had graduated from that to having a bath whenever he felt like it, it would have seemed to him a senseless extravagance to have one every day. He certainly felt like one now. While Dick was in the shower he stripped off his heavy woollen underwear with a sign of relief, and stood in the cool breeze with a towel round his waist. Presently he opened his suitcase and stood looking at his clothing ruefully. His woollen cricket shirts and gray flannel trousers were the best he could do; they might be tolerable after dark but he knew now that they would be very hot in the daytime. Still, they were all he had.

Presently Dick King came out and he went in and tried the shower experimentally. He found it strange but not unpleasant and he stayed under it for a long time, gradually reducing the temperature of the water and washing away his fatigue with the sweat. When he came out he was cool and refreshed.

He would have to have some money in his pocket, and they used dollars here, it seemed. He had never cashed a travellers' cheque before and consulted Dick, who showed him where to sign it and told him they would cash it at the desk. He followed this advice when they went downstairs. Then they went to the verandah bar.

"Beer's the cheapest," said Dick. "Not like the English beer—a kind of fizzy lager. But it's what we mostly drink here, on account of the dollar allowance."

In the bar most of the rest of the aircrew were already gathered, with Captain Davies of the *Cathay Princess,* the chief engineer, and the third engineer, a lad called Alec Bourne. Captain Fielding turned to Dick and Keith to introduce them. "This is Mr. King, flight engineer," he said. He smiled. "This is Mr. Keith Stewart. We call him flight engineer under instruction, which means he's come along with us for the ride. He writes for a model paper in London. We're hoping that he'll give us a good spin when he gets back."

The third engineer's jaw dropped, and they all shook hands. The third said, "It wouldn't be Keith Stewart of the *Miniature Mechanic,* by any chance?"

Dick King said, "The very same. You read the *Miniature Mechanic?*"

"I've read it every week, ever since I was a little nipper," said the lad. "I've got every copy since 1948 at home, and a lot on board. Ma sends it to me every week. Fancy meeting you, sir. I never thought I'd do that, except maybe to see you opening an exhibition." He hesitated, and added, "Would you like a beer, sir?"

A beer was just exactly what Keith Stewart needed, and while it was coming he talked models to the third engineer. "I made a Hornet about two years ago," the young man told him. "I'm working on a Gannet now."

"Did the Hornet go all right?"

"It went fine. I had a bit of difficulty getting it started at the first go off, but then I got a bottle of American fuel, and she goes fine. I got a little airscrew on her for the load."

Keith nodded. "They generally put more ether in the American fuels. If you're using that, I think I should wash out the cylinder with a light oil after each run. I've heard that the American fuels are more corrosive than ours. Put in a drop or two of Three-in-One, or something like that."

The young man nodded gratefully. "Thanks for the tip, Mr. Stewart."

"Where do you work?"

"Oh, in the engine room workshop," the third said. "We've got a six-inch lathe there, and a shaper. It's quite well equipped, really." He paused, and added a little shyly, "If you've got the time to come on board and have a look round, Mr. Stewart, there's one or two of the lads would like to meet you."

"I'd like to do that very much," said Keith. "I'd like to see your workshop." Twelve beers arrived upon a tray carried by a very pretty Asiatic girl in a cheongsam of figured silk. These were distributed around, and the talk became general.

Alec Bourne turned to his captain. "I've just asked Mr. Stewart if he'd like to come on board and see the engines and the workshop, sir."

"Of course." Captain Davies turned to Keith. "There's more model engineering done in that workshop than was ever done on bits for the ship. You should see the commotion when Alec here was trying to get his little engine started up. They had to use the main engines as a starter motor for it, so the chief was telling me."

The third flushed uneasily. "Mr. Stewart designed it, sir. It was the fuel that was wrong."

There was a general laughter. "Come on board any time you like, Mr. Stewart," said the captain.

"That's very good of you, sir," said Keith. "I thought perhaps I'd stick with the rotor and lend a hand unloading that tomorrow morning, and perhaps come down with it to the dock."

"Fine. What are your movements, Mr. Stewart? Are you staying here a bit, or going back to England with the aircraft?"

Keith said, "Well, that's just the point. I really want to get to Tahiti, but I asked Mr. Yamasuki and he said he didn't know of any service from Honolulu to Tahiti. He was going to find out this evening and let me know." He hesitated. "I suppose you don't know of any service, sir?"

Captain Davies shook his head. "I never heard of one. There must be an odd tramp or two, of course. It's got to be Tahiti, has it? You've got some business there, or something?"

"That's right." These merchant service officers would probably be understanding and sympathetic about events following on a wreck. He pulled out his wallet and took the cutting from *The Times* from it. "My sister and my brother-in-law were sailing out here in a yacht," he said. "They got wrecked on an island in the Tuamotus. I've got to get down there and see about things—the grave, and salvage, and anything that might need to be done." He gave the cutting to the captain.

The officers were very interested, and asked a number of questions about the yacht, and about John Dermott. Captain Davies had been an officer of the Royal Naval Reserve in the last war. "I'm almost sure I remember him," he said thoughtfully. "At Invergordon ... or was it Scapa? An R.N. two-and-a-half, in one of the Tribal class. Wait now. The man I'm thinking of had a broken nose, boxing or something."

"That's right," said Keith. "He had a broken nose."

The captain dropped his eyes again to the cutting. "He was a good seaman," he said. "Better than most R.N. It's curious it should have had to end like this."

The three merchant officers turned their minds to Keith Stewart's problem, and discussed it carefully. "There's a fortnightly air service from Fiji through Samoa to Tahiti," said the captain. "You can probably fly from here to Samoa, but it's the hell of a long way round."

"How far would that be?" Keith asked.

"I'd only be guessing. Might be four thousand miles. I'll work it out for you tomorrow when you come on board."

"Sounds like it might be a bit expensive for me," said Keith a little ruefully. "I was hoping there'd be something more direct—and cheap. Something like a cargo steamer taking a few passengers."

Captain Davies shook his head. "I don't know of anything. But I'll find out for you, Mr. Stewart." He handed back the cutting, and Keith put it back into his wallet.

They all turned to the beer. In the buzz of conversation

the chief engineer said to his captain, "There's always Jack Donelly."

"Nonsense," Captain Davies said shortly. "The man's mad."

It seemed to be an unwelcome subject and Keith did not pursue it, but he noted the name. They set to work upon the beer and to a consideration of the unloading and the handling of the rotor from the aircraft to the ship, the air officers being principally concerned to avoid damage to the aircraft by the crane reaching into the fuselage through the door, and the marine officers being principally concerned to get the rotor undamaged into its field magnets and bearings in the engine room. Keith stood a round of beers and was concerned at the inroad that it made into his small store of dollars, and presently they all went to dinner in the hotel dining room.

All who had flown from England went to bed early that night. In the bedroom that Keith shared with Dick the moon was bright upon the mountains, the palm trees rustled continuously, and a warm wind hardly cooler than in daytime blew steadily through the room. Keith unpacked his thick woollen pyjamas and eyed them with distaste. "You'll boil in those, in this place," said Dick King. "I don't sleep in anything, these tropical places. Look, put the sheet over your middle and tuck it in, like this, so you don't catch cold. Then you've got your shoulders, arms, and legs out in the cool." Keith followed his example, fell asleep at once to the murmur of the palm trees, and slept like a log all night.

Next morning he was up with the aircrew and out on the aerodrome with them at seven o'clock. Mr. Yamasuki said, "I have asked about the ships or airplanes to Tahiti. There are no ships on regular service, no airplanes. The next Norwegian freighter is due here on March 3rd."

That was seven weeks ahead. "Nothing before that?"

"I am sorry. It is possible to go to Tahiti by air through Samoa, or else perhaps by Los Angeles. I think either way would be expensive. Pan-American can tell you what the fare is, and the services, at the Passenger Terminal."

Keith nodded. "I'll go and ask them presently." He knew quite well that the answer would be far beyond his means. "You didn't hear of any irregular services—a trading schooner, or anything like that?"

Mr. Yamasuki said, "I have no news of one. Sometimes with a trading schooner there would not be any advance news. She would arrive one day, and stay perhaps three or four days, and let it be known that she was calling at Papeete and other places. One might come today, or perhaps not for six months."

Keith thanked him, and went on working with the aircrew to get the rotor out of the aeroplane without damaging either. It took about two hours to get it on the truck. Most of the aircrew then went back to the hotel to rest and swim and shop on their small dollar allowance for the next two days before beginning the long flight back to England. Mr. Adams and Dick and Keith rode on the truck through the streets of Honolulu to Kapalama Basin, where the tanker was berthed.

There was nothing he could do to help the dockyard engineers get the rotor into the ship, and he went on board with Dick King. The third engineer met them and invited them below to see the main engine room and the workshop and, more particularly, the Gannet engine of Keith Stewart's design which was half finished, a little box of carefully machined unassembled bits. "Half the engine room have had a hand in this," the lad from Dartford said proudly. "Whenever somebody gets tired of reading Peter Cheyney he comes and asks if he can machine one of the pistons. I sometimes think that I'm just managing the job, not making it."

He was in trouble over the crankshaft machining jig. "You said to make it of high tensile steel in the serial, Mr. Stewart, but I can't seem to lay my hands on just a little bit anywhere in Honolulu. The smallest I can find is four-inch bar. Would it be all right to use mild steel instead?"

Keith had had this one before in letters from Andover to Auckland. He picked up the *Miniature Mechanic* from the bench and turned to the jig drawing that he had made in the basement room in Somerset Road, Ealing, with Janice sleeping in the room next door, eight thousand miles away. "I've got a mod for that," he said. "You've got to retain this eighth-inch thickness, here, because of the tool clearance. If you're going to make it in mild steel, make it an L section, like this." He added swift pencil lines to the printed drawing. "It's just a little bit more complicated. You'd have to get out this bit with an end mill—about three-sixteenths. Have you got a mill like that on board?"

The third nodded. "That's easy, Mr. Stewart. I could do that in the drilling machine best, I think. Thanks a lot."

Presently Keith pulled a small box from the pocket of his blazer. "I've got a little thing here that might amuse you." He unwrapped the little Hornet-engined generating set from the rag that wrapped it round, and put it on the bench. "Gee," said the third reverently, "that really is something." He studied it carefully. "What's the engine, Mr. Stewart? It looks a bit like a Hornet."

"It's a Hornet with a different cylinder and piston, cam gear and valves, to run on petrol, and a governor in place of the reduction gear," he said. He picked it up, shook it to check that there was still petrol in the little tank, turned it upside down to prime the carburettor, and flipped it into life with his thumb. The little engine caught with a crackling roar, speeded up, steadied as the pea bulb glowed with light. The noise attracted other engineers from the engine room, and soon the workshop was crowded. Somebody said, laughing, "Has Bill Adams seen this?"

"No—I don't think he has," said Keith.

"Cor—that'll give him something to think about. Anyone can build a big generator set that you can get your hands around inside. Fetch him along, Bert, and ask him how he'd like to service this one!"

Mr. Adams was fetched and stood in reverent awe till the little motor ran out of petrol and stopped, and almost at the same time the dockyard hooter sounded for twelve o'clock, knocking-off time for dinner. Keith wrapped his generator set up again and put it in the box and in his pocket; later he filled the tank with an egg-cup of petrol provided for use in the ship's launch, strained carefully through a piece of chamois leather. The officers escorted Mr. Adams and Dick and Keith up into the wardroom for lunch.

After lunch, as they were sitting smoking at the table over cups of tea and coffee, Captain Davies said, "I've been making some enquiries about your journey to Tahiti, Mr. Stewart. Not very satisfactory, I'm afraid. I can't find out anything about a cargo boat in the near future, and there's no regular service."

Keith nodded slowly. "Mr. Yamasuki said this morning

that a trading schooner might come in at any time. No one would know beforehand she was coming."

"It's a possibility," the captain agreed. "We've been here for four and a half weeks now. There was one just after we came, but she was going to Palmyra. I don't know where she was going after that."

"Where do they tie up, in case one did come in?" asked Keith.

"This one berthed just outside the harbour, just the other side of the Merchant Officers Training School," the captain said. "I think they like to sail in and out if there's a fair wind, save the cost of a tug."

"You don't think there's one there now?"

"Not that I know of. But that's where you'd get news of them, if anywhere. It might be worth a walk along and talking to the longshoremen. They might know more than the harbourmaster."

The first officer smiled. "He doesn't bother much about the small fry."

"The trouble is, I've got so little time," Keith said. "If there's nothing turns up that's within my means I'll have to go back with the aircraft the day after tomorrow."

"More like Tuesday," said Dick King. "Captain Fielding said this morning we'd be taking off at dawn on Tuesday."

"That's right," said Mr. Adams. "We'll be having the test run on Monday. Then if everything's all right he can take me home again."

"It doesn't give much time," agreed the captain.

The second mate said, "Jack Donelly."

There was a little ripple of laughter round the table. Only the captain remained serious. "I wouldn't think of it," he said.

The first officer took him up. "Nor would I, sir, for myself. But I don't want to get to Tahiti as much as Mr. Stewart. As I see it, it's either him or nothing. Mr. Stewart's twenty-one. I don't see why he shouldn't have a look at him."

"I wouldn't be any party to it," said the captain. "If he ever gets his ship out of hock to the harbourmaster he'll just go off and disappear, and no more heard of him, ever. I've seen it all my life."

Keith asked, "Who is this Jack Donelly, anyway?"

The first officer leaned back in his chair. "He's an American from Oregon or somewhere. Maybe he's a fisherman—I wouldn't know. His ship's a sort of sloop rigged fishing boat—a sailing boat. He built it himself. Quite small. I should say that he's a half-caste, and I'd guess that his mother was a Polynesian. He's a big chap, though, and he must be a good seaman because he sailed here from the United States alone—single-handed."

"He's got the mentality of a child of ten," said the captain.

"That may be, sir. He's so dumb that he can hardly string two words together. But he did get here from the United States, two thousand ruddy miles of open sea, and found the islands. You can't get away from that."

"Yes," said the captain, "and you know how he did it."

"I do."

Keith asked, "How did he do it?"

"Got on the air route between here and San Francisco and followed the aeroplanes," the captain said scornfully. "There are about ten flights every day, or more. That's a fine way to navigate."

"Never mind, sir. He got here."

"He won't get to Tahiti that way," said the captain. "There's no air service."

"Is he going to Tahiti?" Keith enquired.

The captain leaned forward. "Look, Mr. Stewart," he said. "I don't want to stand in your way if you want to go and talk to him. But first of all, I'll tell you about Jack Donelly. He came in here about a fortnight ago and sailed right in to this basin as far as he could go till his bow was practically in the street, and tied up just ahead of us. I'll admit he handled his ship well. He came in under sail—he hasn't got a motor—with his warps all ready fore and aft, got down his main and came in under jib, dropped the jib and came alongside sweet as anything, chucked his warps on to the quay, hopped on shore and made her fast bow and stern in two shakes of a duck's arse. It was pretty to watch. I'll agree with Number One here, he's probably a good seaman."

He paused. "Now that's as far as I go. The port authorities were after him as soon as he tied up. He hadn't got permission to berth there, but that was the least of it. He hadn't got any ship's papers at all—no registration, no manifest, noth-

ing. He hadn't got a bill of health and he didn't seem to
know what it was. He hadn't even got a passport. I shouldn't
think he's got any money." He paused. "I think they were
pretty kind to him, all things considered," he remarked.
"They called him a yacht and towed him round into the
yacht harbour."

"How did you come to know about him, then?" Keith
asked.

"He came on board," the captain said. "He came on board
to ask the way to Palmyra and half a dozen other places.
He's got no charts. He wouldn't know how to use one if he
had it. What he's got is a small school atlas with the whole of
the Pacific Ocean on one page, and a pretty dirty page it is, I
can tell you. He picks the biggest merchant ship that he can
see and comes on board to ask the course to the next place.
That's why he berthed just ahead of us. We were the biggest
ship in harbour at the time."

Keith asked, "Did you give him the course?"

"He didn't seem to know where he wanted to go to," the
captain said indignantly. "He just wanted a course to what he
called 'The Islands.' Well, this is an island, but he didn't like
this one, apparently. Too civilized, I suppose."

The second grinned. "What he wants is the vahines. Naked
women."

"That's about the strength of it," the captain said. "He's
been reading the books."

"I shouldn't think he can read," remarked the chief engineer.

"Well, somebody's been telling him stories, then."

Keith asked again, "Did you give him a course, sir?"

"I did what I could for him," the captain said. "I gave him
half a dozen, all magnetic. True courses wouldn't be any
good to him, and no good talking about variation being
different at the end of two thousand miles. I gave him a mean
value for the course to several places. Nukahiva was one, I
remember, and Tahiti was another. Of course, ocean currents
don't mean anything to him."

"He can write—just," the first officer observed. "He drew
a thick line with a stub of pencil on his atlas from here to
each place, and wrote the course along the line. I never saw
such a mess."

Keith wrinkled his brows in perplexity. "But can he find an

island two thousand miles away just with a compass course from here?"

"Of course he can't," the captain said scornfully. "He'll go off and there'll be no more heard of him. He'll die, and that's the end of it."

"I'm not quite sure that I agree with you, sir," said the first officer.

"What don't you agree with?"

"I don't think he'll die. He may get to the wrong place, and he may take the hell of a long time to get there. I talked to him after you gave up, and gave him a beer. I must say, I was rather impressed."

"What was it that impressed you, Mr. Fairlie?"

"Well, for one thing, sir, he knows a lot about birds. Sea birds, I mean."

The captain snorted. "What's that got to do with it? Is this Raft Book stuff?"

"Yes, sir, I think it is. Birds fly from A to B just like aeroplanes. What I mean is, if he gets within a hundred miles of land, I think he'll find it." He paused. "Swell, seaweed, floating mangrove seeds—all that sort of thing. Things that we don't use."

The captain got up from the table. "Well, I've heard everything now, and so have you, Mr. Stewart. If you like to go to sea with a bloke that navigates by mangrove seeds, don't let me stop you." He smiled. "One of the boys will show you where the yacht harbour is, if you want to go there."

He went out, and to his cabin. The others all got up from the table. The first officer glanced quizzically at Keith. "Want to go any further with it?" he asked.

Keith hesitated. "Well—I don't know. Do you think he's going to Tahiti, for a start?"

"So far as I could gather, he didn't much mind where he went. Footloose, you might say."

"Do you think he'll get there?"

Mr. Fairlie stubbed his cigarette out in the ashtray. "It's an opinion, Mr. Stewart. I've got a better opinion of him than Captain Davies has. In some ways what the captain says is right—he's simple. If you like, he thinks like a child ten years old. But he's certainly a good seaman, and he knows a lot about the sea."

"You think he'll get there?"

"In the end—yes, I think he probably will." He glanced at Keith. "It won't be comfortable."

"Would you go with him yourself?"

Mr. Fairlie smiled. "If I was absolutely desperate and had to get there somehow, at whatever risk—yes, I think I would."

There was half a minute's silence in the wardroom. To go back tamely with the aeroplane to Blackbushe, to renounce all chance of getting Janice her inheritance because he was afraid of Jack Donelly, would be cowardice. If he did not at least investigate this line he felt that he would never be able to tell Katie the truth about this journey; at one point he would have to lie, and go on in the same lie for the rest of his life. At the same time, he felt that he was sliding deeper into the mire of the unknown and the fantastically dangerous. Still, there was no need to decide anything until he'd met the man.

"I think I'd better go and have a talk to him," Keith said at last.

6

THE FIRST OFFICER CHANGED OUT of uniform into linen slacks and a light shirt open at the neck, borrowed Mr. Yamasuki's car and driver, and took Keith to the Alawai yacht harbour. They dismissed the car and walked past the rows of sleek motor cruisers till they came to the less opulent end. Mr. Fairlie pointed out a vessel with one mast. "He's still here. I was half afraid he might have left by now."

The vessel that he pointed out was a white fishing-boat type, about forty feet long and very beamy. She had one mast and no bowsprit. She had no pretensions to yacht finish; everything about her was heavy and painted; her metal fittings were all of iron. The sail upon the boom was of heavy red canvas, apparently tanned with oil and ochre. There was an appearance of rough efficiency about her, but in the Alawai yacht harbour she looked like a poor relation.

She was moored stern on to the quay, and a single plank gave access to her deck. Mr. Fairlie stood on the quay and hailed. "Jack Donelly! You aboard, Jack? I've got a friend I'd like you to meet."

He hailed again, and presently there was movement in the cabin and a man appeared at the hatch. He was a very big man possibly forty years old, olive skinned, with tousled black hair and a somewhat vacant expression. He was bare to the waist and wore only a pair of very soiled blue jeans. He blinked in the sunlight and muttered, "Who are you yelling at? I was having a lie down."

Mr. Fairlie said, "You remember me, Jack? Jim Fairlie, from the *Cathay Princess,* the tanker you came aboard the first day in. We had a beer together."

"I haven't got any beer," said the mariner vaguely.

"That's all right," said the first officer. "I didn't come for that. I brought a friend along with me to see your ship. Mind if we come aboard?"

"I haven't got any whiskey either. Haven't got nothing."

Mr. Fairlie said quietly to Keith, "Except methylated spirits, I should think." Aloud he said, "That's all right, Jack. We'll come down, if we may. I want you to meet Mr. Stewart. He's from England."

Mr. Donelly grunted, turned his back on them, and retreated from the hatch into the cabin. "He may be on the booze." Mr. Fairlie said to Keith, "and he's very shy. But there's no harm in him. I think he means for us to go on down."

They walked gingerly down the sagging, teetering plank on to the transom of the vessel, stepped over the horse, ducked under the boom, and stood on deck by the tiller; the vessel had no cockpit. Jack Donelly appeared again at the hatch. "Guy fell in off that plank," he muttered. "Wanted dough for berthing here or sump'n. He got a swim." He threw back his head and laughed, suddenly and a little shrilly, startling to hear. "He wanted seven dollars and two bits, and he got a swim." He went on laughing, and then stopped suddenly. "Tell you sump'n," he muttered. "You tread on the bow warp up forward by the winch," he said seriously, " 'n she goes forward just a tiddy little way 'n then the plank comes off the transom. That's how it's done. But don't tell anybody."

They laughed dutifully. "Has he been back again?" asked Mr. Fairlie.

Mr. Donelly shook his head wordlessly.

"I want you to meet Mr. Stewart, Jack," said the first officer. "His name's Keith—Keith Stewart. He's from England and he's having a look round. I was telling him how you built this ship yourself and sailed it out here from the States."

"Keats," said Mr. Donelly.

"No, Keith, Jack. Keith."

"Keith," said the mariner obediently. "Never heard a name like that before."

"It's a Scots name," said Keith. "Did you build this ship yourself?"

Mr. Donelly grunted.

"It's a big job," said Keith. "Did you have anyone to help you?"

Mr. Donelly shook his head.

"How long did it take you?"

" 'Bout five years. Worked in the lumber mill some of the time, get dough for fastenings and that."

Keith ran his eye over the ship with a new interest. There was nothing that a patient woodworker could not have done over the years . . . except . . . his eye fell on the seams of the deck planking. Each plank was twelve or fifteen feet long and tailored in plan form to fit the washboard and the bulwarks at the outside of the deck, the curvature reducing to a straight edge towards the centre of the ship where the hatch and the skylight of the cabin made a line. Keith stooped and ran his finger along the seam. "How did you get these curves?"

A gleam of interest illumined the dark features. "Router."

"You routed each plank all along its length to fit the next one?" It was not impossible, but it denoted a skill and a love of ships that threw a little beam of light on the character of the man.

The owner grunted in assent. Then he heaved himself out on deck and stood beside them, a massive, powerful man. "Show you sump'n," he muttered. He led Keith down the port side to a point about three feet aft of the mast, went down on his knees, and pointed out a blemish on one plank, caulked with a tarry compound. "That's where my finger come off," he said seriously. He lifted his left hand and showed that the forefinger of the left hand was missing down to the second joint.

"In the router?"

Mr. Donelly grunted. "Boss said I shouldn't have been using the machinery. But how in hell would a guy do these curves without he had a router? That's what I said to him. He couldn't answer that."

"How long did it hold you up?" The job was the thing.

"Two weeks, I guess. Soon as it quit bleeding I could work."

Keith got up from the deck, and the owner got up with him. He looked around, studying everything with a technical eye unpractised in the shipwright's art. "Where did you get the hull lines from?" he asked. "Out of a drawing in some book?"

Mr. Donelly shook his head. "Guy gave me a lot of blue papers with white lines," he said. "I put my thinking cap on, but they didn't seem to mean nothing." He paused. "Got some bits of hardwood 'n made half models over 'n over till I got one right. Took the frames off of that. Got it below still."

It was the old shipwright's approach. Keith said, "Can I see it?"

The man turned and made for the hatch; Keith and Mr. Fairlie followed him down the ladder. Inside, the ship was little but an empty shell. She was fairly new so that the dirt had had no time to accumulate, but she was already dirty. There were rough, unpainted wooden berths to port and starboard, the port one with a palliasse on it that was evidently Jack's bed. There was a cupboard with a deeply fiddled top on which stood a Primus stove and a few dirty glasses and plates. Forward there was a mass of sails and sailcloth and rope in tangled confusion erupting into the living portion of the ship. Aft of the hatch, behind the ladder, seemed to be a tangled mass of nets and cordage. The whole smelt strongly of salt water and of Jack Donelly.

The owner burrowed into the forecastle treading over sails and rope with his bare, horny, rather dirty feet. He emerged with three half models glued and screwed to pieces of hard, fine-grained planking. He showed them to Keith shyly. "These are what I made."

Keith took one from him and examined it critically. Half models of ships were no novelty to him, but he had never examined one that had shown better workmanship. It was about two feet long, made of some hard, dark wood, perhaps mahogany, French polished. He sat down uncomfortably on the vacant berth to examine it the better, squinting along the lines from bow to stern. "You certainly made a good job of this," he said seriously. "I never saw one better."

"You want to make them nice," commented the builder. "Else you get mad looking at them." He took the half model from Keith. "That's the second one you're looking at. This was the first." He gave him another. "I looked at it two weeks, maybe more, but it didn't seem right somehow. Looked like she wouldn't rise to a following sea." He took that model, and gave Keith the second. "I filled out the buttocks a tiddy bit on this one 'n I didn't like that no better, made her look fat-arsed and slow." He took that model away and gave the third to Keith. "So I put my cap on 'n brought the beam back aft a ways, not so much cod's head 'n mackerel tail. Couldn't see nothing wrong with that, so that's the way I built her."

The process of design by eye was nothing new to Keith. There were very fine lines scribed vertically upon the half model that he handled, at intervals all down her length. "You took the frames off this?"

Mr. Donelly dropped his eyes and shuffled one foot upon the floor. "You want book learning for that," he muttered. "It's not right what I told you, I built her all myself. The schoolmaster at Cushman, he set out the frames. But I did everything else."

Keith warmed to this uncouth, dirty man. "You designed her and you built her," he said. "Setting out the frames from the half model—that's nothing. How does she behave at sea?"

"Okay. Bit heavy on the helm first go, so I took a tiddy bit off the boom 'n leach, makes her easier to reef anyways, 'n just as fast."

Mr. Fairlie asked, "You built her at Cushman, Jack? Where's that?"

"Mouth of the Suislaw."

"That's in Oregon?"

"South Oregon," the owner muttered. Interrogation seemed to make him shy and resentful.

Keith reached up and ran his finger along the joint between one of the deck beams and the frame at the side of the ship; it seemed to him that it would be difficult to insert a ten-thou feeler in it, and all the others were the same. "You certainly made a beautiful job of building her," he said.

The owner glowed with pleasure. "I kinda liked doing it," he said. "It took quite a while, but I kinda liked it."

"I know," said Keith. "I like making things. But mine aren't so big as yours."

He pulled the little box from his pocket and unwrapped the generator set and gave it to Mr. Donelly, who handled it as carefully as an egg in his great horny hands. "You made this?" he enquired.

"He designed it and made it, electrics and all," Mr. Fairlie said. "Just like you did this ship."

Mr. Donelly stared at it in wonder. "I never did see such a tiddy little thing," he said. "It doesn't go, does it?"

"It goes all right," said Keith. He took the little engine, turned it upside down, adjusted the tiny carburettor delicately, and flipped it into life with his thumb. It broke into a roar disproportionate to its size, steadied its note, and the pea bulb lit up. He placed it on the bare wood of the cabin floor and it went on generating steadily.

Mr. Donelly went down on his hands and knees upon the floor and studied it, entranced. "Making the electricity," he breathed.

"That's right."

"I seen big ones," he said, "three-cylinder Diesels and that, making electricity." He raised his head. "Say, Mr. Keats, I guess this is the smallest in the world, isn't it?"

Keith said, "It's not the smallest engine. I think perhaps it might be the smallest generating set."

Mr. Donelly broke into a cackle of laughter, and looked up at Mr. Fairlie. "Well, what do you know?" he enquired. "There's the smallest generating set in the world running right here in the cabin of the *Mary Belle!* Folks wouldn't never believe me if I went ashore and told them that. They'd say I was nuts!"

Keith leaned down and stopped it with his pencil, fearing that it might overheat if he kept it running too long without a cooling draught of air. Mr. Donelly bent closer to examine it at rest. "Look at all those tiddy little wires," he breathed as he scrutinized the armature. "All going the same way, and each to the right place." He raised his head. "Mr. Keats, did you think out all that, yourself? The way each had to go?"

Keith nodded. "Everybody to his own job," he said. "I couldn't have begun to build this ship. I wouldn't know where to start."

"You start with the half model. What I showed you."

"Ah, yes. But if I made a half model, I wouldn't know by looking at it if it would make a good ship. Not like you do."

"You wouldn't?"

Keith shook his head. "Not a hope. You've got to really know the sea for that. You must have been at sea all your life."

"My old man," said Mr. Donelly, "he took me offshore first of all when I was six, long lining. 'Course, I was playing around in scows and that with all the other kids before."

Keith nodded. "You build up experience without knowing it," he said. "Then when the fit takes you to build a ship like this, or build a generating set like that, it just comes easy."

Mr. Donelly glanced at him with common understanding from the floor. "Say, you got sump'n," he said. "Building *Mary Belle* was just like it was kinda fun."

Keith reached down and picked up the little generating set, wrapped it up, and put it back into his pocket. Mr. Donelly watched him do it regretfully; he got back on to his feet and sat down on his berth. Keith asked him, "What are your plans, Jack? Where do you go from here?"

"I guess I'm going to The Islands."

Keith said, "I've got a reason for asking that. I want to get down to Tahiti, and then out to an island called Marokota. That's somewhere in the Tuamotus. But there's no regular service and no trading schooner, and anyway I've not got very much money. Mr. Fairlie here suggested that you might be going down that way."

There was a long silence. "Ma came from Huahine," Mr. Donelly said at last. "She said for me to get back to The Islands where I'd meet up with my own sort. So that's where I'm going."

Mr. Fairlie asked, "To Huahine?"

"I guess I'll go there sometime. I don't know where it is."

"It's not far from Tahiti. It's in the same group."

"That's what a guy said one time. Then another guy said it was this place Nukahiva."

"It's not, Jack. It's nowhere near Nukahiva. It's a bit over to the west from Tahiti. I'll give you a chart."

"I got an atlas," said the mariner. He rummaged under the palliasse on the wooden boards of his bunk and produced his one navigational aid. It opened automatically at the map of the Pacific Ocean. "I looked at all the tiddy little names," he said, "but I never see Huahine. I guess they left it out by mistake."

Mr. Fairlie said, "I think it's probably too small to show on the atlas, Jack. If you're going to take Keith along with you to Tahiti I'll give you a chart that shows every island on the way and round about Tahiti. I know we've got a lot of out-dated ones on board."

Mr. Donelly grunted; Keith guessed that he had little use for charts, never having used one. "You want to get down to Tahiti?" he asked.

"That's right."

"Got a bed?"

Keith hesitated, somewhat taken aback. Mr. Donelly helped him out by lifting the dirty corner of his palliasse; it rustled, evidently filled with hay or straw. "Like this."

"I haven't at the moment," Keith said. "But I'll get something."

"There's a bolt of sailcloth you could sleep on but I guess you'd find that kinda hard," said Mr. Donelly.

"I'll get a bed like yours," said Keith. "How much money would I have to pay you for the passage?"

"Well now," said the mariner, "I'd have to put my thinking cap on for that. The harbormaster, he wanted seven dollars and two bits when he come on board and had his swim." He cackled into laughter. "I reckon he'd want more now, what with drying his clothes. Then there's the eats . . ." He sat in evident bewilderment. "How long you reckon it would take to sail to this Tahiti?"

Keith shook his head. "I don't know at all."

Mr. Fairlie asked, "How long did it take you to get here from San Francisco, Jack?"

"Three weeks 'n two days. I had a fair, reaching wind most of the way."

"It's a little bit further to Tahiti," said the first officer, "and you've got to get through the doldrums. You'll need food for six weeks at least."

"I dunno what that would cost," said Mr. Donelly. He lifted his head, and cut the Gordian knot with decision. "Say," he asked, "how much you got?"

"About a hundred dollars," said Keith conservatively.

"Well then," said the ship owner, "the fare's a hundred dollars." He leaned back with the air of one who has concluded a difficult business negotiation.

"We bake every day," said Mr. Fairlie, "but we carry a stock of biscuits in sealed tins, twenty-eight pounds. I'll talk to Captain Davies. Maybe we could let you have two or three of those against repayment in England. Save the dollars, anyway."

"That'd be very kind of you," said Keith.

"I got 'bout half a sack of cornmeal, 'n some grits," said Mr. Donelly. "I guess we could catch fish a day or two 'n dry some of them, 'n salt down the rest. There's plenty sun here, dry the fish. Not like it'd be at home."

"Where would you put them to dry?" asked Mr. Fairlie.

Mr. Donelly looked surprised. "Out on shore some place," he said.

"I don't think they'd let you do that here, Jack."

"Huh?"

"They'd get people on the power yachts bellyaching about the smell."

"They said I was to berth here," Mr. Donelly muttered. "Got a motor boat 'n towed me round."

Keith judged it better to change the subject. "We'll think up something together about the food," he said. "When do you want to sail?"

" 'Most any time," the owner said.

"And you'd be willing to take me along?"

The other raised his head. "You get sick?"

It was better to face it. "I'll probably be sick," Keith said. "How long does it go on for?"

"Two-three days. I get sick after a spell on shore. There's nothing to it."

"I don't suppose I'll be much use to you, at first," Keith said. "I'll do the best I can."

"Can't do better'n that," Mr. Donelly said. "You'll be bringing the tiddy little motor along?"

"This?" He fingered the little box. "Oh yes, I'll be bringing this."

"Move in when you like," said Mr. Donelly.

They arranged that Keith would go into the question of the food supplies with Mr. Fairlie, and presently they left the *Mary Belle* and took a taxi back to the *Cathay Princess*. In the wardroom Mr. Fairlie said, "I think we've earned a beer." He went and fetched a bottle and two glasses, filled them, and raised his own. "I think you're a brave man," he said.

Keith smiled. "So do I. But I liked him well enough."

"There's no harm in him," Mr. Fairlie agreed. "He'll probably get you there. But I wouldn't take any liquor on board."

"I won't."

The first officer eyed him speculatively. "You're technical. Do you know anything about navigation—anything at all?"

Keith shook his head.

Mr. Fairlie sighed. "Well, there's no time to teach you astro navigation. But I'll look out the charts and a volume of the *Pacific Islands Pilot* for you this evening, and give you an hour on them tomorrow morning. You can read, at any rate, and that's more than Jack Donelly can."

Keith left the ship soon afterwards and walked back through the town to the Beachcomber Hotel, looking as he walked for a shop that sold a mattress. The prices did not seem to him to be excessive, but they were all far too good to put into the *Mary Belle*. He knew that he was in for an indefinite spell of hard living, and he had no great fear of it. It was many years since he had suffered much discomfort though as a child and a young man in Renfrew he had known plently of it; to sleep on a straw palliasse upon bare boards would be no novelty to him. The food was a perplexity. Something better was needed than Jack's cornmeal, grits, and dried fish, but what he needed was to him unknown, or how to buy it. He clung to the thought of the sealed tins of biscuit that might come from the *Cathay Princess*.

In his room at the hotel he found Dick lying upon his bed listening to the radio, and told him all about it. "I fixed up that I'd go with him," he said. "He's not as mad as all that."

The engineer raised himself on one elbow. "He's going to Tahiti?"

Keith started to undress, preparatory to a shower. "He'll

go anywhere so long as it's away from here. He'll take me to Tahiti."

"Sure about that?"

Keith sat down upon the bed. "I think so."

"Captain Davies isn't, old man."

"I know. I've been talking to Jack Donelly all afternoon on board his boat. The boat's quite good, you know. What's more, he built her himself."

"He did? Without any help?"

Keith nodded. "Single-handed."

"That doesn't mean that he can find his way to Tahiti from here, though. It's an awful big place, the sea."

"I know." Keith got up from the bed. "I've never done this before," he muttered. "There's no fuel problem anyway, because all he uses is the wind. It seems to boil down to carrying enough to eat and drink for an indefinite time."

"How much water storage has he got?"

"I saw a forty-gallon drum, up-ended, tied to the mast with rope lashings. I suppose that's it."

"How long is the trip going to be?"

"Jim Fairlie says at least six weeks."

"You'll want more than that much water, then, old man."

Keith went into the shower, and Dick lay back upon his bed in perplexity. What Keith did was no concern of his, really, and yet he felt himself involved. In the world of workshops and of amateur mechanics Keith was a well-known man, and that world was Dick's world also. If Keith were to lose his life at sea with this man Jack Donelly, inevitably Dick King would be involved and charged with some responsibility by other members of their common world, for it would be known throughout that world that he had been with Keith in Honolulu. If Keith were to disappear at sea, as Captain Davies had warned him bluntly might well happen, he, Dick King, would be telling a defensive story of their time in Honolulu in the workshops of England for many years to come, excusing himself, perhaps for all his life. He could hear the whispers: "He's the bloke who was with Keith Stewart in Honolulu and let him go off with that crazy fisherman. You'd think he might have done something about it . . ." He did not like the prospect.

If only Keith knew a little more about foreign countries, about the tropics. If only he wasn't quite so raw.

He said no more, but lay there troubled in his mind while Keith also rested on his bed, letting the cool breeze blow over his bare body. It seemed to Dick that there was no escape from the position he was in. Keith had some compelling reason to get down to Tahiti that was driving him to take the most fantastic risk by going with this half-caste fisherman. If he, Dick King, wished to escape the odium of the future, there were only two courses he could take. One was to talk Keith out of it; he did not think that would be possible. The other was to try to make the journey a success.

Presently they dressed and went downstairs for a beer before dinner. Captain Davies was there in the bar with Captain Fielding. Somewhat the same line of thought may have been running in his mind, too, because he said, "Evening, Mr. Stewart. Evening, Mr. King. Beer?"

The engineers said, "Thank you, sir."

The captain said to the girl in the cheongsam, "Two more beers." Then he turned to Keith and said, "Mr. Fairlie tells me that I've got to provision your ship."

Keith was embarrassed. "That's not necessary at all, sir. All he said was that you might let me have some biscuits on repayment in England."

"To help out the grits and dried fish? I don't know if you've ever tried to live for two months on dried fish. It goes bad, of course. Then the thing to do is to put it in a barrel with some salt. You've got to eat it in the end, of course. Some people like it." He laughed. "You'd better come on board tomorrow with a list of what you want, and we'll see what we've got."

"That's very kind of you, sir." The aircraft navigator strolled up to them, beer in hand. "As a matter of fact, that really would be a great help. I was coming on board tomorrow anyway to see Mr. Fairlie. He was going to go over the charts with me."

"Well, that's something, anyway. Bring your list along."

"Thank you, sir. Here's luck." He raised his beer.

"You're going to need it," said Captain Davies grimly.

The air navigator asked, "Is this Jack Donelly?"

"That's right," said Captain Fielding. "Keith's going with him to Tahiti."

"Can he find Tahiti?"

"That's the sixty-four-thousand-dollar question," said Captain Davies.

The navigator sipped his beer in thought. "Has he got a sextant?"

"Of course he hasn't," said the captain. "He looks to see which way the aeroplanes are flying. If there aren't any aeroplanes he looks for mangrove seeds. If there aren't any mangrove seeds he follows his compass, and that's probably wrong." He turned to Keith. "I was right—he hasn't got a motor in the ship, has he?"

"No, sir."

"Well, that's something. I don't suppose he's ever had his compass swung. Just watch he doesn't put a bucket down beside it when he needs it most."

Keith nodded thoughtfully. "I'll watch that, sir. It makes a big difference, does it?"

Captain Davies laughed. "Try it and see."

"Pity about the sextant," said the air navigator. "The track must be just about due south. A meridian latitude would give them quite a lot of information."

"You've got to be able to add and subtract for that," said Captain Davies.

Mr. King drew the air navigator on one side. "I've been thinking about that," he said. "I mean, he's made up his mind to go. A meridian sight for latitude isn't very difficult, is it?"

"It's the easiest sight there is," said the navigator. "You want a sextant and a nautical almanac, and a rough idea of Greenwich time. Then you've only got to add and subtract."

"He could learn to do that, couldn't he?"

"Jack Donelly?"

"No, Keith. Keith Stewart. I mean, look at the things he does in the shop with mikes and sine bars and all that. He'd learn to manage a sextant in five minutes with somebody to put him in the way of it."

The navigator stood in thought. "It's an idea ... where's the sextant coming from?"

"I think I know where one could pick up one second-hand," said the engineer. "You know where King Street crosses Nuuanu?" The navigator nodded. "Well, coming this way, second or third side street on the right, there's a Chinese shop—sells everything, you know. Old clothes, lacquer screens, Bali heads, all sorts of junk. I'm pretty sure I saw a sextant there."

"This trip?"

"This afternoon. I was poking around, get something for the wife."

The navigator stood in thought. "It's an idea. There's not much time to teach him. We could write it all down for him, of course—just what you do. And it should be possible to pick up an old sextant in this place." He stood in thought. "Pity it's got to be this time of year," he said at last. "The sun'll be pretty near the zenith when they get down to Tahiti."

"That makes it less accurate?"

"More difficult, anyway. I tell you what I'll do. I'll slip down to the ship after dinner and have a talk to Jim Fairlie— see if it's worth while trying to stuff something into him."

Keith spent the evening cogitating in his bedroom, pencil and paper in hand. He had no wish to provision the *Mary Belle* with expensive delicacies to which Jack Donelly would be unaccustomed. He knew that if he were to live harmoniously with this man for six weeks in the close association of a very small sailing vessel he must adapt himself to Jack Donelly and live as he did. That did not trouble Keith; what troubled him was that he had little idea what Jack was in the habit of eating. He did not know what cornmeal tasted like or how you ate it, and grits were a sealed book to him, but they were what Jack seemed to eat. It was pretty certain that he would like sweet things, though. He headed his list with— Sugar, 30 lbs—and added—Jam.

He was certain of nothing else, and at the end of half an hour he had only six or seven items on the list. His mind drifted to the navigation hazards that they all seemed so concerned about. He got out the chart that Mr. Sanderson had given him in Ealing, Ealing that now seemed so far away. There were certainly a lot of islands to be passed on their course southwards to Tahiti. They had names that he had never heard before, Malden and Starbuck and Flint, and many others. He supposed they would be coral islands, similar to that which had destroyed *Shearwater*. If John Dermott who was an experienced navigator could not sail through this archipelago in safety, could Jack Donelly?

His hand drifted to his pocket, and he sat in perplexity fingering the case-hardened grey steel egg that he had made for Janice. Presently he got a scrap of paper and measured the distance between these islands. He had a hazy idea that the vertical graduations on the side of the chart gave you some measure of the scale, and by that the closest of these islands were two degrees apart. But how far was a degree? He sat in thought. Anyway, the earth was twenty-two thousand miles round at the equator. He figured with a pencil on the chart. If that was right, the closest of these islands were over a hundred miles apart, about as far as it was from Ealing to Weymouth. That didn't seem so bad. There was a lot of sea to sail on in between.

The difficulty might lie, as the ship's officers said, in finding one of them at all. It was very different in the Tuamotus where *Shearwater* was lost. There the islands all seemed to be on top of each other.

He went to bed before Dick King got back from exploring the night life of Honolulu, and slept fitfully, uneasy and worried. Next morning he was on board the *Cathay Princess* by half-past eight. He found Jim Fairlie and showed him his inadequate list. The first officer took it, summoned the third, and told him to get out a mess list for two men for eight weeks, able seaman's scale, biscuit instead of bread. "We'll compare his list with yours and see how they match up," he said. "There's one thing, though. If you're going to provision the ship, you don't have to pay Jack Donelly a hundred dollars."

He took Keith up to the chartroom on the bridge behind the wheelhouse. "I've got one chart," Keith said diffidently. He unfolded the one that Mr. Sanderson had given him.

"Oh, good. You've got seven eight three." Mr. Fairlie slipped a chart back in the drawer. "Now you want seven eight two and nine nine two." He opened a volume of the *Pacific Islands Pilot* and showed Keith the chart index. "These two—and that one you've got." He paused. "I'd have liked you to have three oh four five as well in case you get set over to the west, but I haven't got it. Maybe you could get one in town—Yamasuki would tell you where to try.

Now look. I'm going to put these two together and pencil in your track. Do you know what I mean by compass variation?"

They worked on together. "Well, there you are," Jim Fairlie said presently. "Your track is one six six degrees, and in theory, at any rate, you don't hit anything. You don't have to sail over any dry land. You're in the clear the first part of the passage. Then you come to all this over to the west— Christmas Island and all that. Keep away from that—they let off atom bombs from time to time. Then you've got to go between Flint Island and the Carolines. They're about two and a half degrees apart—call it a hundred and fifty sea miles. If you're on course you probably won't see them. After that there's nothing till you hit Tahiti."

They stood examining the charts and the *Pilot* for the best part of an hour, Keith making notes busily. In the middle the air navigator came in, greeted them, and stood listening in silence. They turned to the predominant winds, and studied the picture for January. "You should have a fair wind all the way, easterly." The first officer laid his finger on the page. "A bit irregular on the equator, in the doldrums, but steadying again as you get further south. All easterly. I don't know how much leeway that ship makes, but just watch out you don't get set over too far to the west. Jack knows about that, I think. I'd keep edging up to windward, ten degrees at least. You're very unlikely to go much east of track, but you might get down a long way west of it."

They stood in consultation, Keith scribbling down notes. At last he said, "Well, that's pretty clear. It's very kind of you to take all this trouble." He smiled. "The only thing remaining is to know how far one's gone." He laid his finger on the line that marked the track.

From behind them the air navigator remarked, "You've said it, chum."

Jim Fairlie said, "Jack Donelly would probably say he knows how fast he's going from the look of the water, how many miles he does in a day. Take note of that, and jot down what he says for each day. He may not be so very far wrong when you tot it up. But don't depend on him." He paused. "You could trail a log, but then it's not your ship. He might not take to it—probably wouldn't." He paused. "The proper thing for you to do would be to take a noon sight for latitude each day. As a matter of fact, we were talking about this last night."

The air navigator said, "It's dead easy, Mr. Stewart. You'd better let us show you how to do it. Once you've got your latitude upon this course you know how far you've gone, and no argument. Have you ever handled a sextant?"

Keith shook his head.

"Well, you're going to handle one now." The first officer was opening a polished wooden box upon the chart table.

Keith was torn between technical interest and practical considerations. "I haven't got a sextant," he said, "and I'm sure Jack hasn't."

"You can probably pick one up second-hand quite cheap," the air navigator said. "As a matter of fact Dick King's off looking for one now, with Captain Fielding. Look, Mr. Stewart. We don't want to read in the newspaper one day that you're dead. This latitude sight's easy for a man like you. You'd better let us put you in the way of it, and then go off and buy a sextant."

They settled down to show him how the sextant worked. He was accustomed to precision instruments and had no trouble with it upon the stable deck of the fifteen-thousand-ton ship in harbour. In half an hour he was able to bring the sun down on to the horizon and read off its altitude with some accuracy. "You'll find it a bit more difficult on Jack's ship because of the motion," the first officer said. "It's a matter of practice on a ship like that. Or any other ship, for that matter."

They took him through the relevant part of the nautical almanac, and drew a little diagram for him to show what declination meant. "You're behind Greenwich time," they told him. "When you're taking your noon sight you want to use the declination for ten o'clock at night on the same day. Twenty-two hundred. Look, I'll underline it for you each day so you won't go wrong. You can take this copy and we'll get another for the ship." The air navigator bent to the task.

At a quarter to twelve they took him out on to the bridge and made him start taking the altitude of the sun on the horizon over Sand Island. "Never go back," Mr. Fairlie said quietly. "Maximum altitude is what you want."

When they were satisfied that he had got it they took him back into the chart room to do the figuring. "Height of eye here is about thirty feet," they told him. "With you—take about five feet." They underlined the correction for him. "Now—away you go."

He did the sum. "That seems to come to twenty-one degrees twenty-three minutes," he said diffidently.

"North or south?"

He studied the figures. "North."

"Quite sure?"

"I think so."

"Okay. Now put a horizontal pencil line on that latitude, on the chart." He did so. "Not too bad," the air navigator remarked. "You're about three miles north of where we are, up in the suburbs somewhere. Still, it's not too bad."

Keith stared at them in wonder, and at his pencil line. "Is that all I'm wrong?"

"That's right. Twenty-one twenty is the right answer. I told you it was dead easy."

He was amazed and naively pleased that he had done this thing, that he, Keith Stewart, looking at the sun through a precision instrument had established the position of Honolulu on the surface of the earth. He said something of the sort to his instructors. "You're forgetting about longitude," Jim Fairlie said. "I'd like to teach you that, but there's not time. Anyway, it needs a watch and a wireless set and tables. It's not practical, I'm afraid. But learn this thoroughly, and you'll be all right—on the way to Tahiti, anyway."

That afternoon he went off with Dick and the air navigator and bought a second-hand sextant for twenty-seven dollars and a depressed-looking flock mattress for six fifty. Back to the ship to show his sextant to Mr. Fairlie, who spent an hour trying to get out the index error and reduced it to about three minutes, and to have a session with the third officer about provisioning. Subject to the captain's approval, he found that the ship could provide practically everything that they would need on board the *Mary Belle* in the way of food. He mentioned an extra forty-gallon drum for water; the third said that if he got the drum they could steam it out for him. He went and called Mr. Yamasuki, who agreed to find a second-hand oil drum and get it to the ship.

It was Sunday evening. He was tired by the events of the day, but he did not dare to let a day go by without visiting Jack Donelly, lest he should forget about his passenger. He gave the sextant to Dick King to take back to the hotel and went on shore and found a taxi. He picked up his mattress at the Chinese shop and drove to the yacht harbour. Jack Donelly was sitting on the bow of his ship fishing over the side with a hand line; six or seven small silvery fish lay on the deck beside him in the evening light.

"Evening, Mr. Donelly," Keith said. "I brought my bed. Can I come on board?"

The owner grunted. Keith took this as assent and ventured cautiously down the plank, the mattress on his shoulder, keeping a wary eye on Jack Donelly as he went. But the owner went on fishing. Keith carried his mattress below and laid it on the vacant berth, and then went up on deck and forward to his host. "What are you using for bait?" he asked conversationally.

"Maggots," said Mr. Donelly.

Keith sat down on the deck beside him, watching the line. "Where did you get them from?"

"Out the cornmeal sack. There's just a few in there. Don't make any difference."

Keith swallowed spasmodically. "How long did it take you to get these?"

"Not long." He jerked the line sharply, there was a flurry in the water, and he pulled another little fish on board. "They come in here after the muck the boats let go, toilets and that." He baited the hook with another maggot. "You staying to supper?"

"I can't tonight, Jack. I've got things to do back at the hotel. I was thinking I'd move in tomorrow, if that's all right with you."

"Cornmeal fritters 'n fish. Get a few more, 'n there'll be plenty for two."

"I'd like to, but I can't tonight. Look, we'll want another oil drum for water, won't we?"

"What for? We wouldn't be having baths."

"How much did you use coming out here from San Francisco?"

The owner ruminated. "I guess I filled it last at Sausalito. There's still some left. I'd better get a hose 'n fill it up before we go."

"Think you'd have used half of it? On the passage, I mean."

"Might have done. There was plenty left when I came in."

"There'll be two of us this time," Keith said patiently, "and the trip's a longer one from here down to Tahiti. I've got another oil drum if you want it."

"You have?" The owner considered this proposal. "It might be a good thing to have it along," he admitted. "Always use a barrel."

"Where would you put it? Forward by the mast, with the other one?"

Mr. Donelly sat in thought. "Have it aft under the ladder, if you want it full of water," he said at last. "Make her a bit lighter on the helm. I'll have to make some chocks."

Keith nodded. "It's getting steamed out tomorrow. I'll get it on board soon as I can."

"Say," said Mr. Donelly with enthusiasm, "that's a good idea. The one I got had kero in it one time. Been better, maybe, if it had been gas." He paused. "Kero kinda makes you feel sick in the stomach," he explained.

Keith nodded. "They're steaming it on board the tanker," he remarked. "They might do the other if we asked them—the one you've got now. There's another thing, Jack. They've got a list of food they think we'll need for the trip to Tahiti, basing it upon the seaman's scale. I've got to see the captain, but I think they'll let us have the stuff. They say that I can pay for it in England." He pulled the list out of his pocket on two sheets of paper. "That's what they suggest."

Mr. Donelly took the list and glanced at it, uncomprehending. "You read it out," he suggested.

Keith started in to do so. Mr. Donelly sat watching him, bemused, while the words flowed past him. Presently he stopped Keith. "Jam, 'n butter, n' currants," he said. "Kinda rich chow for a ship. We haven't got all that dough."

"It's what they give the seamen on the tanker," Keith explained. "They have to, by law. If you signed on on the *Cathay Princess* that's what they'd give you to eat."

"That so?"

"That's right. I was going to pay for it myself and take it out of the hundred dollars, if that's all right by you."

Mr. Donelly looked at him vacantly. "What hundred dollars?"

"The hundred I was going to give you for the passage. I

could buy the food for us both from the *Cathay Princess* if the captain agrees, and take the cost of it out of the hundred dollars."

"You got two pages there," Mr. Donelly objected. "A hundred bucks wouldn't buy that much."

"I think it will, and leave a good bit over," said Keith, who had already been roughly through the costs with the third officer.

"Huh," said Mr. Donelly.

Keith turned to the list again. "Is there anything that you don't like that I've read out?" he enquired.

"Turnips," said Mr. Donelly.

Keith wrinkled his brows, and turned over the two pages. "There aren't any turnips on the list," he said.

"That so? I never did like turnips."

Keith nodded. "I'll look out and see that we don't get any." He put the list back in his pocket, assuming correctly that Jack Donelly would eat everything else. "When do you think we ought to sail?"

" 'Most any time. Tomorrow, if you like. Sure costs the earth in this place."

"I don't think we'll be able to sail tomorrow, Jack. We've got to get this food on board from the *Cathay Princess*, and the other barrel. I tell you what—I'll probably move in to-morrow, and sleep on board, if that suits you. Then maybe we could sail on Tuesday."

"Suits me," said the owner. He jerked another little fish on board, rebaited the hook with a maggot from a tin, and lowered the line again. "I been thinking," he said presently. He paused a long time after that alarming statement. Then he said, "See that three-stick schooner berthed out there at the end?"

Keith followed his glance. Lying at the end of the seaward jetty there was a fine three-masted schooner yacht. She lay almost in the deep water channel because there was no room and no depth of water for her closer in. She carried a big crew all dressed in whites; her decks were white, her polished brass gleamed in the setting sun. She wore the flag of the United States, and one of the white-clad seamen was standing by the halliard ready to lower it at the sunset gun. Even Keith was impressed by her.

"I see her," he said.

"She's built of wood," said Mr. Donelly. "I guess we'll go aboard her before sailing, 'n check up on the course." He struggled to give voice to what was in his mind. "Ships built of iron," he explained, "they go a different way upon the compass to what ships do if they get built of wood. That *Cathay Princess*, she's built all of iron. I guess she'd go quite a different way to get to this Tahiti than what that schooner would, because she's a wooden ship. She's a wooden ship, and *Mary Belle*'s a wooden ship, so they'd go the same way. I guess we'll go aboard before we sail 'n check up with the captain."

Novice in navigation though he was, Keith suspected that Jack Donelly hadn't got his theory of compass deviation quite right. Still, any second check upon their course was good, and it might be that from the captain of a sailing ship Jack could pick up information about getting through the doldrums which he would not have learned on the seventeen-knot tanker. "That's a good idea," he said amiably.

He left the *Mary Belle* shortly after that, and went back to his hotel. He found most of the aircrew drinking beer with the officers of the *Cathay Princess*, and joined them. Captain Davies said, "Mr. Fairlie tells me that you've turned into a navigator."

"He was very kind," Keith said. "He showed me how to get the latitude."

The captain nodded. "Think you'll remember how to do it?"

"I think so. I made a lot of notes. I'll have another go at it tomorrow, at midday."

"Jack Donelly's in luck. I don't suppose he knows it. But he might get there, now." He took a drink of beer. "Mr. Fairlie show you the victualling list?"

Keith took it from his pocket. "I've got it here. He said I was to see you and ask if I could have the stuff."

"You can have it if you sign a pretty detailed letter saying where and when you'll pay for it," remarked the captain.

"That's very kind of you, sir. Payment in England would be all right, would it?"

"I think so. You'd better come on board tomorrow morning and I'll draft the letter for you to sign while the third gets the stuff on deck. How are you going to take it round to the yacht harbour?"

"I'll have to get a taxi."

"Make Yamasuki take it. He's got nothing else to do."

Beside them Dick King said, "Give you a hand with it, if you like. I've got nothing else to do, either."

Presently they went in to dinner. At the table Keith said to Dick King, "You're still taking off on Tuesday morning?"

The flight engineer nodded. "Seven o'clock take-off for Vancouver."

"You're going back the same way?"

"That's right. Vancouver, Frobisher, Blackbushe."

"When will you be back in England?"

"Thursday midday if the fans keep turning. We'll have been away a week."

Keith said, "I wonder if you'd take a letter back with you, and post it in England? It's just to tell my wife what's happening."

"Why, sure. She should get it Friday morning."

That evening Keith went up to his bedroom after dinner and sat for an hour with his sextant and his nautical almanac and his notes. He rewrote the notes into a progressive and coherent form while the subject was still fresh in his mind, pausing from time to time to draw little diagrams around the outline of an English penny. It was when you came to the equator that you needed a clear head, or when the sun went over the zenith ... Still, if you followed the rules exactly it would probably come out all right. The thing was to practise.

Presently he left the navigation and started a letter to Katie. He could not make it very detailed because he did not want to worry her; the details of his passage to Tahiti were not such as would create confidence. In consequence, his letter consisted mainly of a description of the flight to Honolulu and the installation of the rotor in the ship; his future plans and movements were dealt with in one sentence at the end, in which he said that he had got a passage on a ship going to Tahiti and he hoped to be there by the end of February. He sealed it up and gave it to Dick King to post in England.

Next morning he went with the flight engineer to the ship, signed a letter drafted for him by the captain, looked in on the generator trials, inspected the oil barrel newly steamed out and free from taint, and took another noon sight. They

lunched on board, telephoned for a taxi truck, loaded the oil
barrel and the stores into it, and set off for the yacht
harbour.

Dick had not seen the *Mary Belle* before nor met Jack
Donelly, and he was filled with misgiving. He knew about
sailing boats in theory, at any rate, and he had little confidence in them. They depended solely on the fickle and the
vacillating wind; if the wind didn't blow in the right direction
they couldn't go. They were archaic survivals of a bygone
age. It was true that the wind, their motive power, was free,
but what did that matter in an era of government subsidies?
The right way to get from Honolulu to Tahiti was in a
Douglas with twelve or fifteen thousand horsepower pushing
it along. It was penny-pinching to think of going by the wind
because the wind was free. It was thinking small, and there
was no future in that in these modern times. You wanted to
think big.

He was deeply concerned when he went on board the
Mary Belle with Keith. There was not so much as a wheel to
steer by, nor any seat on deck for the pilot of the craft. A
sort of stick stuck forward from the top of the rudder, which
came through the deck, and you steered by pushing this stick
from side to side so that the ship went the opposite way to
what you pushed. He knew of this arrangement, of course,
but had thought that it had gone out with the dodo. There
was, of course, no engine. He was prepared for that, but the
total absence of all mechanical contrivances shook him badly. Even the bilge pump was a crude affair, square section in
its bore, built up of wood.

It was a hot, humid day. When they arrived the owner was
below making the chocks for the new oil drum; because he
was below and out of sight and because it was hot he was
working without any stitch of clothing on his burly frame. He
had a woodworker's vise arranged upon the side of Keith's
bunk, and the deck of the cabin was a litter of shavings as he
formed the floor chocks curved to the radius of the drum,
using a spokeshave. Keith went on board with Mr. King and
called to him down the hatch. "Afternoon, Jack," he said.
"I've brought the grub."

The woodworker looked up. "Get the barrel?"

"We've got that with us, too."

"Huh." Mr. Donelly stood in thought. "Better bring the

barrel down 'n see if these chocks fit," he said at last. "It's going here." He indicated a spot behind the ladder, which seemed to have been moved forwards.

"We might need a hand getting it on board," said Keith. "It's an awkward thing to handle."

Mr. Donelly laid down the spokeshave and started up the ladder. Keith checked him. "What about a pair of trousers, Jack?" he said. "There's ladies about."

"Huh?"

Mr. King said, "They'll put you in quod if you come out on deck without your trousers on."

"This place makes me sick," said Mr. Donelly. "You see some of the girls on these hooch ships. They don't wear practically nothing." Grumbling, he turned and pulled on his soiled trousers, and came out on deck.

They got the drum on board, Jack lowering it quickly and expertly from the quayside with the two ends of a warp around it, and lowered it down through the hatch into the cabin. Dick King and Keith carried all the rest of the stuff on board; there was no room to stow anything below till Jack was finished with the oil drum so they stacked it all by the tiller. There was little more then that they could do till Jack had finished except watch him through the hatch, which they did for a time. He worked on oblivious of their presence. Both Keith and Dick King were impressed with the quality of his woodwork; he worked accurately and quickly, putting a loving finish with a few strokes of glasspaper on each chock before laying it aside. Presently Keith leaned down the hatch and told him that he was going on shore to say good-bye to the ship's officers and to the aircrew, but would be back later. Mr. Donelly only grunted in reply, intent upon the job.

7

KEITH MOVED INTO THE *Mary Belle* that evening. The installation of the new oil drum was finished when he arrived and it was ready to be filled with water in the morning. There had been no opportunity to get Jack's drum steamed out, that had once held kerosene, for the *Cathay Princess* was due to sail for Yokohama in the morning. Keith was to regret most bitterly that he had not taken action upon that earlier when he drank his first cup of coffee.

They stowed the tins mostly beneath the bunks, the tins of biscuit going in the forecastle and the perishables in the one cupboard. The cooking equipment of the *Mary Belle* consisted of a frying pan and two battered saucepans; there were two chipped enamel plates and an inadequate supply of knives and forks. Keith found them sufficient for his needs, however, because Jack Donelly ate mostly with his fingers.

They supped off tinned sausages and beans, cooked by Keith, followed by a half loaf of stale bread that he discovered in a locker, and a tin of jam. As he had suspected, Jack Donelly was a voracious eater; he ate everything in sight and then leaned back with a contented sigh. "You cook good chow," he said. "What you got in that wood box?"

"A sextant," Keith said. "I've got some charts here, too." He opened the box, took out the sextant carefully, and gave it to his captain, who handled it gingerly.

"I seen them in shop windows," he observed presently. "Marine stores and that. You know how to use it?"

"Not very well," Keith said. "They put me in the way of the noon sight on board the tanker."

"Huh." Mr. Donelly handed the mystery back to him. "Tells you where you are, don't it?"

"Not quite. Not unless you're better at it than I am. But I think it may tell us how far we've gone."

Jack Donelly said, "Well, I can tell *you* that." He turned to the soiled wooden bulkhead at his side and showed a long vertical line of pencil-scrawled figures. "That's how far we went each day coming from San Francisco."

Keith got up and examined the record with interest. "How did you know how far you went each day?" he asked.

Mr. Donelly said, "Well, each day after sunrise I'd sit down and put my thinking cap on and reckon we were doing five knots yesterday morning, say, four hours, well that makes fifteen knots." He paused in thought, and then started counting on his fingers rather expertly. "No, that makes twenty." He went on, "Then around midday maybe it fell light and then I'd reckon up that. Then maybe I'd heave to in the night, catch up a bit on the sleep, 'n reckon on a knot or maybe a knot and a half. So then I'd tot it up for the day 'n write it down up there."

Keith was deeply interested. "How did it come out?" he asked. "I mean, how did it compare with the real distance when you got here?"

"I never got it added up," Mr. Donelly admitted. "Sometimes I'd try adding all those figures up, but it always came out something different to last time." He reached for his atlas and scrutinized the dirty page of the Pacific Ocean. "It says here two thousand and ninety-eight," he remarked. "A guy came on board one time, said he was from a newspaper. He added it up and wrote it underneath."

Beneath the horizontal line, written neatly in another hand, was the figure 2237.

"That makes it about a hundred and fifty miles too much," said Keith in wonder. "Less than that—about seven per cent."

"You don't go straight all the time," said Mr. Donelly. "You get way off course 'n then that makes it more."

Keith nodded. "I think it's very good indeed," he said. He sat in wonder for a moment. If you took off a bit, say, four per cent, for course deviations, then Jack Donelly's estimate of the distance made good was only three per cent in error, and that error was on the safe side. "How do you know how fast the ship is going through the water?" he asked.

"My Dad taught me. He used to know."

"Do you look at the waves she leaves behind, or something?"

"I dunno. Just how she goes."

He could not explain himself, and Keith did not pursue the subject. Jack's dead reckoning was clearly most important to them; Jim Fairlie had warned him that at that time of year the skies might well be overcast as they got further south, making the noon sight impossible. If he could only get an occasional sight as a check on their progress they might well depend more on Jack's estimates than on his sights. "We'll do this again," he said.

Mr. Donelly ran a dirty finger down the woodwork. "Put another lot of figures right alongside, there," he said. He was seized with doubts. "Think you can add them up right, all those tiddy little numbers?" he asked.

"I can have a try."

"Huh." There was a pause, and then the captain said,

"You bring the little motor along, what makes the electricity?"

Keith nodded. "I've got it here." He reached into his suitcase and pulled out the box, unwrapped the model, and set it going with a flick of his thumb. He placed it on the floor, and Jack Donelly got down on his hands and knees and gazed at it, entranced. "Smallest in the world," he breathed. He looked up. "That's right?"

"I think so."

A disturbing thought crossed the captain's mind. "How long does it go on one fill of gas?"

"Ten or twelve minutes." He added, "I've got a bottle with me."

"A bottle of gas?"

Keith nodded.

"We could run it every day?"

"I think so." He let it run till the miniature tank was dry and it stopped, and then put it in its box on the fiddled top of the cupboard. "We'll keep it there."

He washed the dishes, a proceeding which his captain obviously considered to be quite unnecessary. The cabin was dimly lit by a kerosene lamp in gimbals, too dark for reading if there had been anything to read. They sat on deck for a while, smoking and listening to the radio music from the yachts in the row, brought to them by the cool, scented breeze. "Get the hose along first thing, 'n fill the barrels," said Jack Donelly. "Then we're all set to go."

Keith thought about ship's papers and the strange thing called a bill of health, and decided that they were matters which concerned the captain of the ship, and not himself. He asked, "How much paraffin have we got—I mean, kero?"

"Kero? There's a jerrican. I guess it's still about half full."

"I'll get it filled up tomorrow." Four gallons, he thought, should take them to Tahiti since there was only one Primus stove and the cabin lamp. "I saw a store at the end."

"I wouldn't buy nothing there. They'll skin you alive."

"Is there any other place I could buy kero?"

"I dunno."

They retired to bed soon after. Keith found that Jack's preparations for the night consisted simply in taking off his pants and lying down upon his dirty mattress with a soiled blanket ready to pull over if he felt cold. Keith followed his example, having made a pillow of some of the clothes from his suitcase, and put out the lamp. He was tired, but for a time he was kept awake by the strangeness of his surroundings, the hardness of his bed. The wind blowing steadily from the east kept the main halliards tapping rhythmically against the mast, the water lapped against the ship's side by his ear with little liquid noises; from time to time as the ship moved in her moorings the rudder in its pintles made a clunking sound. He did not know what any of these noises were except the lapping water, but Jack Donelly was already asleep so they were probably all right.

This was Monday, Monday night. It was only on Thursday morning that he had left his home in Ealing, but how far away it seemed! Even Katie seemed distant and remote, and Janice in whose interest he was here, hardly more than a little wistful dream. He tried to reckon sleepily how many thousand miles he was away from his workshop in Somerset Road, and gave up the attempt. Eight or ten thousand miles, perhaps. But he still had the case-hardened egg that he had made for Janice, the grey egg, safe in a little box within his suitcase.

The warm wind blew softly through the cabin, scented with frangipani and salt water.

Presently he slept.

He woke in the dawn to the sound of Jack Donelly getting out on deck and the sound of a thin stream of water falling by the ship's side, and realized that he was out on deck without a stitch of clothes on. He got up, put on his trousers, and put his head out of the hatch. "Are you allowed to do that here?" he asked mildly.

"Morning," said his captain. "Isn't nobody around. Cleaner'n doing it in the bucket."

Since there was only one bucket on board to be used for washing and all other purposes, Keith could not but agree. "I think I'll go ashore," he said.

"Up the end there, by the store. How you sleep?"

"Fine."

Keith put his shoes on and took a little walk. Returning to the ship he asked, "What would you like for breakfast?"

"Cornmeal fritters," said Mr. Donelly.

"You'll have to show me how to do that," Keith said.

He received his lesson over the Primus stove, Jack picking the maggots expertly out of the cornmeal and putting them in a tin for future use as bait. He had a dirty tin of fat smelling strongly of fish, carefully hoarded and poured back after the fry. Keith added some bacon rashers and a loaf of bread that he had bought at the store. To his surprise the cornmeal fritters were very good if you could forget about the maggots, and the coffee brewed by Jack was excellent but for the kerosene. All told, he didn't do too badly, and sat for a while smoking before washing the two plates.

He went off after breakfast with the jerrican for kerosene while Jack looked for a hose along the quayside that he could borrow without permission. The can had only a little kero in the bottom, and though it seemed to Keith that there must be sufficient in the drinking water to get them to Tahiti it was as well to fill the can. He did so at the store and bought a few tinned delicacies that took his fancy, and walked back heavily laden to find Jack with a hose watering the ship.

"I let the forward barrel overflow a little, get rid of some of the kero," he said. "She might need pumping out now, if you've nothing else to do."

Keith bent to the bilge pump, a crude affair with a straight pull upon the plunger, awkward to the novice. It worked well, however, and a steady stream of dirty water flowed out on the deck and away by the scuppers, gradually becoming clearer. Jack finished filling the barrels below and put the running hose on deck in the warm sun, turned it off upon the quay and returned it to wherever he had got it from while Keith continued his back-breaking work. Finally the pump sucked, and Keith rested his aching muscles.

"Guess we're all set to go," said Jack. "You don't know of anything we might want?"

Keith shook his head. "I can't think of anything."

Jack went below and fetched up his atlas, which opened at the soiled page of the Pacific. "Captain Davies, he said to steer one five three," he said, looking at the scrawled pencil figure on the smudged line. "He said that was the same as south twenty-seven east on the compass, but the real course was sump'n different." He sat in puzzled silence, the thinking cap firmly on his head. "I guess we'll go on board the three-stick schooner," he said at last. "She's a wooden ship, same as *Mary Belle*."

Keith asked, "Do you think it would be a good thing if I brought the charts along?"

"Sure," said Mr. Donelly affably. "Can't do no harm."

They set off for the schooner, Jack Donelly clad in pants alone and Keith in trousers, cricket shirt, and braces crowned by the somewhat crumpled Panama hat that he wore on holidays in Cornwall. He seemed pale and fat and undersized in comparison with the magnificent torso of the man beside him, and he was very conscious of his physical deficiencies. Whatever one might think of Jack Donelly's mental ability, and Keith was now beginning to differ from Captain Davies, there was no denying that he was a fine figure of a man.

They walked round the head of the yacht basin and down the long tier of vessels to the immaculate schooner yacht at the end. As they approached her Keith's heart sank. She exuded wealth at every glance, from the polished bronze cap on the end of her bowsprit to the gilt emblem on the top of her ensign jackstaff at the stern. Her paintwork, her varnished brightwork were spotless and brilliant; her halliards were of stainless-steel wire rope running to hydraulic winches at the foot of each mast, her sheets of gleaming white nylon. A wireless aerial ran from the truck of the mainmast to the mizzen and down to the wheelhouse and deck lounge at the stern, from which a television aerial and a direction-finding loop protruded. A deck hand in immaculate white overalls lounged by the varnished gangway leading to the deck. Keith would never have dreamed of setting foot on such a ship himself; he decided that negotiations here were his captain's responsibility.

No such qualms beset Jack Donelly. He marched down the gangway to the deck, Keith following behind. The lounging sailor stood erect. "What can we do for you, brother?" he asked.

Jack said, "See the captain."

"What do you want with him?"

"None o' your business. Just tell the captain I got sump'n to talk to him about."

"You got to say what you want. The captain's busy."

Jack flared into a quick anger that Keith had not seen before. He advanced a threatening step towards the man. "You go tell him."

The deckhand stepped back hurriedly. "Okay, Superman,

okay. But he won't see you till he's finished breakfast. Just wait up on the jetty."

"We'll wait right here."

The man hesitated, and then went towards the wheelhouse door. He almost collided with a woman who came flying out on the deck. "Who's that?" she asked him urgently.

"Coupla guys want to see the captain, lady," he replied. "They won't say what they want."

She hesitated, and then brushed past him and walked quickly to Jack and Keith by the gangway. "You haven't come from Manuel?" she asked. She had bright auburn hair, almost red in the Honolulu sunlight, that probably owed something to art. Keith judged she might have been about thirty years of age.

Jack looked at Keith blankly; the situation was beyond him. Keith said, "We've come to see the captain."

"Oh." She was plainly disappointed. "I was expecting . . . somebody else."

"We just want to see the captain."

She looked them up and down. "Want a job?" She said to Jack, "You're a sailor by the look of you. He might have one for you. I don't suppose he'd have one for your friend."

"We don't want no job," Jack Donelly replied. "Just want to see the captain—ask him about the course down to The Islands."

She stood in silence, her lips drooping. Keith had a queer feeling that at any moment she was likely to start crying. "You're nothing to do with Manuel?" she asked dully.

Jack looked blank, and Keith shook his head. "We've never met him, I don't think," he told her. "Who is he?"

"At the Royal Waikiki Hotel, with his orchestra," she said. " 'Music with Manuel,' every Thursday evening on CBS. You must have seen it. Everyone knows Manuel."

Jack Donelly said, "We just want to see the captain."

She turned away from them and walked slowly to the deckhouse door, and vanished inside. They stood in the sun at the end of the gangway, waiting. Jack smiled thoughtfully. "Like to see her with no clothes on," he remarked. "She'd peel off nice."

Keith laughed. "You're not likely to get the chance."

The deckhand reappeared. "Captain, he's at breakfast," he

told them. "He said to tell you to wait, or else come back again in half an hour."

"Guess we'll wait," said Jack patiently.

They waited for a quarter of an hour or twenty minutes. Then the captain came out of the deckhouse door and walked towards them, a tall, bronzed, efficient-looking man in naval whites and a white-topped naval cap. "You want to see me about something?" he asked. "I'm Captain Petersen."

Jack said awkwardly, "I was wondering if we could check a course with you down to The Islands. I'm Jack Donelly, and this is Mr. Keats, sailing with me."

"Sure," said the captain. "There was a piece about you in the paper. You came from San Francisco single-handed, didn't you?"

"Piece about me in the paper?" asked Jack vaguely.

"In the *Post-Journal,* nearly a column about you and your ship. One day last week. Didn't you see it?"

Jack shook his head.

"I'll get the steward to look through the papers in the cookhouse. Maybe we've got it still. That's your ship up at the end? The white sloop?"

"That's right."

"Where are you bound for now, captain?"

"Going south to this place Tahiti," Jack Donelly said. "Mr. Keats got business to do there."

"Quite a way," said the captain, "but you should find a fair reaching wind, this season of the year. It might fall light and variable when you get down about five north. Then after the equator it might steady up again, still from the east. You haven't got a motor?"

Jack shook his head.

"Oh well, I think you'll be all right. You may get a few days' slamming about in the doldrums. Come into the charthouse and we'll have a look at the course."

They went with him towards the deckhouse door. Keith asked, "Have you got a motor, sir?"

"Oh, sure. We've got a big main Diesel and a smaller one for starting and battery charging. The engine room is quite a show place in this ship."

"How many hands you carry?" asked Jack.

"Nine deckhands," said the captain, "two engineers, one

cook, two stewards, boatswain, mate, and me. Seventeen all told."

They entered the wheelhouse and stood by the chart table. The captain pressed a bell-push and a buzzer sounded below; a steward appeared. "Sam," said the captain, "chase around the ship and see if you can find a copy of the *Post-Journal* about the middle of last week, Wednesday or Thursday, with the column in it about Captain Donelly and the *Mary Belle*. If you find it, bring it here. And—hold it." He turned to Jack and Keith. "Cup of coffee? Right. Three cups, Sam."

They turned to a consideration of the course. Keith was surprised and pleased by the consideration that the American captain of this very fine yacht gave to Jack Donelly's problems. A dumb fisherman from Oregon was clearly no novelty to him; moreover, he had probably been briefed by local gossip in the yacht harbour. He examined Jack's smudged atlas page with interest and with care and turned to Keith's charts with tact, ran out the course for them, and curiously enough arrived at exactly the same magnetic course as Captain Davies had in the *Cathay Princess*. "Guess I needn't have troubled you," said Jack at last. "I thought maybe it would be something different, the tanker being an iron ship."

The captain shook his head. "That's compass deviation. You don't want to stow anything made of iron near your binnacle—an anchor, or anything like that. Take it up forward." They went on to discuss the probable winds, two men of the same country talking the language of sail.

They went on talking for half an hour, sipping the cups of coffee, smoking as they stood over the charts. Keith showed his newspaper cutting about the loss of *Shearwater* and the death of Jo, and told this pleasant man the purpose of his journey. The red-headed woman came up from below dressed for the shore and passed them by, walked with quick steps up the gangway, got into a car upon the quay, and drove off.

"You won't have any trouble," Captain Petersen said at last. "A good, reaching wind most of the way, unless you're very unlucky. You should make better than a hundred miles a day, average. Add a week in the doldrums. I'd say you'll be in Papeete in thirty days." He paused, and then said, "Wish I was coming with you."

Keith asked, "Have you been here long?"

"Too long," the captain said. "Nearly four weeks. We came here from L.A. bound for Tokio and then Manila with the owner, his daughter, and some friends. Four months' cruise, it was to be. But soon as we got here he was talking on the telephone to New York and then to Cincinnati, where the plant is, and he left and flew back East. He'll be back again sometime, but Lord knows when. In the meantime there's just the daughter living here on board, and she's doing no good."

"That's the lady who went on shore just now?" Keith asked. "She came and spoke to us while we were waiting."

The captain nodded. "Mrs. Efstathios," he said. "At least— I always call her Mrs. Efstathios. I don't think the decree's gone through yet."

Jack said, "She was asking sump'n about a guy called Manuel. Seemed to think we ought to know about him."

The captain nodded. "Manuel de Silva," he said reflectively. " 'Music with Manuel.' He was born Mike Simmons, but that was in Puerto Rico so I suppose he felt he'd got a right to a Spanish name. Looks like he's going to be Number Four if we stop here much longer."

He stood in thought for a moment. "Gee," he said, "I wish that I could jump this ship and come down to the islands with you boys."

They thanked this competent man and said good-bye, and went on shore, and started to walk back towards the *Mary Belle*. "Fine ship," said Jack Donelly.

"She was beautiful," Keith said. "I've never been on board a ship like that before. Do you know her name?"

"*Flying Cloud*. Registered in Seattle." He walked a few steps in thought. "She costs somebody plenty."

They walked back to the *Mary Belle* and went on board. In the cabin Jack tucked the school atlas away under the mattress of his bunk, and Keith wedged the roll of charts behind the locker. Jack looked around the cabin. "You think of anything we need we haven't got?" he asked.

Keith thought, and shook his head. "We've got food, water, and kero," he said. "I don't know about the ship."

Jack grunted. "You ever been in a sailing craft like this before?"

Keith shook his head.

"Just keep out of my way, 'n don't do nothing 'less I tell you."

He busied himself for the next half-hour about the deck while Keith stood on the ladder in the hatch and watched. He set the jib in stops, made halliard and sheets ready, set up the main boom and removed the crutch, made fast the main sheet and removed all but two tie-ers from the sail. The wind was blowing from the east down the fairway of the yacht harbour towards the entrance. He took in the leeside bow and stern warps and led the doubled end of the bow warp from the weather bow pile to the stern. Then everything happened in a rush, so quickly that Keith had difficulty in appreciating what was going on. Jack cast off the weather stern warp and then he was everywhere at once, a big, nimble man stripped to the waist, hauling on ropes and casting them off. The *Mary Belle* moved forward smoothly from her berth into the fairway, turned as the jib broke out, and then she was sailing quietly down the middle of the rows of yachts towards the entrance trailing a long rope in the water from her bow, Jack at the helm. "Just gather that rope 'n put it on the deck beside the mast," he said.

Keith did his best with this, and got it all on deck. They turned by the *Flying Cloud* and headed out to sea under jib alone, the wind a little aft of the beam. As they passed the schooner yacht Captain Petersen came out and waved to them from the deckhouse door.

They carried on southwards down the channel till Jack judged that they were well outside the reef. Then he told Keith to get down below out of the way. He loosened the main sheet, cast off the tie-ers from the main, put the ship up to the wind, and ran forward to hoist both peak and main halliards. The big tanned sail slammed and banged about as Keith crouched down below it in the hatch and Jack worked like a demon at the mast. Then suddenly it was over, and they were sailing quietly again, Jack at the helm, the big sail billowing above them. They were sailing much faster now, a little heeled to starboard, making about five knots.

Keith sat in the cabin hatch enjoying the smoothness of the motion in the lee of the land. As he looked around he saw a white launch come out of the harbour behind them. Presently he noticed it was closing up upon them fast, making about twenty knots, a white plume under the raised bow that grew and spluttered as she slammed each wave.

He said, "There's a boat coming out behind us."

Jack turned and looked at it. "Always sump'n," he grumbled.

The launch ranged up alongside them and slowed to their speed. A uniformed man in the stern spoke through a megaphone. "Say, Captain," he said, "you better heave to."

Grumbling beneath his breath Jack Donelly pulled the foresheet up to weather, slacked the main, and put the helm down; the *Mary Belle* came up into the wind and lay quietly with a little forward way. The launch ranged up beside her on the lee quarter only a few feet away. The uniformed man appeared by the coxswain. "Where are you bound for?" he shouted.

Jack Donelly answered, "Hilo."

"You're not going any further?"

"Just to Hilo."

"You've got to get clearance if you go outside the group."

"Don't need no clearance for Hilo."

"No," the officer admitted. "All you need is just pay fourteen dollars and fifty cents."

"What we got to pay that for?"

"Harbor dues, Captain."

"Jeez. I wasn't in the harbor more'n a week."

"Nine days," the officer said. "Your size makes one fifty each day, plus tax. Makes fourteen dollars fifty."

"I dunno as I've got it."

"Then you'll come right back and tell the Judge about it. Come on, Captain—I got things to do."

Grumbling, Jack left the helm and went below and from some secret store unearthed the money. The officer reached out a little fishing net on a bamboo for it and passed back the receipt in the same way. The launch sheered off, put on speed, turned around, and made off back towards the harbour.

Keith asked timidly, "Where's Hilo?"

"On Hawaii. They make all kinds of trouble if you say you're going foreign."

He let draw the jib and the main, and got the vessel on her course again. "You sick yet?" he asked.

"Not yet," said Keith.

"Come 'n take the helm awhile and I'll show you."

Keith came to the tiller, held by a turn of light rope round it from a cleat upon the bulwark, the rope held in the hand. He sat down on the deck as he had seen Jack sit. "Keep looking at the card," he said. He laid a dirty finger on the glass of the binnacle. "That black line, that's the lubber line 'n that goes with the ship. The card, with all them black marks on it, that moves against the lubber line the way you pull the tiller. You see the big thin diamond? Well, not that one but the one next to it; the tiddy little triangle. Not the big triangle, the tiddy little 'un. Keep her about there."

Keith put on his glasses to inspect the binnacle and picked out the tiny numerals, remembered from his navigational instruction, and so identified the tiddy little triangle. He settled down to try to steer the ship, and became engrossed in it. Jack watched him for a time, and then went down and lit the Primus stove. He made a jug of coffee while Keith steered and the island of Oahu grew less distinct behind them, and presently passed up on deck a cup of coffee, a great hunk of corned beef out of a tin, and two inch-thick slices of bread. "You okay?" he asked.

"So far," said Keith.

Jack Donelly grunted. "Guess I'll have a bit of a lie down," he said.

Keith was alarmed. "What will I do if anything happens?" he asked.

"Aw, nothing's going to happen," said the captain. He sat by the galley at the foot of the ladder contentedly eating bread and beef. Then, without ever looking out on deck, he went forward and lay down upon the lee berth, which was Keith's, and went to sleep.

Keith sat at the helm, terrified. He had never sailed a ship of any kind before. Now he was in sole control of this rushing, heaving monster which towered above him in a mass of brown sails and rope whose very function was a mystery to him. He had only mastered one small element of the seaman's craft, that of keeping the appropriate compass mark upon the lubber line, and that only within the last half-hour. He did not know what disaster would ensue if he should let it stray either way. The wind seemed to be increasing and the sea rising as they cleared the land, and the ship was heeling noticeably more. He was scared stiff. He sat there in his cricket shirt and braces with Panama hat upon his head under the brilliant sun of the Hawaiian Islands, the bread and the corned beef untasted on the deck beside him, concentrating on doing the one thing that he had been taught, keeping the tiddy little triangle upon the lubber line. Presently his cup of coffee, now quite cold, left him and slid down into the lee scuppers, still upright.

An hour later he was still sitting in the same position, the ship still rushing along in much the same way under the steady beam trade wind. He was hungry and thirsty, and very sore from sitting motionless on the hard deck. He was less frightened now and his arms were getting tired. He began to experiment with the rope lanyard which assisted him to hold the tiller. If he took another turn around the tiller it eased the grip of his hands. He still had to steer ... but if he tied it, the ship would probably go straight enough for ten or fifteen seconds while he retrieved the cup of coffee from the scuppers. He made a couple of trials, and then, greatly daring, lashed the helm and slithered down the deck upon his bottom to retrieve the cold cup.

By the middle of the afternoon he was taking things more easily. He ate his lunch about three o'clock, and sat on at the helm growing steadily more sunburnt and tired. Below, he could see Jack sleeping peacefully upon the lee berth. Tired as he was, he realized that this made sense since for the next month they would have to sail all night. He could not sail the ship at night; Jack would have to do that, or they must heave to as they had done when the harbourmaster's launch had overtaken them. He must stick it out, and call Jack at sunset, which seemed to come at about six o'clock.

When the sun was about an hour above the horizon he couldn't stand it any longer, and called Jack. The big man stood up in the cabin, yawned, and came on deck. "You done a good spell," he said. "Everything okay?"

"I think so," said Keith. "I haven't touched anything."

Jack Donelly took the tiller. "I got her now. Get down and rustle up some chow. I'll heave her to 'n pull a reef down case it gets up in the night."

Keith got up stiffly and went down below, regardless of what was going on on deck. He lit the stove to make some coffee and got out a tin of pork and beans to heat up for their supper. He had got as far as getting out the bread when he suddenly felt dizzy and faint; the fumes of the stove were nauseating, the motion of the ship intolerable. He struggled on for a little, unable to focus his eyes on anything. Then he was overcome and dashed up on deck to be sick over the lee rail.

He moved back to the hatch when it was over. Jack was tying down the reef points at the boom, and paused in his work. "Gets you, down below," he said affably. "Stay out on deck awhile. I'll get the chow."

"I can manage."

"You'll get sick again. Stay where you are."

Keith obeyed him and sat on the deck by the hatch gradually recovering. Jack finished his chores on deck and went below. Presently he handed up a dirty plate with a great mess of steaming pork and beans on it, a huge hunk of bread, and a cup of coffee. "I don't want anything," said Keith faintly.

"Go on 'n eat it."

"I'll be sick again."

"Sure you'll be sick again. Go on 'n eat it."

Keith took the path of least resistance, and ate most of it, and felt the better for it for the moment. Jack took the dirty plates and cups, wiped them with a filthy rag, and put them back ready for use again. He took the bucket with the lanyard on the handle and sluiced it over the side, left a little sea water in it, and placed it on the deck below beside the head of the lee berth. He lit the cabin lamp and turned it low, then came on deck and took the tiller, let draw the sheets, and got the vessel on her course. It was now nearly dark.

"Get on down 'n get some sleep," he said. "Don't go standing up—lie down right away. You got nothing else to do till daylight."

"You can't sail her all night."

"Aw, if I get sleepy I'll heave to."

Keith took off his shoes, went down below and stretched out on the berth. Somewhat to his own surprise he fell asleep at once. He slept for five or six hours, woke up feeling sick, and got out on deck to vomit over the rail. Jack was sitting smoking at the helm, and the ship going smoothly over the long ocean swell. "Just take her while I get some chow," he said.

Keith took the helm in the bright moonlight and struggled to keep the vessel on her course in the faint light of the oil-lit binnacle. Presently Jack passed him up a mug of coffee and a great hunk of bread spread with jam, and sat below himself finishing up the tin of cold pork and beans. Then he came on deck again. "Guess I'll take her now."

So the night passed for Keith, in alternate vomiting and sleep. He took the helm again at dawn while Jack Donelly slept. In general he was well enough on deck while he concentrated on the sailing of the ship, and he was ill directly he went below. They sailed on all the day under a blue sky flecked with cloud. Once in the afternoon when Keith was lying dozing and exhausted on the lee bunk he opened his eyes to see Jack Donelly wedged upon the other bunk, and realized that there was no one at the helm. To his enquiry Jack said, "She goes by herself okay with the wind forward of the beam. Won't be no harm if we get up a tiddy bit to weather." He pointed at the bulkhead at his feet. "I reckon we made ninety-five miles yesterday, up till dawn today. See where I wrote it down?"

Later that afternoon when Keith was at the helm and Jack below beginning the preparations for supper, he happened to glance up through the hatch. Immediately he stopped what he was doing and came out on deck, and stood looking at the sky. Keith asked him what he was looking at.

"Frigate bird," said Jack. "That's the third I've seen."

Keith followed his arm pointing and saw the bird, very high, flying or gliding on a straight course. "That's a gull, isn't it?" he asked.

"Frigate bird," said Jack. "Much bigger'n a gull. See his forked tail. He's going home some place."

"How do you know that?"

"That sort don't spend nights at sea. They go way out, but they go back to land each night. He'll be down by sunset." He glanced at the sun. "Hour 'n a quarter, hour 'n a half. There's land that way, forty, fifty miles. That's the third I see, all going the same way." He laid a horny, dirty hand vertically across the binnacle, looking up at the flight of the bird and down at his hand. "Just a tiddy bit south of east," he said. "Get them charts of yours 'n see what land that is."

Keith went below and got the chart and brought it up on deck quickly before he was sick. He put the *Pacific Islands Pilot* down on it with the edge pointing a little to the south of magnetic east. "Must be Hawaii," he said. "If we're on course that should be about sixty miles away."

Jack thought about it, watching the bird now disappearing to the east. "I dunno as he'd fly so fast as that," he said. "Reckon we're up to windward just a tiddy bit."

8

THE DC-6B FLOWN BY CAPTAIN FIELDING landed back at Blackbushe about midday on Thursday, just a week after leaving for Honolulu. They could have flown to Speke from Frobisher which would have been more convenient for Mr. Adams, but the landing fees for the aircraft at Speke far exceeded Mr. Adams' fare by rail from London to Manchester, so they took him to Blackbushe with them. They landed back into the cold foggy drizzle of a January day in England; after the languorous sun and warm trade winds of Honolulu the change was little to their liking. "Half-inch thick underwear, fires in the living room, and hot buttered crumpets for tea," said the navigator thoughtfully. "Well, I dunno. I suppose there's something to be said for it."

The crew were tired and ready for a rest. They had flown the best part of their maximum permitted allowance of flying for a month in one week, finishing up with thirty-six hours on end. For most of them there was employment or instruction on the ground in the installations of Blackbushe until they were rostered for another flight, but all were entitled to three days of rest. Dick King would start again upon the overhaul of engines in the shops on Monday morning, but having turned in his logbooks and written his report he was free to go home.

He telephoned to his wife, Ethel, to bring the car to Blackbushe to fetch him. He lived at Egham in a house off Stroude Road convenient both for Blackbushe and for London Airport in case he wanted to change his job, and convenient for Ethel for shopping in Staines. He had brought back little gifts from Honolulu for his wife, a lei of frangipani blossoms in a polythene bag and a bracelet of coloured tropical nuts, unusual in Egham. "I haven't got anything particular for tea," she said as he got into the car. "Anything you fancy?"

He shivered a little in the unaccustomed, raw chilliness of the early dusk. "Sausages," he said. "Pork sausages and fried potatoes." He thought of the navigator. "And crumpets. Let's have lots and lots of crumpets. Got the fire lighted?"

She looked surprised. "I didn't light it yet—it's not very cold. Are you cold?"

"A bit. We'll light it when we get in." Halfway home he thought of Keith Stewart's letter in his pocket, and they stopped and posted it, and bought sausages and crumpets.

When they got home he gave her his presents, and she exclaimed with pleasure at the bracelet and the lei, which was satisfactory to him. While he was lighting the fire and putting the car away she picked the lei to pieces and put the flowers in water in an endeavour to make them last a little while in January England, and then she started in to cook the potatoes and the sausages and crumpets. "I never asked if you had a good trip," she said.

"Pretty fair," he replied. He paused, and then he said, "You remember me telling you about Keith Stewart of the *Miniature Mechanic*, who was coming with us?"

She nodded. "I remember. Did you bring him back?"

"No. He got off in Honolulu. Tell you all about it after tea."

He did so as they washed the dishes in the kitchen, and as he recapitulated to her what had happened in Honolulu the unease grew on him again. It was absurd, of course, and that he realized, because Keith was his own master and if he chose to go to sea with a man like Jack Donelly in a ship like the *Mary Belle*, well, that was that. Moreover, it was all ten thousand miles away, and no concern of his. Yet he was still worried.

Something of his unease communicated itself to her as they sat before the fire. "We got him fixed up with a sextant and the ship's officers showed him how to use it to take a latitude sight," he said. "I hope to God it's going to work out all right."

"Doesn't the captain have to do that?" she asked, puzzled.

"This one couldn't. He was just a sort of fisherman. American," he added, in ultimate disparagement.

"Doesn't the captain of a ship have to pass exams, like in an aeroplane?"

"I don't know," he replied. "Maybe if the ship is small enough you don't. I shouldn't have thought that this chap could read or write." He thought for a moment. "He was a good woodworker."

"However small the aeroplane, you've got to have a licence and pass exams before you can fly it anywhere, haven't you?" she asked.

"That's so. It may be different with ships. This chap couldn't navigate at all. He got to Honolulu from San Francisco by following the aeroplanes."

She was puzzled. "But they fly to all sorts of places, don't they? How would he know that any aeroplane he saw was going to Honolulu?"

"It's the only place they can go to," he said. "They all put down at Honolulu to refuel. You get out in the Pacific west of San Francisco and you see one flying to the west, it's going to Honolulu." He sat in brooding silence.

Presently she asked kindly, "What's the trouble, Dick? Are you afraid they won't get to this place he's going to? What's the name?"

"Tahiti," he said. "That's about the strength of it. It's the hell of a long way—more than two thousand five hundred miles of open sea. Nearly as far as from here to New York. And at the end of it, to find one tiny little island in among a lot of coral reefs you could get wrecked on, like his sister was. To think of starting off upon a trip like that in a sailing ship without an engine, with a skipper who can't navigate!"

"There's nothing you can do about it," she said at last.

"No . . ." He turned to her. "I was with him all the time in Honolulu. We shared a room in the hotel. I've never shared a room with someone who was somebody before—I mean, well known. *You* know." She nodded. "He'd never been outside England before," he said uncomfortably. "For so famous a man—he didn't know a thing, really. Never seen a shower before, or foreign money. He didn't even know how to sleep properly in hot weather."

"Was he nice?" she asked curiously.

"Just like you or me," he told her. "We got on fine." He

sat in an uncomfortable silence. "I ought to have stopped him going on that ship," he said at last. "I didn't quite know how."

She comforted him. "It'll probably turn out all right," she said. "You see."

"I hope it does."

He spent a restless night, much to her discomfort, weighed down by a sense of imminent disaster. He did not know what to do, but he knew that if Keith were to lose his life he would be associated with the tragedy in some small measure. Towards morning, it occurred to him that anyway he should not keep his grim forebodings to himself. Two heads, or several heads, were better than one. If he shared his apprehensions with other people someone might pull some rabbit out of an unthought-of hat, might make some suggestion that would somehow make Keith's journey to Tahiti safer. But who to talk to?

He talked to everyone that he could think of over the weekend, and he talked to all and sundry at Blackbushe when he started work again on Monday, but no rabbit was extracted from any hat. On the Wednesday, when he had been back in England for nearly a week, he took a batch of exhaust manifolds for repair to a firm in Croydon, travelling with them to suggest a welding modification that would prevent certain cracks from starting. He rode with the driver in the truck, arriving in the middle of the morning. He did his business in the welding shop and had lunch in the firm's canteen.

By the time he had disposed of his lunch and his work it was getting on for three o'clock. There was little sense in going back with the truck to Blackbushe for at most an hour of work before knocking-off time, and Keith Stewart was still uneasily in his mind. He rode with the truck driver to Croydon station and took a train to Victoria. An hour later he was walking into the editorial offices of the *Miniature Mechanic* in Victoria Street.

It was not a large office, and it was not modern or well furnished. In the outer office there were a girl and a young man, and two vacant desks littered with bits of miniature machinery, photographs, and pulls from blocks. He asked the girl if he could see the editor.

"Who shall I say?" she asked.

"Mr. King," he said a little awkwardly. "Mr. King of Albatross Airways. He won't know me. Tell him it's about Keith Stewart."

She went into the inner office, and came out followed by the editor. He went up to the engineer. "Mr. King?" he said with outstretched hand. "My name is McNeil. You've come about Keith Stewart?"

"That's right. I thought you might like to know how he's getting on."

"Come into the office. Like a cup of tea?" He turned to the girl. "Make us two cups, Daphne."

They went into the office and the editor gave him a chair. Dick King said, "I'm the flight engineer of the crew Mr. Stewart went to Honolulu with. We left him there when we flew back Tuesday. I thought you might like to know how he was getting on."

"I certainly would. He told me that he'd got a flight with you to Honolulu and he wanted to get down to Tahiti. He had to go there to see about his sister's death."

"That's right."

"Did he manage to get a passage on to Tahiti? He wasn't quite sure about that when he left."

Dick King said, "He did get a passage, of a sort. That's what I wanted to tell you about, really and truly. He was going on a sort of fishing boat. She hadn't got an engine even—just the sails."

Mr. McNeil opened his eyes. "That doesn't sound like Keith. Couldn't he get anything better?"

"Apparently not. We were all a bit worried about it, but he made up his mind so there wasn't anything that we could do."

"It's a very long way, isn't it?"

"About two thousand four hundred miles." He hesitated. "Sea miles, that would be—knots. Close on three thousand land miles, I suppose."

"And he's gone on that in a fishing boat—sailing?"

"That's right."

The tea came. When the girl was out of the room the editor said, "Tell me just what happened, Mr. King."

The engineer considered how to tell his story. "Well," he said, "it was like this. There was this crew of the *Cathay Princess,* the officers, I mean, the ship we took the generator rotor to." Launched on his story he had little difficulty in going on in his own way, and the editor had little difficulty in getting the essentials of the tale. "The chap was kind of simple," said the engineer, describing Jack Donelly. "He built the boat himself and made a good job of her. He's a wood-worker by trade, or else a fisherman. He could be a bit of both. But I don't think he can read or write, and he certainly can't navigate."

Mr. McNeil was puzzled. "If he can't navigate, how's he going to find Tahiti?"

"That's the trouble," said the engineer. "Captain Davies—he's the captain of the tanker we took the generator rotor to—he said they wouldn't get there at all. The first officer, he said he thought they'd get there in the end, but they'd take the hell of a long time." He paused. "It was all a bit of a mess-up, if you get me," he said unhappily.

"But he went off on this ship, did he?"

"I suppose he did," said the flight engineer. "We took off at dawn last Tuesday and they were going to sail the same day. I don't know for sure that they went, but I suppose they did."

"How long was the voyage to take?"

"Mr. Fairlie said six weeks. You'd make it in ten hours in a DC-6, but that's the time he said it would take." He paused. "He did teach Mr. Stewart how to take a latitude sight, and we got him a sextant. And Captain Davies, he fixed them up with food and that."

The editor pursed his lips. It sounded absolutely crazy, and it probably was. He had private troubles of his own that concerned Keith Stewart. It was barely a fortnight since he left England, but already his absence had been felt very much by the staff of the *Miniature Mechanic*. Every other day a batch of letters arrived from Katie that Keith normally would have answered, and which now had to be answered by the editor himself. They were letters from all over the world. Jim McNeil had not fully realized till he had the job of answering these letters from Edmonton and Bulawayo, from Gateshead and Hong Kong, how widely Keith's influence had spread, in what high regard he was held by modellers all over the world. He was uneasily conscious that Keith's salary was perhaps too small; after all, it was only one-third of his own, yet which of them did most for the circulation of the maga-

zine? The overseas subscriptions were increasing every day.
The air fare from Honolulu to Tahiti might not be more than
the book could stand, a hundred or a hundred and fifty
pounds. Keith had been on the staff now for twelve years. It
might be reasonable to stand him that.

He asked the engineer, "How could we find out if he's
actually left?"

Dick King rubbed his chin. "Well, I don't know. I think he
probably *did* sail the day we left."

"I'd like to know for certain." The editor paused. "If I'd
known that he was in this difficulty we'd have given him
some help, I think. I'd have to put it to the Board, of course.
But I think we'd have helped him with the air fare, rather
than see him get into a mess like this."

"You can't fly direct," said the engineer. "You've got to go
by Samoa."

"Have your firm got an agent in Honolulu that I could
cable to?"

"Not that I know of," replied Mr. King. "There's Mr.
Yamasuki. He was agent for the ship, the *Cathay Princess*."

"Any good?"

The engineer thought for a minute. "I don't think he'd do
much for a stranger unless there was money in it for him,"
he said at last. "He didn't seem to want to be mixed up in it
at all. It might be worth a try . . ."

"I'll think it over for an hour or two," said the editor. "I
might think of something better." He took Mr. Yamasuki's
name, talked to the engineer for a few minutes longer, and
thanked him for coming in. Finally Dick left the office to
catch a train to Staines and so to Egham.

Back in his office after seeing the engineer off the prem-
ises, Mr. McNeil sat deep in thought, smoking pipe after
pipe. Something would have to be done about Keith Stewart;
he should have realized that earlier. He should have realized
when Keith first proposed his most improbable journey that
his value to the magazine was such that he must be assisted
to complete it quickly and get back to work again. True, he
had made a half-hearted offer of an advance payment if
Keith should be in any difficulty; it now seemed to him that
in view of his very small salary that offer had been quite
inadequate.

He should have offered him assistance with the air line fare to Tahiti and return—especially the return, because he wanted Keith back at work. It would have been quite a shock to his Board, but he could have pushed it through. Indeed, he would have to push it through now, whether the Board liked it or not. The effect of his penny-pinching was that his best contributor, the man who attracted correspondence to the magazine from all over the world, had had to go off on a crazy trip in the Pacific, on a fishing boat sailed by a skipper who didn't know how to navigate . . .

If Keith Stewart were to lose his life, the effect upon the magazine would be disastrous . . .

He sat in brooding silence. No good crying over spilt milk now. Constructive action was required; the first thing was to find out whether Keith was still in Honolulu or whether he had in fact left upon this fishing boat. Who did he know or correspond with in Honolulu? He searched his mind. There was nobody he could think of. There must be modellers in Honolulu; probably the mail department of the printers could produce half a dozen subscribers to the *Miniature Mechanic* in Honolulu if you included the armed forces. But he knew none of them.

Well then, Americans . . . Americans who might have contacts there. Professor O'Leary leaped to his mind. Professor O'Leary was Professor of Mediaeval Literature at the University of Michigan, just outside Detroit. Perhaps as a reaction from the mediaeval literature, he made models. They had published an article by him once—was it in 1952?—on the construction of his 4¾-inch gauge locomotive model of one of the old wood-burning 4-4-0 engines of the Northern Pacific railroad of 1880. Two years ago he had visited England and Mr. McNeil had lunched with him and with Keith Stewart. He was then completing a model of a Case traction engine, acknowledging a considerable debt to Mr. Stewart for his articles upon the Burrell. He had been lecturing at the University of Hawaii a short time before . . . He had shown them photographs of a very well equipped workshop in the basement of his home in Ann Arbor, with the oil-fired air-conditioning plant in the background, which had interested them as much as the model. Mr. McNeil and Keith had kept in touch with this pleasant reader, who was now ~~d on the construction of Keith's Congreve clock. A

Congreve clock is an antique clock mechanism in which a steel ball rolls upon a zigzag path down an inclined plane and takes half a minute to do so, when the incline of the plane reverses and the ball rolls back again.

Professor O'Leary was the man. He had been in Honolulu lecturing, probably more than once. He must have numerous contacts on the academic staff. Indeed, with his engineering hobby he might well know other modellers in Honolulu or members of the faculty of engineering at the University, to whom the name Keith Stewart would be known. In the professor the editor felt he had a sympathetic contact in the United States who would exert himself to the utmost to find out what had happened to Keith Stewart in Honolulu.

His staff were all departing or had gone by the time he reached that conclusion. He reached for the telephone and rang up his wife in Finchley to tell her that he would be a bit late, and went out into the deserted outer office. He sat down at his secretary's typewriter, put an air letter form and carbon into the machine, and began to type.

He wrote:

Dear Professor,

   You will remember lunching with Keith Stewart and myself when you were last in London, when you showed us the photographs of your Case traction engine and your workshop. I am a bit concerned about Keith Stewart who was recently in Honolulu, and I have wondered if you have a friend there who could assist me in an enquiry.

   The circumstances are as follows ...

He wrote on, putting the case clearly and concisely, explaining about Keith's sister, about his financial inability to pay for his extensive journey, about his free flight to Honolulu, about Jack Donelly and the *Mary Belle*. He ended with a few words of apology.

   I feel we are to blame in some degree in not assisting him with the expense of this journey in view of his long service with the magazine, but you will appreciate that we do not make great profits. We did not think that he would become involved in such difficulties, and we would

assist him now if we could get in touch with him. Do
you know anyone in Honolulu who could cable us, at
my expense, to tell us what the position is? Or who could
get in touch with him if he is still there, and ask him
to cable us?

> Yours sincerely,
> James McNeil

He folded the air letter and sealed it. He glanced at his
watch; there was still time to catch the airmail to New York
if he took it to the Charing Cross Post Office. He put on his
hat and coat, turned out the lights and locked the door, and
went out into the chilly January night to catch a bus to
Charing Cross.

Cyrus Shawn O'Leary got that letter on Friday morning at
his home in Ann Arbor near Detroit. He had no formal
lecture on that day though he had essays to correct. On
Monday he was lecturing upon the debt owed by the Elizabe-
than lyric writers to the early English mediaeval poets, and
on that morning he was engaged in tracing a comparison
between *Piers the Plowman* and the work of John Donne. He
had strayed a little from his line to consider Thomas Campion, the graceful reprobate, and the mail lay unnoticed at his
elbow, and he smiled as he read, for he was still young at
heart:

> I care not for these ladies,
>   That must be woode and praide:
> Give me kind Amarillis,
>   The wanton country maide.
> Nature art disdaineth,
>   Her beauty is her owne.
>   Her when we court and kisse,
>   She cries, Forsooth, let go:
>   But when we come where comfort is
>   She never will say, No.

Perhaps there was enough of that in Ann Arbor; he had
better not stress it to the sophomores. Better to stick to the
religious angle, to the soul-searchings that had followed the
. . . . . He laid Campion aside, and turned back to

John Donne. Outside the snow lay deep; the cars passing in the street made a whisper and a rustle. It was overcast outside with heavy lowering clouds presaging more snow. Spring with flower-decked meadows was the time for Thomas Campion. Winter was the time for John Donne, and for the workshop. . . .

He resolutely turned his mind away from his hobby. John Donne was his business, and he turned to him again, endeavouring to regain the train of thought from which he had been side-tracked. He read the passage again which seemed to him to reflect the Plowman:

> Thou has made me, and shall Thy work decay?
> Repair me now, for now mine end doth haste;
> I run to death, and Death meets me as fast,
> And all my pleasures are like yesterday . . .

That echoed something, surely?

> On your midnight pallet lying,
>   Listen, and undo the door:
> Lads that waste the light in sighing
>   In the dark should sigh no more.
> Night should ease a lover's sorrow;
>   Therefore, since I go tomorrow,
>   Pity me before.

No, that was Housman, much, much later. His mind was wandering today; he could not concentrate. Pallets—he was worried about the method of machining the pallets of his clock—but then that was a different sort of pallet. He did not see how he could hold them in the four-jaw chuck to bore and ream the axis hole, and Keith Stewart had not explained that in the serial. He must be being stupid; there must be some simple way to do that job which every modeller would know. Perhaps if he went down to the basement and had another look . . .

No. He never went down to the workshop in the morning. Get thee behind me, Satan—he must work. If the work would not flow, at least there was the mail to go through, and the essays to correct. He picked up the pile of letters and furtively looked through to see if the new iss

Miniature Mechanic had arrived. It hadn't, but there were two heavy-looking archaeological journals, three local letters, one air letter from his married daughter in Colorado Springs, and an air letter from London, England.

He opened the one from his daughter first and skimmed it through. It was all about the baby and not much else; his wife would be interested. He put it down and picked up the one from London. The back showed it to be from J. McNeil; the name rang a faint bell, but he could not place it.

He opened it, and sat rivetted in his chair as he read. This was really serious, very serious indeed.

He read the letter again and then sat deep in thought, *Piers the Plowman* and John Donne and the remainder of his correspondence unnoticed on the desk before him. The direct appeal stirred him deeply. He was an engineer at heart; if things had broken differently for him he might have been one. He had money; that was the trouble. His grandfather, Shawn O'Leary, had been a railway contractor in the palmy days of expansion; in reaction his father had become a minister in Boston, Massachusetts. Cyrus had been directed to the academic life and he had not resisted; a year at Oxford had followed four at Harvard. Research had come after that, and academic appointments. He did not regret his life, but the urge to make things had been strong in him all the time, inherited, perhaps, from his grandfather who had made the iron roads towards the West. His workshop meant a great deal to Cyrus O'Leary.

He enjoyed his literary work, but the high spot of his visit to Europe two years previously had been the lunch with Keith Stewart and his editor. He had subscribed to the *Miniature Mechanic* for nine years, and in that time he had come to have a deep regard for the design engineer whose lucid, modest, and well-written articles had taught him so much. They did not seem to breed that sort of writer in the United States, and he had wondered why his country with so much engineering achievement did not throw up people of that sort. When he had met Keith Stewart he understood a little better. He had thought from the pleasure that the engineer had given to so many modellers that he would be in the twenty to thirty thousand dollars a year income bracket. When he had met him his regard for Keith was, if anything, increased, but he now realized that his income was three to four thousand, or even less. Few people of such ability in his own country would be content with so modest an income, and perhaps no engineers. The devotion to an art inherent in Keith Stewart's circumstances flowered more prolifically in Europe.

He sat wondering how to deal with this appeal, how best he could help. He did know Honolulu; he had lectured there three times, but the people that he knew there were all literary people. Mr. McNeil had been in error when he had assumed that Professor O'Leary might know members of the engineering faculty in the University of Hawaii. It was the professor's habit to conceal his workshop hobby from his colleagues, even in Ann Arbor. He did not display his locomotive or his traction engine to his fellow professors, fearing that if he did so he would not be taken seriously when he spoke on mediaeval poetry. He would not have dreamed of talking about engineering matters when visiting another university. In consequence the only associates that he had in Honolulu were serious and somewhat impractical students of mediaeval history. He did not know one person there to whom he could turn for an account of the movements of a fishing boat in the harbour.

He left his study and went down to the basement of his house, to the workshop. He had a special bookshelf down there for the copies of the *Miniature Mechanic,* not caring to display them in his study. The row of little magazines was now seven feet long, extending every week; presently he would have to put up another shelf.

He had abstracted from the series the issues of the magazine dealing with the construction of the Congreve clock, and these lay in a little pile upon the drawing bench. He turned them over thoughtfully; it was incredible that a man who could write stuff like that should be so short of money ... He turned to the bench, deep in thought, and fingered the tilting platform of the clock, already assembled in a trial erection in its trunnions. He had made that first thinking it to be the most difficult part; in fact, it had proved to be the easiest. Whom could he turn to for help in this affair? Who else in the United States was an admirer of Keith Stewart? Who else was making a Congreve clock to his instructions?

There was that dairy farmer down in Maryland—he wouldn't be much help. There was Dave Coulson in Indianapolis—he was an accountant. There was the chap that he had met at the Brotherhood of Live Steamers in Detroit, the stockbrokers's clerk in Toledo ... Then—wait a minute, out on the West Coast ... lumber and pulp mills ... what was his name? Hirzhorn—Solly Hirzhorn. Solly Hirzhorn had attended a meeting of the Brotherhood last year, and nobody had realized who he was till after the meeting a week later. Solly Hirzhorn was building a Congreve clock, and he had all the money in the world, and all the contacts, too.

He picked up the tiny pallet that he could not think of how to hold for machining and stood fingering it absently. He should have bored and reamed it first before shaping it to that rather complicated form. Perhaps if he put it in a tin and melted lead all round it he could hold the lead—but then, how would you line it up? There *must* be a simpler way than that. He wondered if Solly Hirzhorn had been caught that way, or whether he hadn't got as far as making the pallets.

As he stood there at the bench of his workshop it seemed to him that Solly Hirzhorn was the one person to whom he could turn. He did not know the lumber tycoon well. He had been introduced to him at the meeting of the model engineering society, the Brotherhood of Live Steamers, and they had talked enthusiastically together about the Congreve clock for nearly a quarter of an hour. Both had then been starting on the project and had been drawn to each other by their common interest, the fat, unwieldy magnate sixty-eight years old and the lean professor of fifty-two. In that quarter of an hour they had become friends, though it was only when they came to exchange addresses at the end of it that each learned who the other was. That was a year ago; they had exchanged cards at Christmas but they had not met again, nor were they very likely to do so.

He glanced at his watch. Half past eleven—that would be half past eight in Tacoma. Not a very good time to call a tycoon upon a personal matter, when he would just have arrived in his office perhaps. He went up to this study again, closed the door, lifted the telephone, and spoke to the long-distance operator. "I want to call Mr. Solomon P. Hirzhorn, person to person," he said. "This is Professor O'Leary. I don't know the number, but it's in Tacoma, Washington. It's Hirzhorn Lumber Enterprises, Inc., or something."

"It's *the* Mr. Solomon Hirzhorn, is it?" she asked.

"That's right. If you get through to his secretary, tell her it's about a clock. I'll take the call at any time convenient to him."

He hung up; five minutes later the operator called again with news from fifteen hundred miles away. "Mr. Hirzhorn is dealing with his mail right now," she said, "and after that he has to fly to a conference at one of the plants. He could accept the call best at his home at five o'clock tonight. That would be eight in the evening of our time. I was to ring her back and tell her would that be okay."

He said that would be fine, and put the receiver down. He could not work that day. Against all his rules of routine, he went down again to the workshop and stood turning over the work of Keith Stewart. So much pleasure given to so many people, in all walks of life ... And yet the man was short of money—worse paid than a professor! It didn't seem right, but that was evidently the way it was.

At eight o'clock he was speaking to the magnate on the telephone. "Say, Professor, this is a real pleasure," said Mr. Hirzhorn. "How are you making out with the clock?"

"Not too bad," said the professor. "I got the tilting table and the escapement made all right, but now I'm finding the clock motion to be quite a job. However, I'll get over it all right. What I wanted to talk to you about was Mr. Keith Stewart."

"He's a great guy," said Mr. Hirzhorn. "Whenever I get in a difficulty I write to him and he comes right back with the answer."

"He's in a little trouble. I thought you might like to know. He's been in Honolulu, but he's probably somewhere in the Pacific at present."

"In Honolulu? What's he doing there? If I'd known I'd have flown across to meet him."

"I got a letter from his editor. Shall I read it out?"

"Sure, Professor. I'm sorry if he's got in any trouble."

Professor O'Leary started in to read the letter from Mr. McNeil. When he was halfway through Mr. Hirzhorn stopped him. "Say, Professor," he said, "this is interesting, but I'd like to see a copy and consider it. Mind if we put it on the tape?"

"By all means."

Mr. Hirzhorn laid down the receiver and called to the next room. "Julie! Say, Julie!" A handsome, Jewish-looking girl appeared at the door. "Get this on the tape, the letter that Professor O'Leary will be reading out. Get the conversation, too—all of the call." In a moment he spoke again. "We're all set now, Professor. If you wouldn't mind starting the letter again."

When that was over he said, "Well, Professor, that'll need some thought. I'll have it copied and think about it, and call you again."

"Can you find out whether he's left Honolulu?"

"Oh, sure. I'll call Honolulu right now. If I can contact him, I'd better speak to him myself and read him out this letter."

"That would be a good idea. His editor, this Mr. McNeil, he's evidently prepared to help him with the fares. He'd better cable his office. But I'm afraid that he'll have started already."

"Well, we'll find that out. Say, if we can locate him I'd be mighty glad to have him visit with me for a day or two on his way back to England. There's one or two things on the clock that I'd like his advice on, and he might be interested to see some of the plants. Would you be able to come over and join us?"

Professor O'Leary said, "Not till the end of May. I've got things I must do here each day."

"Too bad. Well, anyway, Professor, I'll be calling you again."

Mr. Hirzhorn put down the receiver and called for Julie. When she came he said, "Give me all that in type, soon as you can. And say, what's the name of the guy that runs our business in Honolulu, making monkey-pod wood bowls and dishes?"

"Setches, Mr. Hirzhorn. Setches and Byrne, Incorporated."

"That's right. Paul Setches. Well, get that tape in type and let me have it. After that I may want to speak with Paul Setches."

She went out, and he sat on alone in his study, a glass of rye and water with a little ice beside him. He sat, as was his habit in the evening, in front of the great picture window facing to the west. He lived not far from Wauna on an inlet off Puget Sound ten miles from his office in Tacoma. The east side of the house looked out over the inlet, his private airstrip, his boathouse, and his moored motor cruiser; the west side looked over many miles of forest to the snow-capped Olympic range. Here he would sit on the evenings when he had the leisure, and rest a little and watch the sunset light beyond the snowy forests. He had been born a lumber-man, and he loved forests.

He lived very much alone, devoted to his business. His two sons lived in suburbs of Tacoma more convenient to schools and to the main Seattle-Tacoma airport where the executive aircraft of the corporation were housed and maintained. His wife liked Florida and was frequently away there in the winter. He liked Florida well enough and sometimes spent a day or two there with her in the sun, but he could not live for long away from his business and his forests. The girl Julie Perlberg lived in the house with him and managed the ser-vants and worked as his secretary at home. She was an illegitimate daughter of his oldest son, Emmanuel, who had found a job for her in the office of the plant at Marblemount on the Skagit River when she was fifteen years old, conven-iently tucked away in the mountains at a discreet distance from Tacoma. She had the Hirzhorn blood in her, however, and by the time she was eighteen she was virtually running the Marblemount plant. There had been little option but to transfer her to the head office in Tacoma if they wanted to keep a man as manager in Marblemount. There the old man had met her and had taken a fancy to his granddaughter, largely because of her encyclopaedic knowledge of the busi-ness. As he found less room for detail in his mind he had taken her as his personal secretary; his sons approved of this, because they were a closely knit family and theirs was a family business.

His father had emigrated to Seattle from Austria in the early years of the century. Solly had been an enormous, powerful young man who liked work in the woods. He had been a hand faller at the age of twenty and a high rigger when he was twenty-five; he saved his money and at the age of thirty-two he had taken his own lumber concession and had become an employer of men. From that time he had never looked back. Forest after forest had been added to his empire, mill after mill to his payroll. His writ now ran from

Bellingham to Eugene, from Cape Flattery to Spokane. He employed rather more than forty thousand men in the various businesses under his direct control; he owned logging railroads, bulldozers by the score, trucks by the hundred, and many lumber mills. At sixty-two he had a coronary, and his doctors told him bluntly that he must do less work. He must acquire a hobby and live quietly at home for a portion of each day, or of each week.

He had seen this sentence coming, and he knew what he would do. As his business had grown he had bought huge varieties of engineering products, but he had never been an engineer. He had never formed a thread upon a bolt, though in theory he knew how it was done. He had concealed his lack of engineering knowledge all his life by virtue of his native wit, but always he had been uncertain in the background of his mind. If now he had to stay out of the office for a portion of his life he would devote that portion to learning something about engineering, the craft that impinged so largely on his business. He set to work to organize a very spacious workshop in the basement of his house at Wauna where he could learn some engineering quietly and secretly, away from the eyes of the engineers that he employed. Very soon he found out about the English magazine, the *Miniature Mechanic,* and had it sent to him by airmail every week with several other, and lesser, American publications. In a short time he became completely absorbed in his new interest, to the satisfaction of his sons and of his doctors.

He became conscious of a considerable debt of gratitude to the little magazine, the *Miniature Mechanic.* All his life he had heard his engineers speaking casually of milling, and he had not known what the process was. The magazine taught him in the first few issues that came to hand. He consulted with the engineer who maintained their three executive aircraft at the airport, and went with him to a machinery store in Seattle and bought a bench milling machine with a variety of cutters. He got his airplane engineers to install it in his workshop beside the lathe and drill press that he had already bought, and learned to use it; thereafter he could talk on equal terms on milling with his engineers and once or twice was able to correct them, which gave him immense pleasure. In lathe work it was the same.

Of all the contributors to the magazine he held Keith

Stewart in the highest regard for the lucidity of his descriptions and his comprehension of the difficulties of the tyro. Once in a difficulty, which he later realized to be due entirely to his own stupidity, he had dictated a letter asking for advice, hardly expecting to receive an answer. He had got one promptly, brief but helpful; the letter of a friendly man. Encouraged, he had written again some months later, and again, and help had never failed to reach him by return airmail.

This was the mental climate in which he received the sheets of typescript from Julie ten minutes after the call from Professor O'Leary in Ann Arbor. He sat in front of the big picture window in the sunset glow. The girl switched on a standard lamp and moved it to throw the light over his shoulder. He thanked her absently as he refreshed his memory of the call by glancing over her typescript.

"Say," he said at last, "he's got himself into a real jam. I wonder where this fisherman came from?"

"Would you like me to try and find out, Mr. Hirzhorn?"

"No, leave that be. What time is it in Honolulu now?"

"Half-past three."

"Well, get me a call to Paul Setches. If he's not in the office, give his girl hell 'n tell her to find him and tell him to call me at once."

Ten minutes later he was speaking to the president of Setches and Byrne, Inc. "Say, Paul," he said, "this is Sol Hirzhorn. I want you to see if you can contact a man called Keith Stewart for me. He has been staying at the Beachcomber Hotel, but it may be that he's living on a fishing boat called the *Mary Belle* in the yacht harbor or some place." He went on to describe the situation, and read out the letter from Mr. McNeil. "The message is, tell him to contact his editor before going any further, and especially before sailing for Tahiti. After he's done that, ask him if he would call me. I'd like to speak with him. He can do that from your office if he's short of money."

Mr. Setches said that he would make some enquiries and call him back. Mr. Hirzhorn laid down the receiver, and heaved his bulk up out of the chair. He went to the door of the next room, furnished half as sitting room with a log fire and half as office. He said to Julie, "I'm going down into the workshop. If Paul Setches calls again I'll take the call down there. Tell me when it's half an hour before supper, 'n we'll have a drink."

"Okay, Mr. Hirzhorn."

He lumbered off, and went down to his workshop and stood fingering the tilting table of the clock that he had made and burnished with such loving care. He was a slower worker than Professor O'Leary, partly from inexperience and partly from age; on the other hand he was lavish with equipment and spared no expense in providing machine tools for the workshop. He stood fingering the half-machined bronze trunnions that would support the table, his mind far away. Ten or eleven days had elapsed since the *Mary Belle* had been due to sail for Tahiti; there was little chance that Paul Setches would find her still in the yacht harbour. She could be halfway to Tahiti by this time. But how to find a fishing boat in the wastes of the Pacific Ocean, a boat that had no radio?

Chuck Ferris had a yacht, and—yes, it was a yacht in Honolulu. He had been on a world cruise, and had interrupted it to fly back to New York or some damn place. Paul Setches had entertained Chuck Ferris and his party at the Royal Hawaiian, on the old man's instructions, and he had written later to say that the cruise had been interrupted. Sooner or later Solly Hirzhorn meant to fit Ferris hydraulics as a trial installation in one of his mills, on all of the conveyors. Amongst the many accidents that happened in the lumber business a man caught in the flying chains and sprockets of the conveyors was the most horrible; it always made the newspapers in all its gory detail. It created too much adverse comment. Sooner or later he would have to fit a trial mill with Ferris hydraulics throughout, and cut out every chain. It would be expensive; one million, seven hundred thousand bucks was the Ferris estimate for the Flume River mill. Manny was for it; Joe said that it would never pay. His son Joseph was the treasurer of Hirzhorn Enterprises. It was for the boys to decide, but he thought it ought to be tried out one day, in one mill.

He started work upon the backplate of the clock, a thick sheet of brass which involved little but simple cutting and filing. He was, as yet, nowhere near the difficulties which had beset Professor O'Leary. He did not strain his dubious heart by cutting the thick metal with a hand hacksaw, as the

Professor did; among his many machine tools Mr. Hirzhorn
had a little bandsaw powered by an electric motor which did
the job for him in no time. He worked on happily for an
hour or so and made good progress, till the telephone rang
on the corner of the bench. He switched off the machine and
picked up the receiver.

"I have Mr. Setches on the line," said Julie. "Will you take
his call down there?"

"Sure," he said. "Get it on the tape."

A minute later he was speaking to Honolulu. "Well, Mr.
Hirzhorn, I'm sorry to say he's gone. He sailed in this fishing
boat, the *Mary Belle*, on Tuesday of last week."

"Where were they going to?"

"Well, they told the harbor launch that they were bound
for Hilo. That's on Hawaii, in the group of islands. But they
never turned up at Hilo, and the gossip on the waterfront
says they were bound for Papeete, in Tahiti. That checks
with the letter that you read me out."

"Why would they say that they were going to Hilo,
then?"

"I'd say they were afraid of the formalities, Mr. Hirzhorn.
They'd have to have a French visa on their passports, for one
thing, and the French don't like immigrants that haven't any
money. That could be the reason. I wouldn't know."

"What's going to happen when they get to Papeete, then?
If they get there?"

"They'll find themselves in trouble, Mr. Hirzhorn."

There was a long silence. Paul Setches said, "You still
there, Mr. Hirzhorn?"

"Okay, okay. I was just thinking. Did you hear anything
about the captain of this fishing boat?"

"Well now, that's another thing, Mr. Hirzhorn. The Customs officers say he's nuts. The yacht owners down in the
yacht harbor, they say he's a good seaman, but kind of
simple. They don't any of them think he'll find Tahiti. You
see, he's got no radio, no DF loop, no echo sounder, no Iron
Mike—nothing. The ship hasn't even got an engine—no engine at all, not even an outboard. And the captain certainly
wouldn't know how to use a sextant, if he had one."

It was bad. "You're sure Keith Stewart sailed upon this
boat?"

"Sure thing, Mr. Hirzhorn. I spoke with the Customs

officer that went after them in the harbor launch. They left without paying harbor dues. He said Keith Stewart was on board. That's when they said that they were bound for Hilo."

"There wouldn't be any way to get in touch with them, would there?"

"Not that I know of. You see, they've got no radio."

There was another silence while the old man's mind reviewed the situation. "Tell me," he said at last, "is Chuck Ferris's yacht still in the harbor?"

"The *Flying Cloud?* Sure, she's still here. Mrs. Efstathios, Chuck's daughter, she's living on board. Making quite a fool of herself with a bandleader, Manuel de Silva. You know— 'Music with Manuel,' on the TV."

There was another pause. "Well, thanks, Paul. Thanks a lot for what you've done. I'll have to think this over. Maybe I'll be in touch with you again, but that's all for the present."

"Okay, Mr. Hirzhorn. It's been a pleasure."

The old man stood by the bench for a few moments. The conversation had interrupted the thread of thought connected with his work, and now he could not take up his enthusiasm again. He took off his working apron and hung it on the hook on the door, put on his jacket, and went up again to the big sitting room with the picture window. Julie had drawn the curtains to shut out the darkness; she came in from her own office in surprise, for she had expected him to stay down in the workshop much longer. "Will you have the drinks now?" she asked.

"Not yet," he said. "Say, that engineer Chuck Ferris keeps at Boeing—the one who came with him last time. Jim Rockingham."

"Rockawin, Mr. Hirzhorn."

"That's right. You know where he lives?"

"It's somewhere out by Renton," she said thoughtfully. "Elliott, or Maple Valley, or some place like that. I can find out easy enough. Do you want to speak with him?"

"It's more than I can do upon the telephone," he said. "What I'd like him to do is to come here right now and visit with me for a little while. See if you can get him at his home. If so, I'll speak with him myself."

She went into her office and closed the door, and he sank down into his chair before the fire. One million, seven hundred thousand dollars was a lot of money, and on top of that they'd lose at least a fortnight of production from the mill while the conversion was going on. In terms of cash Joseph was probably right; hydraulic operation would put up their costs. But Emmanuel had the right idea. The day was passing when such ghastly accidents could be tolerated in the interest of cheap lumber. People thought much more of human lives now than they used to do. They must convert the Flume River mill for a trial of the Ferris system, but if they were to do that he would see that Chuck Ferris lent his yacht for a few weeks. Chuck had been trying to get his hydraulics into the lumber business for years.

Julie came in again. "I called Mr. Rockawin at his home," she said. "He left this afternoon to spend the week-end with his family at the Mount Rainier Mountain Lodge. Skiing."

"See if you can get him there," he said.

He sat on by the fire. Presently Julie came in again. "Mr. Rockawin is on the line right now," she said softly. She moved the table with the telephone upon it closer to his side.

He said, "That Jim Rockawin? Say, Jim, this is Sol Hirzhorn here. I'm speaking from my home at Wauna. I been thinking a lot about our Flume River mill. I'd like you to drive over 'n have a talk, if you can make it."

It was a royal command and must be obeyed, but it was also dark and snowing at the Mountain Lodge, and fifty-five miles to go. "I'd be happy to do just that, Mr. Hirzhorn," he said. The skiing with his family must be abandoned. "Matter of fact, it's snowing pretty hard up here right now and I'm not too sure I'd make it down the road to the highway. I'll come now if you say, but I'd as soon start with the first light 'n be with you by ten o'clock."

"Okay, Jim. I wouldn't want you to go and break your neck. Come over soon as you can make it in the morning. Meanwhile, I'll be talking with the boys."

They hung up, and Jim Rockawin stood in deep thought by the row of telephones in little counter booths. He was a man of about thirty-five, dressed in ski trousers, slippers, and an ornamental pull-over. This was business; he sensed it. This was the culmination of three years of patient, tactful work. He did not know exactly what would happen in the morning, but he knew this very certainly. Ferris Hydraulics was about to break into the lumber business.

His wife, pretty and kittenish, came downstairs from the bedroom floor, with their two daughters, twelve and ten years old. "Who was that, hon?" she asked.

"Sol Hirzhorn," he replied. "I'll have to go and see him in the morning."

"Oh, honey! Won't it do on Monday?"

He shook his head. "I'm afraid not. Not when Sol Hirzhorn takes the trouble to find me here and ring me personally."

She sighed, but she did not complain further. Men were like that, always putting business first—but after all, Sol Hirzhorn was Sol Hirzhorn. Born and bred in the State of Washington, the name was a household word to her, and she shared in the reflected glory of her husband's coming visit to Sol Hirzhorn in his fabulous home at Wauna. She said, "Well, come and eat, anyway."

"Just a few minutes," he replied. "I'll have to call Chuck about this."

"Oh, honey!"

"He'll be going to bed," he explained. He glanced at the watch upon his wrist. "It's ten o'clock right now in Cincinnati."

She left him, and took the children into the dining room. He turned again to the telephone, and presently he was speaking to his employer in his home. "I don't know what it is he wants, Mr. Ferris," he said. "But it's about the Flume River mill, and it's business."

"Say, that's great news," said Mr. Ferris. "What was it that we quoted for the whole job? Just under two million, wasn't it?"

"One million, seven hundred thousand and some odd dollars," said his representative. "What will I say if he only wants to do a part of it?"

"String him along, 'n call me soon as you can. In that case I'd not go back to New York. I'd fly right out and be with you Sunday afternoon. He shouldn't split that job. I'd try to talk him out of it. It's not giving the system a fair trial."

They talked a little longer. "I guess I'll call you anyway, soon as I get away from him," Mr. Rockawin said. "You'll be home tomorrow?"

"Sure I'll be home," said Mr. Ferris. "This is big news. I'll just sit right here looking at the television, waiting for your call."

Mr. Ferris was a small, dynamic man with auburn hair, fifty-three years old. The war had made him what he was. In 1934 he had been a draftsman in an aircraft drawing office, specializing upon undercarriage legs and on aircraft hydraulics generally. He had considerable inventive genius and even more business acumen. With the growth of aviation he had left the drawing office and had started a tiny specialist business in Cincinnati, working on a shoestring, getting all his machined parts made out by subcontract. He had never looked back. His business had grown astronomically with the war; by 1945 he was the president of a twenty million dollar corporation, with a business that was comparable with that of Solomon P. Hirzhorn.

For years he had wanted to get his finger into the lumber industry, which he considered to be antiquated in its equipment judged by aircraft standards. Moreover, although his business was doing well, there was little doubt that rockets and guided missiles would replace the manned aircraft in the future to a large degree. Guided missiles were not well suited to hydraulic units, and even piloted airplanes were now flying at such altitudes that special precautions, with increased complexity, had to be taken to prevent the hydraulic fluid boiling in the pipes. He had already switched a considerable proportion of his manufacturing capacity to the automotive industry; the lumber business was another one. As a hydraulic engineer, he was turning his attention more and more to things that stayed on the ground.

He did his best to delegate authority, but his business grew too quickly; as soon as he found a man to take one section off his shoulders another enterprise was starting up, needing his guiding hand for the first year or so. In 1952 he had a nervous breakdown and spent three months in a very expensive home. He came out mentally refreshed and fit as a flea, divorced his wife and married another one, and began working sixteen hours a day again. In 1956 he had another breakdown, and went back into the home. This time his doctors impressed on him that he really must do less work and find more interests. They suggested a long sea voyage.

He did not want to die, and so he bought a large schooner yacht, the *Flying Cloud*, that had been built for a cinema magnate who committed suicide for an unmentionable reason. He had actually voyaged in her on his second emergence from the mental home across the Pacific and as far as Sydney. By that time he was so bored that he left her and sank into the deep chair of a Pan-American airliner with an audible sigh of relief; in two days he was back in his office at Cincinnati and at work. Since then he had conscientiously tried to use his big yacht as his doctors had recommended, and he was actually on board her two or three times a year; each time intending a month's cruise or longer. Each time the office drew him back as with a magnet, because he had no other interest in his life except his very fleeting loves.

He sat in his home on Paxton Avenue between the Observatory and the Country Club, and waited for the call from Jim Rockawin. It came at about three in the afternoon, noon on the West Coast. "Look, Mr. Ferris," said his representative, "this isn't just what I thought."

"No business?" asked his employer sharply.

"I think he's going to order presently, but he's not ordering just yet. Emmanuel was there, the eldest son. They wanted to know if they could use the existing powerhouse with the steam plant in it—throw out the steam plant and put our Diesel motors and hydraulic generators in it. It's three hundred and eighty feet from the first conveyor. It's not a proposition, really, but I said that I'd go over Monday and take a look at it with them." He paused. "What Sol Hirzhorn really wanted was something different."

"What's that?"

"He wants to borrow your yacht."

"For crying out loud!" said Mr. Ferris. "What does he want with that? Go for a sail in it?"

"No. He wants to use it. Say, Mr. Ferris, this is going to be mighty difficult to explain over the long-distance line. You got a tape machine there, so you could read it over later and make up your mind?"

"Sure I've got a tape. Wait while I fix it up." There was a pause, and then he said, "Go ahead."

The representative had been collecting his thoughts during the pause, and when he spoke it was clearly and lucidly. "Some years ago Mr. Hirzhorn had a bad spell with his health, and his doctors told him he must get himself a hobby in his home. Well, he started a workshop—not a wood workshop like the rest of us, but a real engineering workshop with lathes, milling machines, shapers, a drill press, oxyacetylene welding, and God knows what. He took me down and showed me. I never saw anything like it. That's where he spends most of his spare time now. He's making some kind of a clock."

The tape reel rolled slowly, steadily, as he spoke. He told the whole story, reading out the carbon copy of the letter from Mr. McNeil to Professor O'Leary at Ann Arbor that he had got from Julie. "Well, that's the way it is, Mr. Ferris," he said at last. "He wants to borrow the *Flying Cloud* to go down to Tahiti and pick up these boys on their fishing boat, and do whatever this Keith Stewart wants to do, and bring him back to Tacoma so that Sol Hirzhorn can talk to him about his clock before he goes back to England. He'll pay you charter money, of course. I know this all sounds screwy, but that's the way it is."

"You think he's going to convert that mill, Jim?"

"I'm sure he is, Mr. Ferris."

"Is he dickering with anybody else?"

"I don't think so. I don't think he'd do that. When the time comes he'll try and beat us down on the price."

"Sure, sure." That was a commonplace. "Well, he can have the yacht, of course. Tell him that right away. Regarding charter money, it won't cost him a cent if he puts an order with us. Otherwise—oh, tell him that we'll let him know. I've never chartered it before. No—tell him he can have it free, as long as he likes."

"Whether he puts an order with us or not?"

"That's right. I shan't be using it."

"I think that's very wise, boss, if I may say so. Sol's going to be very pleased."

"Okay, okay. I'll play this tape back and call Captain Petersen. Now, you go over Monday and string them along. Better call me again Monday night, around six o'clock your time."

Keith Stewart sat on the deck of the *Mary Belle* that Saturday afternoon twelve days out from Honolulu, while Jack Donelly slept below. He was very different now from the fat, rather unhealthy little man who had sailed upon the *Mary Belle*. Five days of seasickness had made him noticeably slimmer and more competent in his appearance. That had been over for a week. He now knew the sails and ropes by name and what they did. He could not yet pull down and reef alone, or he had never done so, but he knew how it was done. He still wore the tattered Panama hat as a protection from the midday sun, and he still wore the cricket shirt at night and when the sun began to burn, but most of the time he went clothed only in a pair of bathing shorts, and barefoot; from frequently stubbing his toes he had charted the position of every eyebolt in the deck and now avoided them. He was a very different man from the Keith Stewart who had boarded the aeroplane at Blackbushe.

By his noon latitude observations and by Jack's dead reckoning he judged that they were now about two degrees and forty minutes north of the equator, about abreast of Christmas Island and probably two or three hundred miles to the east of it. Jack thought that they were closer than that. They had seen a patch of floating seaweed early that morning, and had viewed it with concern. "It could have come from anywhere," Keith had protested.

"Not from the east it couldn't," Jack had grumbled. "Seaweed don't last more'n a few weeks in the sea. I never seen seaweed more'n three hundred miles from land, 'n that only when there's been an off-shore gale. Want to put the thinking cap on for this."

Later, in the *Pacific Islands Pilot,* Keith had found some evidence of an east-going current in the vicinity of Christmas Island at that season of the year. Jack grunted when he told him. "I guess we're well away down to leeward," he grumbled. "Give me a shake up if you see any birds." He went down below to sleep.

Later that afternoon Keith saw something better than a bird; he saw the smoke of a steamer. It appeared broad on the starboard bow on the horizon and grew fairly rapidly. It was the second ship that they had seen since leaving Honolulu, and Keith watched it with interest. Presently he could see the hull above the horizon, and realized that it was going to pass fairly close to them.

He called Jack Donelly from his sleep.

The captain put his head out of the hatch and studied the position. "Bear up a little," he said. He pointed with the flat of his hand at the direction he wanted Keith to steer to

intercept the steamer, or pass close to her. Keith put down
the helm and pulled in the main sheet and then the foresheet.
"That's okay," said Jack. "Keep her as you go."

"What are you going to do?" asked Keith.

The captain looked at him in surprise. "Why, stop her 'n
ask where we are," he said. It seemed the most natural thing
to him. To Keith it seemed an appalling thing to do; this was
a big ship, costing millions of pounds. But he was new to the
sea, and he said nothing.

Jack said, "We'll need a board." He thought for a moment, vanished down below, and reappeared with the lid of
the locker under his bunk, and, mysteriously, a piece of
chalk. "I'll take her," he said, going to the helm. "You write
better'n what I do. Put, 'Want Position.' " A sudden doubt
assailed him. "Suppose they give it on a board in this latitude
and longitude. You know how to put that out upon the chart
'n say where we are?"

Keith said, "I can do that." He bent to his task, making
the letters as bold and clear as he could, and adding the word
"Please," which seemed quite unnecessary to his captain.
Then he took the helm again while Jack went below, and
reappeared with a large flag of the United States, which he
bent onto the burgee halliards and hauled to the masthead
upside down. He viewed it with satisfaction. "It's a great
thing to belong to a wonderful country like the ol' United
States," he remarked. "I mean, you Britishers, nobody
wouldn't know if your Union Jack was upside down or not.
But with Old Glory, there's no mistaking."

The ship drew nearer on an intercepting course. She was a
tanker, light in the water, painted grey all over like a bat-
tleship, and wearing the White ensign. In fact she was a Fleet
oiler that had discharged her cargo at Christmas Island and
was now on her way back to England through the Panama
Canal, but they had no means of knowing that. When she
was less than half a mile away and they could hear the noise
of her engines above the noises of their own passage they
held up their board. Her engines slowed and stopped. Jack
took the helm and put the ship about to windward, and let
all sheets draw, and sailed down the length of her, Keith
holding up their board. From the bridge an officer scrutinized
it through glasses, waved to them in acknowledgement, and

vanished inside. At the stern of the tanker Jack jibed the mainsail and sailed up the length of her again.

Two officers appeared upon the bridge holding a blackboard. The figures on it read, "Lat. 02°05'N, Long. 156° 55'W."

Keith copied the figures down carefully, and went below and set them out upon his chart. He reappeared at the hatch. "We're only seventy-four miles from Christmas Island," he said.

"How far ought we to be?"

"About two hundred and fifty."

Jack waved a salutation to the officers on board the tanker, and they waved back; they heard the engine-room telegraph bells jangle and the big propeller turned in a flurry of foam under her counter. They sailed clear of her stern and got on to their course.

"Guess we'll put her up a point to windward, maybe a point and a half," said Jack Donelly. "I knowed that we was getting down to leeward by that patch of weed."

That afternoon Mr. Ferris called Captain Petersen from Cincinnati. "Say, Captain," he said, "I was hoping to have joined you again before now, but I don't seem able to make it. I got a job for you to do, though. You know anything about a fish boat called the *Mary Belle?* Been in the yacht harbor recently?"

"Sure, Mr. Ferris," said the captain in surprise. "They sailed for Tahiti, maybe two weeks ago."

"How many people were on board her when she sailed?"

"Two, I think. There was the captain, a guy by the name of Jack Donelly. The other was a kind of passenger. English, he was. Flew out here in an airplane from England, and wanted to get down to Tahiti. They came on board here to ask about the course."

"They did? What was the passenger's name?"

The captain rubbed his chin. "Well now, Mr. Ferris—I'll have to try and think. It might have been Keats."

"Keith. Keith Stewart. Say, he's a friend of Sol Hirzhorn, and Sol's all het up about the risk he's taking going to Tahiti in that way."

"He is?" The captain's jaw dropped. He knew all about Sol Hirzhorn and his empire of the forests. "He hasn't any money," he remarked weakly. "That's why he went with Jack Donelly."

His employer replied, "Sol Hirzhorn hadn't any money when he started, nor had I. Now look, Captain. I want you to get going right away 'n follow down the route that he'd have taken to Tahiti. If you catch up with him, that's fine. If you don't, then when you get to this place Papeete 'n he's not there, you start looking for him back along the track. If you reckon they've got wrecked upon an island, visit every island they could be on. But find Keith Stewart."

Captain Petersen's heart rejoiced; he was sick of Honolulu. This was a job after his own heart. "What will I do when I find him?"

"You'll put the *Flying Cloud* at his disposal," Mr. Ferris said. "Keep in touch with me by radio. His sister got wrecked in the Tuamotus or something, so he wants to go to one of the islands."

"I know about that," the captain said. "He told me. He had a newspaper clipping about it."

"Fine. Well, put the ship at his disposal for whatever he wants to do. But when that's over, I want him back in Seattle or Tacoma. You'd better come right back to Seattle with the *Flying Cloud*, 'n mind you bring Keith Stewart with you. Sol Hirzhorn wants to see him, and I've got a big deal on with Sol."

"You shall have him, Mr. Ferris."

"Okay, then, for now. I'll maybe meet you in Seattle when you arrive, or else it might be Jim Rockawin. You know Jim?"

"Sure, I know Jim, Mr. Ferris."

"Well, keep me informed by radio, every two, three days, how it's going on."

"There's just one thing, Mr. Ferris."

"What's that?"

"About Mrs. Efstathios. Will she be coming along with us?"

There was a momentary silence. "Gee," said Mr. Ferris, "I forgot all about Dawn. She with you now?"

"She's on shore some place. I wouldn't know. Maybe the Royal Waikiki Hotel. 'Music with Manuel,' Mr. Ferris."

"I know, I know." There was a pause. "What time is it with you?"

"A quarter of three, in the afternoon."

"It's a quarter of eight with us. The doctor says I got to be in bed and asleep by ten. Say, if she comes within the next two hours, ask her to call me. Otherwise, tell her how things are yourself." The captain made a slight grimace. "She isn't Mrs. Efstathios any more. The decree went through. She can move into a hotel on shore, or she can go along with you, or she can come right home. Tell her that—with love and kisses from Daddy. But you sail for Tahiti first thing in the morning."

"Okay, Mr. Ferris," said Captain Petersen.

9

THE *Mary Belle* MADE A quick passage to Papeete, covering the two thousand four hundred nautical miles in twenty-five days. They carried a fair beam trade wind all the way but for one day of slamming about in the light airs of the doldrums on the equator. They never made quite enough allowance for leeway and passed within five miles of an island which from the latitude they assumed to be Vostok; they bore up two points and passed close to Flint Island. Thereafter they had no difficulty. They sighted Tahiti with the last of the light one evening, hove to for the night and went to sleep, and sailed into the harbour of Papeete next morning.

They had need of all their sleep, because in Papeete every man's hand was against them. On their non-arrival at Hilo the French officials had been fully informed by Honolulu over the radio of their suspected destination, and there was quite a reception committee waiting for them on the quay. The harbourmaster in his launch directed them where to drop their anchor and took a stern warp to the quay. As soon as the vessel was made fast a gangway was put down onto their stern and the reception committee came on board. There was the harbourmaster, an official in plain clothes from the Bureau de l'Administration, an official in plain clothes from the Banque d' Indo-Chine, the port health officer, and three gendarmes in uniform armed to the teeth.

There followed the most unpleasant hour that Keith Stew-

art' had ever had to undergo. Jack Donelly could produce
no ship's papers at all and no carnet, and was told that
import duty would be due upon the value of his vessel on
entry into French Oceania, probably at thirty per cent; he
was also liable to a considerable fine. He had no bill of
health. They would therefore be put in quarantine for thirty
days and refused permission to land during that time; they
would have to pay for the visits of the port doctor to inspect
them each day, and would be fined for that as well. He had
no passport and no visa to visit the islands; that merited
another fine. Keith Stewart had a passport which the police
immediately confiscated. He pointed out that no visa was
required for France; they said that a visa was required for
French Oceania, and he would be fined. They were forced to
produce what money and traveller's cheques they had which
the official of the Banque d'Indo-Chine immediately confiscated, giving them a receipt and stating that accounts would
be opened to their credit, a first charge on which would be
their liabilities to the Administration. After that the ship
was searched very comprehensively by the gendarmes, who
left everything in confusion. The party then departed, leaving one of the gendarmes as a guard at the head of the
gangway. They were given to understand that they would be
towed to the quarantine anchorage later in the day.

Jack Donelly was dazed and bewildered by this rude reception. "I don't see why they want to be so mad about these
tiddy little things," he said. "We haven't done nothing wrong."

"I suppose we set about it the wrong way," said Keith. He
thought deeply for a few minutes while putting the nets back
into the stern locker from which the gendarmes had dragged
them. "I think the thing to do would be to ask to see the
British consul. Your consul, too."

"I dunno," said Jack. "I never had no truck with one o'
them. You ask to see yours first, 'n see what happens."

Keith went to the gangway and spoke to the gendarme. He
knew no French and the gendarme knew no English, so they
did not get very far. "British consul," he said.

The man shook his head. Actually he was trying to convey
the information that there was no British consul in Tahiti.
Failing to get his message through, he tried again. "Sous-
officer viendra," he said. "Aprés le dejeuner. Spik English."

Keith said, "I *am* speaking English." He tried to move past the man to find someone on the quay who would interpret, but the gendarme barred his way with his rifle. Keith returned disconsolate to the deck of the *Mary Belle*. "I suppose we've just got to wait here till something happens," he said.

There was a strong smell of vanilla in the port, and very soon little black iridescent beetles started to descend upon the ship in hundreds; they were everywhere. "They'd be copra beetles," Jack observed. "Ma used to tell me about them, when we were little nippers. They can bite." He shook himself. "Let's have some chow."

They went below and cooked a meal upon an even keel for the first time in nearly a month. Jack was depressed and uneasy. "They couldn't take the *Mary Belle* away, could they?" he asked. "I haven't got no thirty per cent. That wouldn't be thirty cents, would it? I mean, it's something more?"

"It means about a third of what the ship's worth," Keith said. "But don't worry about that. It's just a try-on. The consuls will put that right for us." To console and amuse his captain he got out the little petrol generator set and started it with a flick of his thumb; there was still a little petrol left in the bottle.

Jack Donelly got down on his hands and knees to watch it running. "Smallest in the world," he breathed, entranced. He raised his head. "Those folks who came on board, the guy from the Banque and the guy from the Governor's office and all—they'd have been mighty interested to see this. Maybe we oughta showed it to them. . . ."

They lay moored stern on to the quay for most of the afternoon while Papeete slept; the sunlight on deck was torrid and they sweated it out upon their berths. At half-past three there was a step on deck, and Keith got up. It was the sous-officier, very smart; he held two folded papers in his hand, and gave one to each of them. "Citation," he said. "What you say—summons. To the law court, the Judge. On Monday, at eleven hours in the morning. I will come to fetch you."

Keith opened the paper, but it was all in French. "Can I see the British consul?" he asked.

"There is no British consul in Tahiti," said the man. "He comes sometimes from Fiji."

"Ask about the American consul," growled Jack.

"There is no American consul," said the sous-officier. He eyed Jack, puzzled. "You are American?"

"I'm a U.S. citizen," said the captain truculently. "You better watch your step."

Keith said, "If you're going to take us to court we'll have to have an interpreter. We neither of us speak French."

The man nodded, not unfriendly. "There is here an Englishman, Mr. Devenish, who was consul many years. I will ask him to come and talk to you."

"Will there be an interpreter in court?"

"The Judge speaks good English. Perhaps Mr. Devenish also, he will come."

"Will we get fined?"

The sous-officier shrugged his shoulders. "Perhaps."

"What happens if we haven't enough money for the fine?"

The man smiled. "You will have to get some. Sell the ship, perhaps. Otherwise, there is the prison."

He left them with that to think about and walked up into the town. They sat in the cockpit, dejected, waiting for something to happen. "I don't like all this talk about going to prison," Keith muttered. He had an idea that a permit from the Governor would be needed before he could visit Marokota Island, and prison didn't seem the best place from which to forward an application.

"I'd rather go to prison than have these Frenchies steal the *Mary Belle*," said Jack. "I haven't got no thirty per cent. What they making such a fuss about, anyway? We done nothing wrong."

"I haven't any money to pay fines," said Keith. "But they can't put us in prison. There must be some way out . . ."

"Aw, that's nothing," said Jack, comforting him. "I been in prison. There ain't nothing to it."

Keith raised his head in curiosity. "What did you go to prison for?"

"Rape," said his captain. He struggled to explain himself. "Gloria didn't make no trouble about it. She'd ha' come with me again. But when her Ma turned nasty and she got a lawyer, 'n he said it was rape, 'n they made Gloria say all kinds of things in court. The Judge asked me why I did it 'n I didn't know what to say except that I just naturally wanted to. So he said it was rape, too, 'n give me three months." He stared out over the rippling, sunlit waters of the harbour. "It was worth it," he said simply.

Keith didn't know what to say to that. He grinned, and asked, "What was it like in prison?"

"Okay," said his Captain. "Good chow, 'n not much work. They got the radio in every cell so you can lie and listen to it all the time. Television twice a week, 'n a movie every so often. It's okay." He paused in reminiscent thought. "Gloria would have liked it fine," he said.

Towards evening the harbour launch came back and towed them out from the quay to the quarantine anchorage.

They were sitting disconsolate on deck next morning awaiting the arrival of the port health officer, hoping to negotiate with him for supplies of water and fresh vegetables, when the *Flying Cloud* sailed in. She came from the north, and she came very quickly, for it was one of Captain Petersen's principles in making a passage that he carried sail all the time but whenever the speed dropped below about ten knots he put on his big Diesel to help her along. In consequence he made good more than twice the speed of the *Mary Belle;* he had sailed from Honolulu thirteen days behind them, but arrived in Papeete only a day later.

He sailed into the harbour for he liked to display his fine ship and the seamanship of his crew, the big Diesel ticking over with the exhaust muttering beneath the counter ready to pull him out of trouble if the unexpected happened in the narrow waters of the harbour. But nothing did so. He rounded up neatly into wind heading for a vacant mooring buoy, a dinghy splashed into the water by her side, the square yards on the foremast came down together, the mizzen swung free above the wheelhouse and deck cabin, and in a couple of minutes a coir hawser had been passed through the eye of the buoy and returned on board.

Jack watched all this, entranced. "Gee, that's pretty to watch," he said. "That Captain Petersen, he handles her fine. Great big ship she is, too."

"You're sure that's the same one?" asked Keith. "The one we went on board to ask the course? The *Flying Cloud?*"

His captain turned to him with scorn. "Sure it's the same one. Think I wouldn't know her? See, she's got one topping lift rigged to the end of the mizzen boom. I never see that before. More often they have twins, rigged about two-thirds

the way along. 'Course she's the *Flying Cloud*." He turned to
Keith, a brilliant thought fresh in his mind. "Maybe he'll
come off and talk to us. He was real nice that day. Suppose
he does, let's you and me show him the generating set.
Smallest in the world. I bet he's never seen anything like
that."

He did not come that morning. They thought they saw him
on deck inspecting the *Mary Belle* through field glasses, but
the ships were nearly a mile apart and it was difficult to say.
They thought they saw the woman on deck, too, though they
could not be very certain about that either. Sails were furled
quickly and neatly, a derrick was rigged and lowered a big
motor pinnace into the water, and the captain went ashore to
the Customhouse quay.

There was nothing to be looked at any more. "Let's have
some chow, 'n then lie down," Captain Donelly said. "I wish
that redhead would get in one of them boats 'n come on
over."

The remains of the cornmeal in the sack were now a
festering mass of maggots which neither of them had eaten
for the last fortnight. Keith persuaded Jack to let him drop it
overboard, which Jack did with regret. "Cornmeal fritters are
good chow," he observed. "Maybe we can get another sack
here some place." He scooped up a double handful of the
maggots for use as bait and put them in a tin, and consigned
the sack to the deep. They had a meal, and lay down to
sleep away the heat of the afternoon.

It was about three o'clock when the launch from the
Flying Cloud came alongside. Captain Petersen hailed them.
"*Mary Belle!* Anyone aboard?"

Jack stuck his head up out of the hatch. "Sure," he said.
"They won't let us go any other place."

"Mind if I come aboard?"

"Okay."

The launch drew alongside. Keith joined Jack on deck.
"We're supposed to be in quarantine," he said. "Is that all
right?"

"That's okay," said Captain Petersen. "I've just come from
the Harbor office." He swung himself over the bulwarks onto
the deck of the *Mary Belle*, and turned back to the coxswain
of his launch. "Lay off a cable or so, or else make fast

astern," he said. "I'll give a hail when I'm ready to go back."

The launch sheered off, and he turned to the mariners, smiling. "Well," he said. "You boys have certainly got yourselves a mess of trouble here."

"Aw," said Jack, "that doesn't amount to anything. It's only paper stuff. We haven't done nothing wrong."

There was a momentary pause. "Well," said Captain Petersen thoughtfully, "that's certainly one way of looking at it. It may be the right way." He sat down on the bulwark. "Anyway," he said, "you aren't in quarantine any more. You can move into the quay now any time you like. I'll get my launch to give you a pluck in later."

They stared at him, dazed. "How come?" asked Jack Donelly.

"I got a bill of health for you in Honolulu and brought it along, and put it in with mine," said Captain Petersen. "It's only a sort of letter saying that there wasn't any cholera in Honolulu on the day you sailed. I told the port health officer here that you'd left it in the office by mistake, and they asked me to bring it along." In fact he had had to exercise a good deal of personal charm to soothe the ruffled feelings of the port authorities in Honolulu, but he had got what he wanted in the end. He had been equally successful that morning in Papeete.

In fact he was a frequent visitor to Papeete in the *Flying Cloud* and had built up an enduring friendship with the chef du port over the years. The *Flying Cloud* was a large and an important yacht whose owners expected the captain to avoid irritating delays caused by minor French bureaucracy. There was only one berth in the port that had water and Diesel oil piped alongside and from which a telephone connection could be made, at the Grand Quai, used by mail steamers at infrequent intervals. On his first visit to Papeete he had taken the chef du port out to lunch, and the chef had mentioned the great interest that he took in the affairs of the St. Xavier Hospice des Orphelins. Orphan asylums, said the chef with tears in his eyes, were usually short of money and this one was shorter than most, but they all did what they could to help the little homeless children of Papeete. Captain Petersen reckoned that he knew the form and he was duly touched, so deeply that he had pulled out his wallet there and then and

had given the chef two notes of ten mille francs for him to
take up to the Mother Superior as a contribution, and that
afternoon he had moved the *Flying Cloud* into the berth at
the Grand Quai. He had been stunned that evening to receive
a note delivered by hand containing a note of thanks from
the Mother Superior and a receipt for the full amount. Out
of curiosity he had walked up the mountain next morning
and had found that the St. Xavier Hospice des Orphelins was
a real place, complete with nuns and children. Since then he
had repeated this donation on every visit that he had made to
Papeete, with the result that he had always got the best berth
in the harbour and had had no trouble at all.

He squatted on the bulwark of the *Mary Belle* in the warm
sunlight, a resplendent figure in a clean white uniform. He
dealt first with Jack Donelly. "They tell me that you're
having trouble over no certificate or registration, and no
clearance from Honolulu, Captain," he remarked. "Cigarette?" He proffered an opened pack.

Jack Donelly took one and the captain lit it for him. "I
didn't know you had to have them things," said Jack. "Nobody ever told me. Papers, aren't they?"

"That's right," said Captain Petersen. He turned to the
man beside him. "Tell me—are you Polynesian?"

"I'm a U.S. citizen," said Jack. "I got born in Reedsport,
Oregon, 'n lived there all my life. Eleven of us there was—
eleven that grew up, that is. Seven boys 'n five girls. Dad met
Ma around these parts some place 'n settled down at Reedsport. They got married there, I guess."

"Your mother came from round about these parts? From
these islands?"

"Ma came from a place called Huahine," Jack said. "She
was always telling me to get down to The Islands and I'd be
okay. I guess she didn't know."

"Let me get this straight," said Captain Petersen. "Your
mother was born at Huahine. She must have been Polynesian?"

"I'd say she was. She was always kinda dark, darker than
the other women in our street. Not nigger dark, of course.
Just kinda brown."

"Is she still alive?" asked the captain gently.

Jack shook his head. "Ma died last year. She was always

wanting to get back to The Islands, but she liked the television too, so she was pulled both ways."

Did you tell them you were half Polynesian when you got here yesterday? That your mother came from Huahine?"

Jack shook his great head. "I didn't think of it. Nobody ever asked."

"Have you got anything to show your mother was a Polynesian? Any birth certificate, or anything like that?"

"That's papers?" Captain Petersen nodded, and Jack shook his head. "I got my Navy discharge paper some place," he said vaguely. "Maybe I left it back home. But there wasn't anything about Ma on that." He hesitated. "I dunno that Dad and Ma were ever married, not in church, I mean. But they stuck together over forty years. That counts for something, don't it?"

"Sure," said Captain Petersen. He turned to the man beside him. "Look, Captain," he said. "They can't do a thing to you down here. You're half a Polynesian. The French run this colony for the Polynesians, not for the whites. They'll have to give you back your money. You won't come into court on Monday—they'll withdraw all the charges against you. They won't try and take your ship away from you. They won't expect you to have any papers for the ship. They'll forget about the passport. You rate down here as Polynesian, and this is your country."

"I'm a U.S. citizen," said Jack. "They won't take that away?"

The captain hesitated. "No. But don't talk about it, just at first. Let things get settled down." He paused. "I'll see the chef du port soon as we go on shore," he said. "He'll fix everything for you."

Jack was very pleased. He nudged Keith beside him, and said in a hoarse whisper, "Show him the little generator. Smallest in the world."

Keith nodded. "You tell him," he said.

Jack Donelly turned to the officer beside him. "Say, Captain," he said. "Mr. Keats got something down below we'd like you to see. Smallest motor in the world, it is."

"I'd certainly like to see it," said Captain Petersen politely. They got up from the rail and Jack led the way down below. The captain touched Keith on the arm before going down the ladder. "Would you be Mr. Keith Stewart?" he asked.

Keith smiled. "That's right," he said. "He always calls me Keats. He got it wrong first day."

"Nice guy?"

"One of the best."

"I'd say so, too." He paused. "I'd appreciate a bit of a talk with you later on, Mr. Stewart."

Keith glanced at him in surprise. "Of course."

They went down into the cabin after Jack Donelly. Captain Petersen took a quick glance around the stark bareness of the ship's interior. There was not even any varnish—just the bare wood, getting a bit dirty. There was a minimum of bulkheads and cupboards; the ship was little but an empty shell, devoid of any comforts. Yet she was efficient; the two forty-gallon barrels of water were properly chocked and stayed in place, and the very emptiness of her, the absence of tables, doors, and bulkheads, made it possible to get about inside her in a hurry. He knew fishing vessels, and he liked this one.

Jack lifted the little generator set reverently down from the fiddled shelf. "Take a look at this, Captain," he said. "Smallest generator set in the world. Mr. Keats here, he designed it all, 'n made every bit of it."

The captain of the *Flying Cloud* took it in his hands and examined it with interest and growing respect. He lived at Midlake, close outside Seattle. Here his small son had several model aeroplanes fitted with mass production compression ignition motors, and he had spent many hours contracting a sore finger twiddling the props to try and make them go. He was very familiar with small motors of that sort. This, which he now held cradled in his hand, was something totally different. It was a four-cycle motor, for a start, with tiny valves and valve springs and push rods, beautifully miniaturized, superbly made. The generator was, to him, a little wonder, with its delicately worked commutator and tiny brush gear.

"Does it go?" he asked in wonder.

"Sure it goes," said Jack. "Let's show him how it goes."

Keith filled the little tank with a drain of petrol, inverted the model to prime the carburettor, and flicked it into life with his thumb. The pea bulb lit, the note steadied as the governor came into action, and the model ran on steadily.

"Gee," said Captain Petersen quietly. "I never saw anything like it."

He sat watching the model, deep in thought. He was one of the few people on the West Coast of America who knew anything about Sol Hirzhorn's secret hobby. His wife's youngest sister was engaged to a boy called Pete Horner who worked in a minor capacity upon the maintenance of the Hirzhorn executive aircraft at the Seattle-Tacoma airport. Pete had actually worked upon the installation of the machine tools in the basement workshop of Sol Hirzhorn's home at Wauna, and he had made several visits to the house since then to service minor defects or to take in stocks of materials. He had been warned not to talk about these matters because Mr. Hirzhorn valued his privacy, but inevitably he had told his girl about these visits to the Hirzhorn home, and so they had become known in the family. Captain Petersen had heard that Sol Hirzhorn in his later years had taken to making small engines and clocks in the privacy of a fabulous workshop in his home. He had paid little attention to the rumour, but now it came back to his mind most forcibly.

He watched the little motor till it ran out of fuel and came to a standstill. "Say," he remarked, "isn't that just dandy? I never saw anything like it. Is that right, that you designed it all yourself, and made it?"

Keith nodded. "It's what I do," he said, a little apologetically. "I make things like this, and write about them in a magazine."

"In a magazine?"

He nodded. "The *Miniature Mechanic*. It's an English magazine." He reached over to the foot of the bunk and opened his suitcase, rummaged in it, and produced a couple of copies of the little magazine. "This is it," he said. He gave one copy to the captain, who examined it with interest, and leafed the other through himself. "This is the serial I've just finished now," he observed. "How to make a Congreve clock."

"A Congreve clock?" Captain Petersen was puzzled.

"It's a clock that keeps time by a steel ball running on a zigzag track down an inclined plane," Keith told him. "Only it doesn't keep very good time. It takes thirty seconds for the ball to run down one way—then the plane tilts and it runs back again. It's quite fascinating to watch. Look—there's a picture of it, here. That's the one I made."

Captain Petersen examined it with interest. "You make these things, and then write about them, telling other people how to do it?"

"That's right."

The captain glanced at the date of the issue; it was only six weeks old. "Does this come weekly?" he asked.

Keith nodded.

"Does it circulate in the United States?"

"I don't think you can buy it on the book stalls," Keith told him. "A good many copies, thousands, I believe, go to the States by post to subscribers."

The captain sat in thought. Two days before he had left home in Midlake to come upon this cruise, Yvonne had brought Pete Horner into supper. Sometime in the evening Pete had mentioned that Sol Hirzhorn had started to build some kind of a clock; there had been an order for planished brass sheet five-thirty-seconds thick that he had had to chase all round Seattle for, and take out to Wauna.

He raised his head and looked at Keith. "Say," he remarked, "would you by any chance know a man called Sol Hirzhorn?"

In the hot cabin of the *Mary Belle*, with the strong scent of vanilla all around them and copra beetles everywhere, Keith's mind went back to Ealing nearly ten thousand miles away, to the long hours spent after Katie had gone to bed, answering the correspondence in his "dirty" workshop in the basement, with Janice sleeping in the room next door converted from a scullery. "I've had some letters from a Solomon P. Hirzhorn," he said thoughtfully. "Lives somewhere in Washington. That's the capital, isn't it? Somewhere south of New York?"

"That's Washington, D.C.," the captain told him. "Sol Hirzhorn lives in the State of Washington, in the Northwest. I live there myself. Do you know anything about Sol Hirzhorn?"

Keith smiled. "He's got a secretary with an electric typewriter," he said. "I should imagine he dictates to her from the length of his letters. He's building one of my Congreve clocks following the serial, and he's not very experienced so he writes me a lot of letters, all of which need answering."

"You answer them?" the captain asked.

"Oh yes. If people can't understand the serial and take the trouble to write to me about it, I always send them an answer."

"You must have quite a correspondence," said the captain.

"I have," said Keith with feeling.

Captain Petersen sat in silence for a moment. "I see I'll have to start and tell you things," he said at last. "The first is this. Sol Hirzhorn might be one of the wealthiest men in the United States. I wouldn't know about that. What I do know is that he's the biggest noise around our parts."

Keith stared at him. "What does he do?"

"Lumber," said the captain. "He's the biggest lumberman on the West Coast. He started off from scratch, working in the woods like any other guy. I'd say he's close on seventy years old now, and his sons have taken over the executive side of the business. It's a family concern. God knows how many mills they have, or how many forests they control. I'd simply be guessing if I tried to tell you how many hands they employ in Washington and Oregon, but it's an awful lot. They're quite a family."

"The old man, Solomon P. Hirzhorn—he's the one that's making my clock?"

"That's right. He thinks an awful lot of you, Mr. Stewart. He got all het up about the risk that you were taking sailing from Honolulu to Tahiti in a fishing boat."

Keith's jaw dropped. "How on earth did he hear about me being here at all?"

The captain smiled. "I wouldn't know. He wants you to go visit with him for a day or so on your way back to England, 'n help him with his clock, I suppose. Anyway, he wants to meet you."

"I'd be very glad to meet him," said the engineer. "That clock's quite a tricky piece of work for somebody who's not very experienced. But how did he know I was here?"

The captain leaned forward. "See here, Mr. Stewart," he said. "Guys at the head of a big business with plenty of money and plenty of contacts all over the world, anything they want to get to know about they get to know. Now that's a fact. I don't know how Sol Hirzhorn got to know that you were here. But I do know this." He paused. "He's pretty well out of the business now. He only goes to the head office in Tacoma two or three times a week, they tell me. Other days he might fly out and visit one of the mills, or else fly in the helicopter to one of the clearings where they're cutting. He don't work much. Most of what work he does, he does at home. He's got his grand-daughter working for him as a secretary, a girl called Julie Perlberg. But I tell you, Mr. Stewart—there's not a cat kittens in the State of Washington but those two know about it."

Keith said weakly, "I never knew that he was anything like that. I thought he was the ordinary sort of man who makes models in the evenings—like a dentist or a bank manager."

Captain Petersen nodded. "I guess you did. You made yourself a good friend when you answered all his letters. He got real worried about you, coming down this way. Of course," he remarked, "he knows why you came. He knows all about your sister and the wreck of the *Shearwater*."

"For God's sake!" said Keith.

"There's one more thing I'll have to tell you," said Captain Petersen evenly, "and that's why I'm here. My boss is Chuck Ferris, of Ferris Hydraulics, Cincinnati. Mr. Hirzhorn got so worried about you that he borrowed the *Flying Cloud* from Mr. Ferris to put her at your disposal. My instructions on leaving Honolulu were to find you wherever you were, and put the ship under your orders to take you to your sister's grave on Marokota Island and anywhere else you want to go. After that, if you're going back to England, Mr. Hirzhorn suggested I might take you to Seattle in the *Flying Cloud* in order that you might visit with him for a day or two and help him with his clock." He paused. "I guess this is where I start to say *sir* when I speak to you, Mr. Stewart."

Keith stared at him, dazed. "But that's fantastic!"

"It may seem so to you. It did to me, at first," Captain Petersen admitted. "But I'd say the way to look at it is this. You took a lot of trouble answering letters from a stranger, and maybe some of them were rather stupid questions. I wouldn't know. The fact is that you made a friend, and now this friend's going to a little bit of trouble to help you. That's fair enough. Look at it that way."

Keith sat in silence for a minute. "Could you take me to Marokota?" he asked at last.

"Sure. Take us about four days to get there. Spend as long there as you like."

"Would I get a permit from the Governor to go to Marokota? I mean, after all this trouble?"

Captain Petersen said, "Forget it. We took the Governor to Bora-Bora one time. I've been to the Tuamotus six or seven times with the *Flying Cloud*. Romantic coral islands—that's what a party always wants to see. Lousy, dangerous places—I wouldn't want any part of them. You'll see more grass skirts in Honolulu than ever you'll see in the Tuamotus. But sure—we can go there."

"It wouldn't be any danger to the ship?"

The captain shook his head. "Not a bit. I'd take a pilot from here, somebody who knows the islands. There's no lagoon at Marokota that would take the *Flying Cloud*. We'd have to lie off under the lee, and send you in with the launch. But there's no difficulty about it."

"Is it inhabited?"

"Probably not. It's got a few palms on it—coconuts. I think they come over from Kautaiva in the copra season—gather the nuts. I don't think anybody lives there permanently."

"Do you think I could get a headstone for the grave made here, and take it with us?"

"Why, yes. There's a Chinese stonemason in the town, does that kind of work."

"Would that take long?"

"A day, maybe. Suppose we get on shore before so long, and give the order tonight, he'd have it finished by tomorrow night."

"How much would that cost?"

"I wouldn't know. You'd have to argue that one out with Mr. Ferris and Mr. Hirzhorn." He turned to Keith. "See here, Mr. Stewart, sir—I know the way you're fixed. Mr. Hirzhorn knows that, too. I got a radio from Mr. Ferris that all expenses, of whatever nature, go on the ship. I'll give you an account of what you might call personal expenses when you leave the ship, and you can settle it with them." He paused reflectively. "You might have quite a job."

They went up on deck and he hailed the launch. "I got a

cabin ready for you, Mr. Stewart," he said. "When will you be moving in?"

"I'll stay here tonight," said Keith. "I've got a lot of things to fix up with Jack. Would it be all right if I come on board tomorrow?"

"Sure," said the captain. "I'll be moving into the quay tomorrow; we'll need water, and top up with Diesel fuel. Come aboard any time you say."

The launch came alongside. He turned to Jack Donelly. "How would it be if we give you a pluck into the quay right now, Captain?"

"Suits me," said Jack. "Say, would there be any place where I could get a sack of cornmeal here? We've run out."

Captain Petersen thought for a minute. "Lim Hung Foo," he said. "He's your best chance. He's a marine store, nearly opposite your berth, but he sells everything. I think he might have it."

Half an hour later the *Mary Belle* was berthed again stern on to the quay with the chef du port smiling all over his face, and Keith was walking up with Captain Petersen to see the Chinese stonemason. He printed the simple inscription on the back of an envelope; the old stonemason took it and read it carefully, letter by letter. "Understand," he said, "parfaitement. Demain, le soir. Will be finished."

They walked back to the quay, and met Jack Donelly on the way to his ship carrying an enormous sack of cornmeal on his back as though it had been a feather. "Bit coarser'n the last sack," he said. "I like it that way. And not a maggot in it!"

"That'll be a change," said Keith.

"Good thing we saved some maggots from the last sack," Jack said practically. "Else we wouldn't have no bait. A bit of fish goes good with cornmeal fritters."

Keith arranged with Captain Petersen that he would move into the *Flying Cloud* when she berthed in the mooring; the captain got into his launch and went off to the schooner, and Keith went on board the *Mary Belle* with Jack. After depositing the sack of cornmeal in the forecastle, Jack came and stood in the hatch looking at the big yacht at the mooring buoy. "Captain Petersen, he didn't say nothing about that redhead coming ashore tonight, did he?"

Keith laughed. "No, he didn't. I don't even know if she's on board. She probably stayed in Honolulu."

"She's on board," said his captain positively. "I seen her."

Keith had expected him to have bought a bottle of whisky with the sack of cornmeal but he did not seem to have done so; alcohol was not his major weakness. To take his mind off other matters Keith went below and started up the little generator set, and with the noise of the engine Jack joined him at once, and sat looking at it entranced. "Smallest in the world," he breathed. "Captain Petersen, he liked it fine. But then, he's a seaman. He handled that schooner beautiful coming up to the buoy—just beautiful. I never seen it done better. Stands to reason that he knows a thing or two. He knows when something's worth looking at. Smallest in the world!"

Presently Keith said, "I'll be leaving you tomorrow, Jack. You heard what he said? I'll be moving into the *Flying Cloud* in the morning."

"Fine ship," said Jack. "You make him learn you how to sail her, like I learned you how to sail the *Mary Belle*."

"I'll be sorry to leave you," Keith said. "Where will you go now?"

"I guess I'll head for Huahine. Over to the west, ain't it? Shows on them charts of yours?"

"That's right. It's only about a hundred miles away, a little bit west of northwest on the compass." He paused. "I'll leave you the charts. They might come in handy."

"Say, thanks." The captain took them gingerly. "These things take a bit of understanding," he remarked. "Just show me where it says Huahine."

"There."

"Oh, I see." He pointed to the compass rose upon the chart. "Is that what tells you which way to go?"

"That's right. See, a little bit west of northwest." He traced the course with his finger.

"They don't put that on the atlas," Jack observed. "Wonderful the way they think of things, ain't it? Something new each year."

He rolled up the charts presently and put them away. "There's one more thing," said Keith. "I'll be moving out tomorrow. We'd better do some settling up."

"What's that?" asked Jack.

"You remember I was going to pay you a hundred dollars for the passage, when we talked about it in Honolulu? Well, then there was the cost of food."

"That's right," said his captain. "You bought all the chow except the cornmeal which was mostly maggots anyway, which didn't cost me nothing. That squares it off."

Keith said patiently, "The chow didn't cost a hundred dollars. Most of it came from the *Cathay Princess* at English wholesale prices. There's a good bit owing to you."

"Aw, forget it," said his captain. "You sailed the ship half the time. I didn't pay you no wages."

Keith stared at him helplessly; he knew better than to cross this man. "That's not right," he said. "We agreed I'd pay a hundred dollars for the passage. The food came to about forty dollars. There's about sixty dollars due to you."

"I got plenty to be going on with," said Jack. "I got forty, fifty dollars to get back out of that bank tomorrow."

"I'd like to pay you what we said," said Keith. "Honestly I would."

"Okay," said his captain amiably. "You pay me sixty dollars when the bank lets go of it. Then I pay you seaman's wage, sixty dollars a month and keep. You give it me if you can get it from that bank, 'n I give it back to you. Then we'll be all square."

His mind was made up and there was no use arguing with him; Keith had had this before. "I tell you one thing," he said presently. "I'll leave the little generator set here, in the *Mary Belle*."

Jack stared at him. "Leave that here, with me?"

"That's right. This ship hasn't got a motor. She ought to have one."

"Gee, Mr. Keats—I couldn't take that!"

"I won't want it, Jack. I'd like you to have it." He did not have much difficulty in persuading his captain to accept it. The big man held it reverently in his great hand. "Smallest in the world," he breathed. "Say, I wonder what they're going to think of this in Huahine!"

Keith glanced at the bottle, which was practically empty. "I'll get another bottle of petrol tomorrow sometime, and some lubricating oil, and a little oil can. Then you'll be all fixed up."

They slept presently, and in the morning Keith spent a couple of hours cleaning up the ship, which certainly needed it. Then he went up to the bank with Jack Donelly and, somewhat to his surprise, they were both repaid their dollars in full; he was not to know that Captain Petersen had been active in the city before him. In the bank he went through the ceremony of paying Jack Donelly sixty dollars for his passage and Jack counted it out carefully and paid it back to him as wages. They then went back to the *Mary Belle* and Keith picked up his suitcase.

"I'll be back on board this afternoon," he said. "I'll bring that bottle of petrol and the oil can."

He set off carrying his suitcase towards the *Flying Cloud*, now moored at the Grand Quai taking on water by a hose. A white-clad sailor from the yacht came hurrying to meet him, and took the suitcase from him.

He walked down the gangway onto the deck of the *Flying Cloud*, an incongruous figure perspiring in his rather inexpensive blue suit purchased in Ealing and suitable for the English climate. Captain Petersen came out of the wheelhouse and welcomed him aboard. "I'll show you your cabin," he said. "It's the one that Mr. Ferris uses normally, with a private bath. I think you'll find it comfortable."

In the luxury of the cabin Keith said diffidently, "I think I'll have to get something lighter to wear—tropical clothes of some kind. This suit's too hot altogether, and I can't go round this ship in a pair of bathing trunks, like I did with Jack Donelly."

"Lots of them do that," remarked Captain Petersen. "You'd be surprised. Middle-aged women, too, in not much more." He glanced at the blue suit. "That suit will be fine for Tacoma in the winter, and we'll probably be there before long. Clothes are a problem on this kind of trip." He opened the door of a big wardrobe. "Say, Mr. Ferris, he leaves quite a bit of stuff on board, and you're much the same build. I'd pull out some of these suits, see if they will fit you before buying anything. It's not worth it, just for a few days."

Keith glanced at the array of gleaming Dacron and silk tropical suits, the white neckties, the white shoes. "Are you sure that will be all right?" he asked.

The captain nodded. "Sure. I'll get everything washed and

cleaned before he comes again. He'd want you to have the use of the things, and there's no sense in buying anything."

He left Keith in the cabin. He had a very welcome shower, his first for a month, and dressed in the soft linen and the light hot-weather grey suit of a wealthy American. He went out a little self-consciously and up into the deck lounge, where he ran into the thirty year old red-headed woman that he knew as Mrs. Efstathios. She got up to welcome him.

"Say," she said, "you must be Mr. Keith Stewart. I've heard such a lot about you. My name's Dawn Ferris, and my pop owns this ship. He never uses it, but he just likes to have it around. Aren't those his clothes you're wearing?"

Keith was embarrassed. "I hope it's all right," he said. "Captain Petersen told me it would be."

She laughed. "Sure. Everyone that comes on board uses Pop's clothes. He's never here to use them himself. Say, I remember when you came aboard in Honolulu, only I didn't know who you were then. When did you arrive here?"

"We got in the day before you. The day before yesterday."

"You must have made a quick trip—we didn't waste any time. Mr. Hirzhorn, he got really worried about you going in that little boat, without any motor or anything. Say—that big ape who came on board with you—I forget his name. Is he here, too?"

"Jack Donelly? Oh yes, he's here. The *Mary Belle*'s moored further up the quay, that way. You can't mistake her; she's the only boat that's got tanned sails."

"Is that so? I got some shopping to do presently; I'll take a look and see. Captain Petersen was saying we'd be leaving in the morning for the Tuamotus."

Keith nodded. "I've got to go there to see about my sister's grave. I'd like to leave as soon as the headstone's finished. That's supposed to be tonight. Will you be coming with us?"

She said, "Well now, I don't know. I've seen the Tuamotus so many times, and it seems like this would be a kind of private party. The captain says he'll have to come back here anyway to bring the pilot back before leaving for Seattle. I was thinking maybe I'd move into the hotel for three or four days while you're away, and explore the island."

"I should think that would be very interesting," said Keith.

"It might be," she said doubtfully. "They all speak French here and I don't, which makes things kind of complicated."

They chatted together for a little in the deck saloon. Then she said, "Time I went on shore if I'm going. Say, if I'm not back on board for lunch, tell the captain not to wait. If I find a decent-looking restaurant that can understand what I'm saying, I'll eat there."

She picked up a broad-brimmed sun hat with a gaudy ribbon, and went off, and up the gangway to the quay. Keith went out on deck and started to explore the polished cleanness of the ship, an entrancing occupation. The boatswain found him and showed him the anchor winch forward and the winches at the foot of each mast. "All hydraulic from a central power generator in the engine room," he said proudly. "Used to be manual, except the anchor winch which was a great big electric cow of a thing. When Mr. Ferris bought the ship, first thing he did was rip all that lot out and send down his engineers from Cincinnati to make a proper job of her. She's all hydraulic now, steering and all. Ferris Hydraulics."

Keith was very interested indeed, and spent some time examining the winches and their reduction gears, which evoked his admiration for their clean and efficient design. From the deck the boatswain passed him on to the chief engineer, who took him down into the spotless engine room to show him the power generator, the main Diesel, and the stand-by Diesel. He spent an hour of sheer delight down there, and was finally discovered there by the steward telling him that lunch was ready. He had spent the morning with machinery so clean that he hardly had to wash his hands.

He sat down happily to lunch with Captain Petersen, and gave him the message from Mrs. Efstathios.

On shore Dawn Ferris wandered through the town, looked unintelligently at the big cathedral, wandered back to the waterfront and looked at the French frigate with the sailors with red pompoms on their naval caps, and wandered along the quay looking vaguely for a restaurant, past the rows of native fishing boats and yachts. Near the end of the row she came upon the *Mary Belle*, which she recognized by the tanned sails. Jack Donelly was sitting on the foredeck with his legs dangling over the side, fishing with a handline; a little pile of small, silvery fish lay on the deck beside him. He did not believe in buying food when there was food in the sea. He wore a pair of old blue jeans and nothing else; with his deeply bronzed torso he was a fine figure of a man.

Dawn stopped, and said, "Hullo, big boy!"

Jack looked up, replied, "Hullo," and went on fishing.

She asked, "What are you catching?"

He jerked a little fish out of the water and added it to the pile. "These."

"Are they good to eat?"

"I guess so. They look all right."

"Are you having them for dinner?"

The conversation was taking his mind off fish, but anyway he had enough. Enough, maybe, for two. "I guess so," he said. "Fish fried with cornmeal fritters are good chow."

She was suddenly weary of the sophisticated meals on board the *Flying Cloud,* and she had difficulty in understanding the French writing on the restaurant menus. "Cornmeal fritters!"

He raised his head. "Say, can you cook cornmeal fritters?"

"Can I cook cornmeal fritters! Try me and see."

He got to his feet, an amiable giant about six feet four in height in his bare feet, all bronzed. "Come on down, 'n let's see how you can do it. I'll fetch the sack aft into the cabin."

In the *Flying Cloud* Keith Stewart was enjoying his first civilized meal for a month, not altogether sorry to be relieved of the somewhat monotonous diet of the *Mary Belle.* Over lunch he told Captain Petersen that he had given the little generator set to Jack Donelly in lieu of passage money. "He's a nice kind of a guy," said the captain. "He may not know much navigation, but he seems to get from A to B without it. Did you help him much upon the way?"

Keith shook his head. "I learned how to take a noon sight for latitude. The officers of the *Cathay Princess* taught me. But the course was only a point or two east of south, and there was never much more than a hundred miles' difference between my sight and his dead reckoning. He'd have got here perfectly all right without my sights."

The captain laughed. "Takes us all down a peg or two. It's

wonderful the way they do it." He paused. "Make a good boatswain," he said thoughtfully. "I'd rather have him in the ship than some of the ones we get."

He sat smoking with the captain for a time, and then went on shore and bought a little oilcan at a hardware store with an empty bottle, and took them to a filling station to get filled with petrol and oil. With these in hand he walked along the quay to the *Mary Belle*. Jack Donelly was sitting in his blue jeans in the companion, looking at peace with the world, and very pleased with himself.

Keith went down the gangplank to the aft deck and stepped over the tiller. "I brought the gas and oil for the little motor," he said. He showed them to the captain.

"Gee, that's real nice," said Jack. "Right kind o' gas and right kind of oil?"

Keith nodded.

Jack was very pleased; everything in the world was rosy. "That'll keep her going a long time."

"I'll just take them down and put them on the shelf," said Keith. "Then you'll be all set."

Jack did not move his big frame from the companion. "Don't go down just yet," he said in a low tone, but distinctly. "Wait while she gets her dress on."

Keith stared at him in horror. "Wait while *who* gets her dress on?"

"The redhead," Jack informed him. "Some foreign name I forget. But she don't talk foreign." He added thoughtfully, "Or act foreign, either." He broke into a happy smile.

Keith thought only of escape from this situation. He thrust the bottle of gas and the oilcan into Jack Donelly's hands. "Here, take these," he said. "I'll come over and see you later."

"Okay," said Jack phlegmatically. "Be seeing you." Friends and women, he knew, never really mixed.

Keith fled up the gangplank and walked rapidly away up the quay towards the *Flying Cloud*. On deck he passed Captain Petersen and said something incoherent about going to lie down in his cabin, and went and hid himself below. His first instinct was to keep well out of sight and avoid a meeting with Dawn Ferris. Whatever her problem was, he didn't want to get mixed up in it.

He lay on his bunk petrified with terror waiting for the

storm to break till the steward tapped on the door and entered at about five o'clock. "Captain says he's sending up a boy with a handtruck to fetch the gravestone down," he said. "He wanted to know if you'd like to walk up with him, see the stone before it leaves the yard."

He ought to do that. Apparently the storm hadn't broken yet. "Tell the captain I'll be with him in a minute,' he said. "I'll just put on my shoes." As he sponged his face he thought of the gravestone and of Jo, his sister, and he thought of how she would have laughed, for her sense of humour had been broad. He was smiling, a little furtively, himself as he left the cabin to meet the captain up on deck.

As they strolled up the hill he asked casually, "Is Miss Ferris coming with us to Marokota?"

"Not this time," said Captain Petersen. "She's seen it all before. She packed two suitcases and moved into the hotel while you were resting. We'll pick her up when we come back here with the pilot, Thursday or Friday."

"She won't be on board for supper?"

"I don't think so. She said not to disturb you, but just tell you hullo, till Friday."

They walked into the stonemason's yard. The stone lay upon the bench all ready for delivery, a slab of purple-coloured slate engraved with the simple inscription that he had chosen. He passed his hand over it; when he had done this for Jo and seen it erected there was no more that he could do for her, except to look after Janice. He would see this stone set up above the grave and then he would go away; it was very unlikely that he would come back to see it again. Still, it was something to have got this far; when he had walked out of Mr. Carpenter's office in Bedford Square he had intended to try and make it but had never really thought he would succeed.

The captain was talking to the old Chinese stonemason who was drawing a little diagram for him upon the back of an envelope to show him how to set up a gravestone so that it would not fall over as the years went by. He arranged that the boy with the handtruck should bring a bag of cement down with the gravestone to the ship that evening, and he paid the stonemason in American dollars to his great content. Then they were walking down the hill again towards the quay in the soft tropical dusk, through the myriad evening smells of Papeete.

On deck the captain turned to him. "I never drink at sea, myself, or in harbor before sunset. But this is after sunset, sir." He smiled. "Would you join me in a highball?"

Keith wasn't quite sure what a highball was, but he appreciated the offer. "Have you got any beer?" he asked diffidently.

"Sure we've got beer. We've got pretty near every kind of liquor in this ship. We've got dark beer, and we've got a kind of lager beer." It was still hot in the harbour and Keith chose the lager; they sat down in the long canvas chairs on the aft deck and the steward brought them iced beer and rye on the rocks.

Presently Keith asked, "What time are we going off in the morning?"

"Any time you say," Captain Petersen replied. "Have you got any more to do on shore?"

"No. I'd like to get away as soon as possible." Before the Dawn Ferris storm blew up, he thought. He found it impossible to imagine what was going to happen to Jack Donelly, or himself. If he were to complete his mission to Marokota, however, the sooner he put a considerable distance between Dawn Ferris and himself, the better. "Sail tonight if you like," he said.

"I've got it all fixed for tomorrow morning first thing," said Captain Petersen. "Hands to breakfast at six, pilot on board at seven and get under way. Then we have breakfast about half-past eight, when we've got sail set and all clear." A sudden thought struck him. "Would you be likely to feel sick? We could have breakfast here any time you say, and get under way after."

"I shan't feel sick,' said Keith. "Not after a month in the *Mary Belle* with Jack Donelly. At least, I don't think so. No, that would suit me fine."

He spent that evening with the captain, dining with him quietly in the big saloon, sitting with him on deck in the vanilla-scented tropical night, watching the reflections on the water. He heard a good deal about Captain Petersen's family and home at Midlake, and the captain heard a good deal about Keith's home in Ealing, and about Katie, and about Janice, and about the wreck of *Shearwater*. Captain Petersen had already picked up local information about that in Papeete. "They had bad luck, Mr. Stewart," he said simply. "When that hurricane blew up they were in just the worst possible position they could be in, with no sea room for the change of wind." He sat in thought for a minute. "I believe in that position I'd have turned right around and headed back to the southeast with the engine at full power, and chance it turning south before it got to me. I think that might have been a better bet, but it's hard to say. But anyway, they'd only got a little motor, hadn't they?"

Keith nodded. "That's another thing," he said. "From what I hear, the motor was taken on shore from the wreck and covered up. It's probably worth something. If I could get it back to England I could work on it myself and recondition it. Do you think we could get it on board and take it with us to Seattle, and ship it home?"

Captain Petersen considered the matter. "We can't berth there to get it on board," he said. "We've got to lay offshore while you're on the island, and send the launch into the lagoon. It won't be much good now, you know. Not after being in the sea."

"I'm not so sure," said Keith. "Things like that often look a fearful mess with external damage and corrosion, but when you strip them down, they're not so bad. It's got wet liners to the cylinders, so they're replaceable quite easily in England. New pistons and liners, and a coat of paint. It might fetch a couple of hundred quid by the time I've done with it." He paused. "Enough to pay my passage back to England," he said smiling.

"Oh, sure." It was difficult to keep remembering that this intelligent little man who had travelled half across the world and who was thought of so highly by so many influential people, had practically no money at all. "How much do you think it would weigh?" he asked.

"Three or four hundred pounds. I shouldn't think it could be more."

The captain nodded. "I should think that's about it. We can do that, Mr. Stewart, if that's what you want. I'd beach the launch in the lagoon. Then we'd need six or eight hands ashore and some baulks of timber, get it in the launch and rig a wire strop around it." He thought for a minute. "Bring it off to the ship—that's easy. Then to get it on board from the launch to the ship in the open sea . . ." He thought deeply. "I'd make up special coir bolsters, four of them, pretty thick and about eight feet long, for the launch to ride against while we lift the motor on board with the launch derrick. That'll be okay. We can fix that for you, Mr. Stewart."

"There wouldn't be any risk of damage, would there?"

"Only paintwork, at the most." He thought again. "We can fix that when we come back into harbor here at Papeete before sailing for Seattle. Get some planks when we get back here, too, and knock up a packing case for it, so it'll be all ready to ship back to England from Seattle."

"That would be fine," said Keith. "I'd give it a bit of first aid before closing up the case. Wash it well out with fresh water, crankcase, cylinders, and all, and leave it to dry in the sun and the wind. Then pour a lot of oil into each cylinder and fill the crankcase up with oil. I don't think she'll have come to much harm."

"Maybe we're too apt to scrap things in the States," said Captain Petersen. "The engineers can lend a hand with that."

They sat in silence for a time. "There's just one other thing," said Keith. "Marokota is uninhabited at this time of year, isn't it?"

"So they tell me," said the captain. "There's no regular settlement upon it. The people come there every now and then to pick up the nuts, but they make the copra upon Kautaiva. They happened to be there when *Shearwater* got wrecked, but of course they couldn't do anything."

"I know . . ." He hesitated. "Would it be very difficult for me to spend twenty-four hours alone upon the island, after we've set up the gravestone?"

The captain turned his head. "There's no difficulty in that from my point of view, if that's what you want to do. We shall be standing off and on offshore. We can do that for a week if needs be. But there's nothing there, you know. I don't know even if there's any water."

"I could take that with me, with some sandwiches . . ." He turned to the captain. "I don't suppose I'll ever come back here again," he said simply. "I don't suppose that Janice —Jo's daughter, who's going to live with us—I don't suppose she'll ever come here. I want to take a lot of photos—an awful lot of photos, from all kinds of angles, and that'll all take time. I'd rather not be hurried by having other people about. I'd like to have your little rowing boat and go out to the wreck and take some photos of that. And—well, she was my only sister. I'd just like to be there alone for a bit."

"Sure," said Captain Petersen, a little huskily. "I'll get a pack made up for you—blankets. It could be cold at night. Beer, water, sandwiches. What we could do is, go in in the launch with the gravestone, towing the dinghy behind. Set up the gravestone and leave you with the dinghy, go back to the ship. Then come off again next day and load up the engine into the launch, and pick you up. How would that be?"

"That would be grand," said Keith. "I could make a good inspection of the engine in an hour or so and decide if it's worth taking back to England. If the engine room could let me have a few spanners it might help."

"Sure. You got plenty of film?"

Keith nodded. "I've got three new rolls, over a hundred exposures. I got them here today. I'll be all right for film."

He went to bed soon after that and slept soundly in Chuck Ferris's cabin, the first night that he had had in comfort for about a month. He wondered, as he went to sleep, about Dawn Ferris; no complaint had come from her, or if it had Captain Petersen had not told him. Perhaps the omnipotence of Sol Hirzhorn could protect him, even against that. In any case, apparently they were leaving in the morning. He must take things as they came. He slept.

He was roused by the bustle on the decks at dawn, had a shower and dressed in an open-necked shirt and slacks, and went up on deck. The steward found him and brought him coffee and biscuits, and he stayed on the aft deck out of the way of the seamen watching the processes of getting the ship to sea. It was all very different to the *Mary Belle*, a matter of ordered movement controlled by an occasional whistle from the boatswain. The pilot came on board, dark skinned and French speaking, and was welcomed by the captain. Then the main Diesel started below his feet with a rumble that steadied to an even purr. The springs were taken aboard, bow and stern lines singled up and brought back on board by a harbour boat. Captain Petersen moved into the wheelhouse, the stern lines were cast off, the engine room telegraph bell sounded, and the *Flying Cloud* moved forward from her berth into the main waters of the harbour. She turned and made for the entrance, hoisting the mainsail as she went, followed by the foresail and the mizzen, causing Keith to retreat into the deck saloon.

From Tahiti to the Tuamotus is a dead beat into the easterly trade wind at that time of year. Captain Petersen put his vessel under all plain sail and kept his engine going hard, taking in the mainsail for the hours of darkness. The distance to Marokota is about three hundred miles, and it took them four days of hard slogging against the wind, a restful and invigorating four days for Keith. He learned a good deal about the management of a large schooner yacht, and took the helm for several spells to the interest and amusement of the captain. He found that sailing the big schooner was not very different to the sailing of the *Mary Belle* once you had got accustomed to the wheel instead of tiller, and the size of her, and the speed.

They were approaching Marokota Island on the evening of the fourth day. Captain Petersen hove to at sunset, unwilling to venture in among the reefs in the hours of darkness, and they lay hove to all night with the engine stopped so that they could hear breakers but with an engineer on watch ready to start up if necessary. With the first light they got under way again, and by ten o'clock they were hove to under the lee of the island, on the west side of the encircling reef.

Captain Petersen stood at the door of the deckhouse staring at the reef through glasses. He lowered them and handed them to Keith. "That's the wreck," he said. "She went on from this side. Just past that grey coral, where you see those timbers sticking up. That must be *Shearwater*."

Keith stared at the timbers, washed by the sea. It seemed incredible that this should be all that remained of the yacht that he had been on board in the Hamble River, only six or seven months before. He lowered the glasses. "Would I be able to get near her from the other side?" he asked.

The captain lifted the glasses again. "I should think so, in the dinghy. It's on the lee side of the island so there's not much sea." He lowered the glasses. "It looks quite calm in the lagoon." He hesitated for a moment. "Like me to come with you in the dinghy?"

Keith shook his head "I'd rather be alone."

"Okay."

They rigged the launch derrick, put the coir bolsters over the lee side, and, steadying the big launch with guy ropes, watched their opportunity and put her in the water. They lowered the gravestone cased in a wooden frame into the launch with the sack of cement, a breaker of water, a pick, and a couple of shovels. Then they lowered down Keith's pack for the night, and dropped the ten-foot dinghy into the sea with a small davit. The captain got down into the launch with Keith, four seamen joined them, and the launch cast off and made for the narrow passage through the reef into the lagoon, towing the dinghy behind.

The chief engineer leaned upon the rail with the second, watching the boats as they went into the shore. "If he comes off with that engine in the morning we'll have to carry it on deck," he said. "Get Sammy to lash a tarp down on the deck, somewhere there." He jerked his head. "Don't want to get the deck messed up with oil and rust."

"Okay," said the second. "I'll see Sammy. Beats me what he wants with all those tools."

"Going to examine it," he said. "See if it's worth salving."

"With a hammer and cold chisel and a hacksaw?"

"Loosen off the nuts that got rusted up, or cut them off. That's what he said."

The second turned from the rail. "Shouldn't think the engine would be worth the salving, after treating it like that."

In the sunset Keith Stewart sat alone a little distance from the grave. He had done all that he had to do, and he had taken a good many photographs of the grave, the island, and the wreck out on the reef. He had turned the motor on its side, and he had taken off the sump, cleaned out the interior, and put it back again, replacing all the bolts and screwing them up tight. Darkness was approaching and he had finished all the major jobs. He sat eating his sandwiches upon the beach, and drinking his beer. In the morning he would take a few more photographs, and then he would be ready to return to England.

The gravestone stood erect behind him, set in a wide box of semi-liquid concrete, stayed upright with ropes to pegs driven into the coral sand. They would leave it so. The concrete would set into a solid mass when they had gone; the ropes would slacken off and rot away in time, but the stone would stay erect to mark the grave with its simple inscription to be read by any who should come to Marokota.

He finished his meal and sat looking out over the tropic sea in the fading light, a little sadly. That was the end of it. This was the end of something that had begun in a slum street of Renfrew near to Glasgow on the far side of the world, through the joys and tears of childhood, the Tiller Girls, John Dermott and the naval life, and Janice. Who could have thought that it would all end here, on an uninhabited island in the Pacific Ocean?

He got to his feet and moved over to the grave. He took the steel egg from his pocket, the grey, case-hardened egg that he had made for Janice back in Ealing, on the evening he had told her of her mother's death. "Jo," he said quietly "this is one of the eggs I made for Janice to go with the duck. It's the only thing I've got of hers to leave with you. And Jo—I'll do my best."

He scraped a little hole before the gravestone, and buried the egg in the sand.

10

THE *Flying Cloud* SAILED BACK into the harbour of Papeete three days later, having made the voyage downwind under sail alone. For much of the time Keith Stewart had been working on the engine secured on deck upon a tarpaulin, assisted by one or other of the engineers. They had removed the cylinder head and washed out the cylinders with fresh water and had hosed out the crankcase, Keith rejecting a proposal that they should take off the sump again as being quite unnecessary. They had dismantled the magneto in the engine room and discovered that all that it required was a new contact breaker; they had assembled everything again and filled the crankcase and the cylinders with oil. By the time they sailed into the harbour the engine was ready for crating for shipment to England.

They approached the harbour in the late afternoon.

In the wheelhouse Keith asked Captain Petersen, "How long will we be here?"

"You got anything you want to do?"

"No. The sooner I start home the better."

The captain nodded. "It's too late to go into the quay now —it'll be dark. If there's a buoy to spare I'll lie on that for the night. Go into the quay first thing in the morning. We'll want to top up with Diesel oil and water, and a few stores. Get some planks and timber for the packing case, put a little paint on the ship's topsides where the coir mats rubbed, pick up Miss Ferris, get a bill of health and clearance, and send a radiogram to Cincinnati. It ought not to take us longer than a day. I'd say that we'll be on our way day after tomorrow."

Keith nodded. "Say good-bye to Jack Donelly."

"Sure. See if you can find out where he's heading for, and if we can do anything."

They sailed into the harbour before sunset with the motor ticking over, and rounded up to a vacant buoy. When the bustle of mooring and stowing sail had subsided a little the captain came aft, to find Keith on the aft deck with the glasses in his hand. "Funny," he said. "I can't see the *Mary Belle* anywhere. She's not in the place where she was."

The captain scanned the shore line and the moored vessels, then took the glasses from him and searched with them. "She's not there," he said positively at last. "He must have sailed some place."

Keith was disappointed. "I didn't think he'd have done that. I wanted to thank him, and to say good-bye."

"Maybe he's gone out fishing, be back tomorrow," said the captain.

The men were putting the launch into the water with the derrick. "Guess I'll go ashore and take the pilot," said the captain. "See the chef du port and tell Miss Ferris that we're back. You like to come along?"

They went in in the launch and stepped out onto the concrete steps that led up to the Customhouse quay. Here they said good-bye to the pilot and shook hands with him; he went off up an alley in the dusk. There was a light on in the office of the chef du port and they went in. The chef was still there, and he got up to greet them.

"Well, we're back, monsieur," said Captain Petersen. He

offered cigarettes and lit them for the chef and Keith. "We're at the buoy right now, but tomorrow I'd like to move into the quay."

"Certainement," said the chef. "Tomorrow at what hour?"

"Eight o'clock?" The chef made a note upon his pad, and they went on to discuss the refuelling of the *Flying Cloud* and her clearance for Seattle.

A quarter of an hour later, business concluded, the captain asked casually, "What's happened to the *Mary Belle?*"

"She has depart," the chef said. "Sailed."

"Sailed? Where for?"

The chef shrugged his shoulders. "Who can say? Native boats, they do not need clearance. They come, they go. Some say Huahine, but that I do not know. In the Isles sous le Vent—anywhere. Raiatea, Tahaa, Bora-Bora—anywhere. Perhaps even to Samoa in the end. That one, he makes long voyages."

They stared at him. "I didn't think he'd have gone off like that before we got back," said the captain.

The chef shrugged his shoulders. Then he glanced at Captain Petersen, a glint of humour in his eye. "We have many years been friends," he said, "and we have laughed together. I hope you will laugh now." He hesitated. "He took a passenger."

A terrible thought occurred to Captain Petersen. "Who was that?"

"A lady from your ship, Mlle. Ferris, avec la tête châtaine."

The captain stared at him aghast. "For the Lord's sake!" he said quietly. "Well, what do you know?"

"The more I see of women the less I know," replied the chef du port. "At my age it is better to stick to wine."

"When did they sail?" asked the captain.

"Two days after you," replied the chef. "One night only she stayed at the hotel. Then she moved into the boat. They bought many choses de cuisine. Then they sailed the next day."

"Over to the west? On a westward course?"

"That is true."

They stood in silence for a minute. Then the captain turned to Keith. "I guess this is just a bit outside my province," he said. "I'll have to put this to Chuck Ferris in a radiogram, where do we go from here." He stood conning the words over. "It's going to be a mighty long one, too."

They left the chef du port and went up to the hotel, hoping to find that Dawn Ferris had left a suitcase there, indicating an early return. The captain went in to enquire at the desk, and came out in a minute or two. "No suitcase, and no note," he said shortly. "Too bad."

He led the way to the Bureau des Postes et Telegraphes. The office was closed, but there was a light inside and he hammered on the door. A half-caste clerk came at last and told him that the office was closed. A mille changed hands and opened it, and the captain stood in worried thought writing three pages of a radiogram to his employer. He made a copy, paid the charge, and went out into the dark, vanilla-scented street with Keith. "I don't know what we do now," he said, worried.

"Go back on board, sit down, and have a drink," said Keith.

"I guess that makes sense."

They walked back in silence to the steps, hailed the motor launch, and went off to the schooner in her. On the aft deck the captain rang for the steward, ordered the evening drinks, and they sat down in the long chairs in the warmth of the tropic night, looking at the lights reflected in the dark waters of the harbour.

At last the captain broke the silence. "If I'd thought a million years," he said, "I'd never have thought of this one."

"I would," said Keith. "Knowing Jack Donelly."

"I guess you know him better than I do."

They drank. Then Keith asked, "Has she ever done this sort of thing before?"

"I wouldn't know—well—yes. I'd say she must have done. She's been married three times. There must have been—incidents."

"What did her husbands do?"

"I think the first one was a college boy in Cincinnati. He went into real estate. The second was a rancher somewhere near Helena, Montana. That lasted quite a while—she had two children, but I guess the country got her down. Then there was Efstathios, but that didn't last long."

"What did he do?"

"Oriental rugs and carpets in New York City. They called him Count Efstathios, but I don't think he was a count at all."

"Nice chap?"

"Small guy with black hair and a little black mustache," said Captain Petersen non-committally. "Good dancer, I should say. He wore brown patent leather shoes. I never saw shoes like that before." He paused. "They didn't go with the ship," he said.

Keith laughed. "And now it's Jack Donelly. Well, he'd go with the ship."

"Berthing with the seamen," said the captain. "But—I don't know. The rancher, Gort or Grant, some name like that, he was a great big guy and pretty dumb. Maybe that's the way she likes them, after all."

They sat in silence for a time. "What worries me," the captain said at last, "is, where do we go from here? My last orders were to sail for Seattle, taking you along to meet Mr. Hirzhorn. Well, that's right the opposite way to Hauhine and Bora-Bora, and there's hundreds of islands down that way, all the way through Samoa and Tonga to Fiji and New Caledonia." He paused and took a drink. "If I'm supposed to go and look for her," he said, "it could take the best part of a year. And what about you?"

"Don't worry about me," said Keith. "I could get back from here some other way."

"I do worry about you," said the captain practically. "I've got a home at Midlake just outside Seattle, and I want to see my wife and kids. I'm not losing any sleep over Dawn." He paused, reflectively. "I bet she is."

There wasn't much that they could do about it except to await an answer to the captain's radiogram. They sat in the warm darkness drinking rather more than usual in their perplexity, and then went down to dinner. They came up on deck again later and sat in the long chairs on the aft deck smoking Chuck Ferris's cigars till it was time for bed. Keith went down and slept well, a little amused, but Captain Petersen spent a bad night.

They moved into the quay next morning and began to take on Diesel oil and water. In the middle of the morning a radiogram arrived in answer from Mr. Ferris. It was refreshingly direct:

King size deal pending with Sol Hirzhorn so sail immediately for Seattle bringing Stewart along stop keep contact with Rockawin and be sure advise him date arrival time and berth stop you weren't hired to monitor Dawns lovelife but appreciate your concern leave her settle it her own way stop am arranging credit for her with the Bank of Indo-China Papeete suggest you tell harbormaster ask him to inform her as opportunity occurs.

Ferris

The captain showed this telegram to Keith, who read it with interest. "Well, that's the way it is," he said. "We kiss Dawn good-bye, and she goes sailing out into the far blue yonder with Jack Donelly." He stood for a minute in thought. "I guess I'll go on shore and take the chef to lunch, 'n show him this," he said. "It's time Chuck Ferris gave a bit more to the Orphelins, anyway."

Keith asked, "What's this about the king-sized deal with Sol Hirzhorn? Am I in on that?"

"I wouldn't know," said Captain Petersen. "Maybe I ought not to have shown you that." He paused. "One thing," he said. "Sol Hirzhorn's getting an old man, but he still owns the business. It's quite clear that he thinks a lot of you—as an engineer. My boss—Chuck Ferris—he sells engineering. Maybe Sol Hirzhorn's looking to you for a fresh mind on his problem—whatever that is. Maybe Chuck Ferris knows it. I wouldn't know. It's just an idea I got."

"I see," said Keith thoughtfully.

"Anyway," said the captain briskly, "we sail for Seattle in the morning."

"How long will that take?"

"About three weeks. It's quite a ways from here."

"Will we be going into Honolulu?"

The captain shook his head. "I'll have to do some figuring this afternoon, but I can tell you right now what the answer will be. North from here until we're clear of the Tuamotus at Mataiva. Then make all the easterly we can while we're in the southeast trades. Cross the line about Longitude 145, maybe. Then a thousand or twelve hundred miles of beating up against the northeast trades, tracking due north—if we're lucky. After that, gales and fog and rain and radio bearings to Cape Flattery—all kinds of rough stuff. Then home, and a few days skiing on the spring snow. Just lead me to it!"

He went on shore to lunch with the chef du port alone and to get the necessary clearances. Keith lunched alone in the saloon and strolled along the quays. He bought a tinted coral necklace for Janice and a bracelet of polished beans and shells for Katie, souvenirs of his travels that did not cost too much because he still had no idea how he was to get back to Ealing from Seattle. The one thing that seemed clear to him was that he hadn't got enough money for the fare, however he might travel. Still, he was getting a good lift on the homeward track by going in the *Flying Cloud* to Seattle. He was not very worried now about the homeward journey; one way or another he would make it.

Twenty days later the *Flying Cloud* entered the Juan de Fuca strait in a rainstorm at about ten o'clock in the morning, running into relatively sheltered water before a strong westerly wind. They drove in with the mizzen furled, the mainsail close reefed, and the fore topsails doing most of the work, an engineer on watch beside the motionless Diesel. They passed, by radio bearings, about four miles north of Cape Flattery and never saw it, and carried on down the strait all day, gradually coming into calmer water. On deck they carried the engine from *Shearwater* in a packing case constructed in the first days of the voyage, one side secured by screws for the benefit of Customs, lashed down on deck beneath two thicknesses of tarpaulin.

In the early afternoon they passed Port Townsend and entered the calm waters of Puget Sound. The rain stopped and the clouds lifted to a thin, watery sunset light as they ran down past Edmonds, heading south under mainsail and jibs, the topsails furled. With the last of the light they approached Seattle, furled the main and started the Diesel, and finally dropped anchor in the quarantine section of Elliott Bay just north of Duwamish Head.

The captain came out of the wheelhouse as the chain rattled out. "We'll be staying here all night," he said. "It's a bit late now. Harbormaster, port health officer, and Customs—they'll be off about eight in the morning. I reckon we'll have breakfast at half past seven. Then after that we move into a berth."

"What about this chap Jim Rockawin?" asked Keith. "We had to let him know."

"That's so. I sent him a radiogram four days ago via San Francisco. I've got a shore connection now on VHF. I guess that this might be as good a time as any, try and get him at his home."

Ten minutes later he was speaking to Jim Rockawin, who in turn rang Julie at the Hirzhorn home near Wauna. "Oh, fine," she said. "I'll tell Mr. Hirzhorn. He's down in the workshop right now. Can I fix everything, or would you like it if I put you through?"

"I don't want to disturb him unless you think he'd like to speak to me."

"I don't think there's anything that we can't fix between us, Mr. Rockawin. Mr. Hirzhorn has been looking forward to Mr. Stewart visiting with him for a few days, and he'd like you to bring him right out here, with his suitcases, as soon as you can get him off the yacht. He's kept the next four days free of all appointments. He thought perhaps Mr. Stewart might care to take a look around some of the plants with him."

Jim Rockawin was deeply impressed. He knew that Sol Hirzhorn thought a lot of this British engineer; he had not realized that his regard went so far as to allocate four days of his time to him. The thought flashed through his mind that, inevitably, in that four days they would discuss the Flume River mill, and the proposal to convert it to Ferris hydraulics. Keith Stewart was important to Chuck Ferris, and Chuck ought to know about it.

He said, "It would probably be midday before I get him off the yacht, past Customs and all the rest of it. Suppose I give him lunch in the city and bring him out to Wauna in the afternoon?"

She said evenly and directly, "Mr. Hirzhorn doesn't like secret hand-outs, Mr. Rockawin. What's more, he always gets to hear about them in good time, or else I do."

"Say," he expostulated weakly, "we wouldn't think of anything like that."

"That's fine," she said. "I'll expect you in the middle of the afternoon, and we'll get the room made up. Mr. Hirzhorn will be very pleased when I tell him. He's very grateful, very grateful indeed, to Mr. Ferris for lending his yacht. Don't go and spoil it."

"I won't," he said thoughtfully. "The job's good enough to stand on its own feet."

"I'm sure it is," she said. " 'Bye now."

Jim Rockawin put down the telephone and sat in thought for a few minutes. His first reaction had been that if Sol Hirzhorn was going to take this British engineer all round his plants and talk to him about the Flume River mill, they should get hold of him at once. He should call Chuck immediately. Chuck would probably drop everything and fly out to Seattle to meet Keith Stewart at lunch tomorrow; Chuck could be pretty impetuous at times. Now, after talking with Julie, he was not so sure that that would be a very good idea. He had a notion that nothing he or Chuck might say to Keith before he got to Wauna would remain long unknown to Julie or Sol Hirzhorn; in Seattle they were playing on their own home ground. Better, perhaps, to take the matter straight, and leave Chuck out of it.

He did not call his boss.

He was on the quayside when the *Flying Cloud* berthed at about ten o'clock next morning. He knew Captain Petersen well, and greeted him cheerfully as he went up the gangway. "Hi, Joe," he said. "How's everything?"

"Good and bad," said Captain Petersen. "Jim, this is Mr. Stewart."

"Glad to know you, Mr. Stewart." They shook hands. He turned again to the captain. "What's bad, Joe?"

"Dawn," said Captain Petersen. "You know she skipped it?"

"I did hear something," Mr. Rockawin admitted. "Got another guy?"

"And how. Is Chuck mad with me?"

"I don't think so."

"He will be when he hears the whole of it," said the captain apprehensively.

"He knows most of it already," said the engineer. "He did get a bit upset after he got your radio, so he called Sol Hirzhorn and told him all about it. They're pretty thick, just now. Sol put Julie on to find out what she could about this Jack Donelly. She got a line on him from the manager of the forest down on Taylor Butte, and then she called a guy they've got called Paul Setches out in Honolulu to get a line on him from there. I'd say Chuck knows most of it now." He smiled. "The worst that Julie managed to find out was that he got in prison once for three months for rape, and she reckoned that was a put-up job."

"That's one I didn't know about," said the captain. "Three months isn't much for rape."

"It wasn't much of a rape, according to Julie," said Mr. Rockavin. "She says the girl's been giving her mother hell ever since."

Captain Petersen was immensely relieved. "Well—gee, I'm thankful that I haven't got to tell Chuck much."

"He's not worrying. She's left three husbands and she'll leave this one if she wants to. But—you never know. This one might stick."

He turned to Keith Stewart. "Say, Mr. Stewart," he said, "Sol Hirzhorn's looking forward to you staying with him a few days before you go back to England. He wants to talk to you about a clock he's making, and he wants to take you around and show you something of the Hirzhorn enterprise. Is that okay with you?"

"Of course," said Keith. "I'd like to meet him. I had some letters from him back in England."

"Well, that's fine. If you can get packed up I've got my car right here. What I thought we could do is drive around a bit so you can see Seattle, and then have lunch, and then drive out to Wauna in the afternoon. That's around fifty miles, to where Sol Hirzhorn lives."

"That sounds fine," said Keith. "There's just one thing. This case has the engine from my sister's yacht in it, that got wrecked in the Tuamotus. I want to get it shipped back to England."

"Perkins and Durant," said Mr. Rockawin. "They'd be the best shipping agents to handle that. It's passed Customs inwards?"

"That's right," said Captain Petersen. "We took the top of the case off for them this morning. There's their mark."

"Oh well, then, it won't have to go in bond. I'll get a truck along and take it to their warehouse. Leave it to me. I'll bring you out the documents to sign."

The steward brought Keith's suitcase up on deck. Keith turned to Captain Petersen. "I don't know if I'll be coming on board again," he said, "but I suppose I shan't. I'd like to say, thank you, for all you've done for me."

The captain said, "It's been a real pleasure having you aboard, Mr. Stewart, and having your company. And say, that trip down to Tahiti was a pleasure too, not to mention ending up back here at home. I'd have cut my throat if I'd been stuck in Honolulu for much longer, acting as a houseboat while Dawn made eyes at Manuel." They shook hands. "I'll be seeing you one day."

Keith went down the gangway with Jim Rockawin to the car, the steward following with the suitcase. "I guess we'll go up through the city first of all so you can see the sort of town it is, up by Lake Union, across the canal, take a look around the university, then back down Lake Washington. Then back by Boeing Field and have lunch in the city." He paused. "Say, if you could get Sol Hirzhorn to spare you for a day, I'd like to take you into Boeing. There's stuff there classified you couldn't see, of course, but there's plenty that you could. And there are engineers in Boeing know about your writing in the magazine. They'd be real glad to show you around."

They drove round for an hour and a half, and finished up in the grill room of the Olympic Hotel for lunch. Keith was a little daunted by the magnificence of the hotel and completely overawed by the prices on the menu, far from his Ealing way of life. He was equally astounded by the size of the spareribs when they were placed before him; it seemed impossible that he should eat all that, as indeed it was. Towards the end of his meal, he said to Mr. Rockawin, "Tell me, Mr. Rockawin—"

"Jim," the other interrupted smiling. "We get pretty quickly here to where it seems kind of formal, even rude, if you keep on using the surname. That's unless there's a good big difference in rank. I don't suppose I'll ever get around to calling Mr. Hirzhorn Sol."

"All right, Jim," said Keith. "Tell me—what does Mr. Ferris do?"

The representative brushed the ash off his cigarette, which gave him a moment for thought. "Hydraulic engineering," he replied. "Ferris Hydraulics, Inc., of Cincinnati. Ever heard of them?"

Keith nodded. "Is that the same Ferris?"

"There's only one Chuck Ferris," said his representative. "He's my boss."

Keith searched his memory. "Aviation mostly—and motor cars?"

"Well, that's the way it used to be," said Mr. Rockawin. "Automotive products are up each year, both in the United States and on the Continent of Europe from our Laeken plant, in Belgium. But aviation products are declining— they're way down from what they used to be. That's general in the industry, on account of airplanes flying higher. But we get by."

Keith thought for a minute. "I'd like you to know that I'm very grateful to Mr. Hirzhorn and to Mr. Ferris for sending the *Flying Cloud* down to Tahiti," he said. "It was a tremendous help. We were really in trouble—quite bad trouble— when Captain Petersen turned up. I don't think I'd ever have got out to see my sister's grave or to set up a stone without his help. It meant a lot to me."

"Well, that's real nice to know," said Mr. Rockawin. "Mr. Hirzhorn, he'd be glad to know that, if you tell him." He paused. "I think when people get older," he said, "they kind of get more mellow. They kind of like to give help in return for help they get. And Sol Hirzhorn, he's mighty interested in that clock."

Keith nodded. "It was very good of Mr. Ferris, too, to lend his yacht."

"Oh, sure," said Mr. Rockawin. "But Chuck's not building a clock. He lent the *Flying Cloud* just in the way of business. It's Sol Hirzhorn that you want to thank."

"Captain Petersen showed me a telegram he'd had from Mr. Ferris," Keith remarked. "It was in Papeete, when we were so worried about Dawn. It was all about Dawn. But Mr. Ferris did say one thing. He wanted the *Flying Cloud* to come straight back to Seattle with me on board, because he said he had what he called a king-sized deal pending with Sol Hirzhorn."

"He said that, did he?" Mr. Rockawin sat in thought for a moment, wondering if it was wise to take a line so very different to that which his employer would have taken. "Well, that's true enough, Mr. Stewart," he said at last. "There *is* a contract pending between Mr. Ferris and Sol Hirzhorn. You know that already." He paused again.

"Whether you come into it or not, I wouldn't know. In any case, I'm not going to tell you a thing about it. You'll be staying with Sol Hirzhorn for the next few days. If he likes to tell you about it, well, it's his business and that's okay with me. But I'm not telling you about Sol Hirzhorn's business from this end." He smiled. "Julie would know all about it by the time we get to Wauna."

Keith asked, "Who is this Julie? Captain Petersen said something about her once."

"Julie Perlberg," said Mr. Rockawin. "She's a Jewish girl I think—quite young. Twenty-five, maybe. She's the old man's private secretary, sharp as a needle." He paused. "I've heard it said that there was some kind of tragedy, I don't know. In any case, that's only rumor. If true, she'd be his granddaughter." He paused. "She lives at Wauna in the house with him—his wife's away in Florida most winters, so she runs the house servants. She goes to conferences with him, taking shorthand notes. You might say she's his eyes and ears right now." He laughed, "And say, they're mighty sharp eyes and mighty long ears."

Keith smiled with him. "Long enough to hear what's going on in here?"

"She's quite capable of having someone put a mike into that bowl of flowers," said Mr. Rockawin. "Although I don't really think she works that way. She'd know by just looking at us if we'd talked about the deal." He paused. "She's sharp, like all her family."

"We'd better not talk about it, then," said Keith.

"I'm not going to," said Mr. Rockawin. "I told you that."

He paid the check and they went out of the hotel to the car at the parking meter where the policeman was just making out a ticket for staying too long. Rockawin talked him out of it by introducing Keith Stewart as an English visitor, which so intrigued the policeman who had been in England in the war that he forgot about the ticket. They got on the road for Tacoma and on southwards down the fringes of Puget Sound. It was the first time that Keith had been in the United States and he was amazed by the high standard of living, at any rate in visible, material things. The size and beauty of the motor cars, the number of them, the size and quality of the roads, and the enormous number of great

four-wheeled trailer caravans; these things impressed him
very much indeed.

They drove through the industrial city of Tacoma at
the head of Puget Sound and over the toll bridge across the
Narrows out into the country again. Presently they left the
road and turned into an inconspicuous lane or drive marked
only by stone pillars by the roadside, and went on winding up
the hill through a forest of fir trees. After half a mile they
came out on to an open hillside, a place of grass and granite
outcrops with a little snow upon the ground, and with a
magnificent view over to the snow-covered Olympic Mountains to the west. There stood the house, a long, low stone
building, two stories in the front and single storied at the
back by the slope of the hillside, a house very much larger
than appeared at the first glance. Below it lay an inlet of the
sound with boathouses and a moored motor yacht, and by
the water's edge there was a long airstrip with a hangar by
the road that led down to it.

Jim Rockawin drove up to the front door behind the house
and parked the car. A manservant in a green baize apron
came out and took the suitcase, and they went towards the
house. A stout, elderly man came forward to meet them.
"Mr. Stewart, isn't it?" he said. "This is a real pleasure.
We've exchanged letters, but we've never met before. Say,
take off your coat and come right in." He paused. "I'm Sol
Hirzhorn."

They went into the huge living room with the great picture
window looking out over the Olympics. "Mr. Stewart, would
you like a cup of tea?" he asked. "I know you Englishmen
drink tea in the afternoon."

Keith said, "Don't bother about that for me, Mr.
Hirzhorn. I've been away from England long enough to get
out of English ways."

"We often have a cup of tea around this time," said Mr.
Hirzhorn. "It's getting so it's quite a habit in the office." He
raised his voice. "Say, Julie!" She came into the room. "Mr.
Stewart, I'd like you to meet Julie Perlberg. She does all my
letters to you. Julie, this is Mr. Stewart. Say, would you tell
Jake to get us English tea, with cookies or sump'n?"

"I'm glad to know you, Mr. Stewart," she said quietly. "I'll
see about that right away, Mr. Hirzhorn."

Keith walked over to the big window. "What a wonderful view," he said. "I've never seen anything like it."

"I built the house for it," said Mr. Hirzhorn simply. "I saw it first when I was quite a young chap and I used to go all over for the cutting. Lumber—that's my business—you know that." Keith nodded. "Nineteen twenty-two— or twenty-three, would it have been? I can't just remember. I'd have been thirty years old or so about that time, and married about five years. I thought then that I'd like to have a summer camp up on this hill. Well, then that wasn't hardly practical with a young family and not much time to spare, but I never forgot about it. I got to realize that it would take a lot of money to live here and work at the same time. But anyway, I couldn't get it out of my head, and in 1936 things got so I could buy the land as an investment, so I'd got it, anyway."

"How much land is there, Mr. Hirzhorn?" Jim Rockawin asked.

"Twelve hundred acres. A little more, I think—twelve hundred and thirty-six, far as I remember. Sarah said it was a silly thing to do because we'd never live there—it would cost a fortune." He laughed. "Well, then the fortune came, 'n I never wanted to travel or go horse-racing or anything—just build the house and live in it, 'n go on working. And that's just what I did."

Julie came into the room behind them. "Tea will be here in a minute," she said softly. She went through into her own room, leaving the men talking.

She closed the door, and went to a tall cabinet of steel drawers. She selected a file marked *Stewart* and took it to her desk, and opened it again to refresh her memory.

One of her jobs was to protect her employer, who was also her grandfather. She never sought to influence his judgement; she worked rather to get him the maximum of information with the least effort on his part. They had few contacts in England, but she had quickly discovered that there was an agency in London which specialized in finding out particulars of individuals in connection with hire-purchase credit. The first document that they had sent her read:

Keith Malcolm Stewart. Born, Renfrew, Scotland, 1915. Lives now at 56 Somerset Road Ealing Middlesex, a four storey ten roomed house which is his property.

The house was purchased for £3,200 in 1943 by Mr. Stewart and subdivided. The top two floors are let at a rental of £2.15.0 per week. There is a mortgage of £2,200 on the property at 5½%. Mr. Stewart is married and has no children of his own but has one daughter apparently adopted recently.

Mr. Stewart worked as a fitter in the aircraft industry till 1946. He then became a free-lance technical journalist working principally for a magazine called the *Miniature Mechanic*. His income is estimated at about £700 per annum. His wife works whole time as a shop assistant in Ealing. With the rental of the leased portion of the house, the family income appears to be about £1,100 per annum.

Mr. Stewart does not bet or drink to excess. He does not own a car. He appears to live within his means, and has a good reputation in the neighbourhood.

This report reached Julie while Keith was on his way from Honolulu to Tahiti with Jack Donelly, and she was amazed. First she was surprised by the invoice sent with the report which was for twenty-five shillings, only about three and a half dollars. Secondly, she was staggered by the smallness of the income, only about three thousand dollars from all sources including the wife's earnings. And then, to go and adopt a child, upon an income like that!

She had taken the report at once to show to Mr. Hirzhorn. He had read it with interest. "A guy with his ability, he could earn a better wage than that," he remarked presently, "even in England. I guess it's just he kind of likes his work, better than making money. There's nothing wrong with that." He handed back the report to Julie. "You know sump'n? I'd like to see some photographs. Photographs of the wife, of the adopted kid, of the house, of the street, of the garden of the house so I can see if he keeps it clean or not. Photographs of anything that you can get."

"Okay, Mr. Hirzhorn," said Julie. "We'll have to have them here within two weeks or so. They should be able to do that. I'll write today." She paused in thought. "I'll say we want it in a hurry. I think I might put three ten-dollar bills in with the letter. Kind of help things along."

Four days later a pavement photographer took a picture of

Katie in Ealing Broadway as she went into the shop, in spite of her smiling denials. Janice got photographed by a strange man on her way home from school to her surprise, and the house and street were taken from all angles, including the back garden. A week after that a sheaf of photographs arrived on Julie's desk at Wauna in the State of Washington. By the time Keith Stewart got there his hosts knew quite a lot about him.

She put the file back into the steel cabinet and locked it up. The little man looked like what the file and photographs had told her added to what she had gleaned from sundry issues of the *Miniature Mechanic*; an honest little man of lower-middle-class suburban type, content to go along upon a miserable salary for the sake of doing the work he loved, with a wife who was prepared to work in order that he should maintain that way of life. There was no deceit about this man.

That was important, for she had little confidence in Chuck Ferris. He was too anxious to sell his hydraulics, to get into the lumber industry. Jim Rockawin was better, but not much. One million, and seven hundred thousand dollars for the conversion of the Flume River mill was quite a contract, in anybody's language. She knew that production at the Cincinnati factory was declining on account of the reduction in aviation contracts; she knew that they laid off a thousand hands last month. Ferris Hydraulics had indulged in too much salesmanship, and made Julie suspicious. This lending of the yacht ... A million, seven hundred thousand dollars was a lot of money.

She had not mentioned her misgivings to her grandfather. Her business was to take his orders, take the load off him where she could, and get him information. She knew, however, that the same misgivings had occurred to him; there had been too much salesmanship. Chuck Ferris would have done better to have charged a charter fee for the *Flying Cloud*. His refusal to do so had undoubtedly held up the contract for the Flume River mill; the old man smelt a rat. He had delayed a decision till a fresh mind was brought to bear upon the problems of the mill, for fresh advice. He had been waiting for Keith Stewart, to see if this insignificant little engineer from England could say anything useful.

She got up from her desk. She had decided in her own

mind that he was honest; that was where she stopped. Whether he was competent was a matter for her grandfather to decide.

She went out into the living room. The men seemed to have finished drinking tea, and Jim Rockawin was getting up to go. She went through to tell the houseman to clear away the tea, and came back to the hall in time to bid Jim Rockawin good-bye. She went on into the living room to pull the curtains over the great picture window and to light the lamps, for dusk was falling now.

Sol Hirzhorn came back into the room with Keith. "Like to have a look at what I'm doing with your clock, downstairs?" he asked.

"I'd like to very much, Mr. Hirzhorn," he said. They moved towards the door.

Julie said quietly, "Drinks will be on the table here at seven o'clock, Mr. Stewart, and dinner is at seven-thirty. Mr. Hirzhorn usually goes to bed at nine."

"You see how she keeps me on a string," said the old man.

"That's what I'm here for," she said equably. She smiled. "I generally go down to the workshop about ten minutes of seven, and chase him out. Otherwise he'd be there all night."

The two men went down to the workshop in the basement. It was a long room, more than forty feet long, but only eight or nine feet wide. There was a long workbench for the full length of it lit by windows in the outer wall, and these windows looked down the hill over the sea inlet and the airstrip. The back wall was of light construction, separating the workshop from the heating plant and from the laundry of the house.

In this long shop was every machine and hand tool that a modeller in metal could desire, from lathes and a milling machine to oxyacetylene welding and soldering irons. Keith stood and took it all in with a practised eye, from the clock parts laid out on a white cloth at the end of the bench to the racks of raw materials on the back wall. He had never before seen anything like it in a private house, and not in many institutions; its completeness staggered him. He turned to the old man by his side. "You've certainly got a beautiful set-up here," he said. "Did you do all this yourself?"

"No," said Mr. Hirzhorn. "I'll be straight with you. When I first got interested eight years ago I had the bench put in, and got the South Bend lathe, and fixed that up myself. Well, then when I got going and got really stuck into it I decided on a whole raft of things I ought to have. I was new to it, you see, and the lathe took me a month to get fixed up the way I wanted it. So then I figured by the time I got the shop fixed up I'd probably be dead, and nothing done. So then I got along Clem Harrison who runs our aviation section and told him what I wanted, and he made the plan and got the things for me, and put it all in with his boy, Pete Horner. I wouldn't like you to go thinking that I did all this for myself, with my own hands."

"Very sensible," said Keith. "You've certainly got a fine shop."

"You like it?"

"It's the best I've ever seen, in any private house. That's the clock, over there?"

"On the cloth. That's as far as I've gone so far."

Keith moved over and picked up the tilting table. "You've made a good job of that," he said examining it. "A beautiful job. How did you get the burnishing so flat and even?"

"Lapped it on a sheet of plate glass with oil and fine grit Carborundum," said Mr. Hirzhorn. "Then I finished off with metal polish."

"On the plate glass?"

"That's right. I thought this was the part folks would be always looking at, so it ought to be finished good."

Keith nodded. It was better finish than on most of the examples of the clock that he had seen. He picked up the trunnions and the rocking arm, examined them, and laid them down. "You're getting on quite well," he said. "These are the four plates?"

"That's so. They've got to be burnished, but I won't do that till all the holes are drilled." He hesitated. "They don't get seen so much," he said. "I thought I'd do them on a polishing mop."

Keith nodded. "That's quite good enough. These bevels. Did you make them yourself?"

"No," Mr. Hirzhorn admitted. "I got Clem Harrison to have them made for me. I do spur wheels, but I never did a bevel wheel."

"They aren't so difficult," Keith said. "But they do take time. I often get mine made in a shop where they've got proper tools for it." He turned over the parts. "You're getting on quite well," he said. "I should think you must be about halfway through. What's the next part to be tackled?"

"Bobbins and armatures," said Mr. Hirzhorn. "I never wound a coil before, and I don't know how I'm going to make out. Forty-six gauge is mighty fine wire to handle when you can't see so well."

"I know," said Keith. "It's better not to handle it at all. It's so easy to get kinks. I made a coil winder for mine. It's quite a simple thing. The wire passes from the spool through soft wood grips tightened by a spring, to give the tension. Then that traverses along the slow feed—the pitch just bigger than the wire diameter. Reverse direction with the tumbler reverse at the end of each row. Like this." He seized a piece of paper and began to sketch, Mr. Hirzhorn watching intently. Suddenly he stopped drawing. "Look—you don't have to make one. Get on with the ninety-five- and twenty-tooth wheels next, and the maintaining gear. As soon as I get back to England I'll put my coil winder in the post to you, air mail." He moved to the South Bend lathe and examined it. "You'll have to make a little plate fitting and put it on the tool post, here. I shan't be using it. You can post it back to me when you've done with it."

"Say, that's mighty kind of you," said Mr. Hirzhorn. "I've been kind of frightened of those coils, and yet I want to learn to do them. You know how it is."

Keith nodded. "They aren't difficult," he said. "Use the coil winder, and pick a gauge of wire to suit a slow feed on the lathe, and run in back gear at your slowest speed. There's no magic in forty-six gauge." He examined the gearbox on the lathe. "Look, this one here gives an advance of four thous per rev. Forty-four gauge is 3.2 thousandths diameter. I should use this gear with forty-four gauge wire. You won't have any difficulty. Mine took about an hour to make each coil."

An hour later Julie came down to the workshop. She came in unnoticed by the men and stood behind them for a little, watching and listening. The visit of this English engineer was a good thing; there was no doubt of that. She had been troubled from time to time that the circumstances of his life compelled her grandfather to pursue his hobby and his interest alone. Every evening he went down into the workshop alone. She could not share his interest with him, nor could his wife. It seemed all wrong to her that he had nobody to play with, but that's the way things were. She knew it for a solitary occupation, in that he wanted to make the whole clock himself, but his pleasure in Keith Stewart's visit pleased her very much indeed.

She said quietly, "Drinks are on the table, Mr. Hirzhorn."

The two men started, and turned to her. Sol Hirzhorn said, "They can't be," and looked at his watch. "Oh, well . . ."

They went obediently upstairs with her and washed their hands in the cloakroom. Over the drinks before the big log fire Sol Hirzhorn said, "I was wondering if you'd care to take a look at one of the mills tomorrow, Mr. Stewart. Ever seen a lumber mill in operation?"

"I don't know anything about the lumber industry at all," Keith said. "It's all new to me. I'd like to very much indeed. But I don't want to take your time."

The old man shook his head. "I want to go and see this mill myself. We've got an engineering problem there needs sorting out. I think we'll go into the office first of all while I look through the mail, 'n you can meet the boys—my two sons, Emmanuel and Joseph. They do most of the work now. And then we'll go on to the mill. Julie!"

"Mr. Hirzhorn?"

"Julie, we'll want the car half after eight tomorrow, for the office. You'd better come along. Then—say ring the aviation section, say I'll be coming to the airport and I'll want the helicopter at ten o'clock for the Flume River mill. Maybe we'll drop in at the Eight Mile Cut in the afternoon, so Mr. Stewart sees the whole process."

"Okay, Mr. Hirzhorn. Will you want Jim Rockawin along?"

"No. We'll leave him out this time. But say, if Manny's free I think he might come. Call Manny after the airport, and if he's home I'd like to speak with him."

She moved the telephone to the small table by his side and put it by the glass, and went into her office, closing the door. Five minutes later the buzzer sounded quietly, and the old man picked up the receiver. "The helicopter will be ready at ten o'clock," she said. "I have Mr. Emmanuel on the line now. Will I put him through?"

"Sure." There was a click and Mr. Hirzhorn said, "Manny? Say, Manny, I've got Mr. Stewart with me now, the British engineer that I was telling you about. That's right. I'm coming in the office, see the mail, first thing and let him meet you and Joe. After that I'm taking him to see Flume River. Would you be able to come along?"

"I think so, Dad." There was a short pause. "Bill Schultz of Euclid, he's coming in the morning about the new trucks, but it's all financial. It's more up Joe's alley than mine. I'll call Joe presently. If that's okay with him, I could come."

"That's fine," said Mr. Hirzhorn. "I'd like you to be there if you can make it. Time we made up our minds. I kind of thought that telling Mr. Stewart all about it might help to make up our own minds. You know what I mean?"

"Sure, Dad. I'll call Joe, and if he doesn't think he'd like to handle it I'll maybe call Bill Schultz and put him off a day. It's not that urgent."

"Okay, Manny. Give my love to Rachel. See you in the morning." He put down the receiver.

They dined simply in a great dining room rather too ornately furnished, full of oil paintings and clocks, served by the manservant, Julie dining with them. "My wife, Sarah, she'll be sorry to miss seeing you," said Mr. Hirzhorn once. "She gets this sciatica each winter in the cold and wet, and nothing seems much good except the sunshine and the warmth. She used to go down into California, but she likes Florida best. I go and see her there once in a month or six weeks, but there's nothing to do there." He smiled. "No business and no workshop. I like it here. She likes it, too, excepting when it's cold. She'll be back around the end of April, soon as it fines up."

They went to bed early, and Keith slept well in the deepest, softest bed that he had ever slept in, in the intense stillness of Wauna. By ten minutes to nine next morning he was in the head office in Tacoma meeting the two sons, Emmanuel and Joseph, treated as a very honoured guest. They left Julie in the office and went on at half-past nine to the Seattle-Tacoma airport; by ten o'clock they were outside the private hangar labelled "Hirzhorn Enterprises, Inc." with the helicopter standing on the tarmac in a little drifted snow, saying good morning to the pilot. "We'll want to go to the Flume River mill," said Mr. Hirzhorn. "We'll be there for lunch. Then if there's time we'll look in at the Eight Mile Cut. We'll be going back to Wauna after that, but it might be close on dark. Maybe we'd better go home in the Cessna."

"Okay, Mr. Hirzhorn," said the pilot. He spoke to a ground engineer and the father and son got into the machine in the back seat, putting Keith beside the pilot. The pilot got in after them, the doors were closed, the engine started, the rotor revved up. Presently the pilot moved the big lever in his right hand gently up and they were in the air and moving ahead slowly. He put the helicopter in a climb and they set out towards the east and north.

The flight was a delight to Keith, who had never been in a helicopter before. It took about fifty minutes over mountains and up shallow valleys filled with the unending forest. In the end a river showed up ahead of them and buildings marked by a great plume of smoke and steam, a railroad, and a small town beside. Mr. Hirzhorn reached forward and touched the pilot on the shoulder. "Circle around a bit," he said. "I want Mr. Stewart to take in the whole set-up before we land."

The pilot nodded and put the aircraft into a right hand turn around the plant at about a thousand feet, while Manny explained the layout to Keith; the logs coming down the river, the log pond, the jack ladder from the log pond to the mill, the drying kilns, the lumber stores along the railroad tracks. Then they had seen all that was to be seen from the air, and they came in to land softly on an open space reserved in the car park.

They spent two hours in the sawmill seeing the whole process as the logs four feet in diameter were sawn into planks and taken away for kiln drying or stacking, while the offcuts were turned into pulpwood for newsprint. The Hansel debarker, ripping the bark off the logs by jets of water, interested Keith very much. The saws, both bullsaws and bandsaws, were well within his experience though on a vastly larger scale than any he had seen before. He spent some time in the saw-sharpening shop talking to the head sawyer about set and cutting angles for the various types of wood to be cut, information that he stored away in his mind. The flying carriages, operated by four-inch roller chains running over great sprockets, appalled him, but he did not say so at the time.

They lunched with the manager and the secretary at a table reserved for them in the canteen. No drinks were served, for the whole plant was dry. Emmanuel apologized to Keith for this omission. "We're kind of strict on that," he said. "This is a company town. We've got 'most everything else that folks would want—a dance hall and a movie theater and eight stores—but not a liquor shop. We find that liquor and a sawmill don't go well together."

"Do you have many accidents?" Keith asked. He had been shown a very comprehensive little first-aid room.

"Not more than what's average to the industry," Manny replied. "You get gangs felling the tall timber in the forests, or walking around on logs in the log pond, or dealing with quick-moving saws like what you saw—you'll get more accidents than in the automotive industry, for an example. We try and keep them down."

"There hasn't been a fatality in this plant since it was set up," said the manager. "That's seven years."

"That's so," said Manny. "That's partly due to Lou here. But he's got a modern plant to help him. We had three at Viper Bend in the last year."

Sol Hirzhorn leaned forward, and they all deferred to him. "Say, Mr. Stewart," he said, "you've been around a bit. What do you think of safety in this plant, coming to it fresh? Now that you've seen it?"

Keith paused before answering, thinking over all that he had seen that morning. "I don't think you could do much better with the saws," he said at last. "With big saws running at that speed, you'll always get the bloke who gets careless as the years go by, and puts his hand in one. You can't help that—except by cutting out the drink, as you do. The thing I didn't like were all those chains."

Emmanuel and Lou glanced at each other. The old man asked, "You mean the roller chains that work the carriages?"

"That's right. I saw that they were well lubricated. How do they get greased? You don't keep stopping the plant?"

"They get greased nights and midday when the plant's stopped for dinner," said Lou, the manager. "They'll have greasers working on them now. In between, a guy goes around with a slush can and a brush upon a five-foot stick, and puts it on with that."

"Does the stick ever get caught up? Some of those chains were going thirty miles an hour."

"Sometimes. Not very often."

"Does the greaser ever get caught up with it?"

"Not here," said Lou definitely. "Not in the seven years that I've been manager."

Sol Hirzhorn said, "Say, Mr. Stewart, do you know anything about Chuck Ferris? Ferris Hydraulics, in this mill?"

Keith faced him. "No, I don't," he said. "I know that Mr. Ferris has a contract he's negotiating with you. I asked Mr. Rockawin if he'd tell me what it was, in case I put my foot in it, and said the wrong thing. But he wouldn't tell me. He said it was your business."

There was general laughter. Sol Hirzhorn said, "Good for Jim. Manny, would you be able to come back to Wauna this evening? I don't think we'd lose anything by telling Mr. Stewart what's proposed, now that he's seen the plant."

"Sure, Dad." He thought for a moment. "I'll call the office, and have them send the plans out to the house. They can call Rachel, too—tell her I'll be late."

They left in the helicopter after lunch and flew for twenty minutes eastward up the river. They came to the Eight Mile Cut, a timber camp, and put down on a level platform built of logs with a plank decking specially for the helicopter. They got into a truck with the young manager and were driven a mile or two through the devastated forest to where the felling was going on.

This was wholly strange to Keith; he could make no useful comment and he said so, though he found it full of interest. He watched a couple of Douglas firs about a hundred and fifty feet tall as they were felled, watched the branches being lopped off by men standing on the trunks working with axes. He tested the edge of an axe and found it as sharp as a razor. He watched the bulldozers pulling the logs down to the lake and rolling them in, to be made up into rafts by the boom-men and floated down the river to the log pond at the mill.

The work seemed to him to be excessively dangerous, but on enquiry he found that the Hirzhorns were not worried by accidents in the forest cuts. They said that the accident rate was lower than in the mills, possibly due to the average age of the men being lower; most of them were unmarried anyway so that accidents made less trouble. Keith thought that the monotony of work in the mills might have something to do with it. In factory work when men get thinking of other matters than the job in hand accidents were apt to happen, but out in the forest where no two jobs were ever quite alike men kept alive to the chance of a tree rolling over and crushing them.

They drove back to the helicopter in the truck and took off for home. They landed at the Seattle-Tacoma airport as cars on the main highway were beginning to put on their lights, changed into the Cessna waiting for them on the tarmac, and landed on the strip below the house at Wauna a quarter of an hour later. The car was there to meet them and take them the few hundred yards to the house, Sol Hirzhorn being forbidden to climb hills. An hour and twenty minutes after leaving the forest cut a hundred miles away they were seated with cups of tea and cookies before the fire in the great living room at Wauna.

Julie had come back to Wauna from the head office in Tacoma in the car, and had brought with her a great packet of plans and specifications from Ferris Hydraulics, a file of correspondence, and a sheaf of photographs. She had laid these out upon the table in the middle of the room; she showed them to the men and retired to her own office. When they were warm and comfortable before the fire Sol Hirzhorn said, "I'd like you to know the way things are at the Flume River, Keith."

"I'd like to hear it, Mr. Hirzhorn."

The old man paused in thought. "It started over a year ago," he said. "I got an invite to attend a demonstration of rockets at this place Cape Canaveral in Florida, Thor and Atlas and things like that. Well, I don't know anything about rockets or satellites or space vehicles, or what you call them, and not much interested either, but an invite like that don't come very often and I was taking Sarah to Palm Beach, so I decided I'd go. I didn't understand much of what I saw or what they told me either, but one thing did interest me. They had one of these things lying horizontal on the launching base while they serviced it and did things to it. Then they had to lift it up into the vertical position for fuelling and firing. It was eighty or ninety feet long, and they put it up vertical with two great hydraulic jacks, one on each side, all in next to no time. Those jacks must have been thirty feet long, the extension, I mean, and I never see jacks go so fast." He paused. "Well, you know how it is. You know at the first sight it might be useful in the business but you don't know what it is you've got in mind. So I asked the officer showing us around who made the jacks, and he said, Ferris Hydraulics." He paused again.

"It wasn't till the middle of the night I thought that if those jacks could push at that speed they could push our carriages in the mill just the same, 'n cut out every chain. I don't suppose you ever saw a man caught up in a four-inch roller chain that runs over a sprocket, Mr. Stewart?"

"No," said Keith.

"Well, you don't want to, either. I got in touch with Ferris Hydraulics, and Chuck Ferris he came down with his engineers, and left them with us for a week. I guessed it would be best to try it out in the one mill for a start, and we picked on the Flume River. Well, what they proposed was that we didn't stop at the carriages but put hydraulic motors on the saws as well, worked off the same hydraulic mains, from the same plant. Well, that's attractive in some ways although it's a big increase in the costs. I don't care about high-voltage electric motors in a sawmill much more than the chains. Six hundred volts can kill a guy quite quick, and you take an eight-foot bullsaw, that'll take close on two hundred horsepower. You get a saw break and hang up and things are apt to happen." Keith nodded. "Well, with the hydraulics they just put a sort of safety valve across the mains and no one's likely to get hurt, no damage to the motor either. I don't care about high-voltage current in the mill, any more than the chains.

"Manny's got the drawings and the specifications on the table there," he said. "I wondered if you'd care to take a look at them."

"I'd like to very much," said Keith. "I don't know that I'd be able to help much, you know. It's not as if I was a consulting engineer."

"No. But you've been around a bit. I'd appreciate it if you'd look the scheme over."

Keith crossed to the table with Emmanuel and they started

to discuss the scheme, while Sol Hirzhorn sat on in his chair before the fire. They started on the plan of the mill, then turned to the Ferris drawings and the specification. It was all straightforward enough to an engineering mind, a well prepared scheme, easily comprehensible. It was good, too; Keith Stewart liked the look of it. It was one which would remove most of the apprehensions which had troubled him that morning in the mill. It would certainly make the work safer.

"What happens to the waste heat?" he asked Emmanuel at last.

"What's that?" asked the mill owner.

Keith turned to the specification. "The power going into the hydraulic system is the brake horsepower of these Diesel motors, the prime movers," he remarked. "Six thousand five hundred horsepower."

"That's so."

"That's the power going into the mill when everything's going at full blast. Well, of course, nothing works at hundred per cent efficiency." Emmanuel nodded. "I don't know what the efficiency of these hydraulic rams would be," said Keith thoughtfully. "The motors might be ninety per cent. Suppose we guess that as the figure for the whole mill—ten per cent power loss. That means that when the plant is going at full blast, six hundred and fifty horsepower has to be got rid of as waste heat."

"Seems a lot," said Emmanuel.

"I don't know that it is," said Keith reflectively. "Not in the scale of the whole job. I suppose it goes into the hydraulic fluid. I saw something about that." He turned over the pages of the specification. "Here it is. Maximum temperature of the fluid, 100°F."

"That's what these intercoolers are for, I think," said Emmanuel. "They've got them stuck around behind each motor and each ram, with water from the river running through them. Here's the drawing of the water mains and pump."

"I see." Keith took the drawing and studied it. "That's all right. This is the drawing of the intercooler . . . In two sizes." He studied the dimensions. "It's not very big . . ."

"I wouldn't know," said Emmanuel.

Keith smiled. "Tell you the truth, I don't know either." He

sat in thought. "How hot does it get there at the mill?" he asked. "Outside, I mean—on a fine day in summer?"

"Oh, it gets quite hot," said Emmanuel. "The guys outside, they work in pants and undershirts. Eighty degrees, I'd say—maybe eighty-five. It's right down in the valley, so you don't get much wind."

"That'd be the inlet temperature of the hydraulic fluid by the time it got from the power plant into the mill," said Keith thoughtfully. "It must go in at round about air temperature."

"I guess it would," said Manny.

Julie brought the tray of drinks into the room, and the two men crossed over to Sol Hirzhorn by the fire. "How did you make out?" he asked.

"I'd like to think about it just a little bit," Keith said. "The trouble is, I don't know much about hydraulics, and they know just about everything there is to know. There are one or two things I don't understand, but that's probably my fault." He paused, and took a drink. "I'd like to read that specification through quietly after dinner, by myself."

"Do that," said Mr. Hirzhorn. "I'll be down in the workshop starting work on the gear wheels."

"Not after nine o'clock you won't," said Julie firmly. "You've had quite a day."

Keith settled down after dinner at the big table in the middle of the room, while the old man retired to his workshop and Emmanuel sat in a long chair before the fire smoking a cigar. He read the specification through twice and did a little figuring on the back of one of the drawings. At the end of it, when Julie went downstairs to flush Sol Hirzhorn from the workshop, Keith was as much in the dark as he had been before.

He got up as the old man came into the room. "I'm sorry," he said simply, "but I still don't understand these intercoolers. I'd say they were too small and they should be about three times the size. There's almost certainly some factor here that I don't understand."

"Could be," said Sol Hirzhorn briefly. He turned to his son. "Manny, how would you like to take a run up to Cincinnati with Mr. Stewart, show him the hardware 'n talk to the engineers?"

"When, Dad?"

"Tomorrow, I guess."

Emmanuel reflected for a moment. "I could do that," he said. "Go in the office first and catch the United plane midday, flight 183, thirteen zero five. Gets in around nine o'clock their time, sleep in the hotel 'n see them in the morning. Back here next night. We could do that if you like, Dad."

"I'd be kind of happier, now this has been raised," the old man said. "If we don't get it cleared up we might be worrying about it all the time." He turned to Keith. "Could you do that for us?" he asked. "It seems asking rather a lot."

"I'd be very pleased, Mr. Hirzhorn," said Keith. He smiled. "I'd be very glad of the chance of walking through the Ferris works."

Sol Hirzhorn turned to Julie. "Better call United now and make the reservations. Make them for the return flight, too,"

"Okay, Mr. Hirzhorn."

The organization went smoothly into effortless action. Keith spent the next morning in the workshop going over all the details of the clock with Sol Hirzhorn. At twelve-thirty the Cessna was waiting on the airstrip to take him across the water to the airport. At twelve-fifty the pilot escorted him to the booking hall and handed him over to Emmanuel. Ten minutes later he was sitting in the DC-7, and at nine-thirty that night he was in his bedroom at the hotel in Cincinnati over two thousand miles from Wauna.

He had a morning of absorbing interest in the Ferris plant next day, and finished up with considerable admiration for the design and manufacture of the hydraulic motors. The morning ended with an office conference presided over by Chuck Ferris, a small dynamic red-haired man that Keith had no difficulty in recognizing as Dawn's father. The chief engineer was present with one of his aides, a Mr. Monnington.

Keith said he didn't quite understand the intercoolers. "That's all right," said the chief engineer patiently. "The cold river water comes in here-from the main, picks up heat, and comes out here, and back into the river. The oil comes in here, and goes out here, a whole lot cooler."

Keith said he understood that. "What puzzles me is the heat transfer balance," he said. "I take it that the hydraulic fluid goes into the intercooler at a hundred and ten degrees? That's the maximum temperature you work at?"

"That's so," said the chief engineer. "In the case of the biggest motors that would be the outgoing temperature."

"And it goes into the power generator about eighty degrees?"

"More or less."

Keith stared at the drawing, still puzzled. "Well, what's the temperature rise in the cooling water, then?"

The chief engineer glanced at his aide. Mr. Monnington said, "Fifty degrees. Fifty-five under extreme conditions."

Puzzled, Keith said, "It can't go higher than the temperature of the oil, or it couldn't do any cooling. What's the inlet temperature of the water?"

"Fifty degrees," said Mr. Monnington. Emmanuel stirred, but left the talking to Keith.

"That seems on the cold side for summer temperature," said Keith.

"It's general in these rivers," said the engineer. "Maybe you don't get the same conditions in England. This is snow water, made by melting the eternal snows upon the Glacier Peak."

Emmanuel leaned forward on the table. "That's baloney," he said candidly. "Flume River doesn't rise from Glacier Peak. Flume River rises in the Troublesome Mountain, not much higher than five thousand feet. All the snow's gone from Troublesome by the end of April, most years."

He paused, and then he said, "Tell you sump'n. I went fishing up the Flume two years ago, in August, ten or fifteen miles above the Eight Mile Cut. Trout fishing. We didn't catch anything because the water was too hot, the fish wouldn't stir. So there was only one thing to be done, see? We stripped off, 'n went in for a swim. Real warm it was—I stayed in half an hour or more. I guess the water in that river, in the Flume, the one we're talking of—I guess it was seventy-five degrees or more, that day."

There was a dead silence in the conference room of Ferris Hydraulics, Inc.

Sol Hirzhorn took his call to Chuck Ferris next morning in Julie's office because he didn't want Keith Stewart to hear what was said. The girl started the tape recorder as he lifted the instrument and stood back in the room.

He said, "That Chuck Ferris? Morning, Chuck. The boys tell me they had quite a party with your engineers."

"That's right," said Chuck cautiously. "About the intercoolers. There was a difference of opinion on the inlet temperature of the water."

"Manny tells me that he's putting on a swimming party at the mill next August. Girls and all."

"I know, I know," said Mr. Ferris. "Quit ribbing, Sol. My boys had the rivers mixed up. We're redesigning the intercoolers for your plant right now. That won't hold up the job, and our quotation stands. There's quite a bit more copper will be needed, but that's our mistake and we pay for it."

"That's fine," said Mr. Hirzhorn. "Mr. Stewart that I sent to Cincinnati with Manny, he was very much impressed with what he saw."

"Well," said Mr. Ferris, rather relieved, "that's nice to know."

"Really impressed, he was. He had a long talk with Manny on the plane on the way back. They didn't put much importance on this intercooler business, now that's all cleared up. They advised me to go right ahead and sign the Letter of Intention so the attorneys could draw up the contract. There's only one point to be settled now."

"What's that?"

"Who's going to pay Keith Stewart?"

There was dead silence on the line. The tape rolled on.

"He's not on your payroll and he's not on mine," said the old lumberman. "He isn't going to be on mine, either. I asked him to look over the scheme as a friend. He said he didn't understand why the intercoolers were so small, so I sent him up with Manny to see your boys. Well, they found that there'd been a mistake in your office."

"I know, I know," said Mr. Ferris. "You think he ought to get something?"

"I sure do. Kind of a consultant fee."

"What were you thinking of?" asked Mr. Ferris cautiously.

"One per cent on the contract."

Mr. Ferris leaped in his chair. "Jeez!" he exclaimed.

"That's—that's over seventeen thousand dollars! He's not a guy that's in that sort of money!"

"See here, Chuck," said the old man evenly, "a guy's worth what he earns. If he'd not spotted that the intercoolers were too small they'd have gone into the plant the way they were. Next July or August we'd have had to stop production for a month or more while you put the job right. Maybe we'd have had a law suit over it. There's big money involved. Do you know what one day's production from that mill is worth?"

"I know, I know," said Mr. Ferris petulantly. "Still—seventeen thousand dollars! That's three Cadillacs!"

"If we'd had a lawsuit over this, 'n you lost, it would have cost you fifty Cadillacs," said Mr. Hirzhorn.

"Sure. But there isn't going to be a lawsuit. We've got the new design laid out in the drawing office right now. I was in there just a few minutes ago."

"Sure there isn't going to be a lawsuit," said Sol Hirzhorn. "Maybe there isn't going to be a contract either. My son Joe, he said right from the start we should have had some competition in on this."

There was a pause. "You really feel that this guy's contribution rates seventeen thousand dollars?"

"I certainly do," said the old man. "If those intercoolers had gone in as the old design we'd have been up for ten or fifteen times that amount. And it wouldn't have been me who paid it."

Mr. Ferris threw in the towel. "Okay," he said. "If that's what you think right, well, that's the way it is, Sol. That'll be okay with us at this end."

"Well, that's fine," said Mr. Hirzhorn. "Jim Rockawin, he's got the Letter of Intention typed out already. If he brings it to the Tacoma office tomorrow morning I'll sign up, and he can sign for you. Then we'll get it right over to my attorneys. There's just one clause needs adding, seventeen thousand dollars payable to Mr. Keith Stewart for consultant services. Oh—one thing more. Mr. Stewart will be leaving for England day after tomorrow, so Jim Rockawin had better bring the check along with him, with the Letter of Intention. Seventeen thousand dollars."

He put down the telephone and leaned back, a little weary. Julie came forward from the back of the room. "He won't know if he's coming or going," she said softly. She turned off the tape recorder. "Shall I do a transcript?"

"May as well," he said. "We'll have it at the office in the morning, case they have second thoughts."

"They won't do that," she said. "They want this job too much."

He got up from his chair. "He's earned it," he said. "A guy has a right to be paid for the job he gets mixed up in, whether he's accustomed to that scale of dough or not." He smiled. "Pay off his mortgage."

"It'll do more than that," she said. "It's three times the value of his mortgage."

"Well, he'll have a little bit of loose change, then."

"Is he going back to England day after tomorrow?" she asked.

"That's what he wants to do."

"Had I better get busy with the reservations for his trip?" she asked.

He nodded. "Yes, do that."

"On the office?"

"Why, certainly. On the travelling overhead."

"Okay," she said. "I'll see him presently. I've got the mail right here, Mr. Hirzhorn, if you'd like to see it now."

Half an hour later while Sol Hirzhorn was getting ready to go into Tacoma for a business lunch appointment she called Keith Stewart to her office. "There's two or three things," she said, businesslike and efficient. "First, Jim Rockawin called yesterday. He's got some shipping documents he wants you to sign, about the engine salvaged from your sister's yacht."

Keith nodded. "He was going to get those."

"Well, you've just got to sign and it's all through. The engine will be shipped upon a British ship sailing Thursday of next week, the *Clan McAlister,* to London docks. He's having it consigned to you, care of Perkins and Durant in London. Is that okay with you?"

"Fine," said Keith. "When can I sign the documents?"

"Well now, that's another thing. Mr. Rockawin is coming to the head office tomorrow morning to sign the Letter of Intention for the Flume River contract. Will I call him and tell him to bring the documents along with him then?"

"That would be fine."

"Okay, I'll do that. Mr. Rockawin has been talking with some of the Boeing engineers, and they certainly would like to take you through the plant one day. Would you like to do that tomorrow afternoon?"

"I'd like to do that very much, if Mr. Hirzhorn can spare me."

She glanced at her diary. "He's got a business lunch today, and another one tomorrow. He won't be back here either day till around five o'clock." She smiled. "I know that he'd appreciate an hour in the workshop with you then." She stood in thought a moment. "Suppose we fix Jim Rockawin for ten o'clock tomorrow morning. Signing the Letter of Intention and your shipping documents won't take more than half an hour. He could take you on then to lunch with the Boeing engineers and see some of the plant. Then I'll have the Cessna at the Boeing Field at a quarter after four to bring you right back here."

"Well," said Keith, "that'd be grand for me. But it's putting everybody to a great deal of trouble."

She shook her head. "The airplane and the pilot would be standing idle in the hangar. Manny's got meetings in Seattle and Joe hardly ever flies. I'll fix that. Now there's another thing, Mr. Stewart, and that's about your consultant fee." One of her duties was to deal with awkward or embarrassing matters for her grandfather.

"My what?"

"Consultant fee, Mr. Stewart. Mr. Hirzhorn asked you to look the Ferris plans over and you discovered a mistake that had to do with the intercoolers. To check on that you had to go to Cincinnati. Well, the Ferris crowd *had* made a mistake that would have cost both parties a great deal of money if it had gone through. Mr. Ferris reckons that your technical services rate a consultant fee, and he called Mr. Hirzhorn about it this morning," she said, lying like a good personal secretary. "They reckoned that one per cent of the contract would be a reasonable figure—that's seventeen thousand dollars. Is that okay with you?"

Keith was dumbfounded. "But that's absurd!" he exclaimed. "It's much too much!"

"It's what's usual in this country," she said off-handedly. She could lie beautifully, with a perfectly straight, businesslike expression. "If you want to talk Mr. Ferris out of it you'll have to go to Cincinnati. But there's no reason for you to do that. It's in line with fees paid every day for consultant technical services."

"I'll have to think about it," Keith muttered.

"Jim Rockawin's bringing the check out with him tomorrow morning," she remarked. "It's probably made out by now. That's because Mr. Hirzhorn told Mr. Ferris that you're on your way back to England. They fixed between them that would be a reasonable fee, and there's a clause in the Letter of Intention about it."

"It's much too much for the work I did," he repeated.

"That may be so in England," she remarked. "I wouldn't know. I can tell you one thing, though. If you want the Letter of Intention altered in the morning, Jim Rockawin will have to call Mr. Ferris in Cincinnati and you won't get to Boeing in time for lunch. I'd leave things the way they are, if I were you." She paused. "There's one more thing. Mr. Hirzhorn said you'd be leaving us day after tomorrow. Will you be going straight through to London?"

Keith nodded. "I've got to hurry home. I've been away too long."

"Too bad that you can't stay a little longer," said Julie. "Maybe you'll be over again. I'll call United and book you on the flight to Idlewild, New York, that connects with the night Pan-Am flight to London. Okay?"

"Wait a bit," said Keith. "I don't know that I want to fly. I was thinking that I'd have to go by train and boat."

She said, "But you flew out to Vancouver and Honolulu, didn't you?"

"I got that free," he said. "At home—well, I don't live like you do here."

She said, "I know it." She eyed him kindly. "You mustn't think that everybody in the U.S. lives like Mr. Hirzhorn," she said. "One day, maybe I'll get married, and then I'll come down with a bump. Mr. Hirzhorn has a right to live like this. He's built up a great industry, and that's about the only real interest he has, except the workshop." She paused. "I asked him about the reservations and the tickets," she remarked. "He said to put them through the office account."

Keith paused for a moment, untangling her unfamiliar words. "You mean, he wants to pay my airline fare back to London?"

She smiled. "Not personally, of course. He said to me to put it on the travelling overhead at the office. But that's what it adds up to."

"I can't let him do that," Keith said. "Not with seventeen thousand dollars of Mr. Ferris's money in my pocket."

"You want to learn arithmetic," she said. "If this goes in the office overhead it gets deducted from the profit before tax is charged. Mr. Hirzhorn won't pay twenty per cent of these fares. If you pay, you'll pay it out of your net income, one hundred per cent. That doesn't make sense."

She paused. "Don't refuse him when he wants to do this little thing," she said gently. You've given him a lot of pleasure with your letters and the clock. Let him do this for you."

11

KEITH STEWART LANDED BACK IN England at London Airport three days later, eighty days after he had left England from Speke. He passed through immigration and customs and took the airline coach for London. He stopped the coach and got off at the end of the South Ealing Road and got on a bus. Shortly before lunch time he arrived at his house in Somerset Road carrying his suitcase. It looked a little small now, and a little tawdry, but he was very, very glad to be back.

He let himself in with his latchkey, for Katie would be at the shop and Janice would be having lunch at school. For the first time in months he could relax. He put his suitcase down, took off his coat, and went down to the basement. His clean workshop was untouched, the machines bright and shiny, ready for work. In the dirty workshop there was an enormous pile of correspondence on his desk, but outside the daffodils were nodding in the sunshine and the wind. He looked into Janice's room, that once had been the scullery. The plastic duck still sat upon the four eggs, multicoloured, in the basket-work nest upon the table by her bed.

It was very good to be home.

He made a cup of tea and a couple of pieces of dripping toast. There was one job that must not be delayed. He put on his coat after the little meal and went out again. He walked a quarter of a mile to the shops of West Ealing, and into the local branch of the Westminster Bank. Before the eyes of the astounded cashier he endorsed a cheque for seventeen thousand dollars, and paid it into his account.

He walked back to the house and let himself in. He took his coat off and went down to the workshop, and stood for a time in thought. He had brought back with him a few of the Ferris drawings of the hydraulic installations at the Flume River Mill, and his mind was playing upon those. The hydraulic motors might not be too difficult to make in model scale . . . and would be something new and up to date for readers of the *Miniature Mechanic*. Suppose he took the 20-cc. Gannet engine as a basis, or any engine of about that power. Suppose he coupled the power generator on to that, aiming to deliver a quarter of a horsepower, working at a pressure of three hundred pounds per square inch, as a first guess . . . Then a miniature hydraulic motor driving something or other—a small bandsaw, for example—a tiny replica of the great bandsaws he had seen in the mill . . . Start off with a bronze casting, like this . . . He seized a pad of paper on the desk and began to sketch.

An hour later he heard the gate clang and heard Janice's footsteps on the path to the front door. He went upstairs and let her in before she could open the front door with her key. She dropped her satchel of school books and flew into his arms. 'I'm glad you're back," she said.

He hugged her clumsily. "Miss me?" he asked.

She nodded. "Mm." And then she said, "It's been dull, not having anything made."

"You been all right at school?" he asked.

She nodded. "I'd have come home early if I'd known you'd be here," she said. "We play hockey for the last hour now, Mondays and Thursdays. This is Monday, so we've been playing hockey. But if I'd known you were here I could have come home after school."

"Like hockey?" he asked.

She nodded again. "Aunt Katie bought me a lovely hockey stick with a green and yellow handle, new. Diana's got a new one, too. She's awfully good at hockey."

She struggled out of her coat. "I must put the kettle on because Aunt Katie will be coming home."

He glanced at his watch. "She won't be home for an hour."

"She gets off an hour earlier now," said Janice, rushing to the kitchen to fill the kettle. "She started doing that when you went away because she said she ought to be at home when I get back from school because you weren't here, but I'm a big girl now, aren't I? And then they started taking eight and tenpence from her pay packet each week because she left an hour early. Wasn't that mean of them?"

Together they laid the kitchen table and put the macaroni cheese in the oven to heat and got out the bread and the butter and the jam and the cherry cake. Across the table she asked suddenly, "Did you go to where my Mummy and Daddy were buried?"

"Yes, I went there," he said. "We had a stone made and put it up to mark the grave. I took a lot of photographs for you, but I haven't had them developed yet. I'll take them up to London, to Kodak, tomorrow or the next day. Better not trust them to a local photographer."

"Were they buried on the island?" she asked.

"Yes," he said. "On the island with the sea all around. Nobody lives there. You see, it's only a little island, and there isn't any water for people to drink, so nobody else can live there."

She stood looking at him. "Can you hear the sea from the place where they're buried?"

"Yes," he said. "You can hear the sea all round."

"I think that's nice," she said. "They always liked the sea."

"I left the grey egg with them," he said, "because I thought they'd like to have something that was yours. I buried it just underneath the sand."

She nodded. "They'll like that."

That was the end of it. She did not speak about her father or her mother again till they showed her the photographs ten days later.

Katie came in before the kettle boiled. "Keith!" she said. "Why didn't you let us know? I didn't really think that you'd be home for another month. Where have you come from?"

"There wasn't really time to write," he apologized. It was out of their economic way of life to send cables about the world. "I came from the other side of America, right through. I left there ... yesterday morning, I suppose. Times get a bit mucked up."

She wrinkled her brows. "Flying?"

He nodded. There was much to tell her, but it would have to wait till Janice was in bed. "You've got so *brown*," she said in wonder. "Whatever have you been doing? Out in the sun?"

"That's right," he said. "I'll tell you about it later."

Janice said, "Diana went to Bournemouth with her Mummy and Johnnie, and they all came back ever so brown. Can we go to Bournemouth some day, Aunt Katie?"

"We'll go there one day, dear. Perhaps next summer." Then they went in to tea.

After tea Keith unpacked his suitcase and got out the little presents he had bought for them in Honolulu and in Papeete, and gave them to Janice and to Katie. There was so much to tell them that Katie allowed Janice to stay up for half an hour longer, but it was a school day next day, and Katie took her off to see she washed her ears and neck properly in the bath after playing hockey and to see that she brushed her teeth and said her prayers and went to bed without reading. Keith washed the dishes while all that was going on, and when Katie came up from the basement room where Janice slept they were free to talk. "First thing," she said practically, "have you got any money, Keith?"

He nodded. "I was trying to sort it out on the plane," he said, "but it's all foreign, so it wasn't too easy. I didn't have to spend very much." He pulled a muddled sheaf of notes from his breast pocket, with a black wallet of traveller's cheques. He shuffled the pack. "There's a pound note," he said, pulling it from the mess. "And there's another. These things must be francs. You see what you can make of it." He passed the lot to her.

She opened the little wallet. "There's forty pounds here that you haven't used!" she exclaimed.

"Is there? I knew there was a good bit left."

"Well, thank the Lord for that," she remarked.

"Are things tight?"

"Not worse than they've been before. We don't owe anything. I've got a little over three pounds in my purse. But there's ten guineas to pay next month for the school. Still, this will put us right. I think we've got about eight pounds in the bank."

"We've got more than that," he said comfortably. "I paid in a bit over six thousand pounds this afternoon."

"That's Janice's money," she replied. "We can use that for her school fees, but we can't use it for living on ourselves. We'd better open another account for her money."

"It's not her money," he retorted. "That's coming along later. This is ours."

It was midnight before they went to bed.

Next morning he wrote a letter of thanks to Mr. Hirzhorn and packed it up with the coil winder in a little box to go to him by air mail. He spent most of the rest of the day in sorting out his vast pile of letters and answering the most urgent ones, thinking regretfully of Julie in her office in the house at Wauna and how she would have made a meal of them. Perhaps, he thought idly, one day Janice would become a secretary and would be able to help him. He gave up the correspondence early in the afternoon, and turned for relaxation to the design of the hydraulic models.

Next day, rested and refreshed, he took his hydraulic sketches up to Mr. McNeil in the office of the *Miniature Mechanic*, and told him most of what had happened on his journey, and about Sol Hirzhorn and his Congreve clock. They lunched together at a nearby Lyons, and talked about the serial that Keith proposed for the hydraulic mechanisms. "We've got quite a few subscribers in the Seattle and Tacoma district," he told his editor. "They told me that there are six or seven in Boeing alone."

"I'll get hold of the subscription figures," said Mr. McNeil thoughtfully. "I think a serial on model lumber mechanisms is a good idea—especially if you incorporate the bandsaw. After all, that's useful in the workshop, too. Besides being something really up to date for the Canadians and the Americans . . ."

Keith stayed quietly at home for the next six weeks, catching up with his work, developing the hydraulic models, and writing the serial. Then the *Clan McAlister* docked, and he was called down to the docks to see his packing case through Customs. Presently it was delivered to the house in Somerset Road upon a truck. He got the truck driver to help him roll the case on short lengths of steel bar from the workshop through the front gate and the front garden, and down beside the house to the back garden, where they left it in the middle of the garden path. Keith gave the driver five shillings for his help.

Next morning, after Katie had gone to the shop and Janice had gone to school, he unscrewed the sides of the packing case. The engine seemed in fair condition, though a good deal of external corrosion was evident all over it. He got an enamel basin from the kitchen and drained the oil from the crankcase, spilling a good deal on the garden path to Katie's subsequent annoyance. She wasn't too pleased about the condition of the basin either, which she used for washing vegetables.

He had no chain blocks to lift the engine with, nor any ropes or tackle. He undid the main holding-down bolts from the wooden bearers, put a couple of coal sacks where the head would hit the ground, and turned it rather roughly on its side using a length of one-inch round steel bar as a crowbar. In that position he could undo the bolts holding the sump in place.

That afternoon he rang up Mr. Carpenter, the solicitor, at his office in Bedford Square. "This is Keith Stewart speaking," he said. "You remember? Commander Dermott's brother-in-law."

"Of course I remember, Mr. Stewart. You've been away, haven't you?"

"Just a short holiday," Keith said. "You know those diamonds that we were looking for?"

"I do."

"Well," said Keith. "I believe they've turned up. My wife Katie—she was turning out the box room yesterday and she found a suitcase that she didn't think belonged to us, full of clothes. She showed it to me when I got home and they were uniforms and things like that, and books and things. It must have been one that John left behind he hadn't told us about, or we'd forgotten. Anyway, there was a litle box in it full of white stones, cut like jewels, if you understand me. Do you think they'd be the diamonds?"

"Did you count them?" asked the solicitor. "How many of them are there?"

"Half a minute, and I'll count them now," said Keith. There was a pause. "Forty-seven," he said.

"That is the number of the stones that Mr. Franck sold to John Dermott," the solicitor replied. "I should think you probably have found them, Mr. Stewart. That's very fortunate, very fortunate indeed."

"What had I better do with them?"

Mr. Carpenter thought for a moment, "They'll have to go back to Mr. Franck as soon as possible," he said, "to be sold for the benefit of the estate. We shall have to re-open the matter with the Estate Duty Office—but that comes later. I'll ring Mr. Franck at once. Could you bring them up to my office tomorrow morning, if I ask him to come round? Say about ten-thirty?"

"That's all right for me," said Keith.

"You'll have to be careful of them tonight," said the solicitor. "If they're the diamonds, they're worth twenty-seven thousand pounds. It's just like having so much cash in the house with you. Does anybody else know about them?"

"Not a soul," said Keith. "I haven't even told Katie. And there's no one in the house now, to hear us talking."

"Well, be careful of them, and don't tell your wife or anyone. You'd better take a taxi in the morning, straight from your house right up to this office. I'll expect you at ten-thirty."

Keith walked into the solicitor's office next morning, dressed in his soiled old raincoat and holding his dirty old felt hat in his hand. There was a florid man with Mr. Carpenter, with curly black hair, middle-aged. They both got up when Keith came in. The solicitor said, "Good morning, Mr. Stewart. Mr. Stewart, this is Mr. Franck, of Rosenblaum and Franck, the diamond merchants."

Keith said, "Good morning," and shook hands.

Mr. Carpenter asked, "Did you bring those stones up with you, Mr. Stewart?"

"I've got them here," said Keith. He pulled a little cardboard box out of his jacket pocket and gave it to the solicitor. Mr. Carpenter opened it, glanced inside, and handed it to Mr. Franck.

The diamond merchant took it, glanced at the contents, and frowned. He took a monocle magnifying glass from his waistcoat pocket and fitted it in his right eye. Then he selected one of the largest stones and carried it to the window for a better light. He stood in silence for a minute scrutinizing it. Then he scratched it with his thumbnail and examined it again.

"What's this yellow stuff all over them?" he asked.

"I don't know," said Keith. "That's how I found them. Is there something wrong?"

"There's this yellow, gummy deposit on them," said the diamond merchant. "Have they been stored in oil?"

"Not since yesterday," said Keith truthfully. "That's all I know." He paused, and asked a little anxiously, "Would it matter if they had?"

Mr. Franck shook his head. "It'll polish off. I can scratch it off with my nail. They're diamonds all right," he said. "At least, this one is."

He came back to the desk and put the stone in the box with the others. From his attaché case he took a little black leather case, opened it on the desk, and erected a tiny set of scales with minute weights handled by a pair of forceps. He weighed them all together, very carefully. Then he pulled a typed list from his pocket and consulted it. "Ninety-seven carats," he said thoughtfully. "The diamonds that I sold Commander Dermott totalled ninety-two carats. But then, they've got this deposit on them now . . ." He took the two largest stones and weighed them carefully, and the two smallest stones, again consulting his list. He counted them for number.

Finally he put the lid on to the cardboard box and put away the scales. "I think there can be very little doubt that these are the stones I sold Commander Dermott," he said. "I can't be absolutely sure until we have them polished and examine each stone individually. I should like to take them and have that done, giving you a receipt for them, of course. Then I suppose that you would want them to be sold?"

A few minutes later he left the office, taking the diamonds with him, asking the office girl to call a taxi to the door. Keith said, "Well, I'll be getting along. You'll let me know what happens?" He got up and reached for his old, shabby hat.

The solicitor got up with him. "You're looking very well," he remarked. "Much better than when I saw you last. You must have been out in the sun."

"I had a bit of a holiday," said Keith defensively.

"A very good thing to do," said Mr. Carpenter. They moved towards the door. "Tell me," he said, "did you ever do anything about the engine that was salvaged from your brother-in-law's yacht?"

"I had it shipped home," said Keith. "I've got it in the garden. But it's not much good, not really."

The shadow of a smile appeared on Mr. Carpenter's face. "I don't suppose it is, not now," he said. He moved to the door with Keith. "I wish some of my other clients took their trusts as seriously as you have done," he said. "I think Commander Dermott made a very wise choice of a trustee."

Janice still goes to Miss Pearson's school in West Ealing, but she is entered for the Royal Naval School for Officers' Daughters at Haslemere and she will go there next year. After that, Katie would like her to go to Oxford or to Cambridge if she can get in, and Miss Pearson thinks she probably will. Katie says that that's what Jo would have wanted for her, and she may be right.

Jack and Dawn Donelly are married in a kind of way, though there is still a little doubt about Jack's marital status. They live on Raiatea Island in the Isles sous le Vent, at the southeast corner, on Baie Hotopuu. They lived first on the *Mary Belle* at anchor in the bay, mostly on fish and corn-meal fritters, but presently Chuck Ferris sent the *Flying Cloud* to Raiatea with a prefabricated house for them broken down into small sections for deck cargo, and Captain Peter-sen helped them to put up the main structure before sailing for home. The completion of this house has kept Jack busy woodworking, which he does very well, and he in turn has kept Dawn busy for she had three children in one calendar year, twin girls in January and a boy in December; I believe there is another one on the way. Of course, she lives some distance from a pharmacy. Chuck Ferris is sending out another house to them, to make a bit more room.

Sol Hirzhorn has just about finished the Congreve clock and is thinking about starting off on the hydraulic models in Keith's serial. Julie still works for him and looks after him in the winters when Mrs. Hirzhorn is in Florida. He would like Keith to come out to the West again and bring Katie and Janice with him for a few weeks' holiday. Keith has deferred this until Janice is a little older, but Julie writes privately that Sol really means it and that Joe says that in view of Keith's professional services the fares would certainly be chargeable to Hirzhorn Enterprises, Inc., so Keith will probably accept the invitation in a year or two.

Keith finally sold the engine salvaged from Shearwater for sixty pounds, but it took him six months to do so. It cost him fifty-nine pounds eight shillings and tenpence in shipping charges from Seattle, so that he made a profit on the transaction.

Katie no longer works in Buckley's drapery shop in Ealing Broadway. They discovered that the interest on the sterling equivalent of seventeen thousand dollars just about equalled her wages at the shop, and that all Janice's expenses were amply covered by the interest on her own money, relieving them of the burden they had willingly assumed. At the same time Keith's correspondence throughout the world was growing to such an extent that some days he did nothing but write letters. So Katie gave up her job and bought a typewriter and a tape dictating machine, and took charge of the letters. She is not a Julie Perlberg and she never will be, but Keith by sitting in his chair and talking into the microphone can clear the heaviest mail in an hour or so, and the letters get done somehow.

If you happen to be in the tram from Southall or from Hanwell at about nine o'clock on a Friday morning, you may see a little man get in at West Ealing, dressed in a shabby raincoat over a blue suit. He is one of hundreds of thousands like him in industrial England, pale faced, running to fat a little, rather hard up. His hands show evidence of manual work, his eyes and forehead evidence of intellect. A fitter or a machinist probably, you think, perhaps out of the tool-room. If you follow him, you will find that he gets out at Ealing Broadway and takes the Underground to Victoria Station. He comes up to the surface and walks along Victoria Street a little way to an office block, where he climbs four flights of stone stairs to the dingy old-fashioned office of the *Miniature Mechanic* to deliver his copy.

He will come out presently and take a bus to Chancery Lane, to spend the remainder of the day in the Library of the Patent Office. He will be home at Somerset Road, Ealing, in time for tea. He will spend the evening in the workshop, working on the current model.

He has achieved the type of life that he desires; he wants no other. He is perfectly, supremely happy.